Alex Gray was born and educated in Glasgow and is the author of the bestselling William Lorimer series. After studying English and Philosophy at the University of Strathclyde, she worked as a visiting officer for the DHSS, a time she looks upon as postgraduate education since it proved a rich source of character studies. She then trained as a secondary school teacher of English. Alex began writing professionally in 1993 and had immediate success with short stories, articles and commissions for BBC radio programmes. A regular on Scottish bestseller lists, she has been awarded the Scottish Association of Writers' Constable and Pitlochry trophies for her crime writing. She is also the co-founder of the international Scottish crime writing festival, Bloody Scotland, which had its inaugural year in 2012.

Alex Gray

THE STALKER

sphere

SPHERE

First published in Great Britain in 2019 by Sphere
This paperback edition published in 2019 by Sphere

1 3 5 7 9 10 8 6 4 2

A CIP catalogue record for this book
is available from the British Library.

ISBN 978-0-7515-7228-5

Typeset in Caslon by M Rules
Printed and bound in Great Britain by
Clays Ltd, Elcograf S.p.A.

Papers used by Sphere are from well-managed forests
and other responsible sources.

Sphere
An imprint of
Little, Brown Book Group
Carmelite House
50 Victoria Embankment
London EC4Y 0DZ

An Hachette UK Company
www.hachette.co.uk

www.littlebrown.co.uk

To Suzy.
Follow your dreams,
for dreams do come true.

That night, a child might understand,
The deil had business in his hand.

> From 'Tam o' Shanter'
> by Robert Burns

PROLOGUE

Darkness, *be my friend,* he whispered, though he doubted any noise escaped his lips, the words mere thoughts, lost in the gathering gloom. She had left the window open again, a clear invitation to let him climb up on top of the water butt and pull himself inside the room where only a flickering candle gave any light.

He could smell it from where he stood, the rose and bergamot drifting like invisible smoke into the night air. And he could have sung the words, too, had he wished, the rhythmic beat from her music drowning out anything else. She would be sitting cross-legged on the floor, dark hair twisted in a knot at the nape of that slender neck, earphones discarded by her side, eyes closed as she attempted the relaxation exercise she performed every evening around this time.

A passing crow flapped silently by, its wingbeats a mere shadow, a black glove flung upwards on a current of warm air. But there was no wind tonight; all was still, the very air close and waiting as though holding its breath in anticipation of what was to come.

There was only the slightest sound as his feet met the wooden rim of the water butt, the blood singing in his ears drowning out any peripheral noises.

It was time, he told himself over and over; time to test her will, time to offer what he had to give. Time to take what she owed him. He stepped back down and crossed to his waiting car. It had taken a lot of planning but soon she would leave that room and come outside, then he would open the door and invite her in. Her regular taxi had been dispatched long since and she would never know the difference. Later he would be waiting once again and this time he would ask her the question that would make him complete.

And, should she refuse?

Then darkness would cover her completely and for ever.

CHAPTER ONE

It was like being at her own funeral.

Maggie Lorimer shuddered. Where on earth had that thought come from? She glanced back at the audience in front of her, men and women who had come out of friendship or a sense of loyalty. Even, perhaps, out of curiosity. Similar to the sort of attendance you'd see outside a crematorium . . .

Stop it, an inner voice scolded. Maggie swallowed hard. This was supposed to be one of the happiest days of her life. No, it *was* one of the happiest days. She smoothed down her velvet skirt, the dark green chosen in a moment of caprice to match the book jacket. Nerves, she told herself; just nerves, that's all. Yet the sudden morbid thought had taken the edge off the excitement she had felt all day.

Looking out at the crowd of people waiting for them to begin, she gave a deep sigh to calm herself then smiled as she experienced an unfamiliar tug of pride. Every seat had been taken.

The shop window downstairs had posters proclaiming that

tonight was the launch of Margaret Lorimer's debut children's book, *Gibby the Ghost of Glen Darnel*. 'Free but ticketed', the chalk board at the door had told any passers-by. Only half an hour ago she had stopped and gasped at the display of brand-new books piled right in the middle of the aisle. *Her* books! Holding the first printed copy in her hands had been special, but this made her want to laugh out loud. *Wicked*, her kids at Muirpark Secondary might have said. Her book was there, in a real bookshop, alongside the work of hundreds of other authors, as if she actually belonged.

The bar staff had been giving out drinks to the stragglers as Lucy, her agent, and Ivy, her publicist, escorted her along to the theatre area and Maggie had given a small wave, recognising Sadie Dunlop, the canteen lady from Police Scotland, all dolled up for this special occasion.

Heads turned and people grinned when she passed down between the two aisles of seats. They had all come to cheer her on; and now that she looked out from the stage, Maggie spotted several colleagues from school (and quite a few of the kids), friends and neighbours, even Audrey Ellis, from along the street, though Maggie suspected that was out of sheer nosiness. There was a cousin she hadn't seen since Mum's funeral ... perhaps that was where the strange thought had come from. All these people from different parts of her life. There were women she hadn't seen for ages, and some men, too, though several faces were unfamiliar to her.

And then she spotted the one person she most wanted to see.

There he was at the end of a row, preferring to take a seat at the back, his long legs stretched out. Bill. She had surprised him with this book, she remembered with a smile, the news of its publication coming right at the end of one of his successful cases. Next to her husband were a few other police officers of their acquaintance: Niall Cameron and his nice wife, Eilidh; Betty and Alastair Wilson; and several other men and women from Stewart Street Police Office as well as the Major Incident Team in Govan. Solly Brightman and his wife, Dr Rosie Fergusson, were right at the front, however, faces wreathed in smiles. The book was dedicated to Abigail and baby Ben, though Maggie and Bill's godchildren were both at home. It was a school night for Abby and in any case she was still too little to read about Gibby, the little ghost boy who had taken the children's publishing world by storm.

Maybe that was why there were so many strangers here? Ivy, her publicist, had sent out a press release insisting that there was a lot of interest in this Glasgow teacher turned author. Only last weekend Maggie had gazed in astonishment at the double-page spread in the *Gazette*'s Saturday supplement, her picture staring out at her, the delighted expression unmistakable.

'Ready?' Lucy asked quietly, a slight nod to catch Maggie's eye.

Another deep breath and a proper smile, just as Ivy had told her, then she watched as Lucy rose to her feet, the murmurs from the audience immediately dying down, the spotlight now focused on the stage.

'Good evening and thank you all for coming. My name is Lucy Jukes and I have the pleasure of being Maggie's agent. When I first read the manuscript of *Gibby the Ghost of Glen Darnel* I knew at once that here was a writer with a great imagination and an ability to make her words conjure up pictures in the mind of a child. I have to tell you,' she turned and looked at Maggie with a brief smile, 'I was quite blown away by the story and I am sure that anyone reading it for the first time will agree that a superb new talent is born!'

The sudden applause that followed made Maggie's cheeks burn. It was something she had not prepared herself for, despite all of Ivy's pre-publication hype, this sensation of being the centre of attention and actually not quite deserving it at all. For a moment Maggie wished she were anywhere else but here, the object of so many eyes watching her, faces looking at her as though she were now someone special just by having a book published.

It's nerves, she repeated to herself, *simply nerves and excitement now that this moment has arrived.*

'Thank you,' Maggie murmured, taking her place behind the lectern. She swallowed and then caught sight of Bill at the back of the room. He nodded, just once, and she took another deep breath. *You can do this*, his eyes seemed to tell her.

'Thanks, all of you, for coming tonight. It's really rather overwhelming!' She shook her head so that a ripple of sympathetic laughter rang out.

'I'd like to read a little from the book and I hope you like it,' she added, smiling more confidently as she opened the book at the page she'd marked with one of her own new bookmarks.

Then, as she began to read, it was more like being back in the classroom, the words measured carefully, the different voices bringing the characters to life, and Maggie Lorimer knew that everything was going to be just fine.

The small stage was little more than a raised dais, the two figures seated side by side. Once the reading was over the lights went up and members of the audience were invited by the agent to ask all sorts of questions.

Oh, there were plenty of questions he wanted to ask, heart thudding with excitement, but for now it was better to listen, to remain another anonymous punter sitting in a darkened corner of this room where all eyes were on the slim, dark-haired woman sitting on the stage. She had neat ankles, he noticed, and shapely legs, though that skirt just below knee length suggested a sort of modesty. The lacy top glimpsed beneath her jacket was more promising, however, like a camisole that could be ripped off easily, revealing a warm body beneath. A schoolteacher. A woman who ordered kids about. He drew his legs together, feeling the warmth beginning. *This time, surely this time...?*

She was exactly what he wanted. And he would not rest until he made her submit to his will.

The table where Lucy directed her had a large vase of white lilies, making Maggie think again for a moment about death and funerals.

'Glass of wine?' Lucy asked. 'White or red?'

Why not? Maggie thought suddenly. It was her night. She deserved it, surely?

'White, please,' she agreed, then looked up as Ivy came to hover over her, ready to hand her each book, turned carefully to the page with the publisher's logo at its foot. There was so much to learn about this publishing business, Maggie had sighed earlier that day to Bill, but right now, with Ivy by her side, she was happy to greet every person in this long queue that had her book in their hand.

'Gosh,' she exclaimed, looking up at Betty Wilson, 'three books!'

'One for us, one for Kirsty and James and just sign the third one. It's a present for a friend,' Betty explained.

'How are they getting on in Chicago?' Maggie asked.

'Loving it,' Betty replied. 'We miss seeing them, mind you, but Kirsty wants us over again next month.'

'Privilege of being retired,' Maggie murmured.

'Aye, well, we worked hard for that and Alastair's got a decent pension.'

Betty smiled and gathered up her books then leaned forward, tapping Maggie on the shoulder. 'You look lovely tonight, lass,' she told her. 'Well done. So proud of you.' Then she was gone, another taking her place.

Sandie, her best pal at school, thumped several copies of the book on to the table.

'All for the school library,' she said with a grin. 'Manson reckons the juniors will enjoy it,' she added. Keith Manson,

8

head teacher of Muirpark Secondary School had sent his apologies earlier in the day and Maggie had felt a certain relief. She got on well enough with the man but he was a real authoritarian and her nerves had been stretched enough.

Who would you like me to dedicate it to? became like a mantra, the question posed to each new person who came to the signing table.

Sometimes she was told to 'just sign your name', like the chap in the raincoat who stared at her for a moment then scurried off as soon as she had written in his book. He was a stranger, but one of several who may have come at another's behest or simply out of curiosity. Seamus from the bookstore had reminded her about the different book groups that met here in Waterstones, so really it should be no surprise to meet new people.

'So many folk I don't know,' she whispered to Ivy.

'Well, remember, these are first editions,' Ivy retorted. 'Could be worth a mint some day.'

Maggie shook her head and smiled. No, she was not one to crave fame or fortune, despite Ivy's best intentions. If you believed your hype you could be coming down to earth with a crash, she had told herself. Yet, in an idle moment, Maggie wondered if J. K. Rowling had felt like this on the evening of her first Harry Potter launch.

She had looked forward to it for weeks and yet now, lying here in bed, Maggie was glad that it was all over. The applause, the kind words, the dinner afterwards in Rogano with Bill and her publishers . . . it had all been magical, creating memories she would treasure. Tomorrow she would begin the tour of bookshops all across the country, leaving Bill behind. She snuggled in to his side, feeling his arm encircle her waist in response.

'I'll miss you,' she whispered.

'Don't be daft,' Bill replied. 'Just go out there and enjoy yourself. You were fabulous tonight and you'll wow audiences everywhere, just wait and see.'

Maggie sighed, half in pleasure and half because what she had said was true. The fortnight's Easter break would be swallowed up by Ivy Thornton's plans for this tour and she knew a moment's regret that they would be apart for so long.

Price I have to pay, she thought. For what? Success? She blinked in the darkness. Was that something driving her on? Tonight it sometimes felt as though she had changed into a different person. Being on stage and behind that signing table, she had drifted into another world. Since Maggie had become an author she had the feeling that everyone was looking at her with new eyes, as though she were suddenly deserving of respect. Well, inside she felt just the same.

A movement by the bed and a familiar sound made Maggie reach out her hand to feel the soft fur of Chancer, their old ginger cat. With a purr he responded to her petting then silently leapt up on to the bed and began to circle himself carefully before settling down by her feet.

I'll miss you, too, she thought, closing her eyes.

*

Their bedroom curtains were open. If he had a ladder he could climb up and peer in. What would he see? Two people in bed together? The thought made him clench his teeth.

The figure beneath the street lamp raised a hand in silent salutation then slipped quietly away, shadows taking him into the dark.

CHAPTER TWO

I t was one of those mornings made for climbing a hill, binoculars slung around his neck. The April skies were devoid of any trace of cloud, a shimmering brightness against the horizon where the sun had risen, the air warm and fragrant with the scent of hyacinths in a tub beside him. Bulbs that Maggie had planted in the late autumn. Lorimer sighed as he closed the front door behind him. *Too bright, too early*, he could almost hear his late mother speaking the words. Well, this was the west of Scotland and the weather was capricious to say the least. If he had set off for the hills there was no doubt he'd have packed waterproofs. Yet Lorimer's thoughts were still on the journey his wife was making at that moment. The publicity woman had picked Maggie up half an hour earlier, the birds still in chorus, and by now they would be out of Glasgow and heading north while he made his short journey to the MIT office in Govan. In his mind's eye he followed their route through Dumbarton, along the dual carriageway to the Stoneymollan roundabout with its sculpture of white flying gulls. Maggie always gave such a sigh of pleasure as they drove around that particular landmark, towns left behind, the hills ahead beckoning. They had travelled that road many a time together but now she was with Ivy Thornton. Lorimer pressed his lips tightly together thinking of the PR and how Maggie had allowed her to take the lead the previous evening. The publishing world was new to them both and he supposed the Thornton woman was just doing her best to promote Maggie's book, but something in her manner had jarred with the detective superintendent. Was it her tendency to cut in whenever Maggie began to show signs of modesty? She had been pleasant enough towards him, but he'd felt the scarlet-lipped smile had been a little forced when Ivy had looked at him and her eyes had dropped under his questioning gaze as if there was something she did not wish to share. Still, perhaps he ought to give her the benefit of the doubt, despite his natural inclination to analyse another person's behaviour. His wife was more than capable of looking after herself, he told himself, a faint smile hovering across his mouth as he remembered their earlier conversation.

Maggie, practical as ever, had taken out a frozen meal before she left, reminding him there were several more in the freezer. She'd shaken her head and smiled at him ruefully. 'Bet you dine out on takeaway curries instead,' she'd murmured as he'd drawn her into his arms for a hug. She knew him so well, this wife of his. Lorimer grinned, as he drove away from their home. He glanced up for a moment, his attention caught as a lone heron slowly flapped its great wings against the pale morning skies. The bird had its destination in mind, just like him, but it was free to go where it pleased and right now, William Lorimer wished he were beside his wife and heading towards the hills.

Becoming head of the Major Incident Team here in Glasgow had meant time away from home for Lorimer, too, as the unit could be required anywhere, Police Scotland covering every inch of the country. But today he expected to be in the office, with paperwork to prepare for a forthcoming trial. The streets were busy already; even at this early hour Glasgow was wide awake and ready to roll. As he skirted Pollok Park, Lorimer wished once again that he could turn off and spend some time away from the job. The idea made him slip off the main road and take the single track that wound through the park. A short cut, he persuaded himself, though these speed bumps would hardly help him to make better time. The fields and trees on either side were beginning to show signs of spring, a few new leaves tentatively unfurling, though many of the branches remained bare. Further ahead he saw the shapes of shaggy beasts grazing in the long grass: Highland cattle that lived in this oasis of peace in the middle of Scotland's busiest city. The road forked to the right past the Burrell Collection but Lorimer headed on, past the Police Sports ground then out again towards his destination.

He sighed as the traffic made him stop and wait. It was a pity that the entire school break was being used for Maggie's book tour but perhaps they would manage a weekend out of town when it was over. A faint smile worked across Lorimer's face, crinkling the corners of his blue eyes. She'd been amazing last night, a real star, and the pride he had felt had been tinged with something else. Surprise? Perhaps. After all, Maggie had written the book secretly, waiting until it had been accepted for publication before she had told him about it. And there was something else, a feeling of sadness, regret that her mother had not lived to see this day. She'd have been so proud.

The familiar sight of Ibrox football stadium, home to the famous Glasgow Rangers, hove into view and minutes later Lorimer was driving towards the red-brick building on the corner of Helen Street, close to Bellahouston Park. *The dear, green place* was the phrase someone had coined to describe Glasgow and so it was, though several cases that had come Lorimer's way had involved decidedly unpleasant incidents amongst these quiet, leafy enclaves.

Lorimer had hardly sat down behind his desk and opened the laptop when there was a knock on his office door.

The tall, rangy figure of DCI Niall Cameron stood there, papers in one hand and a serious expression on his face.

'Just came in, sir,' Niall said, and Lorimer motioned him to sit down.

'Female found over there,' Niall tilted his head in the direction of the far-away wall.

'Bellahouston?' Lorimer felt a prickle across his scalp. Only minutes ago he had been thinking about the shadowy sides of Glasgow's parkland and here there was another grim incident to take in. It was as if a sixth sense had been telling him about it already. He shook his head, chasing off any fanciful notions, and skimmed over the details on the pages Cameron had thrust his way.

White female, possibly in her thirties. Strangled with what appeared to be her own scarf and pushed under a line of shrubbery.

'Uniforms called it in, sir. Less than an hour ago. One of the park keepers discovered the body. Forensics are there now.'

'Major Incident need to be involved?' Lorimer asked, his eyebrows raised in question. The body of a young woman found in Queen's Park some months previously had been dealt with by CID as a one-off. The culprit was never located and the case was still live, though it would most likely be downgraded as time wore on and other cases piled up on the investigating officer's desk. But, if this poor woman's death had been at the hands of the same killer, then they might well be called upon to reclassify the whole thing. Any danger to the public made a case top priority, but why would a senior investigating officer turn their case over to the crack team at the MIT? As a DCI back in Stewart Street, Lorimer had dealt with cases of multiple murder without resorting to the MIT.

'Why has it come to us? Surely this ought to have been given to DCI Fraser Urie, the SIO in the Queen's Park case?' He frowned.

'Urie's off on long-term leave,' Cameron explained. 'He was involved in a bad road accident. But that's not the only reason this has landed here.'

'Oh?' Lorimer was immediately alert to the expression on his DCI's face.

'There's a missing person report too,' Cameron told him, his face serious as he handed over a second sheet of paper.

Lorimer read the details and stared at the photograph then immediately rose to his feet. 'Better get ourselves over there right now. If this turns out to be who we think she is all hell's going to be let loose.'

He swept up his coat as they left the room together, his thoughts on what awaited them in the nearby park.

The grass was still dew-spattered as they made their way across to the white forensic tent and Lorimer could feel the edges of his trousers soaked through already. The earlier brightness had indeed held a suggestion of rain to come and now the sun was blotted out completely. Several white-suited figures loomed out of a mist that had descended across the park, one of them heading their way.

'Sir.' The face beneath the forensic hood was one of the Fiscal's young assistants, a woman whose name Lorimer could not remember. They took the suits from her outstretched arms and in moments he and Cameron were fit to enter the crime scene, their wet shoes covered in bootees.

Lorimer could hear people talking inside the tent and as he approached he recognised the voice of the woman who was leaning over the victim, her accent unmistakable. Dr Daisy Abercromby, the Aussie pathologist, turned as he entered the tent.

She gave him a brief nod then returned to speaking details into her recording device.

'... time of death to be established,' she said, then switched off the tiny machine and stood up. 'Poor woman's been here for at least two nights, I reckon,' Daisy murmured before turning to see the men from the MIT.

'Big guns out this morning, eh?' she remarked, eyes meeting Lorimer's own. 'Something special bring you across the road, Superintendent?'

'Possibly,' Lorimer agreed. 'I'll tell you more once I've seen the victim.'

Daisy Abercromby frowned. 'You know who she is?'

In answer, Lorimer stepped forward and the pathologist made room for him to examine the victim.

The woman was lying on her back, arms by her sides. Her attacker had been kneeling on the victim's body, Lorimer thought, seeing the bruised flesh on the gap between her leggings and the cropped sports top. The cause of death was easy enough to see, the ligature around her neck a twisted silk scarf. Long dark hair had drifted across the victim's face and with one gloved hand, Lorimer gently swept it aside.

He had never seen a picture of this person until Cameron had handed him that second piece of paper. But now, here in this damp little space, looking down on her pale complexion, eyes wide and glassy, Lorimer knew without any doubt that this was the woman who had been reported missing.

'Yes,' he said. 'I know who she is.'

*

Lorimer had craved a trip into the countryside but as the Lexus took each bend of the Stockiemuir Road he wished that he were not travelling to break the news of the woman's death to her father. In contrast to his sombre mood, the rain clouds had lifted and every hill and mountain was clearly etched against the morning sky, their shadowy blues and greens a harbinger of better days to come. Even the hillsides of tawny bracken had glints of fresh green fronds peeping through with here and there a clump of wild primroses, pale yellow faces shivering in the still cold breeze. Up and down they went, each rise revealing more and more of the hidden secrets beyond the valleys: a glimpse of Loch Lomond, then, higher still, the Cobbler peeping out between twin peaks, its anvil mountain tip clear to see. Then they were driving down again, through little villages where life was being played out as normal: children running in their playground, a tractor in the fields, several hikers ready to tackle the West Highland Way, backpacks shouldered as they took the route from Drymen.

His eyes turned briefly to scan the forest that had been the target of a terrorist gang several years before when Lorimer had been called to investigate a serious plot. It had been replanted after the explosion that had rocked the quiet hillside and already the young trees were showing a dark line against the horizon. Life went on, Lorimer told himself. Nature was a force that would always come back despite the depredations of humankind. But nothing would bring back the girl whose father he was about to visit and the thought made his lips draw together in a thin, hard line.

*

Lord Donovan, celebrated high court judge and friend of several members of the royal family, sat beside Lorimer and wept. Lorimer had last seen him in court, the long wig and formal robes giving him a gravitas that had frequently terrified guilty men and women. But this man bore little resemblance to the authoritative figure that Lorimer remembered and the sounds of his anguish tore at the detective's heart. It was a moment that no father wanted to experience: the facts that he'd dreaded coming to reality.

Lorimer waited, his hands ready to offer more tissues from the big box on the table in front of them. He and Hilary Johnston, the family liaison officer, had driven out immediately to the small village in Stirlingshire. They would try to keep the press at bay but it was only a matter of time before this news hit the headlines. Patricia Donovan had been a favourite of the tabloids, a party girl whose lifestyle was at odds with her upbringing. *Boarding school then a year away in Switzerland*, Hilary had read the brief notes aloud as Lorimer had driven them out of the city and through the winding country lanes. Then rumours of drugs and rehabilitation centres; a sad story that was all too familiar. Patricia had dabbled with fashion modelling after an acting course and had even enjoyed a bit part on a TV drama, but she had seemed happier being in the sunshine, aboard the yacht of some oil tycoon or on the arm of a perma-tanned actor. More trouble with drugs had brought her back to Scotland and lately she had been a patient at the Priory Hospital in Glasgow. Was that the link, perhaps? Had Patricia Donovan flirted with low life in her attempt to buy drugs? Had she become a victim because of the company she'd kept?

Arthur, Lord Donovan, would likely ask these kinds of questions and Lorimer had to be ready with his answers.

The judge raised his head, eyes red with weeping and caught Lorimer's blue gaze.

'Why?' he whispered hoarsely. 'Why?'

Lorimer reached out and placed his hand across the other man's arm.

'I don't know,' he replied. 'But I promise we will do our best to find out.'

Donovan grasped Lorimer's outstretched hand. 'Was it because of me? Does someone want revenge? We've had plenty of hate mail over the years, of course.' He shook his head wearily. 'Goes with the territory. Lock up a bad bastard and they'll try to blame you for their own misdeeds.'

'Have there been any particular instances …' Lorimer began.

'You mean miscarriages of justice?' Arthur Donovan sat back against the leather sofa with a sigh. 'One or two in my whole career, but none that laid the blame at my own feet.' He shrugged. 'I've handed out heavier sentences after appeals, of course; lighter ones, too, whenever that was justified. But this …' He slipped his hands away, covering his face again and groaning. 'Dear God, why take away my girl? Why Tricia?'

Lorimer swallowed hard then licked his dry lips before continuing. 'The first victim,' he began.

Donovan raised his tear-stained face to the detective superintendent.

'What about her?'

'Same age as your daughter, same long, dark hair . . .' He let the words hang in the air for a moment as Donovan's mouth hung open, the man's eyes wide with shocked disbelief.

'You mean . . . ?'

'It's possible that Patricia was deliberately targeted, not for who she was but for what she looked like,' Lorimer said gently. 'We'll need to ask you a lot more about your daughter, however. I'm so, so sorry,' he said, echoing the words he had uttered earlier to this father whose dead child Lorimer had seen lying on the cold, wet ground.

CHAPTER THREE

Perth was such a lovely city, Maggie thought as they crossed the bridge over its fast-flowing river. The hotel Ivy had chosen had been a treat, too, Maggie's top-floor room a penthouse suite where she might have held a small party had there been anyone to invite.

She pursed her lips, scolding herself for that moment of ingratitude. Ivy was striding ahead, mobile phone to her ear as Maggie followed. The woman was all efficiency, there was no doubt about that, and she had tried hard to make Maggie feel as though she was an important person to the publisher. Yet there was still that feeling of being an imposter. *It's not happening to me*, she'd thought again the previous evening when she had stood up to address that crowded theatre. *I don't deserve it*, she'd told herself when the bellboy had set down her case and she'd stared wide-eyed at the massive suite. The view from her window looked over the river and in the darkness the water had twinkled under the street lamps, the city's wet streets gleaming with the rain. After the initial thrill had come a stab of loneliness, particularly when Bill's voicemail had kicked in and he had not returned her call, even though Maggie had lain awake for what seemed hours.

It was the lot of a police officer's wife, she knew. Waiting patiently for him to come home and now fretting about why he wasn't able to answer her calls.

She almost bumped into the publicist as Ivy turned around, waving her phone in the air.

'See this!' she exclaimed, handing it to Maggie. 'Your husband's been busy.'

Maggie took the phone from Ivy's heavily be-ringed fingers and looked at the screen.

'A murder,' she murmured.

'Not just any murder,' Ivy's voice rose in excitement. 'Daughter of a high court judge, no less! Boy, can we make something of this!'

'What do you mean?' Maggie frowned. 'What's it got to do with—' She broke off, her confusion clearing as she read the meaning in the woman's words.

'Oh, no, don't get me involved in this, please,' she said.

'If we don't someone else will,' Ivy assured her firmly. 'Famous debut author's husband heading up a major crime investigation? The papers will be all over it.'

Maggie squirmed uncomfortably at being described as *famous*. She wasn't and probably never would be. But the publicist seemed determined to have her own way. And surely Ivy, with all her years of experience, knew what she was doing?

'So ... what ... ?'

'We send out a press release as soon as we can. Terribly sad to hear of tragic death of such a young woman. Every confidence in your husband to find the killer, yadda yadda ...'

Ivy took back her phone and gave Maggie a quizzical look. 'Can't put the genie back in the bottle, honey. It's happened and we just have to go with it, make the best of what's there.'

Maggie bit her lip and nodded. What had she expected? To continue in her little bubble of self-confidence, swanning from bookstore to bookstore, stepping on to different platforms just talking about her little ghost boy? Well, yes, she thought. That was exactly what she'd had in mind. Two weeks of this then back to school to resume her role as Mrs Lorimer, English teacher at Muirpark Secondary. Carry on writing the next story when she had the time and perhaps do this trip all over again the following year.

'Come on, coffee while we decide what to send out,' Ivy said firmly, taking Maggie's elbow and steering her across the street towards the big shopping centre and another Waterstones bookshop.

Lorimer sighed as the telephone message repeated that the person called was unavailable. Only to be expected, he thought. She was so busy travelling here and there. Last thing she would want was her phone buzzing in the middle of a talk. He glanced at his watch. Two more minutes and he would have to head along the corridor to the boardroom and face the barrage of the press. Next on his list, though, was a

25

visit to DCI Urie. He was anxious to hear what the man would make of this latest murder, although he already anticipated a bit of flak over the MIT's involvement. No officer liked their cases being taken over, no matter the circumstances. However, given DCI Urie's current leave of absence, the man might just welcome Lorimer's input.

Yesterday he had left Arthur Donovan in that big house on the edge of Kippen, Hilary staying on until Donovan's estranged wife arrived. The man had gripped his hand as they'd stood on the doorstep and Lorimer had seen the despair in the judge's eyes. It had been hard to ease his fingers out of the man's grasp. It had happened before, bereaved parents using Lorimer as an anchor when they felt helplessly adrift.

Now he owed it to Donovan to pick his words carefully, not to allow the press any false speculation, and above all, not to say or do anything that might make it harder to locate the perpetrator of these unforgiveable crimes.

The room was packed, as he had anticipated, familiar faces from several of the papers seated, photographers each side of the room where chairs had been set out for the occasion. Lorimer nodded in recognition as he swept past a woman from the *Gazette*, his expression giving nothing away but the seriousness of the crime about to be discussed.

There was the usual tremor of anticipation as the assembled men and women looked to the front of the room where Lorimer had chosen to stand. Right outside a helicopter was flying low: some poor soul being transported to the

26

nearby Queen Elizabeth Hospital, perhaps; the sound of life and death.

'Thank you all for being here this morning,' Lorimer began, casting his gaze around the seated journalists, their notebooks at the ready. 'I have only a little to say.' He raised a hand as the murmur broke out, silencing it immediately with a severe look.

'The body of Patricia Donovan was discovered, as you all know, in Bellahouston Park and we are now engaged in trying to find the person who committed this foul crime. Before you ask any questions, may I point out that we are of the opinion that this may be the second death at the hands of the same killer. That being the case, our attention will be divided equally between both of the victims.'

'Oh, aye,' a sarcastic voice called out. But Lorimer chose to ignore that for now. Of course the MIT's involvement had come about because of whose daughter Patricia Donovan had been, but what he had said was absolutely true. The first victim, Carolyn Kane, had received plenty of column inches after the initial discovery last August but as the weeks rolled by the woman's death had become less and less newsworthy as no new evidence had been offered to the press. An unknown accountant, a grieving fiancé. They'd milked it for what it was worth but Carolyn Kane's death paled beside that of the daughter of a high court judge, a victim who would doubtless make double pages and more.

Lorimer looked out at them all, a wave of disgust making his stomach clench. They were like harpies sometimes, eager to pick over the more grisly bits of news, their main aim to sell newspapers to the masses, themselves hungry for blood and gore.

The questions that followed were exactly those he had anticipated. Why was the MIT involved? Did Judge Donovan think it might be a revenge killing by someone he'd sent down? How had the women been murdered?

He managed to deflect most of them successfully enough, giving the journalist who asked the third question a pitying look as he gave the standard reply.

'You know we cannot divulge any details while a case is ongoing,' he said a trifle wearily. Of course they all knew that but someone would ask the question anyway, just to put out feelers.

Then the woman from the *Gazette* surprised Lorimer completely.

'Hear your good lady wife is making a name for herself in the world of children's literature,' she began. 'Any chance she'll turn to crime fiction?'

Lorimer shook his head, lost for words for a moment. 'Doubt if she'd want to,' he replied.

'But, surely she's got loads of research material . . . ?' the woman persisted.

Lorimer ignored her and pointed to another hand that was raised at the back. The conference was not about Maggie, nor about him, but about the victims of crime and that included two sets of grieving parents, not to mention friends and colleagues whose lives would never be the same again.

He took several more questions, answering them tersely, before winding things up and thanking them again for attending.

Then, before they could follow him, Lorimer swept out of the room, his long legs taking him back to the sanctuary of his office, flash bulbs popping beside him.

The woman who answered the door smiled at him and stepped back to allow Lorimer to enter her home.

'He's through in the lounge, Superintendent.' Mrs Urie nodded towards a door leading off the hallway. 'Can I get you a coffee?'

'Thanks.' Lorimer smiled. 'Just black, no sugar.' He hesitated. 'How is Fraser?'

'Och, he has bad days and good days. The operation went well but he's still very tired ... itching to get back to work, of course. But that isn't going to happen any time soon.'

She stepped ahead of him and pushed open the lounge door, addressing a man sitting in a high-backed chair facing the bay window. 'Fraser, Superintendent Lorimer's here to see you. I'm just going to make the pair of you some coffee.'

'Come on in, Lorimer. You'll forgive me for not getting up,' a deep voice grumbled from the armchair.

Lorimer walked across the room and stood by the window, looking down at the chair where DCI Fraser Urie was seated, one leg propped up on a footstool, the heavy plaster cast partly covered by a fringed blanket.

'How are you, Fraser?' Lorimer bent down to shake the

man's hand. It was cold and clammy and he heard a sigh as Urie's fingers slipped from his grasp.

'Ach, I cannae be doing with this, Lorimer. Stuck here day in, day out. It's doing my head in. Only so much daytime television a man can take, you know?' He tried to chuckle but the sound spluttered into a cough instead.

'Your wife tells me the operation went well, though,' Lorimer said, pointing to the leg encased in plaster.

'Pinned and set in three places,' Urie agreed. 'Great surgeon, I have to say. But there's still the chance I might not walk properly again. They won't know what nerve damage has been done till the leg heals.' He looked at Lorimer and then down at his hands. 'Only two years till I retire. Don't suppose I'll get back into action again anyway ...' There was a tone of bitterness in the man's voice that made Lorimer feel only pity for the DCI.

Lorimer didn't tell him how lucky he was to be alive, the car crash on the motorway leaving one man dead and Urie struggling with multiple injuries. The man had undoubtedly had time to reflect on that but evidently had now sunk into a depression about his future.

'Have they suggested Castlebrae?' he asked, referring to the police rehabilitation centre in Auchterarder where he himself had been following a particularly traumatic case.

'Oh, aye, that's definitely on the cards once the plaster's off,' Urie agreed. 'Now, let's get down to it, Lorimer. You're not here to ask after my health, are you?' He attempted a smile and this time succeeded in uttering a small, dry laugh.

*

The coffee cups were set aside and Lorimer was seated close to Urie, listening as the DCI explained what had taken place following the death of Carolyn Kane the previous summer.

'We did everything possible.' Urie sighed, running a hand over his grey stubbly hair. 'Closed off the park right away. Bloody great space. D'you know it's a hundred and forty-eight acres?'

Lorimer nodded, allowing Urie to continue.

'Threw everything at it. House-to-house in all directions, set up a static caravan at the gates as an incident room and logged hundreds of witness statements, most of them absolutely no use at all, of course,' he added gloomily. 'What CCTV there was only showed the victim entering the park. We never saw anyone that might have been her killer. Not a trace on any camera.' He sighed heavily.

'What about the fiancé?'

'Nah, ruled him out, though he came in for a grilling at the start. Odd type of man. An actor, you know. Don't know what she saw in him, frankly, but then I'm getting old. What do I know about a young woman's taste in fellows? Our own girl married a butcher from Perth. Nice enough lad but not what I expected. I suppose nobody ever thinks anyone is good enough for their girl, eh?'

'No suspects . . . ?'

Urie shook his head. 'Oh, we interviewed plenty of folk. Friends, colleagues, neighbours. All said exactly the same thing. Carolyn was a nice girl who was saving up to get married. Good at her job, well liked by all and sundry.'

'A stranger killing, then?'

'That's what we concluded,' Urie agreed. 'The worst sort to detect, especially if there hadn't been any previous history of violence. But now . . . ?'

Lorimer forced a wintry smile. 'Aye, now things might have changed. Your killer seems to have picked himself another victim, one that bears an uncanny resemblance to Carolyn Kane.'

CHAPTER FOUR

Arthur Donovan had spent better days watching criminals sweat in the confines of the high court, his wig becoming heavier as each hour passed, the irritation he had felt with his learned friends strutting back and forth nothing compared to this present horror.

He had never been a man to suffer fools gladly but the presence of these police officers, some of them a bit rough around the edges, was oddly comforting rather than annoying. They were so damned young, he'd caught himself thinking as the detectives had introduced themselves, explaining what they were doing in and around his home. Sign of my age, Donovan had told himself, but there was no mirth attached to the thought, just a sigh of regret for the passing years. At least the woman, Hilary, was a bit older. Probably nearing retirement; didn't they all leave at about fifty these days? She'd been by his side ever since Lorimer had left, not asking too many questions, letting him feel that it was all right to break down and weep whenever he could not help himself.

I need to be busy, he'd thought this morning, but the overwhelming inertia had made him slump into the same chair as yesterday. The very act of washing and dressing had been almost too much, his fingers fumbling with buttons and zip, the comb through his sparse grey hair clattering on to the glass-topped dresser as he'd glanced at his own reflection.

Now it was a matter of waiting. Moira would be here soon, Hilary had assured him, the taxi from Stirling station bringing her back. If she'd been here in the first place, maybe this would never have happened ... Donovan bent forward, head in his hands. He must not think like that. Nobody was to blame for the way their only daughter had turned out. Patricia had been eighteen when Moira had announced her departure, old enough to understand that her parents living together was no longer a viable option. And Moira had a new man in her life ... someone who was going to be there for her ... London ... a new start ...

He had heard it all that day as he'd emptied the decanter of whisky drop by drop, not offering any rebuke, just listening to her voice (her *reasonable* voice, he used to mock) telling him what would happen and why he was not to make a fuss. And of course he hadn't done any such thing, it being against the nature of a man like him. He wasn't given to swearing or shouting, although the shards of glass from that decanter had been hard to sweep up in the hours after she'd left.

Odd how their daughter had chosen to remain here with

him when he'd expected her to go with her mother to London. But, no, Patricia wanted to be in Kippen where she might see her friends. It was a small community and she had been happier here than anywhere else, Donovan realised with a pang. She'd attended the local primary school but then they had sent her off to Glenalmond as a boarder, only seeing her at weekends and holidays, a pattern that had suited both parents. Those earlier days had been fun, though. He remembered the excitement of dark October nights when she'd scampered off, dressed up in a witch's costume, to join the other village children for Hallowe'en on their annual rounds of those houses that opened their doors to other people's children. The one opposite the primary school with its cunningly carved pumpkin lanterns, that had been their favourite . . . but never here in the big house with its darkened shutters and Virginia creeper shivering in the moonlight. If only . . .

Donovan rubbed eyes that were sore with weeping. It was useless to indulge himself in regrets now, clawing at his soul like this. The choices they had made had seemed for the best back then. Would Patricia have become a different young woman if she had gone to the local comprehensive? Studied at university like Caitlin and Ailsa, her old school friends, both now doctors doing some good for the world not *racketing about on the arm of some gigolo* . . . Had those been his harsh words? Donovan closed his eyes. She had been such a disappointment to them both, their lovely girl, her life seemingly wasted on riotous living like the Prodigal Son.

He started at the sound of wheels on gravel and pushed

himself up from the chair. Moira was here. And he would have to face his estranged wife, both of them equal now in their loss.

Hilary was waiting in the porch as the door of the taxi opened and Lady Donovan stepped out. She had expected an older woman but the figure emerging from the silver Skoda looked far more than her sixty-eight years. Moira Donovan was stick thin, silver hair cut short, accentuating her features. Gaunt, was Hilary's first impression and her heart went out to the woman who had lost her only child in such a brutal way.

As she stooped a little to pay the taxi driver, her silk scarf slithered to the ground and Hilary stepped forward to pick it up. For a moment their eyes met and Hilary saw the crêpe-like flesh on Moira Donovan's neck, felt the cold fingers as they clasped her own.

'I'm Police Constable Johnston; we spoke on the telephone,' Hilary said, stepping aside to allow the woman to walk on unsteady feet into what had once been her home.

'Yes.' Lady Donovan swept a disdainful glance over Hilary and then looked away as she marched purposefully past and into the large reception hallway. Brittle as glass and possibly just as hard, Hilary decided, though in her long experience the family liaison officer had seen many bereaved folk put on a brave face just to stop from losing it all together.

She hovered behind the woman as Arthur Donovan stepped into the light, a frown on his face as though for one moment he did not recognise Patricia's mother. Then, giving a little cry,

Moira Donovan moved forwards and Hilary saw the judge take her into his arms.

'Oh, Artie, why? Why?' Hilary heard the catch in her voice before Lord and Lady Donovan slipped into the sitting room, closing the door behind them. They were only mortals, like the rest of the population, Hilary had reminded one of the younger officers earlier that day. A big house and a lot of money did not make anyone immune from the troubles that life could bring. And, she'd added darkly, murderers don't usually discriminate.

Whoever had taken the lives of these two young women had targeted them deliberately, looking for a certain type of female, the liaison officer had decided. Hilary had taken several courses at the University of Glasgow over the years and she was well versed in the psychology behind crimes like this. Lorimer hadn't said in so many words, but Hilary suspected that the person they sought could have been following each of these women for a long time before the attacks that had taken their lives.

She knew what she would put her money on, Hilary mused, drifting back to the kitchen, ready to put on the kettle yet again. A stalker, she decided. A dangerous individual who believed himself in love with women who might never even be aware of his existence. Then, when they rejected his advances, something snapped inside him. And he killed.

'I'm sorry, I had to switch my phone off,' Maggie began.

'It's okay, I get it,' Lorimer replied gently. 'Anyway, how are you? How's the tour going?'

'Great. The theatre was packed last night and I had the most fantastic suite in this hotel ... Wish you'd been there,' she added and Lorimer could hear the wistful note in her voice.

'It's pretty full on down here,' he told her.

'I know. We saw the news. That poor young woman ...'

'Two young women,' Lorimer corrected her. 'But I probably wouldn't be involved had it not been that our second victim is Arthur Donovan's daughter,' he admitted. 'Those on high deemed it necessary to involve the MIT. Want it cleared up yesterday if we can. You know the score.'

He heard the sigh. Sure, Maggie understood the pressures a case like this presented and the time it took him away from her.

'Just as well you're doing something nice while I'm in charge of this one,' he told her.

'Thanks,' she replied. 'Ivy's being so sweet, bigging me up at every turn.' Lorimer heard her chuckle. 'Sometimes I actually feel she means all the flattering things she says. Then I have to tell myself that she's probably done this a thousand times for every author.'

'Well, who's to tell that your book isn't going to be a massive hit?' Lorimer argued. 'The reviews you've had so far have been very complimentary.'

'Oh, sorry, have to go. Ivy's tapping her watch. Looks like we're on our travels again. Speak to you later?'

'I hope so. Love you,' Lorimer murmured.

'Love you, too,' she replied then there was sudden silence as the call ended.

He put his mobile on the desk and drew the paperwork towards him. Every member of the team had been given an action: the backgrounds of both Carolyn Kane and Patricia Donovan were being thoroughly investigated; any hint that each woman had been troubled by a stalker would be given special attention. So far there had been nothing of that sort but the detective superintendent felt that sooner or later they would find a link between these two victims other than their physical appearance and the manner of their deaths. Their phones and personal computers were being examined carefully by their best IT officers and every family member, colleague and friend was being questioned in the hope that something might turn up to push the case forward. It was hard for the Kane woman's family to relive this investigation all over again, hard too for Urie's original team who had been replaced by his own crack officers. The Chief Constable had insisted that the MIT take charge and his expectation was that Lorimer and his team would soon have it all neatly wrapped up.

His thoughts strayed to the scene in Bellahouston Park and to a case from his early days as a DCI when the bodies of three young women had been discovered one after another in a different Glasgow park, discarded like so much rubbish. The man who had committed these crimes was still languishing in prison and would stay there for some years to come, Lorimer told himself. Still, it was worth checking whether that particular killer had managed somehow to obtain his freedom.

No, he was told several minutes later, the date for parole had never been fixed and it was unlikely that the prisoner would see his freedom for another decade at least. Ah, well, it had been worth a shot.

What were they left with? A stranger, someone that might never have come in contact with the police. Lorimer sighed. It was like chasing a shadow. But they would work on every last detail until something was found that could bring this man into the light.

CHAPTER FIVE

'She didn't have a bad bone in her body,' the blonde woman insisted, sniffling into a handkerchief. 'Carolyn was lovely. Ask anyone who knew her,' she added, glaring at the two detectives, defying them to contradict her statement.

'You say you'd known her since you were children,' DC Davie Giles said, his eyes on the woman, willing Angela Hitchens to tell them as much as she could.

The woman nodded, glanced up at the good-looking detective constable who was regarding her earnestly and gave a tremulous sigh.

'That's right. I'd just come up from England with my family and starting a new school wasn't the easiest thing I'd ever done,' she continued. 'Carolyn was there for me right from the start ...' She gave a sob and shook her head. 'Still c-can't believe I'm never going to see her again,' she gulped.

'How old were you then?' DS Molly Newton asked, her

tone steady but not harsh, Davie noticed, regarding the DS with interest.

'Almost ten. We were both in Primary Five.' She looked from one to the other. 'Carolyn was really popular,' she added. 'She didn't have to make friends with a complete stranger. Everyone liked her, you know? And it was the same when we went to uni. Always there for me.' A brief smile crossed the woman's face, softening her features for a moment. 'We had so many boyfriend problems back then.' She shook her head. 'Then Carolyn found *the one*.' She extended her left hand, displaying her own large solitaire engagement ring. 'She, she ... was going to be my bridesmaid, just as I was going to be hers ... '

Davie Giles glanced at his colleague for a split second but Molly did not take her eyes off the woman, focusing on her body language, no doubt. Was the dead woman's best friend really the person they ought to be talking to, Molly had asked him earlier. What about work colleagues? People that might give a less biased opinion than this childhood friend. He thought briefly back to another case when he had been paired with Kirsty Wilson, daughter of a retired DI. He'd had hopes of more than a working relationship but Kirsty had made it clear she was destined for another guy ... Molly was probably a better partner for him, Davie decided; cool and detached, a former undercover officer who brought a lot more experience to the job and, he reluctantly admitted, could teach him a thing or two about police work. That was the thing about this job: you were always learning, especially about the vagaries of human nature.

'When will they let the family have her funeral?' Angela

Hitchens asked now, this time looking straight at Molly and not at Davie. 'There was a memorial service but it's been months now and no one has mentioned Carolyn's funeral.'

'That's a matter for the Crown Prosecution Service,' Molly told her tactfully. It was hard to voice the opinion that sometimes a funeral ought to go ahead even when a murder case like this was still live. Now, there was even more reason to retain the dead woman's body in the mortuary as comparisons would be made by the pathologists and forensic scientists. Molly avoided the woman's eyes as she murmured, 'Carolyn's family will be advised as soon as that becomes a possibility.'

'This other woman ...' The blonde gulped and caught Molly's eye. 'They're saying it's the same man ... '

'We're working on that premise,' Molly agreed. 'Some details are similar,' she added. 'Now, if you could give us a bit more information about the men in Carolyn's life ... ?'

Davie Giles watched as the woman sat back in her chair, the very act of withdrawing a sure sign that she was reluctant to answer them. And, he knew, it revealed that the question disturbed her more than a little. Had she been asked questions like this before? Had the original officers probed as deeply as they were doing now? Lorimer seemed to think they had but just the same, Davie was eager to see if they could find something new to help push the two cases along.

'Was there anyone bothering her? Harassing her, perhaps?'

Angela dropped her gaze and Davie saw the way she chewed her lower lip: an inner struggle to tell the truth or protect her friend, maybe?

43

'Not harassing, I wouldn't call it that . . . ' she mumbled.

'Who . . . ?' Molly Newton leaned forward, dipping her head so that the woman was forced to look up and meet her eyes.

'She said it didn't amount to sexual harassment. Those were the very words she used,' Angela insisted.

Someone at work, Davie guessed. They knew that Carolyn Kane had been an accountant in a busy city-centre office, steadily working her way up towards partnership, a possibility that would never now be realised.

'Who is this?' Molly repeated. 'And why didn't you mention it when the police questioned you the first time? We'll find out from someone else in the firm if you don't tell us, but it's already months since your friend died and every minute in a murder investigation counts. You do know that, don't you?'

Angela sniffed again, wiping her nose with the crumpled hankie. 'It was her boss,' she whispered. 'Carolyn told me he fancied her, told her she'd be better off with him than with Jake. I honestly never dreamed he might be involved. Carolyn really thought a lot of him, you see.'

Davie said nothing. He knew from the original case file that Jake Richardson, the dead woman's fiancé, had been subjected to hours of interrogation after the discovery of Carolyn's body in Queen's Park, his flat in Shawlands a mere five minutes' walk from the crime scene.

'Name?' Molly's tone was brusque but they were not there to mop up this woman's tears, Davie reminded himself, but to investigate her best friend's death.

'Finlay,' she said slowly. 'Stuart Finlay.'

'Thank you,' Molly said gently. 'I know this is hard for you but, believe me, your information could really help us catch whoever did this to Carolyn.'

'You really think it could have been him?' Angela's eyes widened.

'We cannot comment on that,' Davie interjected. 'It may be that we simply have to eliminate Carolyn's boss from our inquiries. She didn't see him as a threat?'

'No,' the woman admitted. 'I told you: Carolyn liked him.' She looked earnestly at Molly, even though it had been Davie who had asked that question.

'She liked everyone ...'

'What do you think?' Davie hazarded as they left the semi-detached house on the edge of Clarkston and headed back to his car.

Molly Newton didn't reply for a moment, her head turning back to glance at the window. Davie followed her gaze. Sure enough the Hitchens woman was standing there watching them both, and even from this distance he could see that her expression was one of abject misery.

'She's obviously finding it hard to come to terms with losing her best pal, even after six months or so,' Molly said at last. 'When you're wee, kids make plans about what they'll do when you grow up.' She shrugged. *I'll be your best maid if you'll be mine,'* she said in a sing-song voice. 'Last thing that young woman expected was for her pal to be murdered. It's knocked her past and her future ...'

'What about this guy, Carolyn Kane's boss?'

Molly shrugged again. 'Wait till we see him,' she suggested, stepping aside as Davie opened the passenger door for her. 'Best never to have any preconceived notions. Despite what we just heard.'

Stuart Finlay was in his late thirties, the youngest partner in his firm, according to their notes, but the man who had stepped forward and shaken their hands did not look anything like the stereotypical image of an accountant. Sure, he was dressed in a smart suit but the silk tie decorated with the repeat motif of a cartoon character wasn't quite what Davie Giles had expected. The Road Runner was a figure from his childhood and, Davie supposed, from Finlay's as well. Now a pair of intelligent blue eyes regarded them both as Carolyn Kane's boss sat in the small lounge that was evidently reserved for informal meetings with clients. Coffees had been ordered, the detectives ushered courteously into the room. He'd taken them here, rather than choosing to sit behind a desk in his office and assume a superior stance. But Stuart Finlay didn't strike him as that sort of man, Davie thought, as Finlay caught his eye and gave a sympathetic smile. He was putting himself in their place, the detective suddenly realised, empathising with the task the police had to carry out. It was a rare quality in a human being, the ability to understand another's point of view so swiftly. Perhaps Carolyn Kane would have been better off with this man than the one she'd chosen to spend her short life with, DC Giles found himself thinking. He sat back, regarding the man in front of him. Was his first impression correct or was Finlay adept at manipulating people, his charisma beguiling even to an experienced police officer?

'I saw the report about the second victim, Lord Donovan's daughter. Are you thinking these two deaths are linked?' Finlay began.

'There are similarities that cannot be ignored.' Once again it was Molly who answered the question but, instead of focusing only on his superior officer, Finlay glanced at them both. More Brownie points, Davie thought; this man knows how to make people feel included in a conversation. Bet he's a great boss.

'We had information that you had been rather over-friendly with Carolyn,' Molly began, but her words, though formal, were at odds with her tone, which was lighter than normal. Was she, too, falling under the spell of this attractive man? What was it Lorimer sometimes talked about? Appearance versus reality? Well, perhaps they were being shown a veneer of niceness that hid something darker. It was second nature for officers like him to be suspicious, but something made Davie want to believe this man to be a genuine bloke.

'That's probably true.' Finlay sighed. 'She was a dear girl and we all adored her. Me more than most.' He smiled ruefully.

'There was never anything that could amount to harassment?' Newton asked.

'My persistence, perhaps?' Finlay asked softly, looking away from them for a moment and staring out at the sky. 'She knew that I admired her a lot. I told her often enough.' He shook his head. 'Have you met her fiancé?' he asked suddenly.

'The police have talked to Mr Richardson,' Davie replied, letting the man think what he liked. Neither he nor Molly had been involved, of course, the first victim's investigation having been undertaken by CID.

'How would you describe your relationship with Carolyn?' Molly asked.

'Unrequited,' Finlay said immediately then gave a little laugh. 'It was well known that I'd have given anything for Carolyn to ditch that guy and take up with me. But I never let it affect my work and neither did she.'

'You're not in another relationship, then?' Molly asked.

There was a moment's silence and Davie saw a shadow pass over the accountant's face.

'I was engaged to be married a long time ago,' he began. 'She was a wonderful woman ... Killed six weeks before our wedding. Car accident. Didn't look as she was crossing the road ...'

'I'm sorry,' Molly began.

'Don't be,' Finlay stopped her, one hand raised. 'About eight people benefited from Jennifer's death. Organ transplants, her eyes ...' He gave a little sigh. 'We had the happiest of times in our young lives. I never thought I would ever meet anyone else that could take Jennifer's place ...'

'But you thought that Carolyn Kane might do that?'

He nodded briefly then looked up as a young woman entered the room bearing a tray of coffees and biscuits. Finlay rose to his feet and took the tray from her, setting it down on the table.

'Thanks, Nadia,' he said as the girl left the room, a brief

smile on her face, dark eyes only on the accountant.

'Young Nadia's from Slovenia,' he told them. 'Part of an international intern programme we have.'

He handed round the coffees before sitting down again.

'Sorry, you were asking about Carolyn. Whether I wanted her to be my wife?'

Goodness, Davie Giles thought. *You didn't duck that question even though you were given the chance with that interruption.*

'Yes?' Newton looked at him intently.

'She had chosen another.' Finlay gave a longer sigh this time, setting down his own coffee cup. 'I could only look from afar and hope that in time she might change her mind.' He looked down. 'Too late now,' he said gruffly, his voice husky with emotion.

'But you did try to change her mind?'

'I never forced my attentions on Carolyn,' Finlay countered, 'never made a pest of myself. We were friends, she liked me and I, well, I loved her ...' He shrugged but his affected nonchalance was belied by the sudden tears in his eyes. 'Not a recipe for success ...' he added quietly, blinking hard.

'What do you make of him?' Davie asked eagerly as they walked down the street from the accountancy firm's office back to the city-centre car park.

'Nice man,' Molly replied. 'Pity there aren't more like him in the world.'

Davie nodded. She'd thought exactly as he had and that was something to be pleased about. Yet meeting Stuart Finlay had only emphasised how many victims there were in a murder case. The killer, whoever he was, had chucked a stone into the calm pool of Carolyn Kane's life and the ripples were still drifting to shore.

It was an image that Lorimer was fond of using and Davie Giles suddenly understood why.

CHAPTER SIX

Casting stones into the water was something he had done as a child, a lone figure at the edge of the sand where his feet sank into the grey mud, whorls left by unseen creatures burrowed deep beneath the surface. Other kids skiffed thin stones, often pieces of grey slate washed up on the shore, trying to see how many times their missile bounced across the surface before disappearing for good. But he had preferred to cast his out one at a time, hearing the satisfying splash and knowing that nobody else could retrieve that particular stone or small rock. Sometimes he would creep up surreptitiously on a younger child who had gathered a hoard of stones or pebbles, wait till they had toddled off to gather more then scoop them up and carry them off, gleeful in the knowledge that a small face would soon be red from bawling out their misery over the theft.

He had always been careful not to be seen and never to be caught.

A *quiet wee boy*, his relatives would muse. *But no trouble.* And that had established his reputation ever since. *A quiet chap, inoffensive,* he'd once overheard one of his colleagues tell a new member of staff. He smiled now at the memory. If only they knew! But, of course, they never would. His secret life was his and his alone to enjoy, his powers subtle and hard to pin down.

He walked into the café area of the bookshop, careful to take a seat at the back where it might seem as if he were simply stopping to read the newspaper tucked under one arm rather than to attend the afternoon talk from their latest author. Rows of seats were already taken up by a group of children and their parents, the free activity no doubt a welcome relief from having to spend a fortune entertaining their kids during the Easter vacation. Hidden behind the newspaper, nobody paid him the slightest attention; an ordinary man in dark clothes who would have been passed by in the street outside without a second glance, nobody remembering what he looked like, nothing about his appearance to make him stand out from the crowd.

The woman was a bit older than he had thought at first when he had seen her back in Glasgow, her details now available on Wikipedia. Married, no children. But he knew that already. And her age was of no consequence. She looked much younger than a woman in her forties, her complexion smooth and unwrinkled, no flabbiness around her waist like some of the women he worked with. He sat back as the lights dimmed and a single spotlight shone on her sitting there on that shallow platform, smiling out at her audience. An involuntary sigh escaped his lips, unheard by anyone but himself. She was perfect, simply perfect. Better than the others, her expression animated as she read what was now a familiar section from her book.

The need to keep his distance was a delicious torment. How he wanted to take her in his arms, feel those curves under his exploring hands ... But for now he would practise restraint and enjoy the endless anticipation of what was to come.

Maggie Lorimer tucked a stray curl behind her ears as she bent to talk to a little boy sitting cross-legged in front of her. This, she told herself, was an unexpected bonus of writing her stories. To be greeted by children like this, their eyes fixed on her as she spoke, was surely a reward in itself. As a childless woman, Maggie had known the heartache of giving birth only to see the premature infants being carried away, each tiny body piercing her heart with grief. David, who had breathed for oh such a short time in her arms, had been their final hope.

'Why did you make him a ghost?' the child asked.

'Well,' Maggie began, 'ghosts are quite special, aren't they? Nobody can hurt them and they can float high above the places they want to go unseen.'

'Except by other ghosts,' the wee boy said with a nod of his head.

'That's right,' Maggie told him, grinning. 'Gibby isn't lonely for long in the story when he makes friends with another ghost. Would you like me to read a bit more?'

'Yes!' chorused the children and Maggie settled back in her seat, turning to the Post-it note that marked the very place she had in mind.

Ivy sat to one side, regarding her newest author thoughtfully. The initial media attention had dried up, and now she, as Maggie's PR, must look for ways to direct attention back to this endearing woman. The story itself was good, no denying that, but children's books were notoriously difficult to market and placing good features in the nationals was like finding hen's teeth. There was something about her, Ivy thought as she watched Maggie's animated face, something that she might be able to use ... and it would certainly bring renewed media focus to the wife of a top cop in Police Scotland.

She took out her smartphone and focused it on Maggie's face. A few clicks later she had what she wanted and was scrolling down on the latest newsfeed about the two women who had been strangled back in Scotland's largest city. It was a big risk, but the publishers would never know. Besides, if she played her cards right they would be patting her on the back and even talking about the bonus that Ivy Thornton knew she deserved.

And, if it all went wrong? Well, what else did she have to lose? *Your last job with us*, that publicity director had told her. But she'd show them how much they needed her; they'd maybe even make her a permanent member of staff.

'Every step you take ... I'll be watching you,' he sang softly to himself as the music filled his earpieces. She had left now, the

other woman chivvying her along as soon as the last child had disappeared from the signing table. The flyer had given details of the book tour so it was a simple matter of following that same route and turning up in another dark corner to observe and wait. Meantime, he stood quietly at the counter, another postcard in his hand, one eye on the retreating figures heading back out of Perth's St John's Centre. Next stop was Oban and then across to the Isle of Mull and a small bookshop in Tobermory. He had already booked the car ferry for the following morning, hoping that the two women might have chosen the same schedule. If not, he would spend time watching them from a distance, binoculars around his neck, waterproofs and stout shoes giving the impression of a keen birdwatcher on holiday. And, should he be browsing the bookshelves for interesting bird facts when a certain children's author just happened to be in this island bookshop, well, nobody would notice him casting lustful eyes at his intended prey.

CHAPTER SEVEN

Anyone passing through the village that day might have paused to look at the tables and chairs outside the tearoom, April sunshine bringing patrons on to the cobbled pavement. Already signs of warmer weather were evident in the pink buds of cherry blossom at the crossroads and the unfurling lime green of beech trees by the village church. An idyllic scene and for some, Moira supposed bitterly, it must feel as though new life was being breathed into the air. Winters could be harsh living here above the snowline, the mountains etched against a pale blue sky and springtime had always been her favourite season in this place. But now anything that evoked renewal or rebirth simply taunted her with the reminder that nothing could bring Patricia back to life.

All the forgotten memories of raising their only child had come flooding back since she had arrived here in Kippen. Moira remembered mornings she had enjoyed at Mothers and Toddlers, rounds of birthday parties and school activities marked by Hallowe'en, Christmas and sports days. That seemed so long ago now, but nothing on Kippen Main Street seemed to have changed very much. Mothers still pushed their prams down the narrow streets, folk she did not recognise smiled and wished her good morning, such a change from London life where nobody spoke to strangers! If only ... She gave a sigh as she walked towards the village store. If she had stayed here, if they had not sent Tricia to board at Glenalmond ... If, if, if ...

The hollow feeling in her chest made Moira clutch her jacket around her for a moment and she stumbled, grasping the back of an old bench to steady herself. That was something that was never going to leave her until her dying day. Seasons might come and go but the aching emptiness of loss would be with her for ever. She had come out just for a little walk, the urge to be away from the big house overwhelming her, and now, as she sank on to the empty bench, Moira was grateful for this respite. The detectives would be back again soon, asking questions, wanting to know what sort of life Tricia had as an adult, particularly the times she had spent in London with her mother.

What could she tell them? The trivia of everyday living, was that what they wanted to know? The messy room upstairs that her daughter had claimed as her own private space, the smell of dope wafting down on occasion, traces of white powder mopped up by Moira herself before their cleaner could find them. The late nights ... Dear God, how often had she stood at the front window waiting to hear a taxi draw up, Charles urging her back to bed? And yet, even that had stopped once Tricia had grown tired of staying with them, preferring her friends, especially those men with whom she had been photographed at wild parties, celebrities clustered around, half dressed and vacant-eyed.

The woman who had once been so proud to be known as Lady Donovan closed her eyes and listened to the little world she had left behind all those years ago. The faint whirr of machinery spoke of a lawn being trimmed, the pad-pad of a dog's paws on the paving behind her and laughter from across the street where a group of cyclists had stopped for refreshments. And yet, how quiet it was! No continuous noise of heavy traffic punctuated by screaming sirens in the melting pot of her chosen city but gentler sounds like the cooing of a pair of collared doves in the trees above. What had she sacrificed for the life away from this timeless place? Had she really been as lonely as she'd once imagined? Carping on about the long hours Arthur worked and how isolated she was. *You don't know what you've got till it's gone,* she thought. If, if, if . . .

Her eyes opened wide and Moira gave a start as she felt someone sit down beside her on the bench.

'Lady Donovan?'

She nodded dumbly, taking in the man at her side, the blue eyes staring straight at her, a kindly expression on his face. Then, the flash of a warrant card so that she knew he was there on business.

'Detective Superintendent Lorimer,' he added. 'Sorry if I gave you a fright. You looked quite at peace with the world just now.'

Moira blinked and drew herself up, appraising this stranger who had the advantage of knowing a lot more about her than she did about him. His hair flopped over his forehead a little giving him a boyish look but the creases between those eyes and the lines around his mouth spoke of a man who had seen too much of the world's grief.

'I'm sorry for your loss,' he said quietly. How often had she heard those words now since that awful day when a police officer had stood on her London doorstep? Yet this man's accent was measured and sincere, as though he could somehow understand just what she was feeling at this very moment.

Almost before the silent tears began he had handed her a clean cotton handkerchief and looked away, allowing her the moment she needed to compose herself. Breathing in, she smelled something male yet fragrant, hints of citrus.

'I ...' Moira began, holding up the soiled handkerchief for a moment.

'Keep it,' Lorimer told her. 'I won't miss it and you can think of me next time you have to use it.' He smiled, one dark eyebrow raised.

Moira shook her head, not in denial but somehow bewildered by the kindness of the gesture. How long had it been since a man had done something for her without seeking a favour in return? She pursed her lips, the natural inclination to cynicism reasserting itself. Of course, he was just buttering her up so he could ask her all sorts of questions about Tricia, that was all.

'Would you like to sit here or go back to the house?' Lorimer asked.

Moira shook her head. 'Neither,' she replied. Then, on impulse she decided. 'Let's go for a walk, shall we? It's too nice a day to be back indoors and we can speak more privately along the road,' she added, nodding towards the hill that sloped gently to her left.

He took her elbow, a moment of courtesy, then stepped out, careful to match her stride. She was still wearing her city clothes, a smart fleece-lined jacket and a scarf knotted around her neck. For a moment Lorimer ground his teeth, the vision of another slim neck flashing into his thoughts. Patricia's mother was doing her best to hold it together, but he would let her weep if tears were needed, gently probing some sore places in order to find out what he needed to know.

To his surprise, Moira Donovan slipped her hand into his arm as they approached the end of a pavement, each of them taking time to look for traffic. A few cars were parked outside the doctors' surgery but nothing impeded their progress up Kippen Main Street, past the old red sandstone primary school with its garland of green vinery, past the garage then the playpark, the pathway just broad enough for them to walk side by side.

She stopped for a moment and turned. 'There,' she declared and pointed. 'Ben Ledi.'

'That's some view,' Lorimer agreed. 'I might have seen this village from the top once or twice.'

'You're a hill climber?'

'When I have the time, which isn't often these days,' he admitted.

'We all went up there once,' she told him, still looking at the panoramic line of hills across the valley. 'All three of us. When Patricia was in Primary Six.'

Lorimer saw her shake her head, her chest rising and falling in a great sigh. It was a good memory, by the expression in those tired eyes. And he hoped that she was being comforted by being here, knowing that her daughter's life had not been all about drug-taking and careering around on the arm of one rich playboy after another. There had been a Patricia Donovan before all of that, a little girl whose ghost still lingered here so long as there were those to remember her.

Solomon Brightman took down the book and smiled. The very first hardback copy, inscribed to them all but dedicated to Abby and Ben. What an achievement! He and Rosie were both proud of their friend's success and glad that Maggie had found something that was hers alone. As a schoolteacher she had gained a lot of satisfaction, her love of literature a precious gift to be passed on to future generations, but the pressure of administration for teachers everywhere nowadays took the shine off a lot of that sort of dedicated teaching. Add to that a husband whose working day stretched into the wee small hours for days at a time and you could understand if Maggie had been dissatisfied, but that wasn't in her nature. He nodded quietly to himself, thinking of the night of her book launch, the radiance in her face and the cheers from the huge crowd that had gathered to wish her well. If anyone deserved a moment in the sun it was Maggie.

The book slipped from his hand, its shiny cover opening up to reveal the author photo on the dust jacket. For a moment Solly frowned. That was ... He took a deep breath and gathered it up, smoothing the cover back into place. For a split second he saw the image of another woman, one whose press photo had graced the front page of today's *Gazette*. He blinked and stared. Maggie's long hair framed a heart-shaped face, eyes sparkling as she had looked slightly away from the camera; a moment of quiet joy captured by an experienced portrait photographer. Yet, hadn't he seen a similar expression on the face of that other woman? One whose life had been so brutally snuffed out?

Solly gave a shudder, thinking of the task that lay ahead: to create a profile of the killer of Patricia Donovan and Carolyn Kane. It was a trick of the light, that was all, or the power of imagination. Too much time spent thinking of those two dead women. And yet, when he closed his eyes and thought of them the face he saw was not theirs but Maggie Lorimer's. A cold shiver ran down Solly's back. What if ...? The idea took hold and stayed there for a moment, trembling as he reached for the phone.

'Nobody really knew her the way I did,' Moira told him, her gloved hands twisting the sodden handkerchief. 'From the outside it looked as though she were having the time of her life but she wasn't, not really.'

Lorimer sat beside her on the old wooden bench at the end the woodland path they had walked; opposite them lay a field where sheep grazed, their lambs frolicking together near the hedgerow. It was an idyllic scene, far removed from the stories he had heard of Patricia Donovan's life. It was not an unfamiliar tale: a young woman pleasure seeking in the fleshpots of London and elsewhere, a moth flying too close to the bright alluring candles until her wings were damaged.

'She craved attention,' Moira continued. 'And she got it, but not from the sort of people who would ever have made her happy.'

'Not from her parents?' Lorimer ventured.

Moira Donovan sighed. 'Oh, we were there to pick up the pieces, pay the rehab bills, that sort of thing,' she admitted. 'But neither of us gave her the time she probably needed . . . '

'Was there ever anyone you thought might have harmed your daughter?'

Moira turned her head and stared at him. 'Are you asking if I knew anybody that might have killed Tricia?'

Lorimer nodded silently.

She turned away once more, staring across the fields, and he wondered just what Patricia Donovan's mother was really seeing.

'I don't think there was anyone I ever met who behaved in an aggressive way towards my daughter,' she said at last. 'But then, I think you need to ask her friends about that, people she saw before she . . . she . . . '

Lorimer resisted the impulse to put an arm around the

bereaved woman's shoulder as she sobbed into her hands; it was not his place.

'This might sound a little far-fetched,' he began, 'but was there ever any sign of someone who might be showing an unwanted interest in Patricia? Not necessarily aggressive, more over-eager. A stranger, perhaps?'

Moira Donovan frowned and for a long moment said nothing. 'I can't remember . . .' she began. Then, 'Wait!' She looked up, a finger in the air, lips parted as though she were trying to recapture a long-forgotten moment. 'There was something. Some silly set of postcards Tricia had been sent from different locations.' She turned to Lorimer. 'As I recall they were all scenes of places she had visited up here, in Scotland.'

He saw her shudder visibly. 'One came from here, a postcard of Kippen. I remember it now, an old picture of the village as it used to be, you know? A sepia print.'

'And how did Patricia react?'

Moira shook her head. 'She laughed. Said it was one of her secret admirers.'

'Were they signed?'

Moira shook her head. 'No. And I don't remember what was written on any of them.' She looked up at Lorimer. 'Unlike many mothers, I never pried into my child's personal mail,' she sniffed.

'What happened to them?'

She shook her head and sighed. 'Who knows? Maybe they went out with the rubbish. Maybe she kept them and took them to her own place in *Glasgow*.' She pursed her lips in disapproval as though even the mention of Scotland's largest city brought a bad taste to her mouth. But then, Lorimer reminded himself, that was where Patricia Donovan's life had been cruelly snuffed out.

'And that was all? No strange telephone calls, nobody hanging about outside the house?'

'If there were she never told me,' she replied, a tinge of bitterness in her tone. Then she looked away again and he imagined the inner struggle, regrets for words spoken in the past, recriminations between two women who had different outlooks on life, a broken relationship that would never now be mended.

There were people he needed to see, friends of the victim, who might be able to give him the sort of information that could push this case forward. Any trace of unwanted attention from a stranger would be the key that might unlock the mystery of who had murdered these two women. But Moira Donovan had seen nothing of that sort of thing in London, making Lorimer believe that her daughter's killer was based in Glasgow where she had been found. The postcards, if they were from anybody sinister, might reinforce that theory.

Perhaps Lord Donovan was right in thinking that he had made enemies over the years when he had presided over serious cases in the High Court of Justiciary. But Lorimer's own inclination was to focus on whatever Carolyn Kane and Patricia Donovan had in common, apart from the brutality of their last moments.

*

'He's out of the office at the moment,' the voice told Solly. 'Can I pass you to DCI Cameron?'

'Thank you,' Solly replied, turning this way and that, the unsettled feeling growing inside him. Lorimer's mobile had been switched off, a sign that he was with someone and couldn't be disturbed? Or was he out of range, perhaps? Kippen could be a tricky place for transmission, Lorimer had told him. *Oot o' the world and into Kippen*, the locals boasted, as if their little village could be kept apart from the troubles of life. But sometimes being out of reach had distinct disadvantages.

'Professor Brightman, how can I help you?' Niall Cameron's soft Lewis accent was like a balm to Solly's ears, its musical cadence at once conjuring up a picture of Lorimer's former protégé.

'I had a thought,' Solly began then paused to gather the right words.

The silence between the two men continued for these few moments, no sign of impatience from Cameron who knew the psychologist's sudden silences well enough now.

'Missing persons,' he said at last. 'I was wondering ... what if there were a missing woman, or even more than one ... someone who resembled the two victims?' *And Maggie Lorimer*, a little voice reminded him, though he left those words unspoken.

'You think he's killed before?'

'It's not outwith the bounds of possibility,' Solly replied carefully. 'The act of killing is often preceded by other serious attacks.'

'Like rape,' Cameron agreed.

'Just so,' Solly agreed. 'I was wondering if any of the team had been instructed to investigate that possibility?' His question hung in the air, both men quite aware that no such missing persons' trawl had been made; only the HOLMES database that might throw up another similar killing somewhere else in the UK had been used.

'It's a good idea,' Cameron admitted. 'Though if there had been any woman of that description missing I'm sure we would have heard by now.'

Solly did not reply. People went missing all the time, often from choice, and the police could not possibly follow up every single wandering female unless their absence was reported and an anxious family persisted in making representations to the authorities.

'Besides,' the Lewisman went on, 'if something similar had taken place, surely a body would have been discovered by now?'

Solly nodded silently. This was true. The killer had simply dumped the bodies beneath bushes, not bothering overmuch to conceal them.

'You're right.' He sighed. 'It was only a thought. Still ...' He left the sentence unfinished.

'If Lorimer thinks this is worth following up, I'm sure he'll put someone on to it,' Cameron told him. Manpower, money ... neither man uttered those words but they both knew that such considerations would be at the front of the detective superintendent's mind once Niall Cameron had passed on Solly's message.

'Thank you,' the professor said before he put down the phone with a sigh. Was he chasing shadows? Perhaps. But the image of Maggie Lorimer's smiling face refused to leave his mind and he gave an involuntary shudder, wondering if his fears could possibly be justified.

CHAPTER EIGHT

The ping from her iPad made Maggie leap out of bed. It was still dark and there were hours to go before their boat left from Oban. It must be Bill, she told herself, pulling the device from its overnight charger and tapping in her private code.

She scrolled down the usual list of retail emails, not bothering as yet to trash them, eyes eager to see her husband's name.

Had she missed it? Maggie scrolled up and down, pausing for a moment on an unknown name, Andrew Dark, alerting her to a Facebook Message from someone she'd never heard of. Since the publication of her book, that was something with which Maggie was becoming familiar; so many new names in the editorial team as well as the artists and marketing folk down in London! He would be one of them, she guessed, moving back to sit on the edge of her bed.

She opened the Message page and read the words beneath a photograph of herself taken at the previous day's event.

Want to play hide and seek? I do.

The words were signed off by a tiny emoji of a Hallowe'en ghost.

She blinked and read it again. Who on earth had managed to leave a message on her Facebook account? The icon beside the name was faceless, suggesting a new user. How odd, she thought. Wasn't there some sort of barrier to deny strangers entry? Didn't you have to acknowledge a person before they could make contact? She shivered a little and drew the duvet around her, slumping back on to the pillows. This had to be a joke, surely? Nothing to do with her publishers at all. One of the kids from school, she decided. Some of them had been at the Glasgow launch. Was there an Andrew Dark at Muirpark Secondary School? She didn't think so but that meant nothing. Kids would enlist the help of any pals outside school.

But was it a school pupil? She looked more closely, recognising the woman who managed the bookstore in the background. This photo had been taken at the Perth event. She frowned, more puzzled than annoyed. The ghost was a juvenile sort of thing, but a little too close to her story where a child was dead and only his ghost remained alive and vibrant, the body mouldering somewhere in the earth below. That last aspect was not something she touched upon in her story; Gibby's past was a closed door as far as he and the readers were concerned, his adventures in the afterlife of far more importance. Maggie pursed her lips, doubly annoyed by whoever had sent this silly message and that there was none from her husband.

She closed down the iPad and thrust it to one side as though it were somehow contaminated. It wasn't worth being bothered about, Maggie decided, glancing at the pale light filtering through the curtains. Another day lay ahead and she was determined to make the most of it. Breakfast at the Manor House promised to be rather special and she was dying to show off the island of Mull to Ivy. If it was warm enough they would stand out on deck and watch as the waves from Lismore lighthouse rocked the ferry then she would point out Duart Castle before they rounded the point and headed to Craignure.

Standing in the shower, feeling needle points of spray invigorate her skin, Maggie closed her eyes, a half smile on her face. It would be a wonderful day; the skies were pale blue with no touch of pink to foretell rain, and she had heard birds chirping in the gardens from her open window. Bill would love this, she decided, wondering if they might manage a night in this hotel together before their annual trip to Leiter Cottage.

Just as she had decided to switch off the shower, the telephone rang out and Maggie grabbed a towel and padded swiftly back to the bedroom.

'Hello,' she said, a question in her tone as she listened for Bill's familiar voice.

There was a silence then . . . was that a sigh?

'Hello? Who's there?' she asked sharply.

Maggie heard a sudden click like the fastening of a lock. Then that continuous drone as communication was cut off.

A wrong number, she decided, putting the phone back on

its cradle and gathering the fluffy towel around her still damp body. But was it?

Someone was playing games with her, silly games that were designed to unsettle. But who would want to do something like that?

Maggie shivered, imagining a voice saying the words she had read on that anonymous message.

Want to play hide and seek? I do.

Ivy was already pouring coffee from a silver pot when Maggie arrived at the breakfast table.

'Sleep well?' she asked. Then, glancing towards the window that overlooked Oban bay, she gave a conspiratorial grin. 'Nice place, eh? Perks of being an up-and-coming author, Margaret,' she added.

Maggie nodded. If this tour was to include lovely hotels like the Manor House, then yes, the perks were certainly a boon.

'I did sleep well, thanks,' she replied, unfolding her linen napkin and taking up the leather-bound menu. For a moment she considered sharing the strange message with Ivy and the telephone call that had been abruptly cut off, but she said, 'How about you?'

'Oh, I had to do some work but when I got off I must have slept like a dead one. Like Little Gibby.' Ivy gave a short laugh. 'Right now, to the serious business of breakfast,' she went on briskly. 'Think I'll pass on the full Scottish since we have a boat ride ahead. But I do fancy the eggs Benedict.'

The moment to confide in Ivy had passed, Maggie reluctant

to voice her disquiet. It was just some silly nonsense, Maggie decided. Nothing to involve her publisher.

'I'll have the full Scottish,' she declared, as a waiter approached to take their order. 'Venison sausages and Stornoway black pudding are too tempting to turn down.' She smiled up at him. 'That will set me up for the day.'

The postcard was already stamped and he had rubbed it along the dusty side of the radiator in his B&B so that it looked a little travel worn. All the tricks he had learned, tiny things to throw off suspicious minds. It was part of the longer journey, what he thought of as a yearning after his flawless woman. This one had no imperfections, not like the ones that had struggled in his grasp, heinous creatures who had let him down so badly. Especially the one who had taunted him, threatening to expose his secrets. Well, she was gone now, any memories dead and buried with her.

He sighed as the boat turned its bow towards the western shore, the dark treetops silhouetted against a blue sky flecked with wispy clouds. He was alone now with his thoughts, the woman who dominated most of his waking hours no doubt back down in the observation deck waiting for the signal to descend to the car-parking area. For a few minutes he had watched her pointing towards the ancient castle, stronghold of the Macleans, keen to show it off to the woman by her side. He had stared at them both, sighing a little as he heard her voice again, proud of the animation in her face as she gazed towards the island.

She would speak to him just like that one day, would look at him with the same warmth. The certainty of their future together made him smile for a brief moment. Nothing would stop him achieving his dream. Not this time.

'That's Leiter Cottage,' Maggie exclaimed as the little white house came into view, the forest behind them, the road stretching out in a curve around Fishnish Bay.

Ivy gave her a quick glance then turned her attention back to the road ahead. 'Nice spot,' she murmured as Maggie craned her neck to see the last of the cottage before the view was swallowed up by a thicket of birches. She looked out instead at the water, the Sound of Mull that separated the island from the Morvern hills and the Ardnamurchan Peninsula. It was a sight she and Bill never tired of and Maggie smiled quietly to herself, calculating the weeks till their next holiday here together. She slipped one hand into her pocket, fingers closing on the pale pink pebble she always kept, its rounded surface smoothed by many Atlantic storms. It was a wee reminder of a day at Calgary with Bill, and Maggie sighed, wondering when they would next walk barefooted along these white sands.

Several times Ivy had to brake sharply as she manoeuvred the single-track road between Salen and Tobermory, slowing down for oncoming traffic and (once) a sheep that simply ran in front of them, its shaggy fleece swaying as it trotted ahead, mad-eyed. Maggie hid her grin as Ivy swore at the beast. It was almost as if the creature had sensed her hostility and determined to be as obdurate as possible. Eventually after several blasts of the horn, it took the hint and sloped off into the grass at the roadside.

At last the town came into view, its pastel-coloured buildings spread along Main Street.

'Hey, that's pretty!' Ivy exclaimed.

'Wait till you see it close up,' Maggie promised. Sure enough, as they descended the Eas Brae and drove along to the far end of the street, Ivy was visibly relaxing, her face wreathed in smiles of delight at the picture-postcard town. Maggie pointed out familiar landmarks like the town clock at the end of the Old Pier where fishing boats lay anchored by the stone wall; the old church, now an upmarket gift shop, its rose window glowing in the midday light, and Calve Island, lying protectively between Tobermory Bay and any fierce Atlantic storms.

'Try to park as close to Tackle and Books as you can,' Maggie advised, but Ivy had to drive all the way along to the far end of the street, past a whitewashed pier and the RNLI station before turning back to find a space close by the railings that separated the road from the deep waters of Tobermory Bay.

It was a thrill to see the shop window full of her books, a couple of posters proclaiming the date and time of this particular stage of her Scottish tour. She beamed as Ivy nudged her elbow.

'See, what did I tell you? Famous in every part of your homeland!'

Maggie shook her head and laughed, not believing her PR's

words in the slightest. Still, it was nice to be acknowledged here, in Mull, a place that lay so close to her heart.

They entered the shop and were greeted by the proprietor and his assistant, hugs for Maggie and handshakes as she introduced Ivy to them.

There was a table set out at the side of the shop facing the doorway and Maggie took her seat there, one hand touching the piles of books that had been artfully arranged for the occasion.

'Tea, coffee?' Barbara, the bookstore assistant, asked. 'Or just a glass of water?'

'Oh, water please,' Maggie assured her, settling herself behind the table and glancing around at the few folk who were browsing in the shop. It held all sorts of books, including a section devoted to fishing and other outdoor pursuits, the shop living up to its name as a supplier of tackle as well as a diverse range of books, children's toys and artists' materials.

Barbara returned a few minutes later with a glass of water.

'Here you are,' she said. Then, 'I think this came for you, though we haven't had the post yet. Must have been overlooked from yesterday's mail,' she added hesitantly, handing Maggie a postcard.

'For me?' Maggie took the postcard and gave a little frown. 'How strange,' she murmured. Barbara hovered for a moment, evidently curious to know more, but a customer at the counter caught her attention and she walked away, leaving Maggie to ponder the mysterious card.

It was like any sort of tourist picture of Perth, a summer

shot with flowers around the High Street, but the handwriting on the back was utterly unfamiliar. Small, crabbed writing with her name and the address of the bookshop (even its post code, the detective's wife noticed) and that scrawl across the left hand side:

See you in Tobermory.

She shivered. It was too much of a coincidence, surely? That silent phone call and the message on her iPad . . . someone was playing tricks on her and Maggie decided there and then that she was having no more of it. The kids at school had far too much time on their hands this Easter break, she told herself. She would deal with it on her return to Muirpark, settle their nonsense once and for all. And yet, looking at the handwriting once again, it did not appear like any of the scrawls she was used to from her pupils, the script more old-fashioned, adult . . .

'Here we are,' the proprietor beamed at Maggie as a troop of adults and children crowded into the shop, lining up to have their copies signed.

She slipped the postcard into her handbag, determined to deal with it when this was all over and life was back to normal once again.

Margaret Lorimer's smile was warm and genuine as she greeted each person at her signing table, Ivy noticed. This woman could really make it to the big time if she played her cards right. The sincerity and time she took obviously endeared her to the reading public and Ivy nodded to herself, satisfied that the tour was becoming more successful with every stop.

She slipped out of the place, leaving Duncan, the bookshop owner, in charge. It was quieter on the street, a few people strolling up and down, but Ivy chose to cross to the railings before taking out her mobile phone and tapping in a number.

'It's me,' she said at last, glancing across the street as more customers joined the long queue snaking out of the bookshop. 'There's something I want you to do.'

CHAPTER NINE

Molly Newton's transition from an undercover officer to a detective sergeant who was often out and about, visible to the public, had been difficult but she was beginning to come to terms with all that now. Following the previous case when she had narrowly escaped with her life, Molly had been summoned to Lorimer's office and told in no uncertain terms how he saw the progress of her future career. It had been a bittersweet moment, praised for her courage but chastened for taking a risk that ought never to have happened. Still, the outcome had been a success and if DS Newton had lost her anonymity in the process, she was at least assured of her boss's support now that her role in the MIT had changed. Working for Lorimer was something a lot of cops aspired to; the detective superintendent was a fair-minded man who had seen plenty of action and taken risks himself, if all the stories were to be believed. Good-looking man, too, Molly admitted more than once, observing her boss as the team sat in the boardroom discussing the next steps in the latest case. He was just the sort of man she liked: tall enough for a woman who tipped five-eleven in her heavy-soled boots, a restlessness about him that she found intriguing, mainly because it was something with which Molly could identify. Pity he was so happily married to that beauty of a wife.

Molly listened attentively to the different reports as they were read out: the dead women's computers had been scrutinised for anything untoward and she was hopeful that John Scott, her favourite IT geek, would have something to tell them.

Molly watched, amused, as the man kept pushing his spectacles up from the middle of his nose, his fingers fidgeting with the edges of a pile of printouts. *Oh, aye*, she thought; *Scotty's found something all right, I can almost smell his eagerness to be up and running with it.*

'John.' Lorimer turned to their technical expert. 'You've got something for us?'

The change in the younger man's demeanour made everyone turn and stare; it was not just his frantic nodding but the long breath taken between parted lips, as though he needed that tiny moment to pause in order to hike up the drama.

'I think they both had a common stranger on their Facebook pages,' the man declared at last. 'May I show you?'

Hardly waiting for a nod from Lorimer, John Scott hurried to the whiteboard at the far end of the room and slid a sheet of paper on to the projector, letting it appear.

'There's nothing to show his face, just the image of a

death's-head moth,' he said, turning to indicate the tiny picture on the screen, the name beside it, *Dave Harkness*. 'And,' he drew another breath as if waiting for a drumroll to precede his next statement, 'whoever posted this took down their identity pretty soon after they'd been posted. There were several posts sending various messages of sympathy about Carolyn but this particular one links both women,' he told them.

The IT expert looked at each member of the team, a glint of triumph in his eyes. Then, sweeping the page away, he replaced it with another.

'Now, see what I found on Patricia Donovan's Facebook stream.'

There was complete silence as all eyes were turned to the illuminated whiteboard. This time, the Facebook user, *Dave Harkness*, had selected a grinning skull over two crossed bones.

'Used on the graves of plague victims,' Scott said helpfully. 'Jolly-looking fellow despite the nasty end these victims must have suffered.'

'What did the original team make of that?' asked Molly. 'Seems odd.'

'I don't think much was made of it at the time, to be honest. People have all sorts of strange avatars these days.'

'What else?' Lorimer asked.

Molly glanced back at him, seeing the arms folded, the slight trace of a smile on his lips as though he were enjoying John Scott's little performance.

'This, however,' Scott said with a smile, 'was written on both women's Facebook page just two nights after they died.'

Like a magician saving his best trick till last, Scott placed the final page under the projector.

GOODBYE, GOODBYE

'Not something that elicited a like or a share, not even a comment. Probably nobody really read the posts except to see if their own was there.' He paused to let his words sink in. 'Not long after their bodies were discovered and the news hit the papers. There were plenty of posts on their Facebook pages after that.'

The words in themselves should not have sent a chill down Molly Newton's spine but the very fact of there now being a link like this between the two dead women made her shiver. Murmurs amongst the team were allowed for a moment or two until Lorimer raised his hand and nodded for the IT expert to continue.

'Interestingly, that was also removed from their pages a mere twenty-four hours after it was posted,' he ended. 'And so far we can find no other trace of a Dave Harkness anywhere on the system linked to either of them.'

'Good work, John.' Lorimer nodded, and the IT man sat down again, red-faced with pleasure as the whole team broke into impromptu applause.

'Now we have confirmation, to an extent, of what we had suspected: Carolyn Kane and Patricia Donovan were both targets of a stalker, possibly the same person that took their lives.'

Molly nodded her silent approval. It was bad practice to

state that something was likely on evidence as tenuous as this and they all knew it, but there had been a feeling amongst them all from the start that both women had died at the hands of a man who had hunted them down over a period of time. She roused herself as Lorimer continued to speak.

'You all know how difficult it is to trace a stranger killer,' he told them. 'There is no match on our database for the DNA found at both crime scenes, contact traces that make it almost certain that the killer of Carolyn and Patricia are one and the same man.'

Everyone watched as Lorimer sat up straight again, hands clasped on top of the table. 'And that is one reason why we are again enlisting the services of Professor Solomon Brightman to create a profile for us.' There were a few murmurs and heads turning to glance at fellow officers.

'Given the pressure we are under to solve this one as fast as we can,' Lorimer had raised his eyebrows knowingly, 'there are plenty of resources at our disposal.'

Molly took a deep breath. The man ought to have been a politician, she thought. That was tantamount to saying that Lord Donovan had pulled strings and every member of the MIT would be required to work their butts off until his daughter's murderer was safely behind bars. But at any rate the powers on high had given the green light to spending what was needed on the case, including the services of that bearded professor Molly had met on a few occasions in this very building.

'We need the press on our side,' Lorimer told them. 'We

have a few very good investigative journalists who still keep some sort of integrity when it comes to handling police investigations. Not all of them are out to make cheap copy,' he added. 'Our press officers are already preparing statements for the nationals but this latest bit of information stays here. Understood?'

Nodding heads and *yes boss, yes sir* showed the solidarity of their agreement, Molly noticed. It was important to follow the detective superintendent's lead. One slip of the tongue could result in days or even weeks of work being wasted, not to mention evidence required at a later date for the law courts.

Lorimer lifted the telephone in his office and tapped in the extension number. A few moments later a familiar lilting voice gave his name and rank.

'DCI Cameron.'

'It's me, Lorimer, can you spare a minute?'

He put down the phone and drummed his fingers on the edge of his desk. Then, taking up a pencil, he wrote the words DAVE HARKNESS on a piece of paper. On the rare occasions when they spent an evening together and found time to do a crossword, he and Maggie enjoyed the cryptic clues with hidden words and anagrams spicing up the *Gazette*'s back page. Now these words seemed to rearrange themselves in front of his gaze.

He made a face and sighed. So obvious when you suddenly saw it and he was surprised that a lateral thinker like Scott hadn't noticed it right away.

'Boss?' Niall Cameron had knocked and then opened the door and Lorimer motioned him to his side of the desk.

'Have a look,' Lorimer told him, drawing a pencil arc between the two names and circling the first letter of each.

'Oh, heck,' Cameron said. 'Not one of us saw that even though Scottie had it up on a screen.'

'*Have Darkness*,' Lorimer said aloud. 'It's a message, don't you think? Something to warn them about what was waiting for them.'

'Professor Brightman will have plenty to say about that,' Cameron agreed. 'He was playing with them, do you think? Or giving them a chance to get away?'

'What if he was hoping for something different? Not to kill them at all but to sweep them off in some deluded dream of his own? Isn't that what stalkers do?'

'And when they rejected his advances, terrified by a stranger's approach, he panicked. Is that what you're saying?' Cameron asked.

Lorimer nodded slowly. 'It makes sense of the times he posted those Facebook messages, too,' he said. 'As if he were consigning them to eternal darkness, knowing they were already dead.'

He gazed past the DCI, trying to understand the workings of a warped mind – and wondering if they would ever know what had really taken place in those Glasgow parks.

The university was far less busy than usual given the Easter break, although several students were still on campus, eager to be prepared for their finals in the coming weeks. Solly had walked a little more slowly than usual, noticing the daffodils blowing in the morning breeze, their yellow trumpets bright against the well-tended lawns around the old buildings. There was a distinct chill in the air, a certain frostiness that was apparent on the verges shadowed beneath the grey walls. Winter in this northern climate had not yet relinquished its grip, he thought, pulling his coat collar across his neck. One day the sun might break through these clouds, giving the semblance of a warm summer's day, the next a wind from the north-east could wreak havoc across the city. It had not been the first time that Solly had been caught out by the vagaries of Scotland's weather and he knew that there were still some weeks before he could be sure of arriving to work without his tweed coat.

The two women had been dressed for the weather, he mused: Carolyn Kane in a summer frock and sandals, Patricia Donovan in leggings and a sports top, her leather jacket discarded beneath the rhododendron bushes nearby. This killer wasn't particular about the time of year he took his victims, something to which Solly had given thought over the previous evening. One thing did stand out, however, and that was the timing of each murder. Whoever had taken their lives had targeted the women during the school holidays. Was that significant or a mere coincidence? For Solly it was one more detail to add to the little he knew but everything helped to build up a tentative picture of the man. The women had been killed at night-time, each on their way home; Carolyn had been seeing her fiancé over in Shawlands, her walk across Queen's Park cut short by the perpetrator. Why hadn't Jake Richardson accompanied his wife-to-be across that expanse of parkland like he normally did? There had been a murder there some years before, after all. That, Solly told himself, was a question that the officers from the MIT would do well to ask.

Molly had hidden her surprise at seeing Jake Richardson face to face for the first time. There was no denying he was a handsome fellow, his brown hair a little scruffy but just the right length to be considered fashionable, the two-day growth of beard giving him a raffish look. He was a little taller than her, she guessed, but with heels on Molly had the satisfaction of looking the man straight in his eyes as he opened the door of his Southside flat. She had long ago learned never to judge by appearances and preferred to listen to what a person had to say as well as to their manner of recounting a particular memory.

'Mr Richardson? DS Newton, DC Giles, Police Scotland,' Molly said, brandishing her warrant card then slipping it back into the inside pocket of her leather jacket. Davie nodded to the man but remained silent for now, letting his colleague take charge.

The man stepped forward a little, hands clutching each side of the doorway, filling the space as though to deny her entry, his handsome face scowling back at her.

'What do you want now?' he demanded. 'It's been months since Caro was killed and you lot have done absolutely nothing as far as I can see,' he told them.

'We have reason to believe that the case may be linked to another more recent death,' Molly told him quietly, looking Richardson straight in the eye, refusing to be intimidated by his bullish stance.

'Oh, aye, some high court judge's daughter gets it and all of a sudden you're jumping to someone's orders. Eh? That what you're telling me?' His voice grew louder and Molly was aware of a neighbour passing on the stairs, looking up at the two figures standing outside the entrance to Richardson's flat.

The actor must have been aware of it too, as he drew back and jerked his head towards the hallway.

'S'pose you may as well come in,' he told them grudgingly.

She and Davie entered the flat as Richardson stood aside and waved them in, a grandiose gesture that held more than a hint of sarcasm.

'In here,' the actor told them gruffly, pointing towards an open door.

Molly and Davie exchanged a brief glance as they entered the large room, clearly the main sitting room with a bay window that overlooked Queen's Park.

'Take a seat,' Richardson said, throwing himself into an easy chair that sat against the light of the window, casting some shadows across his face. Was that a deliberate choice? Molly was alert to each and every detail as she watched the man, reminding herself that he was an actor, accustomed to the nuances of theatrical stagecraft. He would know how to hide himself from their gaze, making him less vulnerable to their scrutiny. Or perhaps this was simply the chair he usually favoured? It was a habit of hers to read too much into a situation, Molly reminded herself.

'Mr Richardson, the case of your fiancée has never been closed,' Molly began. 'And I have to tell you that, yes, the high profile of Patricia Donovan has created a bit of media interest. You may well be doorstepped by the press in days to come,' she added.

Richardson's eyebrows flew upwards in a moment of undisguised surprise.

He hadn't expected me to be so frank, Molly told herself. Maybe he would be a tad more cooperative as a consequence. 'We are not officers from the original investigation,' she continued, nodding towards Davie. 'We represent the authority of the Major Investigation Team in Glasgow. Because there is reason to think that Carolyn and Patricia were targeted by the same killer it escalates the entire case, you see,' she explained.

'Oh.' Richardson sank back against the cushions, his whole expression changing from tense aggression to a moment of defeat. The slumped shoulders and downcast eyes made him look a lot younger than his thirty-two years, Molly thought, in a sudden wave of sympathy. This was a bereaved man who had lost not just the woman he claimed to have loved but his entire future with her. Had they planned more than a wedding? Had a house and kids been part of the dream that had been shattered that fateful summer's night? Another victim, she reminded herself. One of many.

'I am sorry to have to go over such painful memories,' Molly began. 'But there may be something that you can tell us that could help find Carolyn's killer.'

The puzzled frown extended towards Davie who leaned forward and nodded his agreement.

'We are talking to all of Carolyn's friends again,' Davie Giles assured him. 'And one of the things that DS Newton and I are trying to find out about is the possibility that the two women may have experienced the unwanted attentions of the same man.'

'A stalker?' Richardson asked, his head tilted to one side as though he was now interested in what they were asking him. 'Is that what you think? Some weirdo who followed both of them . . . ?'

'That is one theory we are working on,' Molly said in clipped tones, fuming inwardly at Davie. This man was used to publicity. It would never do for him to blab about this to the papers. 'I have to ask you to keep such ideas strictly to yourself, of course,' she added firmly. 'Now, can you please cast your mind back to the last time you saw Carolyn.'

Richardson gave a huge sigh and shook his head. 'How can I ever forget it?' he asked, one hand raised in a gesture that seemed a little too practised to Molly's eyes. This was the actor back on his stage, performing for them, she decided. Nevertheless she would watch and listen to what he wanted to tell them, see how he recounted particular memories and decide if it was the truth.

Richardson stood up and walked across to the window, hands folded behind his back so that they could not see his face.

'I stood just here,' he told them, in a voice that seemed full of genuine sorrow. 'Watched her walk across the road and along to the corner. Knew she'd be crossing the park before it got dark.' He turned to them now, his face serious. 'It was late summer and a nice evening . . . she should have been okay walking home in the park . . . plenty of people about . . .'

'Why didn't you go with her, see her safely home? You told the original investigating officers that's what you usually did,' Molly asked, her words sounding harsh though she had dropped her voice a little in an attempt to soften what was a difficult question.

Richardson winced as though she had actually hit him. 'Don't you think I've asked myself that a thousand times?' he cried. 'God knows if I could turn the clock back then I would!'

'So, why didn't you?' Molly persisted.

Richardson turned away from them again. 'I was waiting for a telephone call from my agent,' he murmured, his voice barely audible. 'Big part in a TV drama I was expected to get . . .'

'And did this agent call you that night?' Molly continued. 'Could you not have taken it on your mobile? Walked Carolyn home at the same time?' She frowned. That didn't make sense. Who stayed in waiting for a landline call nowadays? Some of her friends didn't even have such a thing any more.

Richardson turned around and both detectives could see tears streaming down his face. 'I was always losing phones,' he gulped. 'Pretty absent-minded, I guess . . .'

'So your agent called you that night?' Molly cut in. 'You stayed in to find out about a part. What happened?'

He shook his head. 'Never called. Someone else got it. I could've walked Caro home after all.' His voice was husky with emotion and regret. 'All this time I've been blaming myself for that night ...' He thumped his chest and tossed his head as though lost for more to say.

Molly pursed her lips, unconvinced by the tone of Jake Richardson's voice, the dramatic words and the beating of his breast a tad too staged for her liking.

But her colleague had evidently been swayed by this little performance.

'Don't,' Davie told him, standing up and crossing the room, a paper handkerchief held out to the weeping actor. 'If what we believe is true then your fiancée's killer was an opportunist who was waiting for the moment he would find her alone. You couldn't have been with her every moment of the day.'

Richardson blew noisily into the tissue, nodding briefly.

But Molly Newton had a frown across her brow. Most couples engaged to be married had moved in together by this stage. Why not the Kane woman and her fellow? That was curious, surely? And another thing, in all of the paperwork and photographs, she had never seen a sign of an engagement ring.

'Did Carolyn have a ring? An engagement ring?' Had it been taken, perhaps, by the killer? Molly wondered. And if so, why had that never been made clear by the original investigating team?

Richardson avoided her gaze. 'Couldn't afford one,' he mumbled. 'Would have bought her a beauty one day, of course,' he added defiantly.

'I'm so sorry,' Davie began, shooting a dark look towards Molly as if her question had been out of order.

'I'll never forgive myself as long as I live! Never!' Richardson cried out, thumping one fist against the other.

'Something we are asking all of Carolyn's friends,' Molly went on calmly as though the man's dramatic outburst was not taking place, 'were you ever aware of anyone making a nuisance of themselves, pestering Carolyn in any way?'

Richardson shook his head. 'No,' he told them. 'I never saw anything . . . anyone . . . I promise you.'

And Molly Newton believed him. Was this a man quite wrapped up in himself and unable to see further than his own persona? Maybe he had really been in love with Carolyn Kane, maybe some of these tears were genuine, but as she rose to take their leave, she doubted whether a person like Jake Richardson would fail to move on from this tragedy. He'd find someone else, she decided. Might even try to capitalise on the renewed interest in Carolyn's death. For a moment she wished that the accountant they'd met had been able to win the dead woman's heart after all. Molly gave herself a little mental shake. That was unfair to make such a sweeping generalisation about the man they had just met. Besides, how were they to be sure that Stuart Finlay was as genuine as he had appeared?

And, she reminded herself as they left the flat, even if Carolyn Kane had shifted her affections to her boss, would that have made any difference to her fate?

*

Jake stood at the window watching the two figures walk towards their car. His mouth was dry and he badly needed a drink after that little performance. Had he convinced them? He thought so. But even as he saw their car pull away from the kerb, he continued to follow its progress, wondering what these two police officers were saying at this very moment.

They would never find out what had really happened that night, he told himself with a sigh. Only Carolyn could ever have told them. And now that particular truth was dead and buried.

CHAPTER TEN

The home that Patricia Donovan had lived in was not very far from his own house in Giffnock, Lorimer realised, as he followed the directions on his satnav to Rouken Glen, a park that he remembered playing in when he was wee. The boating pond had been a magnet for Lorimer and his pals back then, all of them eager to show off their prowess with a pair of oars. He glanced at the greenery flashing between trees as he slowed down and turned into the street where Patricia had lived. It consisted of rows of pre-war bungalows, their steep tiled roofs punctured by dormer windows, some extended over the years to provide family-sized homes.

He came to a halt as the satnav voice proclaimed unnecessarily that he had arrived at his destination. The grass at the front had not been cut yet, he noticed, and there were weeds sprouting up through the gravel on the driveway. From what little he knew of Patricia Donovan, he had not expected her to be an avid gardener, probably preferring to go out socialising than spend time tending her flowerbeds. Yet she had been at a sports club the night of her death; that showed some enthusiasm for an active life? Mustn't be too eager to judge, Lorimer reminded himself, locking the Lexus and fumbling for the keys to the dead woman's home.

Reading the dwelling place of a particular person was something he had learned over the years. How they decorated their own space, whether plants and flowers proliferated, the sorts of pictures they chose to display, all of these and more provided clues about a person.

He stooped to pick up a small pile of mail, mostly flyers, from where they had dropped through the letterbox. Riffling through them with his gloved fingers, Lorimer noted the plain white envelopes with business addresses he recognised for what they probably were: bank and credit card statements. No personal handwriting or postcard from an absent friend, he thought with a twinge of disappointment, placing the leaflets for loose covers and the local food stores at the back of the pile and putting them on a nearby table beside a lamp with a Tiffany shade and an empty seashell, its pearly pink surface gleaming softly. He ran a finger across the surface of the wooden table, noting only the faintest trace of dust. Someone had kept the place clean, at any rate, he thought. Had Patricia employed a lady to come in and 'do' for her? Or had Lord Donovan's daughter been scrupulous about her own housework? He stepped forward, his feet loud against the pale wooden floor, and headed for the nearest door. A quick glance revealed a toilet and shower, the dark red carpet and matching painted walls contrasting with the white porcelain ware. Pushing the door a little further Lorimer caught sight of a large colour photograph displayed on the wall opposite the shower. It was Patricia Donovan, all right, scantily dressed and posing for the photographer, a mocking smile on her half-open lips as though she were perfectly aware that the coquettish pose was just a big joke between them both. She'd been a model, of course, and this might well have been given after a particular photo shoot. The woman looked back at him, head tilted at an angle, hands on hips as though challenging him in some way.

What a waste, he thought sadly, remembering the rehabilitation centres and gossip columns full of lurid tales. She'd been recovering from her reckless past when someone had snuffed out that vibrant life, he realised. Jaw hardening, Lorimer resolved once more to find out just who that person was.

The hallway led him to a large lounge-cum-dining-room with a door leading into a smart kitchen. His first impression was of lots of light and colour: the sofa was turquoise with a brightly coloured Indian throw tossed across it and small velvet cushions in crimson and violet stacked into each corner. Again, the flooring was wooden though a pair of Turkish rugs covered the space in front of the sofa and under the dining table and chairs. No photographs adorned the walls here but instead several framed prints, a Jolomo landscape and others chosen, he guessed, for their vivid yellows and blues to match the room's décor. She'd had an eye for colour, Lorimer could see, walking around the room, noting the candlesticks with buttercup yellow candles, their perfect wicks never lit but merely for show. He stopped at the dining table, staring at the thick cotton place mat and folded yellow linen napkin. A table set for one, he thought sadly. Patricia Donovan had been schooled in the old-fashioned habit of dining at her own table, setting herself a place there for meals. There was something about it that made him reassess his idea of the dead woman. Had she been content here in her own home? The place bore all the signs of having been enthusiastically decorated, a house she might have enjoyed for many years to come.

He'd take a closer look later, but a cursory glance into the kitchen showed plain grey units and clean white surfaces with stainless-steel fitments; it might have come out of a magazine, the place was so neat and tidy.

Upstairs there were two bedrooms, one with an en suite bathroom that had obviously belonged to Patricia. There were shelves full of expensive cosmetics here and a spotlight above the wash-hand basin with a vast mirror behind it making the bathroom seem larger than it actually was. The bedroom, however, was huge and Lorimer reckoned that at some point a builder had knocked down a wall to make three rooms into two. There was a faint smell of something sweet and musky that he could not readily identify but, spotting a square glass candle-holder on the windowsill, he strode across and picked it up, sniffing the half-burned-out candle inside. Yes, he decided, that was where this particular fragrance came from. She'd evidently used it often enough for the scent to linger. In one corner lay a rolled-up yoga mat and a pair of headphones, plugged into a socket by the queen-size bed.

Outside the window a birch tree swayed in the breeze, its twigs still holding on to buds yet uncurled. Below, the garden was a mixture of grass and shrubs, a few late purple crocuses closed against the chill air. Directly beneath the window was a water butt, placed by the rone pipe to catch any overflow. He could see the oily water gleaming. A small frown crossed his face: any police officer doing a home safety inspection would have pointed out the danger of having such a thing directly under a bedroom window. A leap from the edge of the butt could allow a skilful burglar access to the room, had a window been left the tiniest bit open. He gave an inward sigh and stepped back again. Worse than that had befallen the woman, but not here, not in the sanctuary of her own home. She'd been killed in that park instead.

The bedroom might be a huge room but it had a cosy feel, too, the white carpet softer underfoot than the laminate flooring throughout the rest of the house, small pillows piled high against the larger ones tilted against a pink velvet headboard, the tones in this room muted pastels and creams. He closed his eyes, breathing in the scented candle, and imagined the woman sitting cross-legged listening to music or something else – mindfulness recordings from one of her rehab places, perhaps? Had she reached somewhere to relax? Had this been a warm and comforting space at night? And, the biggest question of all, had she been stressed by the unwanted attentions of a stalker, needing to banish any fears with her nightly routines?

Several pot plants trailed their leaves from the top of a display cabinet and there were books stacked in the lower shelves alongside a framed picture of Patricia with her mother, the London Eye in the background. What sort of books she had might give him some insight into her personality, Lorimer told himself as he took note of the titles on their spines. A few romances jostled for space with popular crime fiction and a couple of slim hardback volumes about yoga and mindfulness. He took them out, one by one, anxious not to disturb the way she had left them; though why that mattered now he could not really say. It was a mark of respect, he supposed, putting a Christopher Brookmyre back alongside an Ann Cleeves, the volumes clearly sorted in alphabetical order. The dust jacket was a bit creased and he drew it out again, folding the cover back neatly.

That was when he saw them, wedged behind the books: a small pile of postcards.

The rubber band snapped into two pieces as he tried to unfasten it, scattering the cards on to the floor. Cursing himself, Lorimer scooped them up with gloved hands trying to keep the pile in their previous order. They were all picture postcards from different parts of the UK: several were scenes from Glasgow, including the University, Glasgow Cathedral and George Square, and there was one from Edinburgh then two from London (the London Eye again) and lastly an old sepia print of the village of Kippen.

There was no writing other than Patricia's name and some different addresses, including her mother's flat in London, all in the same small, crabbed hand.

Lorimer sat back on his haunches, wondering. Had these been sent by whoever had taken that photo of Moira Donovan and her daughter? Or were they the same ones Patricia's mother had referred to when he had dropped a hint about a possible stalker? Drawing out a plastic bag, Lorimer placed the postcards inside to take back to Helen Street. He would see what their technical experts might make of them.

As he descended the stairs, Lorimer wondered if the dead woman's mother had ever visited this house and known the sort of home Patricia Donovan had created for herself at last. There was no sign of any other person here, no spare tooth-brush in either of the bathrooms, no male fragrance jostling for space beside the Lancôme and Dior. And just that one table setting. As he walked back to the kitchen and opened cupboard doors, Lorimer had the feeling that Patricia Donovan had found contentment living here on her own with her books and her small rituals of mindfulness. Had she tired in the end of the whirl of parties and recreational drugs? Perhaps. He and his team still needed to question her friends and neighbours, piecing together a picture of how Patricia had lived in the days leading up to her death: the same sort of questions that had been asked about another young woman whose future had been cruelly cut short.

A picture of Carolyn Kane's life was slowly emerging, Lorimer realised, as he put together the various reports from his officers. She had been an ordinary enough young woman, successful in her career, planning her wedding, house-hunting with her actor fiancé ... He frowned for a moment. That wasn't ordinary, though, was it? Nowadays most couples cohabited, often for years, before marriage, babies sometimes coming on to the scene before the panoply and expense of a big wedding. Yet these two had maintained their own separate flats, Richardson's in bustling Shawlands, Carolyn's across the park in a leafy avenue off Victoria Road. Why? The detective superintendent pondered the question. Theirs was to have been a church wedding, but as far as he could tell Carolyn had not been particularly religious, certainly not part of any sect that forbade sex before marriage. No, there was something else here that might be worth another look.

Richardson had no firm alibi for the woman's death. Yet there was nothing they could do to pin it on the man. Sure, his DNA was all over her; what did they expect? The couple had spent the evening together after all; Richardson's initial statement showed that they had talked about their future, discussing the wedding during the hours before she'd left to cross the park. But if the actor's hands had been the ones to strangle her, then there were no sign of his prints around her throat. DS Newton had reported on their visit, adding a note that she had felt the bereaved fiancé had exaggerated his feelings for the benefit of the two officers. Not a crime, of course, and perhaps playing a part was second nature to a thespian. Besides, what had Richardson to gain from Carolyn's death? She had been the higher earner of the couple, her prospects within the accountancy firm rosy, whereas Jake Richardson was far from being the big household name he undoubtedly aspired to be. A few TV ads and some small parts in a Scottish soap were the highlights of his CV, his more recent income depending on recording a series of audio books.

Had there ever been a hint of jealousy on Richardson's part? A feeling of frustration that he was standing still while Carolyn was going places in her career? None of the mutual friends that had been questioned had ever mentioned anything of this sort, however. And, why would they? Her death had bound them together, after all, pity for the actor's loss a focus for their collective grief. Perhaps Molly Newton could probe a little deeper, Lorimer thought. She was becoming adept at asking difficult questions. And this morning Newton and Giles were to visit the person that had brought Kane and Richardson together in the first place.

'We were in the same year at school,' Lesley McArthur explained. 'Dan, my husband, knew Jake from his own school days.' She shrugged. 'It was as simple as that, really. Dan asked me if I thought Caro could drive Jake to the wedding, seeing as she lived so close . . . ' She waved her hands in the air, bringing them together as if to say how that meeting had resolved itself. 'We had even spoken about the possibility of them getting together then we said, nah, it would never work, they've got nothing in common.'

'Why was that?' Molly asked, looking at the woman sitting opposite. Lesley McArthur shifted uncomfortably in her chair, adjusting a cushion behind her back. Molly and Davie had travelled out of the city to a new housing estate to see her, on account of her pregnancy.

Lesley made a face. 'Jake always struck me as being pretty full of himself,' she explained, raising her eyebrows meaningfully. 'Caro—' She broke off and looked thoughtful. 'Caro was one of those girls everyone liked. She never made best friends with one person and left another out like some of the wee bitches we went to school with, you know?'

Molly nodded. That sort of childish behaviour was endemic with young girls, their tussle over best friends vying with peer pressure to conform to unspoken rules. She'd thrown herself into sporting activities to get away from the sly looks and whispered words behind girls' hands, her height and awkwardness making Molly Newton the butt of jokes amongst her classmates. *All ugly ducklings grow up into swans*, her dad had told her more than once and Molly remembered this now, all these years later. But Carolyn Kane had been a nice girl, her friend told them, the sort you could always depend upon.

'So, why Jake Richardson?' Davie asked.

Lesley shook her head. 'It surprised us both,' she admitted. 'They were engaged six months after our wedding.' Lesley glanced towards the large silver-framed photograph of her much slimmer self decked in white, her handsome, kilted groom laughing beside her. The woman heaved a sigh and turned back to the officers. 'That was it. Met at our wedding, as I said, then boom! Before anyone knew it they were totally besotted with one another. Well, *she* was, anyway,' she said, glancing at Molly.

'She was a good-looking girl,' Molly replied blandly. 'He must have found her attractive?'

'According to Dan, my husband, Jake hadn't ever shown signs of settling down. One pretty girl after another, played around ...' She shifted uncomfortably again. 'We told ourselves that everyone settled down eventually, even Jake. But I think he found a different sort of attraction in Caro,' she continued slowly. 'Don't get me wrong, she was lovely, but a much quieter sort of person than he was, not his type at all.' She hesitated and Molly waited, wondering what was on her mind.

'If this sounds unkind, then I'm sorry,' Lesley said at last, looking from one of the officers to the other. 'But Caro was exactly what Jake had missing in his life.' She blinked for a moment then added, 'He was forever spinning some story or other, trying to get everyone's attention, you know? Caro doted on him, hung on his every word.' She paused for a moment and chewed her lower lip, as if considering her next words.

'I think her main attraction to Jake was that she was the audience he needed.' She sighed. 'And,' she added, looking at Molly and Davie in turn, 'it might sound a terrible thing to say but I really believe he would have sucked the life out of her *if* they had ever got married.'

'Was there any doubt about that?'

There was another pause then Lesley McArthur nodded. 'I didn't want to say anything at the time. Jake was so upset. But ... I think ... just before her death ... Caro was having second thoughts.'

'What do you make of all that?' Giles asked as they set off from the sprawling housing estate.

'Hard to say,' Molly replied. 'Had he settled for her, really? Was he still playing the field?' She turned and gave him an enquiring sort of look.

'Perhaps she found out he'd been cheating, threatened to break it off? Is that what you're saying?'

'If that was so, then she'd be the one mad enough to kill him, not the other way around. No,' Molly continued thoughtfully, 'as far as I can see all was well with them that night as Carolyn left his flat. He didn't seem to me to feel any sort of remorse other than that he'd stayed in to wait for his agent's call. Who knows what really happened that evening before she left him on his own?'

'And he stayed in to wait for that call. Do you really think he lost his mobile?'

'Perhaps.' Molly made a face. 'My wee brother is like that. Leaves them on trains, buys cheap ones then forgets where he's put them. Careless, just like Richardson. If we believe him,' she added darkly. 'And, if what he says was true then that is one of the many *if onlys* he'll have to live with now.'

Giles shook his head. 'Let's just say that she was the love of his life, okay? Fair enough they were different sorts of people from totally different backgrounds. But maybe that was what a man like him needed? Stability, a woman who would always be there for him?'

'Plus one who brought in a decent salary and had good prospects,' Molly added cynically.

'Aye, that as well,' he agreed. 'But, so what? Loads of women earn more than their partners nowadays.'

Molly nodded absently. 'Might do no harm to talk to some of Jake Richardson's acting pals. Beginning with that agent.'

The theatrical agency near St George's Cross was situated up two flights of stairs in a renovated building that appeared to house a variety of artistic enterprises, including studio spaces. Sounds of voices filtered up the stairwell, punctuated by bursts of an electric guitar. The noise receded as the two detectives reached the dark green door with a brass plaque that proclaimed, D. D. MORGAN THEATRICAL AGENCY.

There was a single bell push set into the doorframe that buzzed loudly when Davie Giles pressed his finger to it. They waited, listening for the sound of feet approaching, but several minutes passed, Davie pressing the bell repeatedly before Molly shrugged.

'Must be out. We can come back another time, I suppose.'

She had just turned away when a voice made her jump.

'Looking for me?' it said softly.

Molly spun round to see a small, fat man standing in the doorway, his beady eyes fixed on them both as though he were sizing them up for a particular reason.

'Mr Morgan?'

'That's right,' the little man agreed with a slight inclination of his head. 'You wished to see me?' he glanced from one to the other then added, 'No appointment, now I wonder why?'

Molly and Davie's warrant cards held aloft were answer enough.

'Ah, the boys in blue,' Morgan chuckled. 'Well, well. To what do I owe this pleasure?'

Molly sensed Davie's questioning glance but did not take her eyes off the agent standing in front of them. He was what her father might have termed dapper, the three-piece tweed suit in a bold check of ochre and brown, polished brogues and lemon yellow shirt topped with a Paisley-pattern bow tie in shades of green and yellow. On any other person this ensemble might have attracted raised eyebrows but it was somehow in keeping with Morgan's rosy cheeks and wispy white hair.

'We want to talk to you about one of your actors, Jake Richardson,' Molly replied at last.

The little man merely blinked at them and nodded, as though he were accustomed to Police Scotland turning up on his doorstep.

Molly resisted a smile, acknowledging to herself that Mr Morgan was either one very cool customer indeed or himself practised in the dramatic arts.

'*Entrez*,' he said with a sweeping gesture of his podgy hand, stepping aside to let the two detectives enter.

'Welcome to my humble abode,' he continued, closing the door and skipping nimbly ahead of them. 'This way,' he declared, pushing open a door and beckoning them forward.

Molly entered a large room where the walls were completely covered with newspaper cuttings and bill-posters from years gone by. It was impossible not to stare at them as she entered, her eyes catching images of several well-known actors.

'Are they all on your books, Mr Morgan?' Davie asked,

wide-eyed, as he pointed to a famous Scottish actor who had enjoyed a film and television career spanning several decades.

The agent inclined his head. 'All mine, dear boy, all mine,' he told him, the smile on his face broadening as Davie responded with a quiet whistle of admiration.

The room was certainly a testament to the man's own success. But was it designed to impress or to intimidate those who entered? As she gazed around, Molly noticed an old chaise longue, upholstered in plum-coloured velvet, an antique desk complete with green shaded lamp and an old-fashioned Bakelite telephone. Floor-to-ceiling curtains in the same dark red material were swept back from the bay windows, fastened by golden tassels. It was like a stage set for a theatrical agent's premises, Molly decided and silently applauded the man's taste in décor.

'Please, sit.' Morgan was gesturing to them both, his shrewd eyes flitting from the rather overawed Davie to Molly, who met his glance with an amused smile. For a moment their eyes met and she perceived that slight nod of recognition as though he had read her thoughts and approved of them.

'Would you like a small refreshment?' Morgan asked coyly as Molly and Davie sat side by side on the chaise.

'No, thank you,' Molly answered for them both. 'We'll try not to take up too much of your time,' she added, noticing the man had already pulled his high-backed captain's chair from the desk and angled it so that he was sitting opposite them.

'Now,' he began, rubbing is hands together, 'poor Jake Richardson. What can I tell you about the boy?'

Molly felt her eyebrow begin to rise. *Boy*? At thirty-two, a similar age as the two victims, Jake Richardson was hardly that. She suppressed the desire to make a comment and pressed on with the main reason for their visit.

'We are investigating the death of his fiancée, as I suppose you know,' she began.

'Ah, yes, the other girl in the park ...' Morgan nodded, his clever eyes gleaming.

He hadn't needed to say much more, Molly realised, trying to keep her annoyance in check. The facts in the newspapers spoke for themselves: the daughter of a high court judge is murdered in similar circumstances to Carolyn Kane and suddenly the big guns of the MIT were pulled out to investigate both deaths.

'Jake Richardson told us that he was waiting for a telephone call from you on the night that Carolyn died,' Molly told him.

'Yes, I am aware Jake told this to the police but I have to tell you that his wait was quite in vain. There was nothing I could tell him, you see.' Morgan spread his hands wide.

'He didn't get the part he'd been hoping for?' Davie put in.

'I emailed him the following day. Before I knew about the tragic event,' Morgan explained. 'I only call clients when I have some good news for them,' he added with a sigh. 'Poor boy. He had so many expectations ...'

Molly frowned slightly. 'Expectations? You mean in his career?'

Morgan paused for a moment, considering. 'Jake is not as good an actor as he thinks,' he said slowly. 'Lovely voice, of

110

course, which is why he makes a modest living from radio work and audio books. But his stage presence ...' He lifted his hands and dropped them again with a sigh, as if to lament the actor's deficiencies. 'Hard to place, especially with so much competition,' Morgan explained. 'So much new young talent here. Our Conservatoire nurtures some of the best in the country,' he added, lifting his chin as though he were somehow responsible for these successes. And, perhaps he was, Molly mused. A good agent would be essential in finding the right parts for actors in order to promote their careers. She glanced up at the walls again, the famous faces staring down at her.

'He must have thought he'd got the part if he waited in for your call?' Davie persisted.

'That I cannot say.' Morgan shook his head. 'I suppose he is claiming that as his alibi?'

'We cannot comment,' Molly replied stiffly.

'No, of course,' Morgan nodded. 'Poor Jake ...'

'Has he gained any further work since Carolyn's death?' Molly asked.

Morgan sat up a little straighter. 'As a matter of fact, he has. A small but lucrative job. Television advert for a major insurance company,' he said. 'Goes out in the autumn. When car registrations change,' he explained. 'Catches the market, apparently,' he added, examining his fingernails as though he were becoming bored by their questions.

'Apart from his acting abilities, what sort of man would you say he is?' Molly asked.

Morgan gave her a smile. 'Oh, vain, like so many of his kind, and desperate for an audience to applaud his sadly limited talents. But a charming boy for all that,' he conceded. 'I really don't think he has much passion for anything other than seeing his name in lights. And,' he added, his face suddenly serious, 'I must tell you I have had a lot of experience with people like Jake Richardson. Many actors have passed through this room,' he declared, waving a podgy hand towards the nearest wall. 'I've seen them come and I've seen them go. I know what makes them tick, you see,' he said, pursing his lips together. 'However,' he added, one finger raised aloft as though he were making a final dramatic statement, 'I could not for one moment imagine that boy capable of murdering his fiancée.'

'I believe him,' Molly said as they buckled their seat belts and prepared to head back across the city. 'And I think he's probably a very good judge of people's personalities, don't you?'

'Aye,' Davie agreed. 'Some character, though. Surely he's been in the game himself?'

Molly threw him a sideways smile. 'Actually, no,' she said. 'I looked him up and according to what I read Morgan never trod the boards, though he came from a theatrical background. Both his parents were actors. He took over their management when he was still in his teens and opened the agency after they both retired.'

'Right. So, what do the initials stand for? D. D. Morgan?'

'Desmond Dylan,' Molly replied with a laugh. 'The mother played Shakespeare's Desdemona and the father was famous for his recording of Dylan Thomas's *Under Milk Wood*.'

'Oh,' came the reply and Molly resisted a grin, guessing that Davie Giles was not one for attending the theatre or reading poetry.

She glanced behind her for a break in the traffic then moved off, knowing that he was probably still bemused by their visit, the agent and his premises a novelty to be shared once they were back in Helen Street. Molly Newton had never aspired to be one of the names on those walls despite her undoubted talents in that direction and the fun with amateur dramatics she had experienced as an undergraduate. She had enjoyed her university years studying English Lit and those same talents had been put to good use during her time as an undercover officer.

Were they any further forward? She pondered the question as the lights changed to red, making her apply the brakes. Richardson still had no definite alibi for the night of Carolyn Kane's death, only the suggestion from his agent that he was incapable of murder. But was that necessarily true? Lorimer would be looking for hard facts to substantiate any claims like this and, Molly told herself with clenched teeth, so far they had none to give him.

CHAPTER ELEVEN

The event might have been one of the smallest on the tour so far but Maggie felt a frisson of excitement nonetheless as she was shown to the seat behind a table, specially set up for her book signing. The day outside was bright and the open door let in wafts of sea air as more and more people trooped in to stand in the queue. If she'd been at home it would have been a perfect day to potter in the garden.

Thoughts of the usual blitz of weeding that was being left to Flynn, their gardener, melted as Maggie took in the ever-increasing line of people waiting for the event to begin.

Duncan, the bookshop proprietor, stepped forward and raised a hand.

'Ladies and gentlemen,' he began, 'please put your hands together for our next author, who is no stranger to Mull. Margaret Lorimer will be here for the next hour, so do take the time to have your books signed and the chance to have a blether with her. Thank you.'

As Duncan stepped aside, warm applause broke out making Maggie blush with pleasure. It was true that they were frequent visitors, though one particular summer when their holiday had turned into a serious police investigation remained etched in her mind. Now she was here in a very different capacity, not as the wife of a senior investigating officer or as another tourist enjoying the sights but as a budding author!

The space in Tackle and Books was too small to give any kind of talk, so Maggie lingered over each book that was thrust into her hands, taking time to speak to every child and adult who approached her. She could tell that some were locals, by their distinctive accents, and Maggie was delighted when she recognised a man from the Tobermory garage bringing his grandson to present her with a book.

What was he? Nine, ten perhaps? A serious face below a thatch of red curls, his jeans tucked into black wellies and a hand-knitted Guernsey giving him the appearance of a small fisherman.

'I like books,' Calum avowed stoutly. 'And my wee sister does an' all,' he added, shoving a small fair-haired child forward.

'Just make the signature out to them both,' their grandfather suggested. 'To Calum and Phaime. Is that all right?'

Maggie did as requested, checking the spelling of both names, just in case there was something she got wrong. She had already encountered both a Sheilagh and a Sheila at one signing and was on her guard.

*

The queue was so slow that at one point he almost lost his nerve and fled from the shop. But that would only make folk stare at him, he reasoned, and drawing attention was something he needed to avoid. The beard he'd bought looked pretty real and the tweed hat covered his own hair adequately enough. A pair of thick-rimmed spectacles completed his disguise, though one day soon he wanted to let her see him as the man he really was. As he waited, the future presented itself in his mind: he would be the quiet man behind her success, the one that was always waiting after these events. The current husband had only shown up for the first night in Glasgow. The man sniffed in disdain. If he were by this woman's side then there was no way he'd be letting her go all over Scotland on her own. His eyes wandered towards the English woman standing just outside the door-way, phone jammed against her ear as usual. Probably talking business with these book people down south. Not taking any interest in her author right now. Or, he allowed himself a small smile of satisfaction, in the individuals in the queue.

One by one she smiled at them, her head bent to write something in each book, a friendly handshake signalling every goodbye. He saw her smile, the heart-shaped face turned up to greet him as he stepped forward and presented his book, the copy turned to the correct page for signing. Her eyes were the colour of the waters out there on the bay, either blue or grey, he couldn't be sure as she returned his gaze.

'What would you like me to write?' she asked him and for a second he was speechless. *From Margaret with all my heart*, he wanted to tell her, but the words stuck in his throat.

'Just sign your name,' he answered then gave a cough, hearing the hoarseness in his voice.

'Giving it as a present?' Maggie asked, her curls tilting to one side as she hazarded a guess from this stranger.

'Aye,' he replied, relief flooding through him as her suggestion gave him the cue he needed to leave.

'Thank you for coming and buying a book,' Maggie told him, offering her hand.

For a tiny moment he hesitated then he took the hand and gave it a little squeeze. Did she understand what he was telling her? Was she feeling anything special from that lingering touch? Her smile gave nothing away, or did it? Could he read something more than friendliness in those sea-grey eyes?

In seconds he was out of the door and walking briskly along the street, oblivious to any other pedestrians, that magic moment replaying in his mind, the feel of her skin against his, warming his blood.

'Well, that was a success,' Barbara, the shop assistant told her. 'Can't remember when we last had an author selling so many books in one day! Well done.'

'Thanks.' Maggie grinned, stretching her back and giving a small yawn. 'I enjoyed that. A lot,' she added, staring at the last of the folk from her queue disappearing out of the door.

'Will there be a paperback later in the year?' Barbara asked. 'Only, we could have you back to sign stock before Christmas. If you had time to visit us again?'

'Maybe,' Maggie answered slowly. 'I teach school during

term time so it would have to be a weekend or during the October break. Ivy will know,' she added, standing up and searching the shop for her PR.

'The wee lady who was with you?' Barbara asked.

'Yes.'

'She's over the road. On her phone,' Duncan's colleague told her, with raised eyebrows and a look that seemed to express the opinion of Barbara's generation that mobile phones had taken the place of ordinary civility. 'Now, how about a cup of coffee? I know Duncan would love to have a chat before you leave and there's just a few copies left … Would you mind signing them too?'

Ivy had kept one eye on the people leaving the bookstore as she continued her conversation. Anybody watching might have noticed how she chewed her lower lip, as if something was on her mind. The bookshop owner appeared in the doorway gesturing with his hand and mouthing 'cuppa'. Ivy shook her head, waving his offer away with her free hand. Let Margaret Lorimer linger there for a bit longer, Ivy decided. It gave her all the more time to firm up her plans with the person on the other end of the line, someone who would remain an unknown figure of intrigue while helping both Ivy and her author to sustain the public's attention.

'It's not enough, you need to up your game. Are you sure you can do it?' she snapped, turning towards the waters of Tobermory Bay, oblivious to the ebb and flow of the tide, the clinking sounds from boats at anchor or the sunlight licking the waves.

Ivy nodded, her thin mouth turning up in an expression of satisfaction.

'It'll be worth your while,' she added. 'Speak to you once it's done. Okay?'

Then, not waiting for a reply, she slipped the phone into her pocket and leaned against the white-painted railing, breathing in the fresh sweet scent of the air, and smiling as though she were seeing the view across the harbour for the first time.

There were flyers at each of their events and he had picked one up at every stop, her picture smiling out at him afresh. Now the latest one was stowed into his pocket, folded neatly so that there was no crease across Margaret Lorimer's face. The man raised his high-definition field glasses to his eyes and gazed across the bay, his binoculars taking in a lot more than the famous view as he turned slowly from his vantage point at the end of the Old Pier. The PR woman was standing by herself now; he could see her leaning against the railing that separated Main Street from the waters below, the harbour wall reaching up only as far as the roadway. Any moment now, he told himself, concentrating the glasses on the open door of the bookshop.

'Where are you?' he whispered. 'Come out and let me look at you.'

Sure enough, her familiar slim figure emerged as though in answer to his call. She lifted a hand to sweep back her hair as a gust of wind caught it, then, looking carefully, she crossed the narrow strip of road and joined her companion. It was impossible to make out a word that they were saying but he did catch the expression on his beloved's face as she threw back her head, laughing at something the other woman had said. Would they remain there? Letting him feast his eyes on her for a little longer?

But that wistful plea appeared to be ignored as they turned and walked away towards the corner of the street and disappeared from view. He could follow them, perhaps, climb that steep brae to wherever they were heading, but to do so invited discovery and he was reluctant to let her see his pursuit just yet.

No, tomorrow they would be leaving the island and heading north. Wherever this tour took them he would be sure to follow.

The end of the pier faced an old grey building, Aros Hall, a sort of community hang-out for the locals, he presumed, as he approached its open doorway. To one side was a huge noticeboard covered with flyers, including the one for that morning's book event. But it was the larger poster that caught his eye. There was to be a ceilidh there this evening. Would Margaret spend the night here, in Tobermory? Heart beating with excitement, he stepped up into the hall, eyes flitting around to see if there was somebody to ask about buying a ticket for the dance.

If she were there . . . ? If he could hold her in his arms . . . ? The scene presented itself to him so strongly that he was certain it must come to pass.

CHAPTER TWELVE

Lorimer made a face as he read through the latest figures for stalking crimes in Scotland. Still, it was a matter of pride that his country had been the trailblazer when it came to legislation. *To give the victim an identity and a voice,* had been the wording of a particular campaign that resulted in making stalking a criminal offence almost a decade ago. England and Wales had followed suit after the success of Scotland's new law within a couple of years, something that most right-minded people saw as progress within society. It was such a grey area, often made more difficult for police when it was a spouse that was involved. Stalking someone out of a sense of longing could be understood to an extent but driving a person to despair with unwanted attention was wrong no matter what relationship had existed beforehand.

Who had given Patricia Donovan such attention? Maybe there had been more than one, he mused. After all, the woman had been the subject of a lot of media coverage and who knew what characters had followed her reckless lifestyle with undue attention? The postcards he had found in her bookcase were being examined for prints but it was unlikely even a decent partial would be found apart from the victim's own. It was one thing to be obsessed by a well-known personality whose photographs were splashed all over the weekly magazines and quite another to act on that. The danger to people like pop stars was well documented: fans taking far too great an interest in their idols, sending messages that could be construed as alarming or menacing. Then, of course, there were those who stalked their chosen victims and stabbed them to death, as had happened on some rare but well-publicised occasions. Young women who had spurned the attention of an over-eager suitor were now statistics among the papers on his desk.

Lorimer pushed them away in disgust. There was nothing that the police could do other than issue warnings or try to have court orders placed so that the stalker was forbidden from going within a set distance of their victim. And how often had that worked? He sighed. A sort of madness may well have overtaken these men, their determination to slaughter their former girlfriend (or whatever they had perceived her to be) outweighing the bit of paper that had been delivered by the courts. Already this year there had been an incident down in London, a young woman in her twenties stabbed to death by her former fiancé for no other reason than that she had taken up with another man. Jealousy, that terrible passion, was at the root of so many crimes of this sort.

Like *Othello*, Lorimer thought; the Shakespeare play that

Maggie taught her senior pupils at Muirpark. His mouth curved in a soft smile as he sat back for a moment, wondering how she was and where the tour would take her next. His fingers slipped under the pile of papers stacked on the upper shelf of his in-tray and found the shiny flyer he had taken from Waterstones on the night of her book launch. A list of dates and venues was printed neatly below Maggie's smiling face. Lorimer shook his head, placing the flyer against the wire mesh tray. She would continue to smile at him while he trawled through this paperwork and later they'd talk, catching up on the event in Tackle and Books.

A knock on his door made Lorimer look up to see DCI Niall Cameron, a Lewisman and one of the most important members of the MIT.

'Niall. Come in.' Lorimer half rose and waved his colleague into the seat by his desk.

The DCI gave a nod and then, as he sat down, Lorimer saw him stiffen, his eyes fixed on the flyer.

'That's—' Cameron broke off then shook his head. 'Sorry, for a moment there I thought that was the Donovan woman,' he apologised.

'What? Oh, this?' Lorimer picked up the piece of paper. 'You thought . . . ?' He frowned.

'There's a real resemblance, don't you think?' Cameron ventured. 'Just that first glance, I suppose. Both dark haired, same shape of face . . . ' He stopped and looked at Lorimer, one eyebrow raised in question.

'Can't see it myself,' Lorimer replied gruffly, placing the flyer down on the desk. Still, he sneaked a little look at the publicity photo before he turned his attention back to Cameron. Was there any resemblance? Perhaps, a little, he conceded.

'We turned up something interesting about Richardson,' Cameron told him. 'Apparently he may have known Patricia Donovan way back when he was just starting out as an actor.'

'How . . . ?'

'We haven't talked to him about that. Yet,' Cameron replied. 'But here's the thing. After the Donovans split up and Lady D went to live in London, Patricia took a drama course in the same stage school that Richardson attended. We checked out the dates and they fit.'

'Doesn't mean they actually knew one another, though, does it?' Lorimer argued. 'How many kids were on a course like that?'

Cameron shrugged. 'Aye, I dare say there were plenty of students doing that sort of thing, but imagine this: two Scottish youngsters both starting out. Surely they would have gravitated towards each other at some point, if only to suss out each other's background? You know what we tend to be like? Find another Scot away from home and we're like long lost brothers.'

Lorimer nodded, remembering occasions when he had attended conferences in London. It was quite natural for the Scottish officers to seek one another out.

'How long ago was this?'

Cameron consulted the paper in his hand. 'About fourteen years ago, now. They would both have been around eighteen.'

'Richardson was about the same age as his fiancée.'

'And Patricia Donovan, yes,' Cameron agreed. 'Why?'

'Is there a chance that these three had met up earlier in their lives? Any overlapping areas?'

'Only this, as far as we've been able to find out,' Cameron told him, giving the paper a little shake.

'And Richardson has said nothing to our officers about knowing Patricia Donovan?' he asked.

Cameron gave a grin. 'Not a thing. Wonder why that would be?'

'Either he wanted to hide that little nugget or he genuinely didn't know her. After all,' he mused, 'Patricia Donovan, daughter of an eminent high court judge, might have been a cut above his social class.'

'Possibly,' Cameron conceded, 'but from what Newton and Giles told me Richardson is a pushy sort of bloke. Not backward at coming forwards if it suits him.'

Lorimer sat back in his chair, swinging gently from side to side as he gave the matter some thought.

'There's no reason to suspect the man of murder, even though his alibi is hanging by a thread,' he began. 'Still, I think we can safely say he may be a person of interest.'

'You want him brought in?'

Lorimer thought about this for a moment then shook his head. 'I think I'd like to visit him myself. Maybe take Prof. Brightman along to see what he might make of our actor.'

This would be the second time in a very few days that the head of the MIT made a visit to the bereaved relation of a murder victim, Lorimer told himself later as he parked outside Solly's home. Lorimer had made the call to Richardson, keen to hear the man's voice, listening for any panic or fear. But there was nothing he could hear other than mild surprise. Still, he was hoping that something more concrete might emerge from their meeting. He looked up to see Solly opening the front door and stepping down to the pavement, a smile on his bearded face.

'This is a surprise,' Solly said as he settled himself into the Lexus. 'Off hunting, are we?' he added with a nod.

Lorimer felt the other man's glance as he looked ahead at the traffic. Solly was a keen observer of humankind and was no doubt wondering what had brought the detective superintendent out of the office on this occasion.

'Want to see him for myself,' Lorimer replied shortly. 'It's not that I don't trust the judgement of my fellow officers,' he continued, 'but you and I are old hands at summing people up and I think it would be helpful if we could eliminate this chap from our inquiries.'

'You already suspect he's innocent?'

Lorimer nodded. 'But I could be wrong. We've both experienced being in the company of villains who were in plain sight, not trying to hide themselves in any way. Still ...'

'The man you have in mind is a stalker, someone who does hide himself away.' Solly nodded. 'But this fellow is an actor and actors have been known to hide their own personalities behind quite different personas.'

'That's why I wanted an expert like you to come along,' Lorimer said, allowing himself a sly grin towards his friend.

Once upon a time he would have expressed deep scepticism over the role of a criminal profiler but nowadays he knew the value of such a person as Solomon Brightman. They had seen a lot together over the years and, although their backgrounds were entirely different, it made sense to harness their talents in a difficult case.

The remainder of the journey through Glasgow passed in silence as the Lexus crossed the Kingston Bridge with its panoramic views west and east along the River Clyde. Solly noted the conglomeration of luxury apartments lining the banks, the railway line running parallel until the road curved away and sped them south towards the leafier suburban enclaves. They slowed down after leaving the motorway and the professor had time to look around him as Lorimer drove towards Shawlands. Here were rows of elegant tenement buildings, grey and red sandstone, but as they neared their destination the ground-floor flats gave way to rows of shops and cafés, some with hopeful umbrellas raised against the Glasgow sun. He looked up at the skies. It was a calm day with some brightness behind grey clouds that might change at any moment. Would their actor be like that? he wondered. Changeable and fickle like this spring day? Or would he be able to see past any façade and assess the man's truthfulness as Lorimer posed his questions?

The apartments at Springhill Gardens were set back from the main road with a parallel area for residential parking and Lorimer swung the Lexus into a vacant space and left his card on the dashboard, should any traffic attendant think about writing out a ticket. Police business really did take precedence over the need to raise revenue from illegal parking, Solly thought. Though, as a non-driver, he was content to allow others such stresses.

'Up here,' Lorimer told him as he flicked the fob towards the car to lock it. 'He'll have a great view of the park,' he murmured, turning to look from the upper windows of the flats towards the tree-lined edge of Queen's Park, a vast green space that stretched up and over the hill to Langside.

Solly gave the park a quick glance before he followed Lorimer to the main entrance where they waited after pressing the entry button. Here, he reminded himself, a young woman had lost her life in the most horrible fashion and he was about to meet her bereaved fiancé. The harsh reality of that struck the psychologist as he heard Lorimer give their names in response to the voice from the intercom and then they entered the dark close and headed towards the stairs.

'I seem to be making a habit of entertaining the police,' Richardson said as he stood at his open door. For a moment his stony expression seemed to indicate a reluctance to let them enter but then, tight-lipped, he stood aside and gestured that the two men should come into his home.

'This is Professor Brightman,' Lorimer began. 'I am Detective Superintendent Lorimer. We spoke earlier,' he added, thrusting out his hand to the actor.

Richardson took it and Lorimer felt the dampness on the

other man's palm as he shook it. Richardson looked him in the eye for a bare moment then turned to nod to Solly.

'This could be seen as harassment, you know,' he began, folding his arms in a gesture of defiance as he glanced from one man to the other.

'That's for you to decide, Mr Richardson,' Lorimer said slowly. 'We are here because of certain information that has come to light, something that I wish you had mentioned to the officers who visited you previously.'

'Oh?' The actor let his hands fall by his side and he moved towards a chair. 'Suppose you'd better sit down and tell me what you mean,' he said, his jaw working.

Solly sat to one side, observing the man but not being directly in his line of vision as Lorimer faced Jake Richardson.

'You know that the death of your fiancée has become more high profile since the similar murder of Patricia Donovan?' Lorimer began.

'Took someone like that to make you folk dig deeper to find Carolyn's killer, didn't it?' Richardson sneered.

Lorimer raised his hands in a placating gesture. 'There's truth in what you say, Mr Richardson, though I cannot find any fault with the original investigation team. But we're here not about Carolyn, but about your relationship with Patricia.'

'What?' Richardson exploded, half rising from his chair. 'What the hell are you on about? What relationship? Are you trying to pin something on me? This is absurd!'

Lorimer refrained from letting his lips twitch into a smile as the man's language became similar to the sort of blustering

129

character he had seen on many a TV show featuring Agatha Christie's famous detective Poirot. Had Richardson played a part like that at any time? he wondered briefly.

'You and Patricia Donovan were at the same stage school in London,' Lorimer said calmly. 'We checked the dates,' he added, raising an eyebrow as though inviting the actor to contradict him.

Richardson opened his mouth to speak then closed it again with a sigh. He did not look at either man as he passed his fingers restlessly through his hair. 'Can't believe this,' he muttered. 'I hardly knew her.'

'But you did know her, didn't you?' Lorimer persisted. 'Two Scots kids down in London, surely it was inevitable you would talk to each other?'

'Aye, I suppose so,' Richardson admitted, his voice sounding more like the Glasgow man he was. 'But that was years ago. I hadn't seen her again, except in the papers, of course.' He sighed.

'She became a bit of a modern celebrity,' Lorimer continued. 'Are you certain your paths never crossed again?'

Richardson sat up at that and regarded the police officer as if for the first time.

'Is that what you're thinking? That I killed them both? That's crazy,' he added, shaking his head. 'It was a terrible thing to happen and, yes, it brought everything back about last summer when—' He stopped abruptly, clamping his lips together and looking down. Was that lest his sudden tears betray him? Lorimer thought that it was. He was adept at telling genuine emotion from crocodile tears and he thought that the young man was really struggling with something at this moment.

'We are trying to find out about both Carolyn and Patricia to see if there are any connections between them,' Lorimer explained.

Richardson nodded. 'Sorry,' he mumbled, 'I can see that now. But it was so long ago and we were just pals, well, not even that really, more like acquaintances. Even then I didn't rate that highly with girls like that. Posh girls.' He gave a slight self-deprecating laugh.

'So, what can you tell us about her, this posh girl from back home?' Lorimer asked, sitting back as though preparing himself for a lengthy story.

Richardson looked down at his hands and remained silent for a few moments as though considering. Was he dreaming up some rubbish or really trying to recall the truth? Lorimer knew that he was dealing with a person whose profession might be described as dissembling, creating illusions of truth. Would anything he said help them now?

'I think she was keen to make friends,' Richardson said at last. 'She wasn't the brash woman you saw on these reality TV shows, all glam and no substance,' he added. 'That came later, I suppose, when she'd learned to fit in with the right crowd.'

Could he discern a shade of bitterness in the man's words? Perhaps, Lorimer decided, listening as Richardson continued.

'She was always asking folk out for a drink, eager to pay her rounds, that sort of thing.' He looked up. 'We were all broke back in those days; students with huge loans to see our way to paying rent and all the rest. But Trish had this house in London where she lived with her mother so it was easy for her to splash the cash, make herself the centre of attention.'

'Were you ever there?' Lorimer asked.

Richardson shook his head. 'No, but she was one of the few who did have a place to go back to, a family, I mean. There were one or two others from London who still stayed at home, but most of us came from *outside*.'

Lorimer noted his emphasis on the word. Had Richardson found it hard to fit in with his southern counterparts? Had he resented the Scottish girl's ability to make friends and become popular?

'Did you like her?'

Richardson glared suddenly. 'What do you mean?'

'Just that. Did you like the person she was back then?'

Richardson nodded. 'Everyone did,' he said at last. 'Okay, she was a bit flash, but she worked as hard as the rest of us even if she wasn't ever going to make the headlines ... Oh, God.' He put his head into his hands. 'I didn't mean that ... what a crass thing to say ... '

'I think it is pretty well known that Patricia Donovan's acting skills were average rather than exceptional,' Lorimer agreed. 'So, you remember her as a hard-working drama student who made friends easily?'

Richardson nodded again. 'That's about it. You know she dropped out after the first year?'

'We do,' Lorimer acknowledged. 'And did you ever meet up with her after that?'

'What are you asking me?' Richardson scowled. 'Did we date, that sort of thing? Not then and not after she'd left, I can assure you.'

'You liked dating pretty girls, though, surely?'

Richardson narrowed his eyes but said nothing in reply.

'A good-looking young man, enjoying the capital, lots of keen students around … I imagine you had loads of opportunities for romantic encounters?'

'You can imagine what you like,' Richardson growled. 'Only time I ever saw Trish again was at a party. She was with some big shot or other. If she saw me there she never looked my way.' He shook his head, the muscles on his face tightening.

'How did that make you feel?' A voice from the corner made Richardson start as though he had forgotten the presence of the professor.

Richardson shrugged. 'I was with a girl, can't remember her name, and we were dancing. Trish wandered past with this fellow and I remember staring at her, willing her to turn round and say hello. So …' He made a face. 'I suppose I was a bit miffed that she didn't. Too hoity-toity by then to remember a mere actor.'

He looked from Lorimer to Solly and then nodded as though understanding something for the first time.

'You're not just trying to see what Trish was like back then, are you? This is to see if I had any motive for her murder. Dear God! What are you people like?' He half rose from his seat, raking his hair again.

'It was a long time to hold a grudge.' Lorimer smiled. 'I very much doubt that you were *nursing your wrath to keep it warm* for all those years,' he added, quoting the famous phrase from 'Tam o' Shanter'.

Richardson sat down again. 'Well, why *are* you here?' he asked, a whine in his voice.

'Any link between Carolyn and Patricia has to be investigated thoroughly,' Lorimer said calmly. 'And this was one such link.'

Richardson took a deep breath. 'I see.' He nodded then lowered his gaze. 'Well, I'm sorry that I can't help you any more. I never saw Trish Donovan again except on the TV and in the papers. Can't say I really felt much about her life.' He sighed. 'But I was sorry that she'd died in such a horrible way,' he murmured. 'Don't suppose I'll ever get over losing Carolyn like that and I guess Trish has left family and friends behind who are going through it all like I did.'

'Some of what he's telling us is the truth,' Solly murmured when they were back in the car.

'Yes, I think so,' Lorimer agreed. 'He's certainly good at acting the part of the bereaved fiancé, if that is an act, but he wasn't so good at playing the outraged citizen, was he?' he chuckled.

'His memory of Patricia was interesting. He called her Trish. Do you suppose that was how she was known back then? To her friends and fellow students?'

'Could be. It's Patricia Donovan on her Equity card,' Lorimer told him. 'Her parents refer to her as Tricia or Patricia.

Most parents use their children's full names; it's their chums who shorten them at school, usually.'

'Were you ever called Billy?' Solly ventured.

'Never. It was always William or Bill. Don't know why. Mum and Dad always called me William then kids at school shortened it to Bill. Nowadays it would be Will, I think.'

'Let's find out if her friends called her Trish,' Solly murmured thoughtfully. 'Or if that was a term of endearment Jake Richardson used. Maybe they were more than just friends back then, eh?'

'One thing we mustn't lose sight of,' Lorimer reminded Solly as he fastened his seat belt, 'Richardson's fiancée bore a startling resemblance to Patricia Donovan.'

'You think he chose Carolyn because she reminded him of a former lover?'

Lorimer raised his eyebrows and gave Solly a meaningful look. 'It's something to consider, isn't it?'

Jake Richardson watched as the big silver car eased out of the parking space and stopped by the entrance to Pollokshaws Road. His eyes followed it when a break in traffic allowed it to merge into the stream and head back towards the city centre. He swallowed hard, feeling the dryness in his mouth. It had been like all those times he had walked on to a lonely stage, sweat pouring beneath a costume, nerves stretched to breaking point as he'd uttered lines rehearsed over and over again.

When the car was finally out of sight, he strode back into the room and bent down to open a sideboard door. The bottle of whisky was cold against his clammy fist and his hand shook as he poured a measure into the glass that had been pushed to one side as he'd shown the two policemen into his front room. The amber liquid burned his throat but he tilted the glass until he'd swallowed the lot. A huge sigh escaped as he stood there. If Carolyn had been alive, she would have been there to hold him, tell him he'd done well ...

A renegade tear escaped from his eye and Richardson dashed at it fiercely with one knuckled fist. For a moment he tried to conjure up the memory of the gentle girl he'd tried to hold in his arms that final evening.

But all that came to mind was the image of Trish Donovan's laughing face as he'd bent to fold her in his embrace.

CHAPTER THIRTEEN

'That was a super night,' Ivy remarked as they turned the corner and headed uphill out of Oban.

'Yes, and a lovely meal too,' Maggie agreed. Duncan had invited them both for dinner at his home on the outskirts of Tobermory before a crowd of locals had arrived there for their monthly book group meeting, chaired by Duncan's wife, a cheerful rosy-cheeked woman.

'What did you say that fish was?' Ivy asked.

'Tobermory trout. Smoked trout. It's from their own shop. Mrs Swinbanks runs that part of the family business. You should look out for it in London,' Maggie told her, 'I'm told all the best restaurants order it from her.'

Ivy nodded. 'You sold every one of the books, too,' she added. 'Everyone back down south is going to be very pleased about that. Sales are doing brilliantly for a first week, by the way.' She threw Maggie a sidelong smile.

'I can still hardly believe it,' Maggie murmured. 'It doesn't seem real. Margaret Lorimer, author, and Mrs Lorimer from Muirpark Secondary School. It's like we're two different people.'

'You said that to the press bloke from the *Gazette*,' Ivy recalled. 'But I bet this time next year you'll be so used to it that you won't give it a second thought.'

Maggie pushed her hair behind her ears and sighed happily. 'I need to find time to finish the next book,' she said. 'I'd planned to write most of it over the summer. Bill just takes a couple of weeks off. When he can,' she said, making a face. 'Sometimes work really interferes with our plans. Crime never takes a holiday,' she added quietly.

'Don't you find that hard? Being married to a senior policeman, I mean?'

'Oh, it's had its ups and downs,' Maggie replied vaguely, turning to stare out of the window, a clear hint that she was not going to be drawn on any details of her married life. She was content with her man and, if there had been times in the past when life had proved difficult, well, didn't all couples have rough patches? Being childless was probably one of their lasting regrets but in the Lorimers' case it had only drawn the couple closer over the years.

Maggie twisted her hair and tucked it into a knot.

'Why d'you do that?' Ivy asked sharply.

'Oh, just to get it off my face. I wear it up at school most days. But sometimes I wonder if I should get it cut short. After all, I'm not exactly a spring chicken any more.'

'Don't be daft!' Ivy remonstrated. 'You look far younger

than your years. Anyone looking at your author pic would take you for thirty. Honest,' she stressed. 'Besides, think of all those publicity shots our photographer took. Mustn't let them go to waste!' she insisted firmly.

'Och, I suppose you're right. Anyway,' she smiled a little smile, 'Bill likes my hair long. Even though it might be a bit old-fashioned.'

'Nonsense!' Ivy said brusquely. 'Think of the Duchess of Cambridge. She's kept hers lovely and long. Just like yours!'

Maggie's smile broadened. She was becoming used to Ivy's flattery, though she still didn't take it too seriously.

Ivy breathed out a silent sigh of relief. If Margaret Lorimer changed her hairstyle, all her carefully laid plans would come to naught. Hopefully she would let it drop, but if there was any more talk of cutting that hair, Ivy would just have to remind her what it had cost the publishers to have these photographs taken. As a new author, still a bit overawed by the whole thing, she was definitely the type to feel guilty at incurring anybody an unnecessary cost.

The road was quiet as they drove through the little village of Connel, the foaming river by the roadside making Ivy glance across for a moment. Tonight they would be in another bookshop, further north, where she had a little surprise in wait for her companion.

She hadn't come! He stood by the railings of the car ferry, a frown drawing down his brows. All night long he had endured the noise of the ceilidh band, sweaty bodies whirling past him as he drank his pints of beer, his beard itching, one eye always on the open doorway of the hall, in expectation of her arrival. Why had she let him down? Hadn't she sensed that he would be there waiting for her? After all, as their eyes had met in that bookstore yesterday, there had been a promise of sorts ... hadn't there? He scowled as a gannet flew by, its wings outstretched. All night he had stayed there until the crowd had merged into an untidy circle for 'Auld Lang Syne' and he had stumbled out of the hall into the darkness.

He remembered the water full of lights, dazzling his eyes and making him turn away, staggering a little as he'd made his way to the guest house and a lonely bed. He'd been so sure of her! Yet now, in the blinding daylight, he feared that she was as bad as the rest of them. *Untrustworthy*, a bitter little voice in his head insisted. An image darkened his thoughts as he stood gripping the handrail: a mound of turf beaten into the earth close to the very spot where he had been betrayed. Yet he must learn to bury that memory as he had buried the body of another treacherous woman. That bitch had only ever wanted money out of him.

No, an inner voice insisted, she wasn't like the others at all. Margaret was kind, loving ... there must have been a good reason why she had missed the dance ... after all, he hadn't known if she really was going to be there, had he? his own reasonable self argued.

Just like the others, the words came to his lips and for a moment he looked left and right, wondering if he had spoken them aloud.

He would find her again easily enough, though. The flyer in his jacket pocket gave details of every stop on her tour. And, somehow, he knew there had to be a way to make her see him for what he was: her lover-to-be, her destiny, her fate . . .

CHAPTER FOURTEEN

'Thank you so much,' Maggie gave another bow and a wave towards the audience, the applause and cheers making her grin with pleasure.

Ivy beckoned from the wings and, giving a final wave, Maggie strolled off the platform and was shepherded by the theatre manager down a flight of stairs, along a narrow well-lit corridor and out into the foyer where a table had been set up.

The signing queue was much longer than any event to date, including the Glasgow launch, and Maggie suspected from the numbers of children that there had been school parties in the audience, not every Scottish council having the same two-week break that she had. Ivy had hinted that feelers were going out to the education authorities to see if they wanted to take the book for their schools, a thought that thrilled her. Maybe some day she might teach children who had read her stories in primary school?

'Just a signature, please,' a voice requested and Maggie smiled and nodded, her neat hand penning the words, *Best wishes, Margaret Lorimer.*

'Thanks.' The man gave a nod and disappeared, but Maggie's eyes followed him for a moment. Hadn't she seen him before somewhere? Or did he just remind her of another bearded man who had attended a different event? She frowned then looked up to se the next person in the queue, the incident already forgotten.

The man reflected in the window grinned back at him. He'd finally done it! She had looked into his eyes and given him a knowing smile. Surely there had been something behind that look? Something that words alone could not express? His heart sang with a peculiar joy as he clutched the parcel to his chest, the slim volume inside ready to join the others. What would she say when the time came to be together? Would she laugh at seeing all of those copies side by side on his bookshelf? But it would be a laugh of pleasure, not of scorn, not like those others who had sneered at his small offerings, rejecting them with disdain. No, Margaret wasn't like that. He could tell. And so could the audience who had applauded her talk this afternoon, loving her natural manner and the way she spoke about her story as though the characters were real to her.

If anyone could understand it would be Margaret.

He swallowed down the sudden emotion threatening to make him choke. By this time next week they might be together ... it only remained to find a way of getting rid of that clinging woman by her side. Somehow, he told himself, looking back over his shoulder, he would send the bitch packing back to London.

As if she had sensed the venom in his gaze, Ivy looked up and scanned the crowds departing from the foyer, but her eyes did not fall upon the man sliding out of her view, collar up to hide his face. For a moment she frowned, then turned back to her task of opening each new copy of Maggie's book for signing, a fixed smile on her face that gave nothing away.

At last the final child had been given her book, the author heaving a sigh as she sank back in her seat.

'Well, done,' Ivy said briskly. 'You've really got the hang of this so quickly, haven't you?'

'I'm used to kids,' Maggie replied. 'Though not ones quite so young as those.'

Ivy nodded. She knew most of the English teacher's life history: married to a senior cop, no kids (though not from want of trying, she'd learned) and a lover of the great outdoors. Perhaps, Ivy thought, as she shifted her bulk uncomfortably on the plastic chair, that was why the woman remained so slender and appeared far younger than her years. Ivy had stopped pretending long ago to be one of the young set that dominated the publishing world down south. Instead, she took what she could in the way of funding for these author trips, spending the publishers' money on good food and the nicest accommodation she could find. Her petrol costs were probably higher than they should be, but Ivy liked this particular model with its heated front seats and plenty of space for her ample figure. However, all this could stop as easily as it had begun. Everyone was focused on streamlining the business, even Margaret Lorimer's publisher, Ivy's most loyal client. After the new CEO took the reins he had announced his intention to cut back on any *dead wood* (how she hated that phrase), insisting on examining each and every expense sheet and looking at ways to trim the budget. Ivy, who had long considered herself the freelance that everybody wanted (something she had dinned into the previous chair's ear), was now faced with the possibility of being tossed out unless she could come up with a very good reason to make them keep her on their books.

She glanced at the woman by her side as Maggie gathered up her dark brown coat and a plaid woollen scarf. If Ivy played her cards right, this woman might well be her passport to a better future. It was just a matter of keeping her head and turning things to her advantage. Okay, the schoolteacher might get a bit frightened in the process but, hey, becoming an overnight sensation with every literary festival in the country clamouring for her appearance would more than make up for that. And Ivy Thornton would be right by her side, indispensable to her for years to come.

'Ready?' Ivy asked, pausing as Maggie buttoned her coat then reached down for the smart leather bag that had rested by her feet during the signing session.

'Yes, all set.' Maggie smiled. 'Where now?'

Ivy began to walk along the corridor to the main exit, considering. 'There's a nice little restaurant I happen to know,' she said. 'Perhaps you'd like to go back to the hotel first, though, and freshen up?' She looked at her watch as though to calculate something. 'I can book for five-thirty and that would give us plenty of time before the library event,' she explained. 'Several book groups attending,' Ivy added, noting the appreciative glances of the theatre staff as they headed for the main door.

'Thanks for coming. You were great,' one of the female staff called out.

'She was, wasn't she?' Ivy replied, smiling her usual smile as a young man held open the heavy door for them.

Then, sweeping out, she grasped Maggie's arm. 'They loved you, Margaret,' she chuckled. 'I think you have an excellent future in this game.'

'Stranger killings are always the hardest to solve,' Lorimer said, conscious of the rows of faces turned to the platform where he stood. The Scottish Medico Legal Society had asked him months ago to deliver this particular lecture and it was an irony lost on none of its members that the detective superintendent's current case involved the possibility of a stalker.

As if reading the expectation written on their faces he continued, 'I will make no reference to any cases currently under investigation.' He gave them a hint of a smile. 'But you really didn't expect me to, did you?'

There was a polite ripple of laughter from the audience, all professionals from the legal or medical profession with a couple of Scottish crime authors whom he recognised sitting near the back of the lecture theatre. 'Yet, despite lack of evidence or anything on our databases like DNA or fingerprints, we treat all murder cases in a similar way.'

Most of the members of his audience were well aware of that, from the Fiscals whom he knew well to the pathologists with whom he came into contact at crime scenes or in the mortuary. Yet they were not here to be entertained either; many of these professionals counted these monthly lectures as post-qualifying education and if he could add to the sum of their knowledge by the end of his hour, then he would be happy to have done so.

'We always begin with what we know about the victim and of course the scene of crime,' Lorimer went on. 'Any clues at all as to how or why the victim came to be at that specific spot can help to determine other factors about the killer. Why did he leave them there? Was there a particular way he had arranged their bodies?'

He turned to the screen behind him and pressed the button that brought up an old scene of crime.

'Some of you may recognise the lower level of Queen Street Station where the body of a sex worker was discovered.' He pressed the button again and panned in to show the hands of the victim clutching a wilted flower.

'You may not be able to identify it right away but it was a carnation, and that, believe it or not, was a signature left by the killer.'

There was a murmured response from the younger members of the audience who had not been aware of this old case

147

of Lorimer's and a few knowing nods from others who not only recalled the series of killings but had been part of the investigation.

'That was a particularly cold, foggy night,' Lorimer explained, 'and I can remember how grateful the team all were for the hot drinks supplied by the station staff.' Another ripple of laughter, sympathetic this time; several of those present had attended crime scenes themselves and knew how harrowing they could be.

'We have several tools in our kit box,' Lorimer continued. 'As well as databases and forensics we often call on criminal profilers to build up a picture of a likely suspect. And, in fact, that is what happened on this occasion.'

He went on to show the image of a bearded man and heard whispers of 'That's Professor Brightman' or 'Mm, Solly . . .'

'Motive, means and opportunity; you will all be familiar with that particular mantra,' he went on. 'The means in each case was strangulation using a garment belonging to the victim and the opportunity . . . well, a dark Glasgow night, a deserted station, girls out to make what money they could by selling their bodies . . .' He gave a slight shake of his head as though to say how sad these circumstances had been.

'But as well as that we had to consider a motive. What was it that gave this particular stranger killer a motive to kill these young defenceless women?'

Turning back to the screen, Lorimer took them through the stages of the investigation where not only had a deranged killer taken the lives of these sex workers, but a copycat killer had used it for his own ends. Slide after slide showed images of the scenes of crime and the proximity to the railway, a spot that had been notorious back then for women of the night.

The last slides had been shown, then Lorimer had taken questions from the floor. At last the members were applauding enthusiastically and the secretary came forward to close the meeting by offering her vote of thanks and presenting Lorimer with a square black box containing a paperweight with the society's logo engraved into the glass.

'Pub?' Iain Mackintosh, one of the Fiscals, asked.

'Sure, why not?' Lorimer agreed. Maggie was away on her tour and Flynn, their gardener, would have fed the cat before leaving at teatime so he was free to join the others for a quick drink. It would have to be something non-alcoholic as he was driving home later, but the camaraderie of the Fiscal and some of the others would make a pleasant change as they sat in one of the pubs on Byres Road.

There was a crepuscular glow in the sky, the opalescent blue making black silhouettes of the buildings around University Gardens. Mackintosh was quiet as they stepped through the gloom down towards Ashton Lane where bright lights and the sound of music wafted up: the place a magnet for students and staff alike at any time of the session. Once upon a time they had both been students here, full of youthful enthusiasm and high ideals. Lorimer glanced across at his companion: Mackintosh still had a fervour for justice that lesser men and women lost on their way to the top of their profession. Had he kept his own idealism intact? He hoped so.

They were entering Ashton Lane when the Fiscal spoke again.

'Hear that wife of yours is doing rather well. Saw her picture in the *Gazette* recently.'

Lorimer grinned. 'Aye, that came as a bit of a surprise. Maggie had been writing her story for ages, even had an agent before she broke the news about a publishing deal.'

'You'll be able to retire any time you want, then. Live off her earnings,' Mackintosh remarked.

'That's what everybody seems to be telling me,' Lorimer countered. 'But she'll have to pen a bestseller before that happens. Children's authors don't make vast amounts of money.' He paused, expecting the usual comments about Harry Potter and J. K. Rowling.

'So she'll be keeping on her own job, then?'

'Oh, definitely. Maggie's a dedicated teacher and, besides, this writing career of hers happened partly because she'd spent so much time on her own,' he admitted.

'My wife plays bridge,' Mackintosh replied. 'Quite a demon at it, too.' He nodded at Lorimer. 'Our working lives don't follow any sort of patterns, do they?' he added.

Lorimer shook his head. *Crime never takes a holiday*, he often told the cadets at Tulliallan Police College, a warning to them that family life could and would be disrupted and not to expect a nine-to-five routine if they were to become good officers.

'She's on tour right now,' Lorimer said, a touch of pride in his voice. 'The publishers wanted her to do events and signings all over Scotland to begin with. Maybe next year when her second book comes out they'll take her further afield.'

'That's good,' Mackintosh said as they reached the door of the pub. 'They're obviously investing time and money, then. Maybe she'll find herself choosing between teaching and being an author one day after all?'

Lorimer raised his eyebrows in a moment of doubt. Maggie had been quite firm when he had asked the selfsame question: she wanted to teach for as long as she could, she had told him. Muirpark was a big part of her life, not just her day-to-day job but allowing Maggie the camaraderie she enjoyed with friends there. The idea of leaving to spend her days alone at home was not something she relished.

Iain Mackintosh was ahead of him, already at the bar to place their orders, the noise from the place almost drowning out the fiddle music from the rear of the pub. Lorimer looked around for an empty table and then strode across to a darkened corner. One quick drink of ginger beer and lime then he'd pick up the car from where he had parked further along Byres Road and set off for home. It would be silent there and cold; no Maggie waiting with her ready smile for a hug and telling him what she'd prepared for dinner. And, for a moment, Lorimer wondered why Maggie had not protested more at the long lonely nights when he had been working on a case. He gave a sigh, acknowledging that it was his turn to spend time alone but hoping in his heart that she was missing him as much as he missed her.

*

The room was just as welcoming as the others; Ivy seeming to have a nose for just the right type of hotel. Maggie flopped down on the bed, her fingers smoothing the cream-coloured counterpane. Closing her eyes she gave a deep sigh and thought about that evening's library event. Another success, Ivy had told her proudly. And she was right. There had been so many eager children in the audience, asking questions about her little ghost boy after she had read excerpts from the story. And, Maggie told herself, she was thoroughly enjoying the whole experience of travelling around her home country, speaking to children.

If David had lived he would have been a young man by now, bringing home some nice girls to his mum and dad, no doubt. Maggie felt the prickle of tears against her eyelids and brushed them away crossly. What had she to cry about? She had a great job besides this fledgling career as a writer. And there was Bill waiting for her at home. She was so lucky compared to so many of her colleagues, like her friend Sandie, whose husband had up and left her and their son. And the boy had been a pretty handful for a few years, though he was now settled in a good job and earning enough to treat his mum once in a while.

Count your blessings ... wasn't that the start of the old hymn they used to sing at Sunday school? Another sigh, but this time it was one of contentment, not for what had been lost.

The ringtone of her mobile made Maggie sit up suddenly, slide off the bed and grab her handbag. A quick rummage found the phone and she clasped it to her ear, hoping to hear Bill's voice.

'Yes?' she asked breathlessly, eyes shining in anticipation.

For a moment there was a pause and her smile faded. Had it been a wrong number? There was no click to show the line was disengaged.

Then, a voice spoke, a voice rough at the edges.

'I'm going to come into your room,' he growled. 'Then I'm going to take down your panties and f—'

Maggie clicked the red button, cutting off the words.

A wave of heat flooded her body.

Then she began to shiver as the nausea hit her.

Before she knew it, Maggie was on her knees retching into the toilet pan, hands holding the sides, aware of her arms shaking, her body trembling ... that voice in her head playing over and over, its menacing tones refusing to let her go.

Bill ... she had to tell Bill ... Maggie thought, scrambling to her feet and turning on the cold tap. She swished water across her mouth, her cheeks, across her weeping eyes. Towelling her face, she looked around for her overnight bag. That taste of sick in her mouth ... she needed to wash it away ...

Her legs felt like water as she stumbled across the room and unzipped the bag, hands desperately searching for her toilet bag, her toothbrush ... the need to clean her mouth uppermost in her mind.

Maggie retched again as she opened her mouth to brush her teeth, then the minty flavour seemed to calm her, though the hand that held the toothbrush was shaking.

When the phone rang again, she jumped, terrified.

But this time she would be ready for him.

'Maggie? Are you there?'

The sound of Bill's voice made her sink on to her knees on the carpet, weak with relief.

'Maggie?'

Lorimer sat on the stairs, Chancer the cat butting his orange head under one hand. They had talked for a good while, Maggie weeping at first, her garbled account of the filthy nuisance call only making sense after he had talked her through it gently stage by stage. He could still hear the gulps as Maggie had tried to calm herself, the terror of the experience still real in her head.

And, she'd told him, it wasn't the first time something rather sinister had happened, explaining the strange message on her Facebook account and the telephone call with no voice on the other end.

'Someone playing silly buggers,' Lorimer had told her firmly. 'Could it be kids from school?'

'That's what I thought at first,' Maggie admitted. 'But this wasn't a schoolboy, Bill. This was a grown man. And the voice ...'

He imagined her shudder, wishing that he could be with her at this moment, hold her in his arms, protect her from whatever idiot was trying to scare her with these obscene threats.

Gradually Maggie had described the voice. 'It wasn't a Scottish accent,' she decided, 'more like someone from down south.'

'Any particular region?'

He heard the sigh.

'Sorry, sorry, I'm not very good with regional dialects but it wasn't anything discernible like Cockney or Geordie.'

'Any trace of a foreign accent?'

'No. Definitely English. Though it could have been someone faking it, I suppose.'

'Have you told Ivy?' he asked.

'No, I'm still here in my room. What do you think? Should I bother the woman or just keep it to myself?'

'Up to you,' Lorimer replied. If talking it over with another woman made her feel better then Maggie would follow her instincts. She was a woman of great common sense, not easily frightened, and so this incident was grim enough to be taken seriously. 'Why don't you call her up, have a glass of wine downstairs together?' he suggested. 'Settle your nerves ...'

'Mm, think I'd rather raid my minibar and settle down for the night. *And* I'll keep my phone switched off till tomorrow morning,' she replied.

At last he could hear the steadiness in her tone, a return to the calm and sensible wife he knew so well.

'Love you.'

'Love you, too.'

But as he put down the phone he was acutely aware that neither of them had uttered the word that was on each of their minds.

Could this be a stalker pestering his wife?

CHAPTER FIFTEEN

Lorimer woke from an uneasy sleep and stretched out his arm. But Maggie was not there, he realised, she would be in her hotel. The dream disappeared in broken fragments as he rubbed his eyes and then rolled back over to look at the bedside clock. Four a.m. He sighed and closed his eyes again though he guessed that sleep would now elude him. Thoughts flooded into his brain, questions mainly that he had asked himself the previous night. Who had targeted his wife? Why? What might happen next?

Early on in Lorimer's police career he had been called to the house of a young mother, distraught at repeated nasty telephone calls to her home during the day when her husband was at work. He and an older officer had tried to reassure her, asking about the voice (a local accent, he remembered the woman had told them) and taking down notes about her circumstances. The woman's baby was only weeks old and the incident was bound to have upset her more than usual,

156

in her vulnerable post-natal state, Lorimer's fellow officer had advised him. That incident had been followed by three more of the same, all targeting young mothers in the same area. Some quick detection had noted that each of the women hung out their babies' tiny garments to dry on garden washing lines, something that a passer-by might notice. It was one of the things they had in common, apart from their location in the same part of town. The perpetrator had been caught after he had made one final call to the first victim. The girl and her husband had taken the police advice to change their number to ex-directory, this being a time when mobile phones were not yet a substitute for landlines. Therein lay the caller's downfall.

By this time CID was involved and Lorimer learned that the woman's husband had come home to find her in a state of terror, sobbing uncontrollably. The officers were quick to respond and the man who had been stalking these young mothers was easily apprehended, turning out to be a telephone engineer whose work in the nearby exchange allowed him access to names, addresses and numbers, even those that had been changed to ex-directory, hence his mistake.

Every large organisation has its rotten apple, Lorimer remembered the SIO in the case telling the woman. *Statistically it is bound to happen in any walk of life.* That, he reminded himself now, had been intended to reassure but all it had done was to open the woman's eyes to the evils that stalked every level of society, giving her more to fear and not less. Stalking was now a crime in Scottish law but that engineer had got a far shorter sentence than he deserved all those years ago.

Lorimer pondered the senior officer's words. Was Maggie a victim of some rotten apple? Should he be comparing that to the numbers in the audiences she was attracting all over Scotland? Perhaps. But who would want to target an author of children's stories? It didn't make much sense. Unless . . .

He turned in bed again, restless now that the thought had entered his head. No, that was silly, this was just a middle-of-the-night idea that would disappear in the common sense of daylight. But DCI Cameron's words kept coming back to him: *Maggie resembled those two victims.* Could it possibly be that the stalker had found his wife and begun to maliciously follow her by telephone or on Facebook? His eyes blinked open and he stared at the ceiling, willing the thought to go away and leave him in peace.

At last, no longer able to bear the silence and the cold space in the bed next to him, Lorimer pulled himself up, grabbed his dressing gown and padded downstairs to the kitchen, intent on making a cup of tea.

The cup that cheers but not inebriates, words on the side of their ancient tea caddy proclaimed as Lorimer spooned the dark leaves into a scalded teapot. A familiar sound made him look down and then Chancer's furry body was wrapping around his feet, a clear signal that meant, *Feed me.*

Soon, mug in hand and cat fed, he was sitting in his favourite chair, looking out at their garden, the back door wide open to let in some cool air. The birds were up at any rate, this springtime season the best for their songs, and Lorimer sat quietly, delighting in making out a thrush then a dunnock from all of the rest of the dawn chorus. And there, that trilling final note from their resident wren, no longer searching for a place to hide from the cold but out and about, seeking a mate perhaps somewhere in the hedgerow. Chancer sprung on to his lap, settling himself round and around then falling asleep with a small sigh of contentment as Lorimer's hand stroked the old cat's fur. He was no longer a hunter and Lorimer was grateful for that as they kept each other company, the birds safe as he watched the dawn emerging, a peachy-pink haze against the dark outline of the trees.

Was Maggie watching that same sky from her Highland hotel-room window? Or was she still asleep? It was far too early to call her and besides her phone would be switched off now, she'd promised not to turn it on until seven a.m. to call him. His mind turned to the stalker. Was he near her? Or was this some clown who only wished to frighten her for a lark? It could be schoolkids, he reasoned once again, bored during their Easter break, somehow having found Mrs Lorimer's mobile phone number and seeking her out on Facebook. Teachers had been targeted like that before, he knew, kids thinking it a bit of fun to annoy (and often frighten) the members of staff at their schools. Nastier things had happened too, Lorimer sighed, remembering a dead girl and a man hounded out of his profession, a case that had divided an entire staff and saddened the community.

He lifted the cat off his lap and placed him gently on the floor then, in three swift strides, he was along the path, tipping the rest of his tea into the flowerbed and taking deep breaths of the morning air. A shower and breakfast then off to work early, Lorimer decided. He would be in Helen Street long before Maggie's call came, his day's work begun.

Her sleep had been disturbed by dreams of the phone ringing and once Maggie had sat upright in bed, certain that she had heard a bell. But all was silent in her room, the windows shut fast against the cool night air. A sense of unease filled her as she stood under the shower, the decision whether to confide in Ivy still to be made. Normally Maggie would have chatted happily to her publicist, asking questions about the publishing world, listening to stories about other authors. But as she dressed for breakfast, Maggie longed to be back in her own home, sitting with Chancer on her knee, sipping her favourite Lady Grey tea. She had never minded her own company, well used to the long hours when her husband was working on a serious crime case and right now, Maggie wished she could sit quietly in the breakfast room without Ivy chatting to her across the table. That was a disloyal thought, she scolded herself, slipping on a pair of comfortable shoes for the drive ahead. Ivy had been terrific at arranging everything and so far they had got along companionably enough.

Downstairs Maggie could hear the clink of crockery, the smell of cooking bacon tempting her appetite. By the time she had spotted Ivy at the bay window, she felt hungry enough to eat a good Scottish breakfast, toast, marmalade and all.

'Good morning.' Ivy smiled up at her, placing her morning paper to one side. 'Sleep well?'

It was the normal thing to ask and for a moment Maggie hesitated then shook her head as she sat down and gathered up the linen napkin.

"Fraid not,' she admitted.

'Oh? Hope you haven't got a poorly tummy,' Ivy sympathised.

'No, nothing like that,' Maggie assured her. 'That meal last night was lovely. No,' she repeated. 'It's something else, Ivy.' She bit her lip then turned slightly to see if they could be overheard but the nearest residents were several tables away, too far to listen in on their conversation.

'I had a nuisance call,' Maggie told her, feeling her cheeks flush.

'Really?' Ivy's eyebrows shot up in an expression of alarm. 'Goodness! Has that ever happened to you before?'

'No. Never, well, sort of,' Maggie continued, a little flustered now she had begun.

'Something happen at home?' Ivy asked.

'No, it was when we were in Oban that it started, I think.' And Maggie related the incidents in the hotel there and the strange postcard that had been waiting for her in Tobermory.

'Well,' Ivy sat forward and looked her client straight in the eye, 'I think you ought to tell that clever policeman husband of yours to sort it all out, don't you?' Her voice sounded full of concern but Maggie flinched at her words.

'Oh, I told him after that horrible call came last night.' Maggie stopped suddenly as a waitress approached asking if she wished tea or coffee and had she decided on anything from the breakfast menu?

Once the young woman had departed, Maggie looked again at her PR. 'He'll not do anything official, of course,' she murmured. 'But he did give me some sensible advice.'

'You don't think you've got a stalker?' Ivy whispered, her tone hushed, eyes shining with the drama of it all. 'That would be cool! Someone fancying you after seeing you at a book launch or in the newspapers,' she continued, evidently thrilled at the idea. 'Not that I'd be surprised,' she added hastily. 'A beautiful woman like you. Bet loads of guys have the hots for you. It's just the weirder ones that cause you to lose sleep, hmm?'

Maggie let out a short laugh. 'I don't think so,' she said, smoothing her napkin down over her knees. 'I've never noticed anybody paying me that sort of attention.'

Ivy wagged a finger towards her. 'That's because you only have eyes for that handsome hubby of yours,' she said. 'Bet you never noticed the blokes in the Glasgow audience hanging on your every word.'

'Oh, Ivy, really!' Maggie protested. 'Nobody took any notice of me; it was the book they were interested in.'

'Ha!' Ivy sat back, placing her hands on the edge of the table. 'You've a lot to learn, lady. This caller has probably been following your tour from the very start. I've seen it before, you know,' she added idly. 'Smart woman dressed to kill for her book launch. Fellows lapping up her every word ...'

'Oh, Ivy, what nonsense!' Maggie protested briskly.

'But that call wasn't nonsense, was it?' Ivy retorted shrewdly. '*And* it kept you awake worrying about who it might be,' she added. 'I think we may need to be a bit more vigilant as we travel about,' she said thoughtfully. 'I'll talk to your publisher's security people, see what they suggest, shall I?'

'Oh, really,' Maggie said swiftly, 'there's no need for that. I told Bill I'd keep my phone switched off except when he's planned to speak to me. Surely nothing else can happen?'

Ivy made a face. 'Okay, if that's what you want, I'll go along with it, but remember, I'll be watching each and every member of your audiences from now on.' She smiled reassuringly then her gaze shifted as the waitress reappeared with two plates full of food.

Maggie looked down at the black pudding and venison sausages, her appetite suddenly diminished. She would eat as much as she could, not let Ivy see how genuinely upset she was about the whole nasty matter.

Across the room, hidden by a copy of the *Oban Times*, a figure sat silently, his eyes flitting towards the window where the two women sat. Something was wrong, he could tell from the cast of Margaret's face and the way she had leaned forward, talking in whispers with the other woman. He turned back to his newspaper and pretended to read the latest stories from the outlying islands, the photograph of his beloved taking up a quarter of a page next to a fulsome report on her visit to the Isle of Mull. She was so obviously happy there, the newspaper's photographer catching that smile lighting up her face. And she would smile again, he promised himself. Once she knew how much she was loved, surely her eyes would shine like that, this time just for him?

*

163

'I don't need to know the details,' Ivy said crisply. 'Just do what has to be done. Got that? And,' she paused, turning to the window of her hotel bedroom and looking out at the mist lifting off the distant hills, 'remember I'm making this worth your while.'

He hadn't mentioned the postcard, but then perhaps that was a little touch of his own?

She snapped the phone shut and thrust it into her raincoat pocket, shivering a little as she regarded the snow-clad mountains and wishing that she had brought more suitable clothing for this cold country. Back in London the sun would be shining, folk out in their cotton frocks, no doubt. Well, one more week and she would be joining them, hopefully returning in a blaze of glory. It might take another day or so, before she alerted her contacts in the press, but that was all to the good. It was time Margaret Lorimer recognised the importance of the media in her fledgling career.

CHAPTER SIXTEEN

One could not always depend on a megalomaniac making mistakes but they often did, their downfall created by that overweening sense of being too clever to catch. Solly would welcome such an occurrence but in the meantime it was his task to create a profile of a man who had sought out and murdered two young women, their physical appearance if not their personalities matching closely. That in itself had interested him, one piece of evidence that told the professor the stalker might not know his victims too well. Each woman's image had been in the press, their photographs a matter of public interest: the *Gazette*'s Business section had run a feature about Carolyn several months before her death and Patricia's face was often in the gossip columns. Too often? Solly frowned. Was he barking up the wrong tree here? Perhaps the newspaper photographs had nothing to do with the stalker. Some readers skipped the Business sections altogether and few men he knew bothered much with the gossip columns.

Yet, there was something nagging at him; what if the stalker had deliberately trawled the newspapers looking for a particular female? That seemed to be one of the few things these two women had in common, if he ignored their relationship with the actor, Richardson.

Solly's mind followed that dark pathway to a possible conclusion. Say the stalker had chosen each of the women solely on their appearance (his ideal female? Or someone resembling a woman from the killer's own past?). If the stalker had tried to liaise with each woman and been spurned, then what might his reaction have been? Someone with a severe mental disorder might flare up and hit out, rejection being anathema to such a person. Is that what had happened? Was this a stranger killing, each woman unaware of the existence of their admirer until he had confronted them in a Glasgow park?

He was still out there. And was he seeking yet another victim? Solly shifted uncomfortably in his chair by the window that overlooked University Avenue. The phrase *serial killer* was on several lips now, notably those in the media who wanted to sell newspapers, but Solly wondered if that was a shade too glib. This man, whoever he was, had intended to follow the women, not to murder them, but to gain something else. The gap between the two killings was too far apart to be a lust for taking lives, he had decided. Plus, the incidents had taken place during the academic vacations. Did this suggest anything? Was he constrained by term times for some reason? It was a possibility that had occurred to Solly right from the start and even now the officers from the MIT were trawling

166

records to see if any member of staff, academic or otherwise, had a history of stalking or at least mental health issues. Theirs was a mammoth task but it had to be done. An investigation of this size meant a lot of paperwork and hours sat at a screen, a far cry from the TV crime dramas that portrayed a few heroic souls chasing after their killer in a couple of episodes.

So far there had been nothing much from the officers at Helen Street other than the sinister message to the victims. Door-to-door investigations and hours of interviewing Patricia Donovan's family and friends had yielded very little. Now Solly was doing his best to create a profile of a man who had enough strength to throttle a young, fit woman and enough savvy to leave little trace of himself behind. The forensic offices at Gartcosh had a small amount of DNA from each crime scene that had not been identified as belonging to anybody connected with the case and so the assumption was that it might have belonged to the killer. It was male and not on any database that they had. A one-sided equation, Solly thought, only completed if and when they caught the person that had committed those crimes. He was only one tool in the box, Solly reminded himself with a smile. That was how Lorimer had once expressed it after reluctantly coming round to the view that criminal profiling was worth the effort. Odd, how the senior officer had been so against this at one time, when now he turned to Solly's expertise for cases just like these.

Perhaps, Solly thought, there would come a day when enough resources were to hand that fewer and fewer crimes would be committed, or at least more villains apprehended, thanks to the upsurge of technology and science in criminal investigation. Meantime he knew that human nature would continue to throw up aberrations like stalkers and psychopaths who were a danger to the rest of society.

Solly sat back, his eyes not seeing the clouds scudding across the Glasgow skies, but rather a darkened park where a man lay in wait for a woman he believed would be the answer to all of his dreams. And a question that so far nobody had been able to answer: what had prompted Patricia to follow her killer into the depths of Bellahouston Park? She had cancelled her regular taxi to the sports centre, did that suggest she had been given a lift there by someone that she knew and trusted? Someone who was waiting in the shadows as she emerged after her class?

Last night's stop had found them in Elgin after a brief signing in Aviemore so today he had to drive all the way across to Aberdeen and Dundee before heading to the Kingdom of Fife. According to the tour flyer, St Andrews came after that, then other towns along the east coast. They would spend a day and a night in Edinburgh, signing at various bookstores and giving a library talk, then it was back on the trail to Dumfries and Ayr before returning to Glasgow with the final stop at Newton Mearns. He gave a sigh that was not without a sense of pleasure. It was one way to spend his precious holiday time and he had not regretted a moment of it. Except . . . His mouth twisted angrily as he recalled how she had failed to turn up at the ceilidh in Tobermory. That had been a low point but he

168

had forgiven her now, blaming it on that stout little woman who dogged her every footstep. Late last night he had filled up with petrol, every light in the hotel extinguished, his silent kiss blown in the direction of what he guessed was her window. Now it was a simple matter of waiting in the car park for the pair of them to appear. He would track them across the country, he had decided, not knowing what hotel they had booked for their next overnight stay.

However, it gave him a moment of alarm when the publisher woman's car did not head away from the town in the direction he'd expected but carried on past the ancient ruins of the cathedral then turned into the gates of a low-lying building. *Johnstons of Elgin*, the sign said. He hesitated just for a second then followed them into the car park, making sure that he drove away to the far side, keeping an eye on where they were. Women. Shopping. He sighed again, wondering which of the women had wanted to make a stop here. A frown creased his brow. It was too dangerous to follow them into the shop; better to wait here then follow them once they emerged.

Maggie smiled as she saw Ivy heaving the carrier bags and placing them into the back seat of her car. Ivy would likely need to repack everything before the journey back down to London, these cashmere sweaters a luxury buy even at the sale prices. She'd been tempted herself at the range of lovely knitwear but had resisted. It seemed only a short time since Christmas when Bill had given her a gorgeous cream-coloured cashmere skirt and matching jersey, tiny seed pearls sewn into the neckline. It was wrapped in tissue paper, carefully stowed in her luggage in case one of their stops occurred during a cold snap. Maggie looked up at the banks of pale grey clouds ahead as they set off towards Aberdeen; were they snow-filled? Elgin and Aviemore were now behind them, the Cairngorms National Park with its white-tipped mountains receding as they headed east.

She glanced in the mirror to see the view as they left and spotted a silver car in their wake. She'd noticed it following them out of Johnstons car park. Someone else who had good taste in high fashion, she decided, though a second glance told her there was only one person, the driver, and it was a man. Must have been in to the café, she thought, then smiled, realising that she was on the point of making up a story about this stranger, something Maggie did more and more these days as ideas flooded her imagination, the stories about Gibby her little ghost boy demanding to be written down.

'That isn't an option,' he told her, slumping down on the sofa with a sigh.

'Why not? He knew Patricia, Lorimer said so. And he was engaged to the first girl, wasn't he?'

Arthur shook his head wearily. 'That was sheer coincidence, my dear,' he said softly. 'Besides, there is no evidence to show he was anywhere near Patricia that night. The DNA—'

'Oh, blast the DNA, can they not just arrest him and be done with it? What are they doing? Can't you make them get hold of him?' Moira's voice rose in a querulous note, reminding

Donovan of the constant bickering that had led to a separation so many years ago.

'It doesn't work like that,' he replied patiently. 'Thankfully in this country a person is innocent until proved guilty and there is insufficient evidence to suggest that Richardson was the person who took their lives.'

He stood up and walked over to the settee, sitting beside his estranged wife and slipping one arm across her shoulder.

'It doesn't help to blame just anyone for what happened,' he said quietly. 'Lorimer and his team are the best chance we have of finding who is behind this, Moira. Let them get on with the job, eh?'

For a moment she was silent then with a trembling sob, she buried her face into his shoulder, letting him pat her back as though she were a child. Life for them both would never be the same again. Yet, in a strange way, it had brought them together, united in this terrible grief.

Martin Enderby whistled tunelessly as he typed up the copy. Ivy Thornton had come up with something that could make tomorrow's headlines, if he could persuade his editor. He smiled, glancing to the side of his desk at the folded newsprint with that image of Lorimer's pretty wife. He'd covered the story a few weeks back, one of their prize-winning snappers catching the author in a flattering light. She'd been a good interviewee, full of enthusiasm and well spoken, so that he'd hardly anything to add to the taped conversation. Martin had liked her immediately, wishing that he'd had an

English teacher like that back in the day. Her good humour and genuine love for her subject had made him revisit some of the books they'd discussed over tea and cake afterwards. He'd only been back at the newspaper for a year now but it had been easy to settle in as a freelance journalist, his track record giving him plenty of juicy stories. If Margaret Lorimer had remembered his name, she hadn't said and Lorimer had not been around the day he'd gone to their home in Giffnock. And he'd been reluctant to dredge up his own story, something that had taken years to forget.

He made a face as he wrote. It was a shame if she was involved in this stalking business and whether it was true or just a ploy to keep the public's attention, he felt a little guilty to be the one that drew their attention back to her in this way.

Martin ran a hand across his head, the scar still there though his hair had long grown over these terrible wounds. He owed Lorimer his life, he thought, the feeling of betrayal rising again. Then he shrugged. If he didn't write it then someone else would and at least he could rack up the sympathy angle, make her appear like a helpless woman in jeopardy. That was so far from how he remembered her, he told himself, shifting uncomfortably in his seat. Margaret Lorimer had been funny, laughing at the daft stories he'd told about other, more pretentious authors and then sharing a few of her own anecdotes about life in the classroom. He'd found her good company and had left the house afterwards envious of the policeman who had such a lovely woman in his life.

Still, this was a job and he'd make the best of it. The editor would be pleased to have first dibs on the story too, Martin told himself, his jaw hardening as he continued to write the words that would appear in tomorrow's edition.

Aberdeen, the Granite City. Maggie looked around her, noticing that even here, on the outskirts, terrace after terrace of residential homes were built from the solid grey stone that gave the city its name. It was somewhere she and Bill had never visited together, their holiday preferences taking them mostly to the west coast. Police Scotland covered the entire country now and so her husband had visited many parts, Aberdeen included. A church spire pierced the pale blue afternoon sky and Maggie let her imagination take her up and up into the cold air where Gibby might be floating, looking down on the grey city below. What would he see? Gulls swooping towards the harbour? The North Sea waves dashing against the rocky shores? She no longer saw the streets narrowing or the traffic slowing them down, her thoughts far away now as the next chapter formed in her mind.

Ivy glanced at the woman beside her. What was Margaret Lorimer thinking? There was no sign of strain in the woman's face; instead there was a half smile as though she were deep in thought. Her silence was restful, though, Ivy had to admit. She'd had other authors that never stopped talking, her head aching by the time a journey ended, their event still to come.

The traffic lights turned to red, forcing her to stop and wait, thinking ahead to where she could park for less than an hour in the city. Perhaps she ought not to have spent so much time shopping back in Elgin, Ivy thought. It was already past the lunchtime rush and they still needed to drive to Dundee before their bookshop closed. At last they were on the move again and she breathed a sigh of relief as Union Street came into view.

Maggie felt as if she had seen the same high street over and over again, except the voices of people around her were entirely different. There was no sign of the sea though a chilly wind crept under her coat collar as they hurried back to where Ivy had parked her car. It had been a quick in-and-out of the shop, books piled on a counter for her to sign, Ivy refusing the offer of a coffee.

'We'll have to be quick in the next place, too,' Ivy told her, taking Maggie's arm and propelling her along the street. 'The parking's a nightmare in Dundee.'

Maggie just nodded, Ivy's experience in this job making her compliant. She gave a rueful smile, however, as Ivy dashed her along. The idea of touring city to city had sounded quite glamorous but the reality was turning out to be rather different, with little time to explore each place. Dundee, with its famous new art gallery, was a city she wanted to see, Maggie thought with a pang of regret. There had been so much in the news about the V&A built along by the harbour but she'd be lucky to catch even a glimpse of the celebrated building.

Aberdeen was soon just a memory of grey walls and a brisk wind along its main street as they headed further south, the road hugging the coastline for a while, Maggie staring out at the choppy waters of the North Sea.

She even failed to notice the silver car in their wake, oblivious to everything but the view from the passenger window.

CHAPTER SEVENTEEN

St Andrews was a breath of fresh air after the hours spent on the road. Their first sight of the North Sea was a haze of pale grey, the suggestion of a shimmer as the road dipped towards the coast, a faraway cluster of buildings hugging the land. Maggie lowered the window a little, savouring the rush of cold air with its hint of woodsmoke from a nearby cottage. A look of annoyance from Ivy made her raise it again, though the woman at the wheel could not see her smile as Maggie turned to stare out of the window. The country road rose and fell, several corners making Ivy slow down and then the trees on one side gave way to farmland and the promise of habitations ahead. A sign for the hotel made Ivy give a sigh of relief. 'Here at last,' she declared. 'The best one of the tour,' she added, a triumphant grin on her face.

Rufflets was a country house hotel on the outskirts of the town, close enough for them to drive easily to the appointments on the itinerary but tucked away in its own expansive grounds, a haven for those wishing to get away from the bustle of everyday life.

Maggie looked around as Ivy checked them in. There was a sense of age here, though the carpets were clearly quite new and the décor up-to-date. It felt, Maggie mused, as if it had once been somebody's home and she almost expected to see the owner stroll into the reception area, one hand outstretched to welcome them. However, it was only a young man in a crisp white shirt and black waistcoat that took their bags and led them upstairs, chatting to Ivy about their journey, fitting the key in Maggie's room before ushering her inside.

The room looked on to a large ornamental garden that stretched down into woodland, the pinks and reds of azaleas reminding Maggie of her own garden back home.

'If there is anything you need, do not hesitate to call us,' the young man was saying as he left her bag on the luggage stand. 'Enjoy your stay with us.'

'Thank you.' Maggie smiled, watching him leave to attend to Ivy whose room was somewhere along the same corridor. She stood at the window, a sudden feeling of happiness that for a little while she would be cosseted here in this delightful place. Her eyes flicked over the room and came to rest on the vast bed, its soft green coverings and matching cushions a taste of luxury. Then she grinned and flopped down, grasping the small teddy bear that had been placed in the middle of the pillows. A gesture of homeliness that made Maggie glad that Ivy had chosen to stay here. She certainly picked the nicest hotels, Maggie thought with gratitude. Ivy had been a little put out by Margaret

Lorimer's insistence that they make a detour to include Tackle and Books in Tobermory, taking a different route from the one Ivy normally preferred. Still, the publicist seemed to have been quite taken with the Hebridean island, perhaps she was paying Maggie back with this lovely country house hotel.

There was time before dinner to explore and Maggie sprung from the bed, heading for her case and rummaging inside till she found her binoculars. Then, buttoning her thick coat, she slipped out of the room, locking it carefully and thrusting the large key into the bottom of her pocket.

Outside she saw an older couple strolling back from a walk around the garden. As they drew closer Maggie noted the gentleman's walking stick and the woman's gloved hands clutching his arm protectively.

'Lovely day,' she called out and they nodded and smiled as she watched them pass through the French doors into the house.

A narrow path took her through the garden and down a few stone steps to a bridge that spanned a swift-moving burn. Looking down into the dark brown water Maggie saw only the constant motion of trailing weeds by its banks, any fish hiding in the shadows. She walked across and suddenly saw that the grass ahead was a swathe of yellow daffodils, their scent catching her breath. Wordsworth's famous lines came into her mind at the sight,

> *Beside the lake, beneath the trees,*
> *Fluttering and dancing in the breeze.*

There was no lake here but there was a sense of movement all right as the flowers swayed together in the wind, dancers all in time with one another.

Maggie stood stock still, another movement catching her eye. Out from the trees it appeared, walking steadily through the long grass, oblivious as yet to the woman standing there. A small deer, its bright flanks freckled with darker spots, tiny horns protruding from its velvety head. Then it stopped, nose quivering, scenting the unfamiliar presence. Maggie watched, scarcely daring to breathe as the deer turned its head and seemed to stare right at her. For a moment they regarded one another, wild creature in its own habitat, the silent woman the intruder. Maggie saw its ears flicker as it watched her. Then, lowering his head, the deer began to crop the grass, apparently unafraid of the human standing at a distance.

Maggie slowly raised the binoculars to her eyes and gave a sigh as the deer was brought into focus, its spotted coat russet against the deep grasses, tiny hooves hardly discernible as it moved along.

Suddenly a blackbird's warning cry made the creature raise its head and in one bound it was gone, into the safety of the trees.

She blinked but the place was empty now save for the dancing daffodils and a flock of pigeons wheeling overhead.

For a moment she shivered, looking into the trees.

Was that the shadow of a person stood watching her?

Maggie froze.

Then the shadow moved and she saw it for what it really

was: a sapling moved by the wind. Every little thing was making her jumpy, she thought, thrusting her hands into her coat pockets. A decent drink, that was what she needed, and the comfort of firelight.

Turning, Maggie made her way back, choosing a different track of beaten earth that led around the perimeter of the grounds then up more steps until she approached the upper gardens with their topiary shrubs lining the stony pathway. Ivy had promised cocktails by the open fire before dinner, Maggie reminded herself, a little reward for their toil. But she knew that the encounter with the deer would be a highlight of this visit, something she would save to take home for Bill.

Ivy put down the phone with a smile. All her plans were bearing fruit. This weekend there would be an extra feature on Margaret Lorimer's book, the public more curious than ever about the author whose husband was involved in murder, she herself the possible victim of a stalker. Maggie's publisher was delighted with the news that the nationals had taken the bait and had promised Ivy that this time next month she would be accompanying a well-known American writer on his British tour, the best hotels for them both. The MD's praise still rang in Ivy's ears though his final words had caused her a momentary pause.

Don't know how you do it, Ivy, he had remarked, his tone less flattering than curious. If he should ever find out ...? Ivy wrapped her arms around herself, suddenly shivering. No one would know. The deed was done and it just remained for the results to emerge. Margaret Lorimer would always think it was the work of some silly schoolboys and by the time this particular author went back to her day job, Ivy would be far away, leaving no trace to incriminate herself.

CHAPTER EIGHTEEN

The newspapers were always spread out on his desk first thing. Joe Riley, the Press Officer, ensured that the senior officers had a handle on what was being printed in the media, just one more thing to take up the beginning of the detective superintendent's day. Riley pursed his lips as he fanned out the papers, well aware of the furore that would ensue once Lorimer saw the article. He'd stuck a yellow Post-it note on top of the *Gazette* so that it would be the first thing the boss turned to and now Joe hovered, uncertainly, wondering if he ought to add *sorry* to the foot of his handwritten note. He sighed. Lorimer's wife had embarked on this literary career of hers and, though it was no fault of her own, she was now in the public eye for all to see. Really, there was not a lot he could do to stop this sort of thing.

Martin Enderby. Joe frowned. The name was familiar but try as he might, he could not recall anything negative about the journalist. A quick Google search would bring it up, he decided, heading out of Lorimer's room before the head of the MIT arrived to begin another morning's work.

'What the—' Lorimer stopped himself uttering another word, too astounded to take in what he was reading.

Police Chief's Wife in Stalking Case

A debut author might expect to garner plenty of new fans after the book launch but one thing Margaret Lorimer did not count on was being the victim of a stalking campaign. Sources close to the writer suggest that several anonymous calls and letters have been sent recently, intimidating Mrs Lorimer during her tour of Scottish bookshops with her publicist. However, the main threat to this popular English teacher appears to be her resemblance to the victims of recent killings, namely Patricia Donovan, daughter of high court judge, Lord Donovan, and accountant, Carolyn Kane.

The sub-editor had inserted three small photographs at the side of the column and, though most readers would take a quick glance at this point in the narrative, Lorimer's eyes had already feasted on them, dismay written clearly on his darkening features.

So far we have been unable to speak to Mrs Lorimer but her publishers issued a statement to the effect that Police

Scotland were aware of the problem and that the tour would continue as planned.

Martin Enderby

Lorimer opened his mouth then closed it again. Martin Enderby! His mind flew back in time to a chase across the grounds of Bellahouston Park, the police helicopter's beaming spotlight catching the man that had slashed Enderby's head and left him for dead. The journalist had disappeared from the radar ever since, though a quick internet search showed Lorimer that he had been freelancing for some time now. Lorimer picked up the paper again, letting a single sheet fall out where the press officer had placed it. Maggie's face smiled out at him from the author interview that the *Gazette* had covered several weeks back and, sure enough, the journalist's name was there for all to see: Martin Enderby. Why hadn't he noticed that at the time? Maggie had read it aloud, excited by the article, and he had failed to reread it for himself, more pleased with the photograph and Maggie's obvious delight than anything else.

A sigh escaped him now. Had he been too busy to notice the byline on something featuring his own wife? A wave of shame warmed his face and neck. Yet, what was he supposed to do? He'd taken her out for a champagne dinner, bought her flowers and made a fuss. *But you didn't read the article carefully enough, did you?* Lorimer told himself. Anyway, the fact that Enderby had been in their home had passed him by at the time. Should he be worried? If anything, Enderby ought to remember the name Lorimer with gratitude. But journos were all cut from the same cloth, he thought bitterly. They could be very helpful during a major case if it suited them but equally obstructive if it didn't.

First things first, Lorimer decided, picking up his mobile then laying it down again with a sigh as he glanced at the clock. She'd promised to call him at seven a.m. from their hotel in St Andrews and there were still a few minutes to wait. Keep the phone switched off, he'd warned her. Not that he needed to; Maggie was well aware of the need to limit calls to her mobile after what had happened.

He picked up the double-page spread once more, rereading the fulsome words from Enderby, saying how lovely his wife was and quoting several phrases from Maggie herself. Anybody would have written the same: Maggie's generosity and good humour were undeniable. It was a good feature, he thought grudgingly, no wonder if it had attracted unwanted attention. Lorimer's mouth drew into a thin line, thinking about Martin Enderby, the man he'd saved from that killer so many years ago. To turn around now and write this second piece, linking Maggie to a stalker. It felt a bit like a betrayal.

He read it again, putting himself in the mindset of a person who wanted to find a woman who looked just like Maggie, a woman who resembled two others that were already dead.

'We don't have the manpower to hedge her about with security,' Lorimer told Niall Cameron. 'Besides, it's the school holidays and Maggie reckons it's probably kids having a laugh.

We'd look like fools if we made too much of this,' he added. *Not to mention seeming to favour my own wife*, the thought remaining unspoken between them.

'You might like to see this,' Cameron said at last, handing his boss a printout. 'Missing women and girls over the past two years. Prof. Brightman's suggestion.'

Lorimer raised his eyebrows. 'Been doing a spot of overtime?'

Cameron grinned. 'Eilidh's on nights just now so I stayed on late and this is what I came up with.'

Lorimer screwed up his eyes as he looked down the list of missing women and their most recent photographs.

'That one, there.' Cameron pointed at the black-and-white image of a dark-haired woman that looked as if it had been taken in a photo booth, possibly for a passport as there was no smile and the subject was facing directly towards the camera.

'Mother reported her missing a week after she failed to turn up at work.'

'What did she do?'

'School kitchen assistant,' Cameron replied. 'Seems she had an erratic work attendance there so nobody was very surprised when she didn't turn up after the school holidays. Mother hadn't been used to seeing her too often. Thought she might have headed down to London since she had friends there but apparently nobody had seen her there either.'

Lorimer's head began to ache. School holidays . . . there was a link there surely? Abruptly his phone rang and he put his hand up in apology.

'Sorry, have to take this,' he said and turning on his heel strode back to his own room and shut the door behind him.

'Morning, darling.' Maggie's cheerful voice made Lorimer grip the telephone harder. It was obvious she hadn't a clue what was going on.

'You haven't seen the papers this morning?' he asked gruffly.

'The *Press and Journal*? No, why, have I made the headlines?' She laughed.

'Something like that.' Lorimer sighed. 'It's the *Gazette*.' And he picked up Enderby's article, conscious of her indrawn breath as he read it aloud.

'Who . . . ? Ah, it must have been Ivy,' Maggie said quietly. 'She's been hinting that I needed a wee boost of publicity.'

'You don't think she's behind this?'

'Goodness, no!' Maggie protested. 'I still think it must be someone at Muirpark. Some daft boys having a laugh at my expense. But Ivy would be the first one to capitalise on it,' she admitted.

For a moment Lorimer considered asking his wife to come home or at least to ask the PR woman to talk to him, but what was the point? The damage was done now and if this was silly lads having a lark just because their teacher looked like the two victims he'd not only be wasting police time but making a complete fool of his team and their investigation.

'Just be careful,' he said at last. 'Don't give any more interviews to the press, okay?'

'Of course.' Maggie's voice was worried now. 'I'm really sorry this is causing such a bother. These poor families have enough to think about without some stupid person using their tragedy as the basis for some teenage nonsense.'

That was typical of her to consider others before herself, Lorimer thought, wishing he could fold his wife into his arms there and then.

'I don't want to sound alarmist,' he told her slowly, 'but if you see or hear anything odd, let me know right away. My phone will always be switched on.'

'There's been nothing else,' Maggie told him. 'Honestly.'

'Okay, but be careful.'

'I will. Promise,' she whispered. Then, 'Love you.' Lorimer felt a pang listening to her voice. Did she sound a little hoarse, as if there were tears not far away?

'Love you, too.'

Maggie put down the phone and stifled a sob. This was so stupid! Why had Ivy contacted the press? She gritted her teeth, angry at the woman for meddling and making a complete fool of her. It was simply playing into the hands of whoever was behind this. She racked her brains, trying to recall any incident when she had been forced to mete out a punishment to any of her pupils, but nothing came to mind. That happened so rarely in her classes; perhaps a talkative student would need a raised eyebrow on occasion but generally Mrs Lorimer had a reputation as a popular teacher, her lessons *full of imaginative tasks that never seemed like work*, an accolade put on Facebook by Kyle Kerrigan, one of her former pupils.

The Kerrigans! Maggie sat down suddenly on the edge of

the bed. The older brothers were a bad lot and the father had been in and out of jail more times than she could remember. Did they still have a grudge against the Lorimers after that awful case that had divided the staff at Muirpark Secondary? But that was ten years ago, she calculated. And Kyle was now a young man, following a successful career as a PE instructor in the army. No, she realised, there was not one pupil in her classes that she would have said had the urge to do anything like this. It was well known that her husband was a top police officer and so perhaps targeting Mrs Lorimer was nothing to do with her personally. Had Bill put away any family member of a pupil in her school? Someone outwith her own classes who harboured bitterness against him? Maggie would be an easy target and seeing her picture in the *Gazette* may well have sparked an idea to pester her in at attempt to get back at Bill.

She lifted her phone again and began to text her husband, smiling wryly at her economy of words, the very exercise that she had given her second years before the holidays.

'It'll do you no harm,' Ivy insisted as she held the newspaper aloft, pre-empting Maggie's protestations. 'If there is a kid at your school making mischief, they'll think twice now before attempting anything else.'

'They'll think twice when I find out who it is!' Maggie replied angrily. 'Wee devils have no right to do things like that!'

'It will all peter out, I'm sure,' Ivy soothed, seeing the dark expression on Maggie's face.

'You really think so?'

'Of course,' Ivy said briskly. 'You'll find today's newspaper in tomorrow's cat litter tray. People have short memories, but we can work this to your advantage, all the same.'

'How do you mean?'

Ivy leaned across the breakfast table and Maggie saw a gleam in her small dark eyes.

'The nationals can run their own version of this,' she declared firmly. 'Maybe just a small bit, but it will be enough to draw attention to your new book. The end of each article will have details of the title and publisher, just like that original article in the *Gazette* when you gave such a brilliant interview.'

'It was Martin Enderby who wrote that as well,' Maggie murmured.

Ivy shrugged her shoulders. 'Good freelance writer,' was all she said as though by contacting him she had done Maggie a favour. 'And that's my job, remember,' she added, fixing Maggie with a glare. 'I'm here to promote your new book and if I had let this opportunity go by then I would have been doing you a disservice.'

Maggie drew in a deep breath, suppressing the words she wanted to express. Ivy's argument was not what she wanted to hear but until the end of the tour in a few days' time she would put up with whatever the woman decided.

'Remember, I'm an old hand at this job,' Ivy went on, lifting her napkin and spreading it across her lap as a waiter approached their table.

*

'Celia Gemmell.' Niall Cameron nodded at the photograph again. 'She worked in the school off and on for a few months then disappeared last year. About this time,' he told Lorimer.

'Any follow-up from Missing Persons?'

Cameron shook his head. 'The mother didn't push them much. Notes taken at the time recorded that she didn't seem overly worried if she never saw her daughter again. Something rotten in that relationship, if you ask me,' he remarked gloomily.

'And thereafter? Any sign of the woman using credit cards or a passport?'

'It wasn't followed up that far. If every missing person was pursued in that manner we'd never get to grips with real crimes.' Cameron sighed.

And it was true enough; there were many reasons why someone would want to disappear, begin a new chapter of their lives without any interference from family members: an abusive relationship, money problems, even a new relationship elsewhere in the country... The list was endless and, besides, people had a right to disappear and begin over if that was their own choice.

'Get on to Missing Persons again,' Lorimer said at last. 'See if there has been any sign of credit card, phone, bank or any internet activity from Celia Gemmell.' He sighed. 'If that's what she's still calling herself.'

He did not need to add the unspoken thought that hung in the air between them: *If she is still alive.*

The photograph lay side by side with the three others now

on his desk: four faces that bore an uncanny resemblance to one another. Carolyn Kane, her bright smile shining out from the newspaper article about her success as a young accountant; Patricia Donovan, face turned coquettishly over one shoulder, the pose practised so often for the cameras; Maggie's delight at her new success evident in those bright eyes and now Celia Gemmell, that small photo showing an attractive woman whose features so resembled the others. Yet there was a sombre cast to Celia's face that was missing from the other three and Lorimer wondered what the school kitchen assistant would have looked like had she smiled into the camera instead.

'Where are you, Celia?' he said softly. 'And who would have wanted you dead?'

The rented flat where Celia had lived had long since been let out again, her possessions dumped in the basement, something that Molly appreciated. It would have been easy enough for Grafton, the landlord, to have chucked them into a skip. As it was, the rooms were now occupied by a different tenant and there was little point in trying to send in a forensic team after all this time. What on earth were they supposed to be looking for anyway? It wasn't as if the missing woman had turned up dead, she fumed, as she carted box after box of Celia Gemmell's stuff back to her car.

'Didn't have an awful lot to begin with,' the landlord said, standing on the pavement watching the detective. Molly glanced up at his face, seeing a tinge of pink grow along the jawline. A guilty conscience if ever there was one, she told herself. Probably he'd creamed off the best stuff and left the rest in case anyone came looking. His words rang true, though. There weren't a lot of clothes and those that had remained were packed into an old suitcase with some shoes and a pair of mud-caked wellingtons thrust into a large polythene bag.

'D'you know if she owned any other luggage?' Molly asked him, watching the clasped hands tightening, the man's nerves showing in a different manner.

Grafton shook his head. 'She arrived with just the one case, I do remember that,' he told Molly. 'But I never saw her leave, you know. She still owed me rent,' he grumbled, letting his eyes slide away from Molly's stare.

The detective paused for a moment. 'Didn't you think that was strange, Mr Grafton? Just disappearing like that, leaving most of her things behind?'

'Not the first time someone's done a moonlight on me,' he huffed. 'And there was only the old woman here to ask questions. Told her what I told you. She just didn't come back one day as far as I can tell.' He shrugged his shoulders. '*She* didn't want any of her things either,' he added. Then, stepping closer to Molly and dropping his voice to a whisper, 'I think there was bad blood between them, you know.'

Molly nodded. Mrs Gemmell was next on their list but first she had to get all of these boxes back to Helen Street for their tech guys to examine.

'Was there anything else? A laptop? Mobile phone?' Molly caught another guilty expression on the man's face. 'Perhaps you put them somewhere else for safe keeping?' she suggested, giving Grafton the opportunity to jump on that idea, a way out if he had nicked them for himself. 'Police have ways of tracing such devices,' she smiled, keeping him in her gaze.

'Ah.' He slapped his forehead in a theatrical gesture. 'Sorry, sorry, forgot all about them!' He scuttled back into the main hall and disappeared, leaving Molly to shake her head at the simple duplicity of human nature.

She had just slammed the boot of the car closed when the landlord reappeared carrying another cardboard box.

'So much on my mind,' he mumbled, handing over the carton, avoiding Molly's eyes as he did. 'Sorry, sorry...'

'Here's my card,' Molly told him, after heaving the box into the back seat. 'If you hear from Ms Gemmell at all, please contact us immediately. And,' she added slowly, 'we may need to talk to you again, ask more questions, all right?'

Grafton nodded miserably, watching her climb into the car, and Molly wondered just what they would find on the laptop and phone. Had he wiped them clean? Put them back to factory setting hoping to sell them on? She gave a sigh as she drove into a space in the traffic. At least they had them, she thought, a small feeling of excitement swelling inside. Celia Gemmell had left them behind when she had disappeared. But had she intended to? Or was her disappearance so sudden that she had not had time to gather up any of her belongings? Worse still, had someone else taken these very choices from her?

*

194

'Nothing, absolutely nothing!' Lorimer shook his head as he let the reports fall back on to his desk. 'What does that tell us?'

Solly raised his eyebrows but did not offer an explanation.

'You think she's dead, don't you?'

The professor looked back solemnly at Lorimer. 'It would be uncharacteristic of a killer to pick on two women so suddenly without having had any previous experience, don't you think?'

'You're assuming our man is some nutter—' Lorimer stopped himself and sighed, the word had escaped him before he'd had time to think. 'Somebody with a mental health problem,' he said instead.

'If he is fixated on a particular type of woman then, yes, it is possible that he has taken other lives before those of Carolyn and Patricia. What bothers me is . . . ' He trailed off and looked thoughtful for a moment. Lorimer waited, accustomed to Solly's long pauses as the psychologist formulated what he wanted to say.

'It's the school holidays,' Solly said at last. 'This missing woman disappeared during the school holidays and that was when our attacker took the other women's lives,' he told Lorimer. 'It could be a coincidence, of course, but as you are fond of telling me, you don't believe in coincidences.'

'No, I don't,' Lorimer admitted. 'So, let's look at this. A woman on the kitchen staff disappears, we don't know where or why, but we do know that she had a habit of poor timekeeping and she was practically estranged from her family. What was that all about?' he murmured thoughtfully.

'Our perpetrator uses school holiday times because these are the only times he has free to follow his prey,' Solly suggested.

'Is he a teacher, d'you think?'

'Or someone who works in a school and gets more time off around then. A janitor? Handyman?'

'We need to talk to the staff at Celia Gemmell's school,' Lorimer said firmly. 'But that can wait till we hear back from DS Newton.'

'Oh?'

Lorimer nodded. 'She's visiting the missing woman's mother. And,' he glanced out of the office window, 'I'd love to be a fly on the wall to hear just what she says.'

Janet Gemmell's home was not quite what Molly had expected. The retirement complex in the small Renfrewshire village had taken the detective by surprise, its creamy white walls and trim gardens full of swaying daffodils much more in keeping with the older properties than any new building ought to be. And yet, the architectural details, like those crow-stepped gables picked out in grey paint, or the leaded windows glazed like several of the grand houses nearby, gave Oakwell Court the traditional look its architect had obviously intended.

Each apartment was situated off a wide octagonal space, the roof partially glazed so that light shone down on the reception hall. Outside each white-painted door lay plant pots, some with simple greenery, others with bright azaleas.

Janet Gemmell's name was fixed to her door on a Rennie Mackintosh style plaque:

J. GEMMELL

It gave Molly an inkling of the woman right away; she wanted to show that she had a hint of class, the detective decided. And it intrigued Molly to see if she was correct.

The doorbell was silent from outside and Molly stood patiently, hoping that it actually worked. Soon enough, the door opened and a small woman stood, her grey hair cut into a severe shape close to her skull, looking up at Molly with an expression that was far from welcoming.

'DS Newton,' Molly began. 'We spoke on the telephone.' She smiled encouragingly.

'Better come in.' The woman's deep voice was gruff, the sort that indicated a lifetime's smoking habit.

'Through here,' Janet Gemmell directed, walking ahead of Molly into a small sitting room that was furnished in pretty pastel shades, the two-seater sofa and matching armchair covered in a floral fabric with pink roses and butterflies. Here and there Molly noticed well-polished silver-framed photographs and an array of china ornaments, the whole effect reminding her of a great-aunt's house where children had been terrified to touch a thing lest it break. Floor-to-ceiling bifold doors led out to a small terrace where a chair and table sat; Janet Gemmell's smoking spot, she guessed, as the sitting room itself had no smell of cigarettes.

'It's about Celia, then,' Mrs Gemmell began, fixing Molly with a pair of dark eyes that held no trace of sympathy. 'What's she done now?'

'You haven't heard from her?'

'Not a thing,' Janet Gemmell snapped. 'Typical of her just to swan off and leave me to pick up the pieces.'

'Oh? How was that?' Molly ventured.

'Had to pay her outstanding rent, didn't I? She pushes off and I have to fork out. Again.' The woman bristled with indignation.

'Celia had a habit of disappearing?'

Janet Gemmell's eyes slid away from Molly's gaze. 'Well,' she began, 'she wasn't what you would call very dependable.'

That was vague enough to be a *no*, thought Molly. 'She didn't disappear like this before, did she?'

Janet Gemmell looked down, hands twisting in her lap. Molly saw the slight shake of the head.

'She didn't even call to tell me where she was going ...' The words came out as a whisper and Molly watched as the old woman swallowed hard, trying to keep her emotions in check. Was this a sort of grief? Or a simmering anger? Hard to tell.

'You reported her missing after she failed to turn up for work,' Molly said, consulting her notebook to check on the dates. 'Yet you didn't persist in asking Missing Persons to locate Celia. Why was that?'

The sigh and the silent shrug were all she gave in answer.

Could she push the woman on this? It might just make her clam up, Molly decided. And that was the last thing she wanted.

'I need to ask you about Celia,' Molly told her firmly. 'We are trying to establish her whereabouts in connection to an ongoing case, so anything you can tell us will help to create an idea of what sort of person she is.' Molly drew in a silent breath, aware that she had been about to say *was*. For now they had to go on the theory that Celia Gemmell was alive and missing of her own volition, no matter what alarm bells were ringing amongst the officers in the MIT.

Janet Gemmell looked up into the detective's gaze, dry-eyed, her stony expression hard to read. Was this a mother disappointed to the extent of bitterness against her daughter? Or had her own life been one of enduring emotional blows until she put up a barrier against any feelings of tenderness? Professor Brightman might have been able to make an educated guess, Molly thought.

'Celia wasn't what I hoped she would be,' Janet began, her eyes flitting to a photograph on the mantelpiece where she and a man sat side by side, a small girl between them, looking solemnly out at the camera.

'We brought her up to be a nice young woman, respectful,' she said. 'But from the time she was a teenager Celia went her own way. Stayed out late at night, didn't come home, sometimes.' She gave a short, mirthless laugh. 'Left home and moved in with a boyfriend till he got tired of her then she came home again.' Janet Gemmell glared at Molly. 'That was the pattern till her dad passed on,' she said. 'He was the soft one, couldn't say no to her.'

But you could, Molly thought.

'I sold the family home and moved in here after I'd had

199

a big operation,' Janet explained. 'It's a decent place to live. Warden on hand if you want her, all the privacy you need.' She shrugged again. 'It's a one-bedroom apartment. All I require.'

And no room for a daughter to stay over, Molly almost added.

'Did Celia come to visit you before she left her previous lodgings?'

There was a pause then the woman made a face. 'Once or twice. I didn't encourage her,' she sniffed. 'Celia was a law unto herself. She'd bring presents for Mother's Day then I wouldn't see her again for months. Fact is, last Mother's Day was the last time she came to see me.'

'No phone calls since then?'

'No, and she never phoned unless she wanted something. We weren't close,' Janet Gemmell said quietly, though that, Molly thought, was stating the obvious.

'Did you know any of her friends? Work colleagues?'

Janet Gemmell shook her head. 'There was a man she brought here once, looked a good bit older than her from what I could see, which wasn't much. He chose to sit in his car, never came in even to say hello.'

'Did Celia give you his name?' Molly tried hard not to sound too eager.

A frown and a shake of the grey head. 'I don't remember.' Then, for the first time, a look of concern flitted across her face. 'Is it important? Has something happened to Celia?'

Molly shook her head and smiled faintly. 'We have no news about Celia. And you know what they say,' she added. 'No news is good news.'

Janet gave a snort. 'Never good news where my daughter's concerned,' she insisted. 'And, if she's got herself mixed up in something she shouldn't then she's only got herself to blame.'

Molly looked at the rising shoulders, noting the tremble on the old woman's hand. Her words were suddenly at odds with her body language and Molly understood that Janet Gemmell was afraid for her daughter.

'Tell me about her work,' she continued. 'What did she do?'

'Could have been so much better than a kitchen hand in that school.' Janet shook her head. 'She was clever at school, just went off the rails before she could take any exams. Waste of time trying to get her to study.'

'Did she enjoy the job?'

'Shouldn't have thought so. Wasn't she always bunking off? Terrible timekeeping. Amazed she lasted as long as she did.'

'But she wasn't sacked, was she?'

Janet Gemmell shook her head. 'They phoned me here, sounded worried, I'll give them that,' she admitted.

Molly nodded silently. Bankbrae Primary School was closed for the Easter holidays but as soon as they could, she and Davie Giles would be questioning Celia's workmates and the rest of the staff there.

'Anything else you can tell me about Celia? Any indication that she intended to go away?'

Janet Gemmell turned her head away and stared out of the glass doors. 'Nothing,' she said. 'Not a thing.'

'Was she a keen walker, rambles in the countryside, that

sort of thing?' Molly asked, remembering the wellington boots in that plastic carrier bag.

Janet Gemmell raised her eyebrows in a look of astonishment. 'Celia? Walking in the countryside? Not if she could help it!' the woman scoffed. 'Why do you ask?'

Molly explained about the dirty boots the landlord had passed to the police.

'Some mistake,' Janet muttered. 'Can't be hers. She never wore anything like that. More of a designer shoes sort of girl, our Celia, not that it did her any good.' She sniffed in a disapproving manner.

Molly tried not to show her disappointment. Had the landlord simply passed her an old bag full of someone else's footwear? Well, the forensic lab would show up any DNA from Celia's other possessions and make a match. *Or not*, Molly thought gloomily.

'Here's my card,' she said, laying it on the glass-topped coffee table. 'If you think of anything else or if Celia gets in touch, please call us right away.'

It seemed as though getting to her feet was an effort, but Celia's mother stumbled to the front door, a determined courtesy to show the detective out of her home.

As the door closed behind her, Molly imagined the old woman scrabbling for her cigarettes and lighter, the bifold doors opening to her sanctuary in the garden. Something wasn't right. But was it simple anxiety for her daughter? Or did Janet Gemmell know more than she had let on, suspecting that the worst had befallen her only child?

CHAPTER NINETEEN

The churchyard caught his eye for a brief moment, the dark red spire looming nearer, cars lining the street so that he had to slow down. A funeral, he thought, noticing the black-clad folk walking towards the church door, a stark contrast to the swathes of yellow daffodils lining the path. An older couple passed by, walking hand in hand, then turned towards the mourners making their way along the footpath.

A memory flickered in his brain, the picture of another cold churchyard, lines of grown-ups waiting for the coffin to emerge from the church, those white and yellow flowers borne on its surface a splash of almost indecent colour to his young eyes. Nobody had held his hand that day, he remembered, though there had been plenty of small shoves against his shoulder as he was eased forward towards the yawning grave, instructed to toss a handful of dirt on top of her coffin once the cord bearers had lowered it into the darkness.

He blinked, the image receding slowly as the traffic

gathered apace and the church was left behind. Yet a sense of gloom had settled on his soul, refusing to shift even though he had set out with a song on his lips and a feeling of anticipation that was almost excitement. She still had the power to do this to him, he realised bitterly. Even after all those years.

He switched on the radio and stared at the road ahead, concentrating on finding the correct lane that would take him to his next destination. The radio station was manned by a cheerful young DJ, his Irish tones easy on the ear, the choice of music suitable for all ages and tastes. *Wallpaper music*, one woman had called it when he'd turned on the radio that day after work. It was a damned sight better than the pounding beat from that souped-up BMW next to him, he told himself angrily, his foot on the brake, stopped at a set of traffic lights. A glance from the window took in a young Asian guy, short-sleeved, windows down, his body moving back and forth with the beat. He hated him on sight, the dark head lifted in a swaying tilt, the casual arrogance in his handsome face. When the lights changed the Beamer tore away, a squeal of tyres leaving him yards behind.

He clenched his teeth, a silent curse aimed at the back of the departing sports car, his ill wish to see it crashed at the side of the road. Serve the bastard right!

The moment passed, however, the ballad on the radio station coming to an end and the news bulletin beginning. One hand hovered over the button to turn it off but he listened instead in growing horror as the newscaster relayed the latest items.

'Police Scotland has insisted that the wife of Detective Superintendent William Lorimer is not considered to be at risk from what appears to be harassment from an unknown stalker. The man heading up the double Glasgow murder has told our reporters that Mrs Lorimer is continuing with her book tour and is not expected to be given any special security provision meantime.

'MSPs at Holyrood have been discussing the latest Fisheries Bill—'

One finger shut off the voice and he stared ahead, rage coursing through his body. Who had been making trouble for his beloved? What sort of person was harassing her? As he drove towards the university town of St Andrews, his mouth was a thin, determined line. No one was going to hurt the woman he had chosen. No one. He would be her guardian angel, protecting her from any sort of harm. With that thought came the image of Margaret Lorimer's face and the grateful look he would see in her eyes.

His mouth softened into a smile as the car gathered speed. Soon they would be together and he would be rewarded for his vigilance with the sweetest of all prizes.

CHAPTER TWENTY

'Celia Gemmell was last seen on the morning of April second last year,' Lorimer began, looking around at those officers who had been able to attend the meeting. 'That was by one of the other tenants where she lived.' He caught the eye of the officer from whom that morsel of information had come, nodding his approval. 'Her mother last saw her in March last year when Celia visited for Mothering Sunday. We have noted that she came with a man who stayed in his car throughout that short visit but there was no CCTV footage to show the make or model. He'd parked in a side street,' Lorimer added, his voice loaded with significance. 'Had he wanted to keep out of sight? Was he intending to take Celia somewhere? We need to find out who that man was.'

The room was quiet, all eyes fixed on the detective superintendent, anxious for the bits of intelligence to merge together.

'The bus stations, train depots and airlines have all been scrutinised and we are pretty certain that if Celia left Glasgow then it was by a private vehicle. *If* she left,' he repeated. 'Thanks to our tech team we know that Celia had not browsed any holiday sites nor places to stay. What she had been looking at before she disappeared, however, was linked to her own place of work as a kitchen assistant in the education authority of North Lanarkshire, specifically Glasgow.'

Lorimer turned to face the officers, hands clasped behind his back. 'Thanks to our technical staff, we know that Celia Gemmell had taken a particular interest in the stages of dismissal, accorded to a member of staff. Now, whether she was worried about her own poor timekeeping or not, we cannot tell. But she also downloaded items relating to the reporting and suspension of teaching staff members.' His eyebrows rose as he saw the general reaction. 'Now,' he mused, 'why would she do something like that?' The question was evidently rhetorical as he continued. 'To my way of thinking Celia Gemmell wanted to know how to report a person who may well have been troublesome to her. Someone who made a pest of himself, perhaps?'

A low wave of sound began as the officers in the room voiced their thoughts.

'I don't believe in coincidences and I do not think it is a mere coincidence that Carolyn Kane and Patricia Donovan died during a school holiday nor that Celia Gemmell disappeared in the Easter vacation this time last year.'

'You think she's dead?' Davie Giles blurted.

'I do,' Lorimer replied quietly. 'We have no evidence to suggest the woman disappeared voluntarily and I think what we must be doing now is searching for a body.'

There was a small silence following his remark then Molly Newton raised her hand. 'Sir, there's a strange anomaly over the woman's boots. They were handed to us by her landlord and for a while I thought they might not belong to Ms Gemmell. They're actually a size bigger than her other shoes. But the lab came back and verified that traces of the same DNA were found in all of the footwear so we do know that she wore those particular boots. Even though her mother expressed surprise at the idea of her daughter walking anywhere in the countryside,' Molly explained.

Lorimer nodded his thanks. An idea was forming in his mind. It might be a bit of a long shot, but there was one person he knew who might very well help him with this particular production.

Police Scotland was fortunate to have so many fine specialists amongst the forensic fraternity and the person Lorimer was meeting at Gartcosh was particularly celebrated for her work in soil science. Professor Lorna Dawson CBE from the James Hutton Institute had agreed to travel down to Gartcosh and as Lorimer emerged from the Lexus in the visitors' car park he looked across to see her walking towards the security gates.

His long legs caught her up easily and soon they were shaking hands inside the booth, waiting for the security officer to check their credentials and unlock the entry gate. In moments they were walking side by side, chatting companionably about Maggie's success and how Lorna Dawson had read about the tour in the *Press and Journal*.

'She was supposed to have attracted a stalker, is that right, Lorimer?' the professor asked as they entered the main door of the Scottish Police Campus and waited by the reception desk for their visitors' passes.

Lorimer made a face. 'Probably a storm in a teacup,' he replied gruffly, not meeting the woman's questioning eyes. 'Maggie thinks it's some bad wee kids fooling around. Bored out of their heads during the school holidays,' he added obliquely.

'What do you think?' Lorna asked quietly, shifting her stance a little so that Lorimer had to meet her gaze.

'Truthfully? I don't know,' he said, shaking his head. 'Okay, the press have made a big deal about how she looks a wee bit like those murder victims, but come on, we all know that their main objective is to sell newspapers. Still—' He broke off with a frown. 'I don't like it, Lorna, and that's all I'll say to you.'

'No investigation then into who might be stalking her?'

'Not officially, no.'

'And,' she paused, a soft smile of sympathy on her face, 'unofficially?'

'Aye, well, we'll see,' Lorimer replied. 'Let's get this investigation over before I begin to worry about a nuisance caller, eh?'

Lorna Dawson simply nodded but he could feel the woman was not fooled in the least by his answer.

It was more than an hour later that they sat side by side in a small room off the curving corridor upstairs, the professor having taken Lorimer through the process that she was suggesting. Janet Gemmell had been asked if her daughter was in the habit of gardening or walking in the countryside, only to be told with a scoff that Celia wouldn't be seen dead in a pair of wellingtons. And yet, it seemed that she had worn the pair she had kept in her flat, new boots now caked with mud from some place. Could this be a clue to the missing woman? Lorimer had thought so and now Professor Dawson would take the boots back to her lab and begin the painstaking search for wherever the mud had come from. It was a fascinating branch of forensics and had even been demonstrated on television, the professor given a walking boot and then challenged to find the exact spot where a team of presenters had buried the matching piece of footwear. The professor had risen to that challenge, eventually pinpointing the very place where it was hidden, much to the amazement of the television crew and the general public.

'What do you expect to find?' she asked Lorimer as they prepared to wind up the meeting.

'Who knows?' He shrugged but then caught the knowing expression in Lorna's eyes. 'Well, okay, if she's been somewhere out in the country once, perhaps driven there by another person, who's to say she wasn't taken there again?'

'It's a long shot,' the professor answered, not adding that Police Scotland was spending a decent amount of time and money to engage her services.

'Yes,' he replied shortly.

'But something tells you that she might be buried out in a lonely part of the countryside?'

Lorimer looked away and nodded. That was exactly what he thought but as yet he could not bring himself to voice that fear.

Meantime his officers were trying to locate other members of staff from the primary school where Celia Gemmell had worked, though the school holidays was making it especially difficult to track most of them down.

'His name is Steven Dewar,' Davie Giles told Molly. 'Been head teacher there for the last fifteen years. Always goes away during the school holidays according to his neighbours in Beith,' he added, pushing a mug of hot chocolate across the table in the café where he had arranged to meet his colleague.

'I had an art teacher like that,' Molly mused, opening the slim packet of brown sugar and stirring it into her drink. 'Got into his car and drove with his wife and kids to Italy as soon as the term ended and came back looking like one of the three tenors. Year-round suntan, he had. Spoke fluent Italian as well, I remember. We went on a trip to Verona with him in Sixth year.'

'Well, this guy maybe does the same,' Davie murmured. 'The next-door neighbour says he lives alone, does his garden at weekends and washes his car, the sort of thing most law-abiding citizens do.' He sighed. 'Other than that I couldn't find out much about him. Still, we'll see Mr Dewar once he has come back from his holiday, I suppose.'

'Have to start with the heidie,' she laughed.

'Meantime I've managed to track down the school secretary,

Mrs Bell. She was quite helpful when I explained what I wanted. Told me that Celia was something of a glamour puss and that all the P Seven boys had a crush on her.'

'You don't think ... ?'

'Eleven-year-old lads? No way,' Davie scoffed. 'Anyway, this Celia sounds as though she was capable of fending off any nonsense from wee boys. Or big ones, for that matter. Mrs Bell says that she came to work dressed to the nines and that you'd never have known it was the same woman behind the kitchen counter.'

'They have to wear these mob caps, I suppose. Health and safety?'

'Aye. She worked in the kitchens during the morning, served the dinners then cleared up. Not a bad job if you can exist on the pay. Starting at ten and finishing before the school bell rings in the afternoon.'

'She must have had another job, surely?' Molly frowned. 'Nobody could pay the sort of rent that landlord was charging unless they had a separate income. And her mother mentioned designer shoes.'

'I've checked to see if she had anything from the social. No widow's pension 'cos she was never married. No invalidity benefit or anything like that. So, yes, our Celia must have made money some other way than working for the education authority.'

Molly sat pondering. 'Her bank account was healthy enough but every deposit was a cash transaction. She must have been working somewhere to get cash in hand.'

'On the game?' Davie suggested.

'Could be. Might explain the hostility from her mother. And why her timekeeping at the school kitchen was so erratic.'

'Did the landlord pass any remark?'

Molly shook her head. 'I don't think he took any interest in his tenants except for the weekly rent being paid on time. Good thought, though. Maybe we should ask around the other tenants in that building. See if Celia brought visitors home on a regular basis. It wouldn't be the first time that a sex worker was bumped off by one of her punters,' she added darkly.

Davie Giles blinked and leaned forward, biting his lip as a thought came to him. 'The other two women ...' he began. 'Is there any chance they might have had a secret sex life?'

Molly snorted. 'Like *Belle de Jour*, you mean?' Then, as Davie frowned at her, she laid a hand over his. 'Sorry, didn't mean to scoff. Human nature is crazy enough for us to imagine that sort of thing but I really don't think the information we have about Carolyn Kane matches that sort of profile, do you?'

He sighed and shook his head. 'Just a daft notion. Anyway, let me tell you what else I found.' He slid a sheaf of papers across the table. 'There's a list of all the members of staff, teaching and ancillary. One PE teacher who is peripatetic, same with the music teacher. They both cover several primary schools in the area. And, yes, they are both away on holiday with their respective families.'

'Apart from the school secretary ...'

'Mrs Bell.'

'Uh-huh. Mrs Bell. Who else is actually at home right now?'

Davie counted them off on his fingers. 'Most of the kitchen staff who all live close by, the janitor and the young lad who works as a handyman but helps out the janitor as and when required.'

Molly sipped her chocolate thoughtfully. 'My money would be on the other dinner ladies,' she said at last. 'Bet they had a good gossip about our missing woman. Tell you what, let's see which of them are at home this afternoon and if they fancy a wee visit from the pair of us? Lorimer doesn't need us in till the meeting at six. What d'you reckon?'

Davie gave her a nod and a grin. It was a long time since he had attended a state primary school but he still remembered with affection the big buxom figure of Mrs McAllister, the dinner lady who had dished out second helpings to hungry little boys. She'd been a wise old bird, he thought. And if there was someone of that ilk in Bankbrae Primary maybe they would find out something to help push along this case.

'Yes? Oh, come in,' the woman stepped aside and ushered Davie and Molly into the neat semi-detached villa around the corner from Bankbrae Primary School. Isobel Malone, the senior dinner lady, closed the door behind them. 'Just made a pot of tea,' she said. 'There's coffee if you prefer that, though,' she added, waving a hand towards a glass door. 'Sitting room's in here,' she said, opening the door and letting out a small white dog that began yapping and jumping up at the two strangers.

'Toots! Stop that at once!' Mrs Malone commanded and the little creature slunk away, tail between its legs.

'Sorry about that. She gets excited whenever there's a new person to see. I'll just make sure she stays in the kitchen.'

Molly was about to say it was okay but Davie frowned at her and she remembered the police officer's allergy to pet hair. If the sitting room was full of stray hairs, Davie would be sneezing all the way back to Helen Street.

Moments later Isobel Malone bustled in to join them, perched on the edge of the nearest armchair and leaned forward, eager to begin.

'You wanted to talk to me about Celia, that's right, isn't it?'

Molly smiled winningly. 'Yes. As I said on the phone, we would appreciate any background information you can give us on Ms Gemmell.'

Isobel Malone narrowed her eyes. 'Something's happened to her, hasn't it? I can tell, you know,' she added, shaking her head slowly. 'Always said that one would come to a bad end.'

'Why was that?' Molly asked.

'No better than she should be,' Mrs Malone sniffed, 'if you get my meaning.' She looked up sharply. 'Too interested in men, I'd say. And wanted all the things that money could buy without having to work for it.'

'But she was working in Bankbrae, in the kitchens?' Davie put in.

'Aye, a wee extra on the side, no doubt, plus whatever she was claiming from the Social.'

'Celia Gemmell had no benefits,' Molly told the woman. 'Are you saying that she had another job that nobody knew anything about?'

'If you call it that.' Isobel Malone looked down at her teacup, her cheeks beginning to redden. 'There's a name for women like her, you know. Not a nice one,' she added.

'Have you any proof that Ms Gemmell was a sex worker?' Davie asked bluntly.

The woman squirmed uncomfortably. 'Well, just what she said, you know. Getting in late for work then smirking in that way she had, hinting she'd been kept late in bed by her latest fellow, would be splashing the cash the following weekend, that sort of thing.' She looked from one of the police officers to the other. 'Everybody knew what was going on, of course.'

'Even the teaching staff?' Molly asked.

Mrs Malone made a face. 'They all thought she was the cat's whiskers, so they did. No, I don't think any of them had any idea about her. Leastwise, none of us ever mentioned it to them. Not the sort of talk you want to spread about, know what I mean?'

Molly hid a smile. She knew exactly what the woman meant. The gossip would be confined to the ancillary staff, no doubt, though surely it would have been only a matter of time before the story crept into the staffroom? Had that been why Celia had trawled the internet looking for information about dismissals?

'Something else I want to ask, Mrs Malone,' Molly began. 'Was there anybody employed at Bankbrae who was overstepping some sort of line? Behaving in a way that might result in them being sacked?'

'Other than Celia?' Mrs Malone shook her head, a

cynical look on her face. 'No, dear, we're a close-knit bunch of ladies. All hard workers. And we have a good janitor in Jack McCormick. The young lad, Jamie, fair pulls his weight as well. No . . . ' She shook her head again, picking up her teacup and taking a sip. 'Celia was the only one that might have been given the heave-ho. If she hadn't pushed off by herself.' She gave Molly and Davie a quizzical look. 'Why all these questions anyway? Has she done something? Got herself in a bit o' bother?'

Molly smiled blandly. 'We want to locate Ms Gemmell in connection with an ongoing case,' she explained. 'As far as we know Celia Gemmell has not committed any crime. And I would appreciate it if you made that clear to your colleagues.'

'Oh, yes, of course,' Isobel Malone clattered her teacup in its saucer, spilling a little tea in the process.

It was, Molly thought, as they made to leave, as if the woman couldn't wait to lift the phone and begin to tell the other dinner ladies about her visit from Police Scotland and the inquiries about Celia, the good-looking woman who had disappeared so suddenly a year before.

CHAPTER TWENTY-ONE

The morning was grey and damp when they set off from Rufflets, the splash of tyres through wayside puddles and the rhythmic swish of the windscreen wipers making Maggie feel sleepy. An east-coast haar had settled over the fields, blotting out any view beyond the still-bare trees that lined the road. Everything was a wash of pale light but for the beech hedges and leaf litter on the woodland floor, its rusty brown the colour of a pheasant's wing. There were few cars on this country road and all, like Ivy, had their headlights on, making them appear suddenly through the gloom and disappear again into the mist. A glance in the rear-view mirror showed twin spots of light, one vehicle tailing them, careful not to draw too close in the murky morning.

Maggie closed her eyes, drifting off in a half sleep, her thoughts on Gibby, her little ghost boy, wondering how he would feel flying above the world on a day such as this.

*

Behind them, watching intently, the driver made sure to keep his speed down, knowing the way they would take, anxious to meet the woman once again at the next stop on her book tour.

The queue had come to an end, the last book handed over, and Maggie was busy signing the extra copies for the bookstore when a shadow fell across her table.

She looked up to see a middle-aged man wearing a beige raincoat stooping over her, briefcase in one hand.

'Sorry,' she began, smiling up at him. 'Thought everyone had gone.' She looked but there was no book in the man's hand. He leaned towards her then gave her a sympathetic smile.

'I heard about the stalking,' he said quietly. 'That must have been a horrible experience for you.'

Maggie felt her cheeks flushing. 'Oh, to tell you the truth I think it might simply have been a schoolboy prank, one of the hazards of being a teacher,' she joked.

'Perhaps you need someone to keep an eye on you, Margaret.' He smiled and gave a low chuckle.

She opened her mouth to tell the man to call her Maggie then closed it again. After all, to the wider world she was now Margaret Lorimer, her Sunday name written in bold letters across her book cover.

'Here.' He passed Maggie a business card and she looked at the writing:

CHRISTOPHER G. STEVENSON
Security with Discretion

There was an email address and a telephone number but no website. Maggie gave a small frown. 'Did somebody send you to see me?' she asked, immediately wondering if Bill had pulled some strings in the private sector.

'Let's just say I will be close by for the remainder of your tour,' he told her. 'Look on me as your guardian angel.' He gave an avuncular chuckle and smiled more warmly at her. 'Nobody will notice me in the audiences but I'll be there, making sure you're safe. Just till you get home again. I suspect you're the sort of lady who loves being at home. Settled and content to be where you feel happiest.'

Maggie's eyebrows rose in surprise. He must have been in the audience during that last question-and-answer session. Somebody had asked her 'What's your favourite place?' and she had thought for a moment, wondering if the answer ought to be one of the stops on her tour. But then she'd replied on impulse, 'Home's where you feel the most content. Where all the good memories are.'

And yet, by the way he was looking at her it was as if this man with the gentle voice already knew her well. But then, perhaps it was his business to find out about whoever he had been sent to protect?

'Does Ivy know . . . ?'

His manner changed a little and Maggie saw a frown cross his face. 'She doesn't need to be bothered about this,' he told her. 'If she asks any questions, then I am just another fan.' The smile returned and Maggie found herself drawn to the man. He was not what she imagined a security officer would look like, his salt-and-pepper moustache and thinning hair giving him the look of someone who was approaching retirement rather than filling his days with the cut and thrust of security work. If she had conjured up a guardian angel, then he could not have looked less like this Christopher Stevenson. But then, a little voice told her, surely that was the whole point of remaining in the background, fitting into a crowded room? Perhaps, beneath the guise of a punter attending a book signing was a man with some expertise in martial arts, for all she knew? Appearance and reality, surely she ought to know about that illusion by now?

Maggie picked up her handbag and pulled out her purse, opening it up and fitting the card into a slot next to her supermarket reward cards. She did not notice the security man's keen eyes on the purse, or the way his eyes flicked across her own details of name, address and phone numbers, beneath a rectangle of clear plastic.

'You didn't see me today,' he reminded her with a wink, then, laying a gloved hand on top of hers, he turned and walked away, leaving Maggie with a strange mixture of feelings. In one way she felt a tinge of outrage that Bill should have sent this man to babysit her, but on the other, surely her husband was doing his best to protect her from any more aggravation?

He was trembling by the time he reached the car park and flopped down into the driver's seat. For a moment back there he had seen these lovely eyes clouded with suspicion. The cards were good quality, though, the print shop making a decent job for him. Perhaps it had been his sudden appearance that had so startled her? Poor, dear Margaret. How awful for her to have lived so long with this policeman, the sort of person that never trusted another soul. When she was his he would rid her of any worries, any lingering doubts.

It would be perfect. *She* would be perfect! He closed his eyes, imagining the cottage with its windows lit up again, lamps winking by the door. Once this book tour was over he would return to his old life, just long enough to make arrangements, have the place done up properly. Then he could let go of all the strain of those past years, watching and waiting for the right person who would make him complete.

'How's it going?' Lorimer asked, his ear pressed to his mobile, a sudden longing to hear Maggie's voice.

'Great – we have plenty more signings to get through but we should be home in another three or four days,' she told him.

'I miss you,' he said softly. 'And so does Chancer,' he added.

'Well, no need to worry about us. Got my own personal guardian angel watching over me, haven't I?'

'If you say so,' Lorimer replied. He would hardly have called Ivy Thornton a guardian angel, but if Maggie was getting on that well with the woman, who was he to complain?

'Anyway, enough about me,' Maggie said briskly. 'Besides, there's very little to tell, different shops, different audiences, but it's becoming a sort of routine and I'll probably forget most of the names of folk we've been meeting by the time I'm home. How's the case?'

Lorimer stifled a sigh. If she had been home they would have sat side by side late into the evening, discussing some of the things he could share with her. 'Molly Newton's shaping up well,' he told her. 'She and Davie Giles seem to have become a good partnership. Quite a lot of intelligence coming through from various sources but nothing big yet.'

'It'll come,' Maggie assured him. 'It always does.'

Lorimer bit his lip, glad for once that his wife could not see the expression on his face. Somewhere out there was a killer, a man responsible for the deaths of at least two people, women who looked in many ways like his own precious Maggie. He gave an involuntary shudder.

'Are you still there?' she asked. 'It's gone very quiet.'

'Still here,' he answered gruffly. 'Counting the days till you're home. Glad you've got company, though,' he added. 'Love you.'

'Love you, too,' she whispered.

He knew then, Maggie smiled to herself. The *company* that Bill referred to must be that nice Christopher Stevenson. Oh, well, she could put up with it for Bill's sake, though a small part of her still felt a little peeved at the idea that he thought she was unable to look after herself.

'Time for drinks.' Ivy was there, her coat over the woman's arm.

'Good,' Maggie replied, getting to her feet. For once she was glad the evening's talk was over and they could relax together in their latest hotel. The image of a warm fire near the bar area came to mind as she shrugged into her coat. 'Let's go,' she said with a grin. 'Let's see what cocktails are on the menu tonight.'

It was late by the time he reached home, the day's work continuing through the six o'clock meeting then that discussion with Giles and Newton regarding the missing woman. He had brought the team up to speed on Professor Dawson's involvement though there had been a few sceptical glances cast in Lorimer's direction as he had spoken about the possible link between the wellington boots and the chance of finding the woman's body.

The sky above him was two different colours, a burnt-orange streak hugging the treetops then a swathe of deepest blue above, the new moon the tiniest arc of white. There was a hint of frost in the air, too, though the day had been bright and the sun warm through the windows of his office that afternoon. Maggie had been travelling through the Kingdom of Fife and tomorrow would see her driving further afield, more signings in the various shops, she and Ivy enjoying the life of an author. It was good that they seemed to be getting on well, although he had not warmed towards the Thornton woman, for some reason. He shrugged as he closed the front door behind him and heard the familiar sound of Chancer meowing for his dinner.

The old cat reared up and he stroked the tawny fur, tickling behind the cat's ears.

'Just you and me again, lad.' Lorimer sighed as he strode

into the kitchen and bent down to find a clean bowl in the kitchen cupboard. It had been another long day and, as he watched Chancer gobbling up the cat food, he realised how famished he was, not having had time to stop for lunch.

'A curry,' he muttered to himself. Hadn't there been some left over from a couple of nights ago?

Minutes later, the meal re-heated in the microwave, Lorimer sat in his favourite armchair, one hand forking food into his mouth, the other switching between the TV channels to see if there was any football to take his mind off the case.

He had wiped the plate clean with the warmed naan, stacked the dishwasher and was sitting back down again, console in hand, when the telephone rang.

'Lorimer,' he said, expecting a voice that would ask him to leave the comfort of his own home and set off for some new crime scene. But there was only silence at the other end, something that made the detective frown. Theirs was an ex-directory number, so who had . . . ?

'Sorry,' a man's voice sounded in his ear. 'Must have got the wrong number.' Then the line went dead and Lorimer gave a sigh of relief. Settling down once again, he found a channel with a game in the English League more than halfway through, the wrong number call already forgotten.

The man smiled, looking at the telephone on the table. It was good to check these things and now he knew that this was the correct number. Perhaps one day Margaret's voice would answer his call. Though, he reminded himself, his plans did not include her ever returning to the home she shared with that policeman.

Professor Brightman sat back and considered the two scenes of crime. Mapping murders often gave a picture of where the perpetrator might live and in this case he had decided it must be Glasgow, on the Southside, since each of the bodies had been found only a few miles apart. Bellahouston Park was hedged about with a mixture of areas from the well-tended enclaves of Pollokshields to the tenements along Paisley Road West and cottage flats at Mosspark. Queen's Park sprawled from Shawlands with its up-and-coming bistros and pricey tenements along Langside and around to Victoria Road, again a bit of a mix of housing but possibly with more residents like the Richardson fellow, Carolyn Kane's fiancé.

He had a map in front of him, red lines drawn between the two crime scenes, the exits from the parks marked in yellow. A frown crossed Solly's face. It was not enough. If they did find a third victim then perhaps he might make sense of a map, see if there was any logic to be had in pinning down the whereabouts of the killer. Celia Gemmell had lived in the West End, but she had worked over in the Southside. He traced the route with an inquisitive finger, stopping at Bankbrae Primary School. It was close enough to both of the parks to make his eyebrows rise thoughtfully. Was there some connection between the two dead women and the one that had been missing for a year? He'd think about that but meantime he needed to concentrate on what they already knew. What had been committed, what had been left undone.

The deaths themselves were interesting. There had been no sign of sexual assault, nothing except for the strangulation, by hands strong enough to overcome each young woman. 'Who are you?' Solly murmured softly. The man had chosen each of these victims, possibly stalked them for some time (during school holidays, he reminded himself) then suddenly killed them as light had faded from the skies. There had been no sign of a body being dragged for any great distance, either, so he must have carried them towards the bushes or else cajoled them there before ... what? Throwing them to the ground? Grabbing them by the neck? He closed his eyes trying to see what the forensic team had pieced together. A man tall enough and strong enough to overcome each healthy young woman, yet no signs of a struggle. Did that suggest they had known their attacker? Had he lain in wait as Carolyn Kane crossed the park to the safety of her home? He must have known where she had been and where she was heading, the site of the murder a bit away from the path that the accountant usually took. And Patricia Donovan? Why had she been there at all, in the thickest part of the trees? The MIT officers had taken footage from the CCTV cameras at the sports centre but all they'd seen was Patricia walking out of the building, looking down at her phone then out of shot, heading away from the car park. Had she been called by someone? Lured away? The police had discovered that her usual taxi had been cancelled that night so either she had come to the fitness class with a friend or she'd taken another form of transport to get there. The officers from Police Scotland had gone over all of those details but so far they'd come up with nothing to explain how she had arrived and why she had taken that turn away towards the trees.

It was a puzzle and Solly felt that they were definitely missing something important. Patricia Donovan's last call was to a number that did not seem to exist, a mobile that may have been trashed after the woman's death. 'You've covered your tracks,' Solly whispered, 'haven't you?' This killer had planned it out beforehand, an intelligent mind taking steps to ensure his own safety from discovery. These did not look like crimes of passion, though some latent emotions may have been working away beneath a calm exterior. These were well-thought out. Why? And what had these women done to deserve such horrific deaths?

Imagination, Solly had told his psychology students, can be a huge force in determining our behaviour. What we imagine another person thinking can become a fact in our minds despite there being no evidence. He had cited Shakespeare's Othello, a man whose imagination had been fed by the evil Iago. Solly shuddered. That had ended in an innocent young woman being strangled to death too. Was jealousy a factor here? But it had been a calculated action, he reminded himself, not one fuelled by the green-eyed monster.

Lorimer had told him about Professor Dawson's agreement to tackle the case of the missing woman, Celia Gemmell, who so resembled the two victims. *And Maggie Lorimer*, a little voice reminded Solly.

He gave an involuntary shudder. *A goose ran over my grave,* he thought. Then, with a sigh, he sat back and looked at the map again. Giffnock was not so very far from Shawlands, was it? Could it be that the stalker lived somewhere on Glasgow's Southside? He took a pencil and traced another line from Queen's Park, stopping when he came to the cul-de-sac where William and Maggie Lorimer had made their home.

The sound of a telephone ringing made him start then he reached out a hand to whisk it from the receiver, lest the noise waken baby Ben.

'Hello?'

'Solly, it's me, Lorimer. Sorry to ring you so late but I wanted to talk something over with you.'

'Not a problem,' Solly replied. 'What's up?'

There was an unaccustomed pause then he heard Lorimer give a small sigh. 'It's Maggie,' he said at last. 'I'm worried about her.'

Solly nodded. This had not come as a surprise. After all, the articles in the newspapers had given Maggie some fresh publicity, though perhaps not the sort either she or Bill wanted.

'Do you think she's in any danger?'

'I don't know, Solly, and that's the truth. She says it must be some daft kids but I've been doing a check on the ones at Muirpark who could be likely candidates and I've drawn a complete blank. Most of them are either away on school trips or studying for exams. Muirpark does a really good job of taking busloads of kids away over the holidays. Even the rascals,' he added.

'Could it be someone who's trying to get back at you for some reason? That would smack of a cowardly approach, targeting your wife,' Solly murmured. 'And you've put away plenty of men and women who would be nasty enough to try that sort of thing.'

Again Solly heard a sigh and imagined his friend running his fingers through his dark, unruly hair.

'Maybe. I do worry that might be the case. But how on earth am I supposed to find the person behind it? A stalker isn't like other criminals. The intent to harm might be there but until then he's done nothing except frighten his target.'

'Is Maggie frightened?'

'I don't think so. She sounded positive on the phone. Said Ivy, her publicist, was watching over her, or something. So, no, I think she's being her usual sensible self. Takes a lot to make Maggie scared.' He gave a small laugh.

'And the nuisance calls have stopped?'

'Well, she's not had any more but she keeps her phone turned off except to call me. And nothing on Facebook. Och, it probably was kids larking about,' Lorimer said at last.

Solly bit his lip as his eyes turned towards the map in front of him. Should he say anything to draw attention to the preliminary findings? Or would that simply cause the good police officer a sleepless night?

'If nothing else happens, maybe you can assume that it was just someone trying to alarm their schoolteacher. A prankster who saw how much Maggie resembles the two women . . .' He tailed off with a frown.

'You're probably right, Solly. Anyway, it was good to talk. Sorry to disturb you. See you soon, okay?'

And then he was gone. Leaving the psychologist with one more idea to consider.

Why would a stalker pick on a particular person for their looks alone? An accountant, a former actress, possibly a kitchen assistant and maybe even a secondary school teacher ... It was not what they had in common that mattered so much as that their appearance was alike. Like what? Like whom?

Solly closed his eyes and began to think.

CHAPTER TWENTY-TWO

His dream was always the same. She was drifting back-wards, away from him, arms outstretched as though in supplication, dark hair floating behind. But he could never reach her. It was too late to make a grasp for those pale hands.

He would awaken, drenched in sweat, the bedclothes damp, his hands clutching the edge of the duvet as though he was squeezing and squeezing. The memory of his fingers around another pale neck came back and he let the cover go with a small cry. His heart was beating loudly and he sat up, trying to feel the cool air on his chest, a trickle of perspiration running down his face. Would he never be rid of her? Was it his fate to be so tormented that he could not forget ... ?

Taking a few deep breaths, he swung his legs over the side of the bed, feet searching for his slippers. Outside the day was beginning, pale light filtering through the thin curtains of the bed and breakfast he had chosen. Soon it would be time to get into his car and follow his destined route. He gave a sigh then stood up, stepping out of his pyjamas and folding them neatly. The night terrors were over and it was time to face the day.

A shower and a decent breakfast then he could begin again. Margaret would be waiting and he must not disappoint her.

CHAPTER TWENTY-THREE

If there was one thing that Lorna Dawson enjoyed it was a challenge and soil science presented plenty of those. She was a lady who smiled a lot, humming under her breath today as she stared into the Light Stereo Microscope. The particles recovered from the wellington boot loomed large under her powerful lens, pieces of a jigsaw that would eventually come together as they were analysed and compared to samples collected from areas within Scotland. She was content to follow the detective superintendent's advice and start with the Glasgow area, though her net would widen as different possibilities emerged. In her experience bodies were buried far enough from human habitation to allow the grave-digger enough seclusion for clandestine burial and to make a complete get-away. It was quite normal to look for sites about fifty metres from a roadside where there was deep, diggable soil: somewhere close enough to carry or drag a corpse to a site that might even be already prepared. The perpetrator could be caught eventually by having traces of his deadly work on footwear or in a vehicle that were a match for soils in and around the burial place.

She had recently given evidence in a murder case where a not-guilty plea had been issued on behalf of a defendant, watching the man subsequently break down in the witness box as her testimony made it clear he had murdered his lover. Should this investigation by the MIT succeed in turning up a body then Lorna could be back in court once more as an expert witness for the Crown Prosecution.

It was later in the day that Lorna sat tapping information on to her report. The soil analysis had thrown up several interesting things, one being the seeds of a garden plant, *Crocosmia Lucifer*, that was often found still thriving long after being abandoned by the sides of country roads. Several different particles of pollen had been identified in the grass – Scots pine, ash, birch – and traces of faeces were present in the soil sample, suggesting the place might be adjacent to grazing land. Now it remained to narrow down the soil type, though if she were to hazard a guess they might be looking at a soil with an organic peaty layer, with sheep grazing nearby, some ancient woodland in the vicinity . . . and a derelict house.

It was a start, she thought, sitting back with a smile. She would keep looking at the land cover maps in and around the city to see what was the likeliest source location for the soil recovered from the boots.

'Think we're getting somewhere,' DCI Cameron told the two detectives. 'One of the teachers is back home, just went away for a few days. Deputy head, a Mrs MacDonald. Stays in Newlands. She's asked to come here to Helen Street rather than have officers in her home.' Cameron gave a shrug. 'No idea why. Maybe she just doesn't want any nosy neighbours asking questions.' He glanced at his wristwatch. 'She'll be here about two p.m.,' he continued. 'Tea and biscuits in the conference room, I think. Okay?'

Janice MacDonald was a forty-something lady with blonde hair swept back into a ponytail, her tweed jacket and jeans smart but casual. She didn't look like Molly's memory of a primary teacher, though they had all seemed so much older when she'd been a kid. As they shook hands, Molly noticed a keen, intelligent pair of hazel eyes behind purple-rimmed spectacles giving her a direct look.

'Thanks for coming in, Mrs MacDonald,' Molly said, gesturing for the woman to sit at the huge oval table.

'My husband's off too,' Janice MacDonald explained. 'He's on child-minding duty today.' She wrinkled her nose. 'There wouldn't have been a moment to talk properly to you at home.'

'How many children do you have?' Davie asked.

The woman gave a smile that showed dimples on her cheeks. 'Four. All primary stage. And a real handful, I can tell you!'

'Do they attend Bankbrae where you work?'

'Oh, no. They all go to the local primary. Think I'd go mad if mine were close at hand all day,' she added.

Molly smiled, warming to the deputy head teacher. A family

236

of four kids and she still worked full time in a promoted post. *Hats off to you, lady,* she thought to herself.

'We're trying to locate a former member of the ancillary staff. A Ms Celia Gemmell,' Molly began.

Janice MacDonald's face changed at once, the smile now a frown, her jaw hardening. She sat back and looked from Molly to Davie then back again. 'She was trouble, that one,' she began. 'But perhaps you know that already?'

'We have heard some rumours,' Molly offered, keeping the details from the deputy head.

'Oh.' Janice let out a long sigh and glanced down at her hands. 'Celia was a terrible timekeeper. I think she would have been sacked if she hadn't decided to swan off for good. But it wasn't just that.' She bit her lip. 'Can I say something that is more gossip than fact?'

'Go ahead.' Molly nodded.

She leaned forward, placing her arms on the polished table. 'We all thought she was trying it on with the male members of staff.'

'The teaching staff?' Davie asked.

Janice nodded. 'Yes. Our dear janitor wouldn't have given her the time of day. Don't get me wrong. Jack McCormick's a lovely man. Everyone's his friend, you know? I just don't see Jack being ... well, that way, with Celia.' She wrinkled her nose in distaste. 'And young Jamie was terrified of her.'

'Then who ... ?'

'We have three men on the staff. Our head teacher who is a bit too long in the tooth for all that malarkey, I'd have thought,

237

the PE teacher and a nice guy from the US who's with us on a two-year secondment. She was always cadging lifts from one or other of them, even poor Mr Dewar.'

'Did they all live in the west end, then?'

Janice nodded. 'Well, Travis, that's my American colleague, has a rented house in Broomhill. Gary Johnstone, the PE chap, lives over in Scotstoun. Gary might be able to tell you more about Celia,' she added. 'I often thought she was a tad *too* friendly with him. A bit flirty, you know?' She shook her head. 'Though I have to say that I never saw or heard of any of our male staff behaving inappropriately towards Celia. She was high-spirited, loved fancy clothes. How she lasted as long as she did at Bankbrae was more of a mystery than why she suddenly left.'

Davie glanced down at the papers in his hand. 'I thought your head teacher lived in Beith, that's surely not on Celia Gemmell's way home?'

'You're right,' Janice nodded. 'It's his family home in Beith. Belonged to his parents, I think. He's got a flat in Pollokshields where he stays during the week, used to drop Celia at the subway station, I think.'

'And he's still off on holiday, I believe?' Molly asked.

The woman nodded her agreement. 'Goes away hill climbing every chance he gets. He's not married, no kids other than the ones he has responsibility for at school.' She made a face. 'Sometimes I envy him that freedom,' she laughed.

'The other members of staff are also still away,' Davie stated.

238

'Are they? I couldn't say. There are a few of us who chat about what we're doing over the holidays but I have no idea where either Travis or Gary were planning to escape to. Travis Quinn is here with his wife and kids but they're off back home to Montana in the summer. You should be able to speak to our janitor, though. He might know a bit more.'

The deputy head had been thanked and walked out to the car park by Davie, leaving Molly to clear away the cups and saucers. She sat on a while, however, thinking hard. If Celia Gemmell had been a bit of a flirt, coming on to these three men, surely she would have been given warnings about her behaviour? Was that why she had been looking up the legal stuff about suspensions? Or had one of them succumbed to her charms then been blackmailed? That might make sense of the regular cash transaction going into her bank account. An account that had not been touched for a year, Molly thought darkly. 'Where are you, Celia?' she whispered aloud. 'And what on earth were you up to back then?'

CHAPTER TWENTY-FOUR

She was used to being looked at now, strangers sitting in rows, listening as she read from her story, then talking to the audiences about what it was like to be a debut author. But there was something about this man that made Maggie uneasy. It was hard to say what age he might be, late twenties, maybe older? He slouched in his seat at the front in a navy blue anorak that appeared far too large for his thin frame, an unsmiling face under a thatch of dirty-blond hair. And he stared. All the time that she was speaking he simply stared at her, eyes steady. It was not a predatory look, though, she persuaded herself, no sort of attempt to flirt or even make eye contact.

She glanced his way, trying to see if he would smile but the head went down and he began to shuffle his feet. A shy man? Or someone who could not bear to make any sort of contact? Maggie had come across boys like that in the past: awkward lads who were in mainstream schooling despite their inability to take part in so many activities. She'd had her share of mentoring bipolar pupils and those on different points of the spectrum whose mental abilities often outstripped their social skills.

There was no small child nearby, he had come on his own, she realised, and that in itself struck her as odd. She tried not to let his presence bother her as the question-and-answer session began, but those eyes boring into her were hard to ignore.

Could this be the person who'd sent her those messages? Called her on her mobile in that leering voice? Maggie shivered then clenched her teeth, annoyed at herself. She mustn't let her imagination make her start to suspect every strange person that came her way. Besides, she had her guardian angel to take care of her, didn't she?

There was Christopher, sitting towards the back of the room, a folded newspaper on his knee. Poor man was probably bored stiff listening to her spiel over and over again. But this chap, seated as close to the platform as he could, looked as though he was hanging on her every word.

As the question-and-answer session continued the man in the navy anorak would turn and stare open-mouthed at whoever was asking a question, never posing one himself.

The crowd had mostly gone now, a few browsing amongst the library shelves, the bookseller gathering up the last few signed copies. After this talk in Falkirk library they were heading to the capital where Maggie had three talks lined up and several local bookshops where copies were waiting for her to sign. Perhaps her agent, Lucy, might be there too. Dear Lucy, who had done so much to bring her little story to the attention of various publishers.

'I like Gibby.' A voice right behind her made Maggie whirl around. It was blue anorak and he was holding his head to one side and looking at her with an expression that made Maggie wonder if the fellow did indeed have some mental problem. His eyes were solemn yet vacant, drifting off to one side as though he were afraid to make eye contact.

'I think it would be nice to be a ghost,' he added, in a soft tone that seemed to confirm Maggie's initial impression. This was a harmless chap, a bit slow perhaps, someone that had found reading children's stories an absorbing pastime. She smiled at him and put a hand on his arm but he immediately shrugged it off as though she had stung him. Aye, she'd been right in her thinking, Maggie told herself, recognising signs she had seen in some pupils over her years as a teacher. Poor man. Couldn't take a personal touch yet he'd had the courage to come up and speak to her.

'I'm glad you like Gibby,' she said at last. 'Thank you for telling me that. A writer doesn't always know when her characters are a success. That's down to you, the reader.'

He stared again then turned and walked away, clearly the conversation was over as far as he was concerned. Maggie shook her head and sighed out loud as he left. Poor chap. Yet it was a comforting feeling to know that she'd reached out to him with her story. She bent to gather up her handbag then as she stood up, Maggie saw that Christopher was standing there, his footfall so silent that she gave an involuntary start.

'This chap bothering you, Margaret? I'll deal with him if he is,' Christopher promised.

'No, no, not at all, really,' she protested, slightly flustered that the security man should be so strident. 'He was just ... ' She glanced along the corridor but the man was gone and she found herself reluctant to explain his disposition to the security officer. 'Just an admirer ... of the book,' she added hastily, seeing Christopher's face darken.

'Right, we're off now.' Ivy swept along and, grasping Maggie by the elbow, she marched towards the exit, Maggie hastening to match her stride. Ivy seemed not to have noticed the security man standing there: did she assume he was just another member of the audience? Maggie saw that Christopher had slipped away quietly, probably practised in making himself unobtrusive, though she had no experience of what these sorts of people actually did. Was he a former police officer? Somehow she did not think so, his manner and appearance so unlike any of the men and women she had met through her husband's work.

When they left the building Maggie glanced behind to see Christopher take a different route and for a moment she felt a sense of release. Perhaps he was tired of this sort of work, babysitting a detective superintendent's wife when there was absolutely nothing to worry about.

Edinburgh, at last. Maggie breathed a sigh of contentment as they entered the city, rush-hour traffic slowing Ivy's car down. It was home to so much history: Mary Queen of Scots,

Deacon Brodie, Burke and Hare ... and Edinburgh was a UNESCO City of Literature, Maggie reminded herself with a warm glow of satisfaction as she thought that she too was now part of that world. A published author, one of the thousands of people whose books were on library shelves. Later in the year she would be returning for the Edinburgh International Book Festival, an event that Maggie loved to come to each year when she could. But this time would be different, she reminded herself: this August Margaret Lorimer would be there as a guest of the festival.

'Almost there,' Ivy said as she drove past the Commonwealth Pool and a long row of fine red sandstone tenement buildings. 'Not the poshest hotel,' she added, wrinkling her nose. 'Edinburgh prices. But it is very nice, I think you'll like it. There's a place to park and the rooms are lovely.'

They slowed down at a set of traffic lights, Maggie wondering where a hotel might be found in this part of the city. Then as the lights changed to green, Ivy turned the car left and soon Maggie saw a more residential street with a detached house on one corner.

'Prestonfield House Hotel is just along the road,' Ivy told her. 'Make it big and you never know, we might get you an overnight there some day,' she chuckled. Maggie smiled back. Prestonfield House was very grand. Maggie had been there once, at a charity function, the old hotel a majestic place, kilted footmen on every corner and peacocks strutting in the grounds. But this hotel looked the sort of place she would feel comfortable, she told herself as they stepped out of the car.

The gardens were neat with tubs of tulips on either side of the doorway, the porch a welcome shelter from a stiff breeze that reminded Maggie how chilly it could be, so close to the North Sea.

A ring on the doorbell met with an instant response.

'Hello, welcome to Ard-Na-Said.' A young man stepped forwards, taking up Maggie's bag and smiling a welcome to them both. 'Miss Thornton, how nice to see you again,' he added, giving Ivy a broad grin.

'This is Mrs Lorimer, our newest author,' Ivy told him.

'Breakfast just in here,' the proprietor announced, indicating the dining room. 'We've put Mrs Lorimer into the Wallace,' he added. 'Just follow me upstairs.' He stepped towards a wide carpeted staircase. Maggie followed, admiring the old house with its historic prints lining the walls.

'Here we are.' The proprietor opened a door wide and ushered his new guest into a well-furnished room complete with four-poster bed.

'Hope you enjoy your stay with us,' the young man said. 'Just let me know if there is anything you need.'

Then he was gone, the door closed behind him and Maggie sank gratefully into a chair by the bed. A story was forming in her head, something to do with a little ghost boy who slept in a four-poster bed ...

It was dark when she woke and for a moment Maggie could not remember just where she was. The dark curtains by the bedposts made her sit up suddenly. What were these ...?

Ah, she sank down again with a sigh, thoughts flooding back. There had been so many different beds over these past few days and Maggie had a sudden longing to be back in her own home, snuggling in to her husband, feeling his warmth next to her cold skin. It was nice of Ivy to have chosen this hotel for her but nothing made up for the yearning feeling of loss that she had at this moment. *I'm homesick*, she thought, breathing in another sigh. There had been a few occasions when she and Bill had been apart, the long sabbatical she had taken over in the US, a couple of school trips and several occasions when her husband had spent time away from home. But somehow this was different. Only an hour's drive away, Bill would be sleeping in their bed, Chancer no doubt curled in by his side. The image gave her a pang. *I want to go home*, Maggie realised, with a sigh. But the tour was not over yet and today would see her in the city as Ivy whisked her from place to place. Just a few days more and Ivy would be heading back to London and she would be back in Glasgow, the Easter holiday over, school beckoning, the seniors' exams taking precedence over her life as a children's author.

Across the Central Belt that separated east from west Lorimer lay awake, gazing at the darkness creeping through the gap in the bedroom curtains. Soon the dawn would herald a new day and he would head into the city. There had been a little progress made on the case now, the missing woman presumed dead, her likeness to the other victims so uncanny that just thinking about it made his jaw clench.

He reached out a hand but felt only the chill from Maggie's side of the bed. Where was she now? He had lost track of her movements but thought it might be somewhere in Edinburgh. Before he left for work she would call him and they would catch up with each other briefly before their respective days began. He hoped she was enjoying herself, meeting lots of children who liked her book. At least Ivy Thornton was there to keep her company, though he still had reservations about the publicist. Had she been behind any of the scares to his wife? Who else had access to Maggie's mobile number? And wasn't it rather odd that these calls had been made just after they had gone on that tour? He heaved a sigh. That was daft. Just because he hadn't taken to the woman didn't mean she had a reason to frighten his wife. Yet it had meant a fresh burst of publicity for Maggie and that fact alone made him suspicious.

The bigger concern was whether Maggie really did have a stalker, however. Her resemblance to the dead women haunted him every time he looked at one of their images. And now, in the wee small hours, that *what if* made him toss and turn with anxiety. To include his own wife in the investigation was out of the question. But what he did with the scraps of his own time was quite another matter. There was someone out there with a predilection for a certain type of woman, a woman who looked just like Maggie. Was she in any danger? He sighed again. It was silly to start being worried when he knew she was safely tucked up in some hotel with Ivy watching over her. *My guardian angel*, Maggie had said. Well, he should just trust the woman from

London and let them get on with their tour. Only a few more days and she would be home. The thought made him feel warm as Lorimer curled on to his side and closed his eyes once more.

The young man in the navy anorak was there again, right at the front of the audience. *Strange*, Maggie thought with a start, though Falkirk wasn't that far from Edinburgh. Still, his presence had begun to trouble her when she had spotted him for the third time today.

Who was he? Why was he following her from venue to venue? And, more to the point, could he possibly be some sort of stalker?

Earlier Maggie had asked one of the booksellers if she knew the man, but a shake of the head and a shrug was all that she had been given. 'We get all sorts,' one of them had said. 'But Emily might know. She knows everyone,' the girl laughed. Maggie nodded. Emily, the events manager with her mane of long red hair, was a definite asset to the bookselling business. Maggie had watched her laughing, cracking jokes with every customer she saw. Perhaps she could answer the question once she had a moment. Or, maybe after this talk, she would see if her follower wanted a book signed. So far he had simply been there, talking to her just once, after the event in Falkirk library.

'Thank you all for coming, you've been a marvellous audience,' Maggie said, giving a small bow as the applause continued. Then, leaving the stage, she glanced down to see if the young man was still there but he had gone.

'Ivy, can you keep them waiting a wee minute? There's a fellow I want to talk to,' Maggie said as they headed towards the foyer where a signing table had been set up. She had caught sight of him, his navy anorak zipped up to the neck, a copy of her book tucked under one arm, and now she walked briskly towards him, waving a hand.

'Hello again, thanks for coming,' she said breathlessly, catching up with the young man. 'I see you have my book, would you like me to sign it?' She stretched out a hand.

He looked at her for a moment and all she saw was confusion in those eyes. Clutching the book to his chest, he shook his head and began to shamble away quickly as though afraid she might follow him.

'Is he bothering you, Margaret?' A voice behind made Maggie whirl around. It was Christopher, appearing from wherever he had been hiding, his usual discreet presence somewhere in the shadows.

'No, no ...' she began. 'It's just ... I think he's a bit ...' She stopped, unsure how to describe the young man. 'He's just ... I suppose he just likes to come to these sorts of events,' she said. 'Nothing to worry about.'

'You're sure?' Christopher asked. 'You've turned quite pale, my dear,' he added, catching hold of her arm for the briefest of moments.

Maggie nodded. 'Just tired. It's been a long day. Look, I must get back, Ivy will be waiting for me to sign all those people's books,' she told him.

She did not look back as the security man followed her

with his gaze then turned and looked towards the door of the theatre, a figure in a dark blue anorak slipping out into the street.

CHAPTER TWENTY-FIVE

The newspapers had written about a stalker, someone that might have designs upon the policeman's wife, so now he was certain what he had to do.

The initial sense of outrage had been replaced by a calm as he followed the figure along the wet Edinburgh streets. The day had begun with a small breeze from the east and a few rays of sunshine had managed to pierce the clouds but now the sky was dark and sleet was falling, the wind whipping it into his eyes.

The figure had continued to walk along the street, head down, hood obscuring his features, never pausing to stop at any of the bus shelters that lined this busy road. He marched on, determined to keep his quarry within sight even though the cold was biting into his face, the wet seeping into his shoes. Any moment now the man might turn into one of the tenement buildings and he would lose him.

The crowds began to thin out as he walked further away

from the city centre, fewer pubs and cinemas in this part of town. And still the man walked along the road, and still he followed, uphill and down again, the sleet now turning to snow, melting as soon as it touched the shiny pavements.

Edwin was cold but he liked to stop from time to time, watching the snowflakes dancing in front of his eyes as he headed for home. The apartments were a long walk from the bookshop but Edwin didn't mind walking, the evening still fresh in his thoughts. That nice lady writer had taken time to talk to him but he had been too shy to hand over his book. Maybe next time.

'Gibby will like this,' he whispered, glancing up at the dark sky, a soft smile appearing on his face. The flakes continued to whirl down like feathers blown from a thousand pillows. The ghost boy in the story might be up there playing with the blizzard, not feeling frozen like Edwin was. 'Are you there, Gibby?' he asked, then began to walk a little faster, head down to avoid the wet snow from hitting his eyes. Once across The Meadows he would be nearly home and into the warmth of his room. His hands fumbled in the anorak pocket for a moment, feeling the shape of his door key. Good. It was there. And soon he would be fitting it into the big black door then climbing the stairs to the apartment he shared with his friends from the Centre.

Edwin never turned around to look behind him, unaware of the pursuer who was watching his every step.

*

At last he saw the man walking across a road towards a dark place where trees and grass made a vacant space between streets. *The Meadows*, he thought vaguely. Wasn't that what they called this open parkland?

Spurring himself on, he walked more swiftly, determined to overtake the man in the navy anorak before he could cross to the other side.

The streets were deserted, no one about in this foul weather. No one to see him tackle Margaret's stalker. Gritting his teeth, he moved faster, anger spurring him on.

She would not be bothered by this creature again. Not if he could help it.

'Hey!' he called out and he saw the man stop then turn around.

Through the blizzard all he could make out was a pale face under the hood. He waved his arms and shouted again. 'Hey! You!'

But the figure, perhaps sensing his intention, broke into a shambling run towards the shadows of some trees.

He quickened his own pace, eyes fixed on his quarry.

Suddenly the man he was chasing tripped on the slippery grass, falling headlong with a cry.

In a moment he was upon him, fists pumping the other man's face, sickening blows that made the stricken man kick out and begin to whimper.

'No, be quiet!' he hissed, but the man's cries only became louder as he thumped him again and again.

'Shut up,' he said between clenched teeth, hands reaching below the hood, searching for his throat. 'Shut. Up.'

In seconds it was all over, the struggle ended, the man limp in his gloved hands.

He looked around to see if there was anyone there but the streets were silent and the pavements bare. *Who would want to be out on a night like this?* he thought, snow stinging his eyes as it whirled in the gathering wind.

The body was already beginning to be covered with white, dark jacket disappearing.

The shadow of this tree would hide it until daylight showed, but for now he had little option but to retreat, hide his own presence there. He glanced up at the sky as he hurried across The Meadows, seeing the huge flakes continue to tumble earthwards. Time to move on. Nature was his ally now and no trace of him would be found here by morning.

CHAPTER TWENTY-SIX

'See there's been a murder in Edinburgh.' Niall Cameron nodded to Lorimer as they sat sipping coffee in the detective superintendent's office, a quiet twenty minutes before the morning's briefing.

'Oh, aye?'

'Young guy was found lying in the snow,' Cameron remarked. 'Lived in one of those sheltered accommodation places.'

'A disabled man?' Lorimer looked up.

'Not physically,' Cameron replied with a shake of his head. 'Radio report described him as mentally challenged but able to live in a supported community. Poor fellow.'

'What happened?'

'Usual sort of report. Investigation continuing. Nearest relatives informed. No name given out yet.'

Lorimer looked out of the window. The sky was a pale blue and though there had been a frost whitening the grass when he had left home there was no sign of the snow that had fallen across the country. The east–west divide marked more than just a difference in attitude and culture, the weather could also be more severe in Scotland's capital city.

Maggie was there now, he thought, recalling her voice from the previous evening's phone call. She had sounded happy. The tour was going well and Ivy had assured her that the size of her audiences were much larger than any she had seen before for a debut author. He made a face. The papers had had a field day over the previous weekend, Maggie's photograph not only splashed across the pages of the supplements dealing with books but along with some of the main news items. That publicity woman had made sure that the public was going to see just how much his wife resembled those two dead women. Thank God they knew nothing about the MIT's search for Celia Gemmell. Today he was hoping to have some communication from Professor Dawson. She had narrowed down the possible sites where the soil on these boots had originated. Now it was a matter of pinpointing the place where Celia had once walked.

Where are you? Lorimer asked himself, the latest news about the Edinburgh murder already fading from his mind.

Emily, the bookseller with the long red hair, seemed different today, observed Maggie, noticing the woman's downcast expression, so markedly changed from the ebullient personality of the previous evening. *Boyfriend trouble?* she wondered, ready to be sympathetic whatever the situation.

It was Ivy who whispered the explanation as they watched the books being set out on a table at the back of the hall.

'Seems like a lad she knew was killed last night,' Ivy told her behind a discreet hand. 'I heard it on the news this morning in my room. Happened in the middle of this very city, can you imagine that?' She gave an exaggerated shudder.

'Poor Emily! Was it someone close?' Maggie asked, glancing towards the bookseller.

'One of her regular customers,' Ivy shrugged. 'Think he was at one of your talks,' she added. 'They say he was mentally challenged, poor bloke.'

Maggie froze. *Could it be . . . ?*

In a few swift strides she was along the aisle and standing next to Emily.

'Your friend . . . ? I heard about the tragic death . . . ?' Maggie faltered. What could she say?

A huge sigh that might have stifled a sob issued from the woman and Maggie laid a sympathetic hand on her shoulder.

'Edwin was in the shop last night,' Emily said. 'You might have noticed him. Always sat right at the front. Probably stared and stared . . . ' She sniffed then rummaged in her skirt pocket for a handkerchief. 'He loved your book,' she added then blew noisily into the hanky. 'Whoever did this deserves to be locked up for ever. I mean . . . he was a harmless soul . . . ' She sniffed again. 'Result of a brain tumour when he was a kid . . . lost both his parents . . . Oh, Lord, how can such awful things happen to one decent human being?'

'Did he . . . ? Was he wearing a navy anorak?'

Emily nodded. 'Never wore anything else, bless him. Like a uniform, it was. Sorry, I shouldn't be bothering you with all of this. Now, let's see if we can open the doors and let in your latest audience. Tickets to the primary schools have gone really well for this event,' she added, rubbing her eyes and attempting a tremulous smile.

Maggie nodded then turned to walk back towards the podium, her heart thudding. So, now she knew his name, but she would never sign the young man's book or know what had happened last night after he disappeared from the bookshop. As a policeman's wife, Maggie was aware that there would be a call for any information following a sudden death like this. Did Emily realise that? She retraced her steps, stopping to place a hand on the bookseller's arm.

'Emily, have you spoken to the police?'

'Why?'

'You need to let them know where that young man was last night before he was killed,' Maggie insisted. 'They need to know all of his movements in the hours leading up to whatever happened,' she explained.

But there would be no need for either of them to do that, Maggie realised, as two figures strolled into the shop followed closely by a female officer in uniform.

'It's me.' Maggie sat in a corner of the bookshop staffroom, phone to her ear.

'Maggie!' She heard his voice and felt an enormous sense of relief. 'Is something wrong?'

'Yes, something's very wrong,' she blurted out. 'A young chap who spoke to me at last night's event was killed not long afterwards. They found his body lying in the snow. Over in The Meadows.'

'I heard about that,' Lorimer told her. 'Grim business. And he spoke to you?'

'Yes. The police have been in here this morning. The event was cancelled.' She sighed. 'Emily wanted to carry on but the police had us all in here . . . I mean the staffroom, that's where I am right now. Oh, Bill! And Christopher hasn't turned up either. Do you know where he is?'

'Who?'

'Christopher,' Maggie repeated, feeling a little confused now, her head still spinning from the questions the detectives had asked her earlier. *Had she felt that Edwin Ramsay was worried about anything? Had he seemed agitated at all?* 'You know,' she insisted. 'Christopher. My guardian angel. Security guy you sent to look after me.'

There was a pause then she heard her husband clear his throat before he spoke again. 'Maggie, I have no idea what you're talking about. I sent nobody to look after you. Who is this man?'

'I told you,' she insisted. 'Christopher. I said I had *him* to take care of me. If you didn't arrange this then who—' She stopped suddenly, trying to remember just what she had said to Bill after meeting the older man whose presence she had found so reassuring these past few days.

'You spoke about a guardian angel, right enough,'

259

he said gruffly. 'I thought you were talking about the Thornton woman.'

Maggie felt herself go weak at the knees and a faint buzzing sounded in her ears as the shock of his words hit home.

'Maggie? Are you still there?'

'Yes,' she replied weakly. 'Oh, Bill, I think I've made a terrible mistake.'

The detective inspector who had spoken to them was looking at her intently. Maggie could see his jaw working and she realised he would probably have torn her to shreds had she not been the wife of Detective Superintendent William Lorimer. DI Morrison was sitting across from her in an interview room, the kind of place that must be familiar to Bill. It was warm and stuffy, the single window barred and covered in metallic mesh, the sort of thing she remembered from Florida to keep out biting insects. But here, in this room with its grey painted walls and scratched furniture, the aim was to keep people in. There was a pungent smell of disinfectant, something that might have been applied to clean up some mess or other, or perhaps the staff mucked these rooms out on a daily basis, the human vermin that came and went spitting on the floor, or worse.

'I'm so sorry,' she said again, her stomach churning with guilt for having been so foolish. A security person with the name of Christopher Stevenson did not seem to exist, Morrison had informed her coldly, the business card something that could have been made up in any of the Quick Print shops that were found in shopping malls across the country.

Who was he? And why had he taken it upon himself to look after her? Maggie's head was aching after the barrage of questions from DI Morrison, a man who looked about her own age but whose eyes had seen more awful things than she ever would, including the dead body of young Edwin Ramsay.

'Tell me again what this Stevenson bloke ... we'll call him that for now,' he added grimly. 'What did he say after you had spoken to Mr Ramsay?'

Maggie bit her lip, trying hard to recall the man's words, her shock at discovering his alias making her head pound. 'He said,' she began, 'I mean he *asked* me if Mr Ramsay was bothering me,' she told him bleakly. 'I thought he was just being sort of over-protective, doing his job ... oh dear ... ' She put her hands across her mouth to stifle a sob.

'It's okay.' DI Morrison sighed. 'Take your time, Mrs Lorimer.'

'He seemed angry,' Maggie recalled. 'As if anyone paying me too much attention was some sort of threat to me. At least, that's what I thought at the time. How I interpreted his reaction,' she explained.

'And what did he do then?'

'Well, Mr Ramsay had gone. I'd hoped to sign his book but he had left. I think Christopher – the man calling himself that – went out shortly afterwards.'

DI Morrison nodded and Maggie looked up at him across the table in this interview room.

'Did you catch any sight of him on CCTV?'

Was that a faint glimmer of a smile behind that stony face?

Morrison shook his head. 'You know better than that, Mrs Lorimer,' he chided her. 'We don't give out information. We ask the questions. However,' he heaved a sigh, 'I think your husband might want to talk to me later, so no doubt you will be filled in on some of our casework. You know not to talk about anything that has passed between us, don't you?'

Maggie nodded, feeling utterly miserable. As a senior policeman's wife she had learned all about procedure over the years but nothing had prepared her for the ordeal of being questioned in a murder case.

'I'm so sorry,' she said again, squirming as her own apology sounded hollow.

'Not your fault. Better folk than you have been conned before,' Morrison told her, his tone a shade gentler now. 'But we need to find this chap. And soon. So,' he stared at her intently, 'if he comes back you must let us know right away. And do not under any circumstances be on your own with him, is that understood?'

Ivy's face was a picture when they at last met up in the hotel, her expression almost one of delight.

'Well?' she began. 'What can you tell me? Is there anything we can use to help the publicity side of things?' she asked eagerly, drawing Maggie on to a chair beside a roaring fire in the same room where they had breakfasted that morning.

'I can't say anything,' Maggie told her stiffly. 'And to be honest, Ivy, if we were to cancel the rest of this tour I wouldn't be sorry.'

'You don't mean that?' Ivy drew back, her mouth open

in astonishment. 'The show must go on, Maggie. Kids are expecting Margaret Lorimer to talk to them about this book, sign their precious copies,' she wheedled. 'Look,' she laid a hand on Maggie's knee, 'I know how horrible this is, but these sorts of things happen in any big city. Just because the guy was at your event has nothing to do with what happened to him afterwards,' she protested.

Maggie remained silent. She had sworn not to say a word to anyone about Christopher Stevenson, or whoever the middle-aged man really was, and she was determined to keep to that.

'All right,' she sighed. 'Where to next?'

'That's my girl!' Ivy beamed at her. 'Just let me settle up here and we'll be on our way. Quite a few Waterstones book-shops for signings then we head down to the Borders country and across to Dumfries.' Ivy gave a sigh of pleasure. 'Oh, wait till you see where I've booked you in tonight.' She grinned.

Maggie failed to return the woman's smile. It had been a long morning, she was tired and anxious and above all she was desperate to see her husband again. But, being a teacher had taught her how to put a brave face on anything from masking a physical pain to brushing aside something more emotional. *The show must go on,* Ivy's words echoed in her brain as the publicity woman left her by the fireside. And she must hide her fears, suspicions and questions. Above all: who was this man who had elected himself as her protector?

'Christopher G. Stevenson,' Lorimer murmured to Solly who was sitting next to him in his Helen Street office.

'Interesting alias,' Solly agreed, looking at the piece of paper Lorimer had handed him with the words scribbled underneath. 'Does he have a sense of humour, do you think, or has he some sort of religious connection?'

'Christopher G. Stevenson' had been replaced by 'St Christopher Evensong', the simple anagram revealing something of the mystery man's mind.

'He saw himself as a friend to Maggie,' Solly tried to reassure Lorimer. 'He was her guardian angel, that's how she described him, yes?'

Lorimer nodded. 'And St Christopher is the patron saint of travellers.'

'Of course, and he may have wished to make that subliminal suggestion to her,' Solly said, half to himself.

'It's too close to these other murders for my liking, Solly,' Lorimer said, clenching then unclenching his fist. *Dave Harkness. Have Darkness.* It's as if this comes from the same sick mind,' he added. 'But it must be a coincidence, surely? Edinburgh, after all, nothing to do with the two victims here in Glasgow,' he muttered, though the expression on his face was at odds with his words.

'Let's get back to this man,' Solly suggested. 'Maggie describes a middle-aged fellow, grey-ish hair, small moustache ... could be a fake one, of course ... but she said he looked nothing like her idea of a security officer.'

'That's right. Her first impression is important but she can be let off for assuming he was good at making himself blend into a crowd. Where did he go after he left that shop? CCTVs in Edinburgh only show him taking the same route as the murdered man. And we have no clear image of his face, just a back view. There's absolutely nothing to show that he followed Ramsay to The Meadows. Besides, the footage isn't that good. Blizzard conditions made for blurry images.'

'Anything fresh from the SIO yet? What about the post mortem?'

'Nothing yet. PM in Edinburgh isn't scheduled till later this afternoon.' Lorimer bit his lip. He'd been told that the victim had no living relatives and it had been down to the warden at the Centre to identify the body as Edwin Ramsay. He pushed aside the half-empty coffee cup on his desk.

'DI Morrison promised to keep me in the loop, though I suspect that was merely out of a sense of professional courtesy rather than a need for a senior officer through in Glasgow knowing his every movement.'

'And Maggie? Is she coming home?'

Lorimer shook his head and sighed. 'Ach, maybe she's better being on the road with the Thornton woman. We know where she'll be on each stop of the tour and if this guy should turn up, Maggie knows to notify the police immediately.'

'The publicity lady knows nothing of this, then?' Solly asked, his expression curious.

'No. Why do you ask?' Lorimer frowned. 'Maggie isn't stupid. Morrison has warned her about keeping quiet to anyone expect me.'

Solly stroked his dark beard and merely gave his friend a

nod. Maggie was strong enough to carry on the tour, even if her PR had no knowledge of the unhappy things going on in her author's mind.

CHAPTER TWENTY-SEVEN

The area on the map she was regarding was further away from Scotland's largest city than she had expected. However, Lorna Dawson knew that a burial site, if that was what it proved to be, was bound to be found somewhere off the beaten track. The soil sample from the missing woman's boot had led her to this place, some miles from the border between Ayrshire and West Renfrewshire; now it remained to be seen if there was any disturbance in or around the ground that might show where a body had been laid twelve months previously. That was for the geophysicists to locate, their expertise in finding burial sites often linked with her own in police investigations. Four seasons of wind, snow and rain could have changed the upper layers somewhat but the deeper strata would have remained fairly constant apart from the hazard of animals like foxes and dogs digging on the site. It would not be the first time in a cold case that the professor had assisted in locating a body only for the police to discover a missing limb or even a skull.

Lorimer would be pleased at any rate, she knew, thinking of the detective who had asked for her help. Whether there was anything to be found there remained to be seen.

'It's a few miles from Gateside,' Lorimer told the assembled team of officers. 'Perhaps some of you are familiar with Hessilhead Wildlife Centre?'

A couple of nods and murmurs told him that some officers knew the area at least.

'I am going to meet Professor Dawson in an hour and then we will see . . . ' He tailed off. 'See if there is any evidence of a burial site.' His determination to locate the missing woman (who now seemed almost certain to be dead) had carried his team along with him, Lorimer realised. It was much more than a hunch, however; the unusual aspect of Celia Gemmell wearing wellington boots let alone traversing a piece of land miles from the city had given all of the team pause for thought.

'Someone took her there,' Lorimer said. 'Celia didn't drive and we do know she had these brand-new boots, something her mother tells us she wouldn't be seen dead in.' A small groan of laughter met his ears and he suddenly realised what an inane comment he had made.

He swept a hand across his brow. 'Sorry, wrong choice of words.' Yet it had helped diffuse a certain tension in the room and, as he continued to allocate actions to members of his team he noticed a renewed energy amongst them. Each and every one was expecting a result from the visit to this out-of-the-way location that Professor Dawson had found. What if he was wrong? What if there was nothing to find and he had squandered precious resources?

Lorna Dawson approached the scene with her soil phone app open, showing the ground beneath her feet. This time there was the unusual signature of a species of *Crocosmia Lucifer*, which indicated either a garden environment or an abandoned garden where the resilient plant still flourished. At this time of year there should be fresh green spikes emerging from the cold winter soil, the corms and seeds beneath the topmost layer.

She stepped carefully along the access path, Lorimer at her shoulder, following the HOLMES database information. Lorna was aware of his presence as she walked fifty metres either side of the roadway, her soil map showing her where to go. At last it took her to a spot hidden from the road where Scots pine and birch trees were in abundance.

She was feeling that familiar tension in her stomach, excitement rising as she realised this fitted what she had seen in the pollen profile.

Then, as she cast her eyes downwards, she spotted the clumps of *Crocosmia*. She grasped the screw auger used to take a soil core. Verification would still be needed but something told her that they were at the exact place where these wellingtons had been a year before.

She glanced up at the detective superintendent at her elbow.

'What is it?' he asked, his voice breathless as though infected by her excitement.

'It's here,' Lorna said simply. 'This fits the profile I

discovered on the wellington boots!' She nodded at him in a moment of triumph. She was confident this particular profile couldn't be found anywhere else.

It did not take the team of officers too long to locate what Lorimer expected. Grasses swishing against their thick boots, the men and women had trawled the area indicated by Professor Dawson, eyes cast downwards, intent on discovering a piece of ground slightly raised from its surrounding turf, grass a shade brighter than the rest.

'Over here!' The call echoed through the woodland and at once all feet hurried towards the voice.

The police officer had already parted the grasses with her gloved hands and was looking up enquiringly as Lorimer and Lorna Dawson approached.

The officers spaced themselves around the patch of ground, an oval shape raised a little higher but easy enough to miss under the leaf litter and winter grasses.

Lorimer glanced back towards the road, noting that the place was entirely obscured by trees and bushes: the perfect spot to bury a body. The wind scattered dry leaves in a swirl from the grave and he heard a nearby birch tree groan as its branches were swept sideways. Had these trees been able to talk, what story would they have told? He could picture the scene: a spade cutting into the turf, a figure bent over digging deeper and deeper under cover of night, perhaps? Lorimer imagined the thud as the body tumbled into the dark hole. And was it Celia Gemmell's corpse that lay beneath the mound by his feet? That was something they would find out soon enough.

He straightened up and nodded at the officers who had brought the spades from their nearby van.

'Okay, let's begin,' he said.

It would take time to confirm, of course, but the decomposed body that had been wrapped in layers of black polythene bore all the traces of the woman that had once been Celia Gemmell. She was fully dressed, the pale pink winter coat and high-heeled boots more suitable for a night out in the city than a walk in the woods. Lorimer had seen the mud caked on those thin heels and in his mind's eyes he followed Celia as she had been marched through the woodland, protesting perhaps as her captor had forced her away from the last sign of civilisation, the road now hidden from sight.

But it was the scarf around her neck that told the final bit of the story. She had been strangled, the arms reaching upwards as though to struggle against the pressure. Her open mouth still looked as though it gasped for breath.

There was a pause as they all looked down at the remains, now lying on the black shroud. There was no sense of triumph and nobody spoke, reflecting perhaps on the enormity of this crime and the waste of yet another human life.

Somewhere in the shrubbery a blackbird cried its warning notes and the moment passed.

White-suited figures lifted the body to one side and Lorimer stepped back to where Lorna Dawson stood.

'Take any samples you need,' he said heavily. 'And thank you.' He sighed deeply, trying to summon up a smile but failing. 'We would never have found her if it hadn't been for your expertise.'

There were SOCOs already searching the entire area so Lorimer stepped back with Professor Dawson to let them have access to the grave. A pathologist had been summoned and soon there would be a tent erected to protect the site from the vagaries of wind and weather though he doubted it would be required to shield the body from any prying eyes, the place was so deserted.

A short walk away, however, showed that this had not always been the case.

'See, what did I tell you?' Professor Dawson smiled up at him, her hand pointing towards the remains of what must have been a dwelling at one time but was now just one crumbling gable end and a pile of rubble with trees and bushes screening it from the burial site.

Lorimer returned her grin, knowing how satisfying it must be to have come to the end of her part in their investigation. He looked back again, appraising the ruined house. The place looked ancient but it might still be worth having a look to see who the original owners had been and how long the place had been derelict. He stifled a sigh; it would be one more task for his team of officers who were already working all the hours they could. Or maybe he would delegate this to the local cops.

When had Celia been here, wearing those wellington boots? Had she been brought here by someone she knew, unsuspecting that previous time? Who was this stalker and what had made him take this woman's life? Lorimer tried to picture the scene. Had the murder taken place here? Or had the woman's body been dragged from a vehicle then buried in those woods? There were so many questions but he felt certain it was this place that held some significance.

'You'll find whoever has done this,' Lorna said suddenly, looking back over her shoulder at the white-clad figures busy round the grave. And Lorimer nodded, realising that the professor was not asking a question but stating her belief in him, a belief he earnestly hoped was going to be justified.

CHAPTER TWENTY-EIGHT

'Edwin Ramsay, aged twenty-seven. Spent the last eighteen months in sheltered accommodation,' DI Morrison said, reading from his report. 'Was a keen reader of young adult and children's fiction, the sorts of stuff that are sometimes given to so-called emergent readers. Poor bloke had been perfectly normal once upon a time,' Morrison remarked with a shake of his head. 'Brain damage put an end to the sort of life he'd enjoyed.' He exhaled heavily. 'God, the things we take for granted. Anyway, Doctor, what else can you add to this?'

The detective inspector was sitting opposite a small man in a tweed jacket who was listening intently to the information. Dr Clements, the pathologist, looked at him and nodded.

'Oh, I can add the time of death, the method of killing,' he assured Morrison. 'He'd been struck several times but the blows were not what killed him. That was manual strangulation by someone strong enough to overcome a healthy young man. Trouble is,' he continued, 'the weather conditions probably made it difficult for the victim to escape. We have been unable to find any traces in the snow which is a pity but he may have slipped and fallen, giving his pursuer the advantage. We'll never know.'

'What about DNA? Any results back yet?'

'We're still waiting for traces to be identified and of course if there is anyone on a database you could strike it lucky.' The pathologist chuckled.

DI Morrison stifled another sigh. A random killing in the middle of a freak snowstorm. Nothing to indicate from his officers' investigation that the Ramsay chap had any enemies or that there was a reason to kill him . . . except for that slithery imposter who had been tagging along with Margaret Lorimer on her book tour. She had indicated that the self-appointed security man had been a bit uptight after Ramsay had spoken to her. And CCTV footage showed that he had taken the same route from the bookshop as the victim. But why? The papers had been full of the story of a stalker and more than one journalist had made the point that the children's author bore a remarkable resemblance to the Glasgow victims. He'd spoken to Lorimer's DCI, a fellow called Niall Cameron, and been told that they were currently investigating the possibility of a third victim. But that was to be kept absolutely quiet for now, Cameron had insisted. Their priority was finding this Christopher Stevenson, the self-styled St Christopher, as Cameron had explained. If this was the killer, then he had previous experience of strangling his victims.

Morrison nodded across the table. 'I'll keep you posted,' he murmured. The pathologist would expect no less, Morrison knew. Clements had a keen eye for crime and was well known as an expert witness for the Crown who pulled no punches when it came to testifying.

'You'll be one of our star witnesses once this comes to court,' Lorimer told Lorna Dawson as they shook hands in the car park, a police car ready to take the professor back to Queen Street station for her train back to the James Hutton Institute.

'Presuming you catch your man.' She smiled at him.

'Oh, we will,' Lorimer assured her.

He watched as the eminent soil scientist gave a small wave from the passenger seat then the car swept along the road heading into the city centre. What now? Celia Gemmell's remains were in the capable hands of Daisy Abercromby and her team, the Aussie pathologist having stepped up to the mark during Rosie Fergusson's maternity leave. Should he inform the parents of Patricia and Carolyn that they had not been the killer's first and second victims? They would try to keep the press at bay for as long as possible and he knew deep down that each set of parents deserved to hear this latest development from his own mouth, not through the medium of any newspaper.

He was just entering the red-brick building once more when he caught sight of Molly Newton striding purposefully towards him.

'Sir.' He looked up at the sound of her voice, knowing at once that there had been a new development of some sort.

'Just had a call from a teacher at Bankbrae Primary School. He's back from his holidays and got our message.'

Lorimer shook hands with the man, glad to feel the strength of the PE teacher's grip. A no-nonsense type was his first impression of Gary Johnstone. Good-looking, too, the sort that wee school lassies might have a crush on. *Big ones, too,* he thought, seating himself in the chair next to Johnstone. Lasses like Celia Gemmell? Lorimer saw a man in his late thirties, medium build, blond hair cut short, clean shaven and dressed in a navy tracksuit with sparkling white trainers.

'Your message said you wanted me to come and discuss a former member of staff, Ms Gemmell,' Johnstone began without any preamble.

Lorimer nodded, pleased that the man had come straight to the point.

'Yes, we wanted your perspective on Celia Gemmell, what she was like professionally whilst she worked at your school, and as a person,' he said.

'Hmm, hard to say, really.' Johnstone sat back slightly as though pondering the idea. 'The kitchen staff were always complaining that she took too many days off on the sick. Then one day she simply failed to turn up for work. Must be over a year ago now,' he mused, gazing into space as though to calculate the exact time.

'Has she done something wrong?' he asked, looking back at Lorimer questioningly.

Was that concern in the PE teacher's expression? Had Celia

277

Gemmell been more than a distant colleague, someone who cadged the occasional lift home?

'Celia Gemmell is part of an ongoing investigation, Mr Johnstone, that is all I am at liberty to say,' Lorimer replied smoothly. 'Can you tell me, from your point of view, what sort of a lady she was while she worked at Bankbrae?'

Johnstone gave a small frown. 'That's something you'd have to ask Mr Dewar. I suppose she worked hard enough, when she was there. I never heard any complaints from the other women about that. But I don't think they liked her very much. Celia always liked to dress up. Me, I prefer the casual types.'

Lorimer remained impassive though Johnstone's throwaway comment was interesting. Had Celia made a play for this good-looking man?

'Anything else that you can remember about her?'

'Well, like I said, she was a very smart-looking woman, anyone will tell you that. Dressed far more fashionably than the older kitchen assistants, made them look a bit drab by comparison.' He chuckled. 'Some of them didn't like that but Celia wasn't one to tone down her appearance just to please her colleagues.'

'Go on,' Lorimer encouraged.

'She was the sort of person that needed to stand out in a crowd, I suppose,' Johnstone continued thoughtfully. 'Don't know much about her background. Not married, though. My P Seven boys all raved about her.

'Actually, I do remember one thing. She lent me an old dress for a production the school was doing. I was cast as the dame in their Christmas pantomime.' He gave a self-deprecating chuckle. 'I do a bit of am-dram, but not a lot of cross-dressing!' he added. 'Come to think about it, she never got that dress back. Think it's still amongst all the props stuff at Bankbrae.'

'I was informed that she sometimes accepted a lift after school,' Lorimer said, changing tack.

'Yes, I occasionally took her home if she was leaving at the same time as me,' Johnstone said, nodding. He chuckled again. 'Celia was not the shy type. She would cadge a lift off anyone.'

'Male and female staff both obliged her in that way?'

'I suppose so.' Johnstone raised his eyebrows. 'Never really noticed. Sometimes she was just standing by my car waiting as if she knew I was ready to leave. I had after-school activities including the panto rehearsals sometimes, so it wasn't like a regular thing.' Johnstone tilted his head to one side and looked straight at Lorimer. 'What has she done, Superintendent? Am I allowed to ask you that?'

Was this man simply anxious for a titbit of gossip to take back to his place of work? Or did he really care about what had happened to his colleague?

Lorimer shook his head with a weary smile. Dewar, the head teacher, would be informed when he returned from holiday that his former kitchen assistant had been dead for the best part of a year. But for now this man and the rest of the Bankbrae staff must remain innocent of such information. But there was someone Lorimer thought he ought to see. Maggie always maintained that having a good relationship with the janitor at Muirpark had helped on many occasions. Perhaps this McCormick fellow knew more about the goings-on at his school than any member of staff. It would be worth making time to talk to him at Bankbrae.

'I'm so sorry for your loss,' Molly began, as she sat beside Janet Gemmell. The older woman's face was a frozen mask, betraying no inner emotion, but Molly had seen shock often enough before to know that the grief would come later, the tears would flow when she had left the elderly lady's home.

'Is there anyone we can call for you?' she asked but that slight shake of the head spoke more than words. Janet Gemmell needed nobody, wanted nobody. She turned slowly to look at the detective and opened her mouth, but all that came out was a small sigh as if those months of waiting and wondering had finally ended, bringing something like relief.

'We'll catch whoever did this to your daughter,' Molly assured her. 'Anything you need to know, just give me a call, all right?' She passed her card to the woman, in case she had lost the original or even binned it. But the trembling hand that laid it down on the well-polished coffee table quickly sank into the folds of her skirt.

'I'll go, then,' Molly said gently, rising from her seat. 'Take care,' she added kindly. But there was no response and the bereaved mother sat immobile as Molly let herself out of the flat.

Maggie heaved a sigh as she wiped her hands on the paper towel. Bill's latest news earlier that day had cast further gloom across her spirits. The murder of that kitchen assistant and the discovery of her body ... Maggie shuddered. It was all too horrible to think about.

In a few days she would be home then the holidays would be over, school term resuming once more. Her thoughts turned to the seniors. Would they have taken time out to relax as she'd suggested? It was essential that their days of exam preparation included some recreation between bouts of hard work. *That's what I need, too*, she thought ruefully. A bit of time out. Tossing the crumpled towel into a pedal bin, Maggie pushed through the door of the toilets and walked through the garden centre where she and Ivy had stopped for a quick break.

The tour was beginning to feel relentless now; day after day she saw different faces looking out from an audience yet her talks had begun to take on a pattern and Maggie heard herself say the same things over and over again.

Whatever had possessed that young man to attend several of her talks? Surely once would have been enough? Maggie recalled his earnest expression, that solemn, unsmiling face, and shuddered. Edwin Ramsay hadn't been stalking her. He had simply found something special in her book and wanted to pluck up the courage to come and talk to its author. That was what the red-haired bookseller had told her. It wasn't Maggie Lorimer that had interested him but Gibby, her ghost boy. Biting back a sudden rush of tears, Maggie hastened out of the garden centre and crossed the car park, hugging her coat around her. Poor, poor fellow. Was he a spirit now, somewhere? A ghost hovering like her imaginary character in a place where time meant nothing and they were no longer bound to the earth? Now the story seemed a small, shallow thing compared to the reality of this man's death. What had once been an exciting adventure into the realm of fantasy fiction palled against this present tragedy.

Maggie looked around, trying to remember where Ivy's car was parked, and for a moment she felt a sense of disorientation, the exit from the garden centre further away from where she had last seen her companion. The place was crowded, not unexpected given that this was a school holiday, and she stopped for a moment to let an elderly man pass by, pushing his wife along in a wheelchair. There was a line of trees at the far end of the car park, that was where they had stopped, wasn't it? Maggie began to hurry across, dodging between the rows of parked cars. Then she stopped, spotting Ivy pacing up and down beneath the trees, cigarette in one hand, mobile phone pressed to her ear. She slowed down, realising that Ivy would have the car keys in her pocket and she would need to wait until after the woman's fag break to resume their journey. Ivy's back was turned, her coat collar pulled up against the chill, so she did not see Maggie walking silently towards her and pausing for a moment, reluctant to disturb her conversation in case it was important.

'She has no idea, I promise you,' Ivy said aloud, flicking ash from her cigarette. 'No. Not a clue. We're quite safe.'

Maggie stood still, holding her breath as she listened to the woman's side of a conversation. Who had no idea? Why was Ivy safe? What on earth . . . ?

The woman turned suddenly and Maggie read the shock in her face as she pulled the mobile from her ear.

'Where on earth have you been?' Ivy asked, shoving the phone deep into her pocket and retrieving the car keys. 'You've been ages!' she exclaimed.

'There was a queue,' Maggie faltered then began to follow Ivy across to where the car was parked, stunned by the woman's aggressive tone.

What on earth was all that about? Maggie asked herself as she pulled on the seat belt and listened to the car engine starting up. There was an uncomfortable silence as they set off, Maggie still stunned by Ivy's change of manner and the expression on her face as she had turned to see her client. Had she known that Maggie had heard her? And, more to the point, was she the subject of Ivy's conversation?

Closing her eyes, Maggie feigned sleep but her mind was very much alert, the years of being a policeman's wife making her look at the facts one by one and piece them all together.

Ivy had been the one constant presence during the episodes when Maggie had been disturbed by some nasty person. She'd had Maggie's number at every hotel stop, too. And the woman had been so insistent at exploiting the stalker situation, hadn't she? What if . . . ? Maggie's mind whirled with the possibilities. Had it been her publicity rep faking these calls all along? And was there someone else, the person to whom she had been talking back there? The man whose voice had seized Maggie with terror and disgust?

Suddenly everything made sense. Had Ivy Thornton been

playing her all this time? Ivy had chosen the nicest hotels, taken her for fancy meals, all the while lulling Maggie into a false sense of security as she plotted how to use her for her own personal gain.

Maggie felt her fists clench in sudden fury. Confronting Ivy with this was pointless, however, and would only lead to an unpleasantness in their relationship, if not worse. She would have to come up with evidence, Maggie thought with dismay, realising for the first time that she really cared about her future as a children's author and wondering if the steps she might take would end her burgeoning career.

Lorimer was glad to see a light on in the main building of Bankbrae Primary School, its blue double doors still wide open. He crossed the playground and stepped into the reception vestibule. The glass partition where the school secretary probably had her office was closed over and the doors leading to the rest of the building were firmly shut. All schools had these safety features nowadays, Lorimer thought sadly, remembering his own schooldays when no fearful figures stalked their corridors armed with guns. The Dunblane massacre, though, had changed things for ever. He pressed a buzzer, hoping that might alert any staff to his presence. Sure enough, a figure dressed in a navy boiler suit came around the corner and stood, hands on hips, regarding him with a frown.

'Hello, can I help you?' the man asked.

Lorimer saw an older man standing on the bottom step, looking up at him. His grizzled grey hair was slightly windblown and he put up a hand to smooth it across his head.

'Detective Superintendent Lorimer,' he said, bringing out his warrant card to show the man. 'I was looking for Jack McCormick.'

'Well, you've found him,' the man replied, a faint smile tugging at the corners of his mouth. 'Come on inside, it's a bit cold out here tonight and I need to check the heating in the classrooms before I go home.'

McCormick pressed a combination of numbers on the security keypad and the doors opened with a high-pitched tone.

'Through here,' he said, indicating that Lorimer should follow him.

The janitor led the way along a maze of corridors and down two flights of stairs. He had a nice voice, Lorimer thought, instantly recalling Maggie's remarks about her so-called guardian angel. McCormick was not far off the age or the description of the man who'd conned his wife.

'Suppose you don't get so many holidays as the teaching staff?' Lorimer ventured.

'Oh, I don't do so badly,' McCormick chuckled. 'Took a few days away here and there. Like to drive about the country, you know. You can keep your Benidorms and all that. Scotland's the best country in the world as far as I'm concerned.'

He ushered Lorimer into a tiny room where there was a small table and two chairs with a kettle plugged into the wall, a shelf above lined with mismatched mugs.

'Cuppa?'

'Don't mind if I do, thanks. Just a black coffee, no sugar,' Lorimer replied, noticing a jar of instant beside a packet of tea bags.

He watched the janitor busying himself with their drinks, remembering Maggie's advice to keep on the side of a school janitor.

'I'm here about Celia Gemmell,' Lorimer told him.

'Celia? Hm, that's a name from the past I won't forget in a hurry!' McCormick exclaimed. 'A right lot of trouble that one, if you ask me,' he added. 'What's she done?'

Lorimer did not answer at once. 'Strikes me that everyone we've spoken to about Ms Gemmell expected her to have committed some crime. Why is that, do you think?'

Jack McCormick scratched his head thoughtfully. 'Well, sorry to say but Celia was a pushy sort of woman. Always making eyes at the fellas. Not my cup of tea at all,' he added hastily.

Too hastily? Lorimer wondered. Was this seemingly nice man hiding a secret? Did that pleasant voice and disarming smile conceal a different personality? He stifled a sigh as he accepted the mug of coffee, wondering for a moment if his judgement was being impaired by anxiety for his wife. McCormick seemed a decent chap though, Lorimer reminded himself, people were not always what they appeared. At the very least perhaps he could shed some light on the woman who had disappeared so suddenly the year before.

It was becoming dark as Lorimer drove home, no wiser about Celia Gemmell than before. Like Gary, the janitor had been frank about the kitchen assistant and her flighty manner but by all accounts there wasn't anyone at the school with whom she had been especially close. Unless, of course, one of them was lying.

Solly laid his baby son gently into his cot, the little boy now asleep at last. Rosie had gone to bed early, exhausted, leaving him to read Abby's story and tuck her in, something that he enjoyed each evening. Ben had taken longer to settle, however, and Solly had walked up and down, humming songs under his breath as the baby had fought against sleep. He tiptoed quietly away from the darkened bedroom, closing the door behind him then sighing deeply. Fatherhood was a marvellous thing but, oh, how tiring it could be! He sank into the worn leather chair by his desk, closing his eyes for a grateful moment. All quiet, he thought, smiling.

The sudden ring of his mobile made him sit up abruptly and grab the phone to stop its intrusive sound.

'Brightman!' he announced, a little cross at the interruption to what had been a rare tranquil moment and anxious lest the noise had woken Ben.

'Maggie? Is everything okay?' He sat forwards, instantly recognising the anxiety in her voice.

'I didn't know who else to call. Oh, Solly, I think there's something rather horrible going on,' she told him.

It had been an interesting conversation, Solly thought as he sat back in the chair, hands folded beneath his chin, pondering

Maggie's revelation. She suspected the Thornton woman of conspiring behind her back, setting up a fake stalker. It made sense, of course – he could see where Maggie was coming from – but the very idea of garnering cheap publicity at the expense of terrifying your own client appalled him. There were people the psychologist knew down in London, good reliable folk in the publishing world, who might dig a little deeper on his behalf, which was why Maggie had called him. His own publications had done rather well in recent years and Solly knew that he was a valued author to his publishing house. Children's books were a far cry from psychology text-books, of course, but he would call his editor in the morning and see what he could find out.

The sun had set behind the town square and all the street lights were on as Maggie and Ivy left the building in the centre of Hawick. There had been a good turn-out yet again, the new author's reputation having preceded her. That was thanks to the extensive publicity, Maggie thought sourly as she followed Ivy to where she had parked the car, nothing to do with the book itself.

'You're very quiet tonight,' Ivy remarked as they settled into the car. 'Everything all right?'

Maggie caught an anxious glance. Had Ivy cottoned on to her mood? Was she still wondering how much of that tele-phone conversation Maggie had heard?

'To be honest,' Maggie began, casting a sideways look and pausing to see what effect her words were having (a worried frown, a lip bitten ... interesting ...), 'I'm feeling quite home-sick.' She watched the brow unfurrow, the exhalation of Ivy's breath showing a sense of relief. Maggie smiled and gave a small laugh that was partly from having read the woman's body language. 'Don't mind me,' she said. 'I'm such a home bird. Missing my man and wishing I was back at home. School will soon be on us and the holiday over,' she said truthfully.

Ivy nodded and then glanced behind her before moving out into the road and driving back to the hotel where they were to stay the night.

'Thought you might be a bit fed up with my company,' Ivy said huffily.

'You've been great,' Maggie assured her. 'Everything so well organised. Lovely places to stay ... ' She sighed. 'Don't get me wrong, I've loved doing this tour but ever since that horrible death in Edinburgh there hasn't been the same urge to per-form for an audience.' She turned to catch Ivy's eye. 'Know what I mean?'

Ivy nodded. 'Horrible,' she echoed, but Maggie thought the woman's tone sounded a little insincere. Ivy Thornton would have been milking that dreadful incident for all it was worth in terms of publicity. *A murder surely trumped a stalker?* Maggie thought cynically, wondering just what tomorrow's newspapers might contain.

CHAPTER TWENTY-NINE

He lay in bed, the clean sheets cool beneath his sweating body. Soon it would be time to make his move, find his perfect woman at last and with her the future he had dreamed of for so long. The black-and-white picture had been cut out neatly and added to the others on his cork pinboard, her face smiling down at him now. With a sigh he blotted out the events of the past few days. Spring was just around the corner, despite the recent snowfalls across the country, and with it surely would come the blossoming of all his hopes?

'Margaret,' he said, the single word hanging in the air above him like a benediction. His hands would caress these tumbling dark curls one day, her smile widening as she looked back at him.

He had waited so long to find her, blundering like a blind man in the dark, eliminating those others who had beguiled him with their pretty faces. That was all they had been, though one woman had been much more to him than a wrong choice. Celia had been a real threat to his happiness and so she had been sacrificed and buried far away from prying eyes.

He gave a groan and turned on his side. He wouldn't think about Celia any more, though the memory of her hands on his skin made him shiver with a guilty delight.

'No!' he cried out, hands around the edge of his pillow, pressing harder and harder as though the stuff beneath his fingers was a white neck . . .

Gasping for breath he let go of the pillow and rolled on to his back once more. He would never let it happen again. This time he was certain of his choice. This time the woman would return his affection.

His eyes softened as he looked at her image on the wall and saw that Margaret Lorimer was smiling back at him.

CHAPTER THIRTY

'Oh, *Ivy*. Yes, we know *her*,' the man chuckled. 'What's she been up to now?'

The professor stroked his beard and wondered how truthful he ought to be. 'I think,' he began slowly, 'she may have set up a bogus stalker for one of her own authors.'

There was a silence at the other end of the phone worthy of one of Solly's own lengthy pauses for deliberation.

'Care to expand on that, Solly? Sounds a little like something out of one of our thrillers, to be honest,' Solly's editor exclaimed.

Solly spoke quietly but firmly, giving the man as much detail as the current police investigation allowed. At last he stopped for breath, allowing his editor to pass comment.

'I can find out who that might be,' the man said. 'She has a few of the young guys in her pocket. My money would be on one of them. Let me ask around. Discreetly, of course. But from what you're saying it seems as if Ms Thornton has been playing nasty little games with your friend. I don't like it.'

'Neither do I,' Solly replied. 'And it really isn't helpful while a genuine murder investigation is being carried out.'

'Young chap in Edinburgh?'

'Mm,' Solly replied, not wishing to enlighten the man any further.

'We'll get back to you, Solly,' his editor promised. 'It's not such a big world down here in publishing, frankly. And I can ask questions of the right people.'

Solly put down the phone and gazed out of his study window. Clouds were moving swiftly across the grey skies and he shivered, wondering if the snow that had covered The Meadows in Edinburgh was heading towards the west.

DI Morrison lifted his office telephone and dialled the number for the MIT, his mouth a small, thin line. It was never a pleasant thing to have to hand over an investigation to another officer but in some ways he would be grateful to be shot of the case, he told himself.

'Lorimer,' the voice said crisply.

'DI Morrison here, sir. I wanted to bring you up to speed with our latest forensic report. I've emailed it to you so you can look at it while we talk.'

'Thanks,' Lorimer replied and there was a short pause while Morrison imagined the detective superintendent scrolling up to his latest email from the Edinburgh office.

'The DNA shows a match for the ones already on your

database,' Morrison said helpfully. He heard the intake of breath and wondered if the Glasgow cop was sitting back, astonished at what the new forensic evidence showed.

'Same killer,' he heard Lorimer mutter.

'Looks like it,' Morrison agreed. 'There was sufficient trace evidence on Ramsay's body to make a match. Despite the killer wearing gloves, enough sweat and saliva traces were picked up from Ramsay's neck for analysis.' He stopped for a moment, glad that the man from Glasgow could not see him draw a hand across his own brow. The image of a killer throttling that poor young man to death would stay in his mind for some time to come.

'I expect you will want us to deliver the victim's body to Glasgow City Mortuary, sir? The paperwork will all be sent electronically.'

Another sigh was audible then Lorimer sniffed. 'Aye, you've done the right thing, DI Morrison. And we're grateful for the head start you've made on the case. This complicates our own double murder, of course,' he added.

Morrison nodded silently, wondering if part of the complication was that the detective superintendent's wife was involved in this latest turn of events. But he was too shrewd to voice that thought. Decisions about Mrs Lorimer's part in all of this would be made much higher up the chain of authority.

'Thanks, again,' Lorimer said. 'I'd update you on things at this end, but we're keeping some things very quiet for now.'

Morrison put down the phone and leaned back in his chair. What was going on in the Glasgow detective's mind right now?

Lorimer had sounded calm enough but he had to be worried sick. He already had a double murderer who was probably stalking his wife and now Edwin Ramsay had been targeted for simply paying too much attention to her. What sort of monster was this? He gave a sigh. It was natural to be curious about how the officers at the MIT were going to track him down and for a moment he wished he could be part of their team and see it all unfold.

Lorimer sat reading the report on his computer screen, taking in the details. There was no doubt. The man that had taken the lives of these women had murdered this poor young man in Edinburgh. A cold shiver went down his spine.

Maggie.

She must have been selected, like those others, for the attention of this madman. He reached for his mobile, thinking only one thing: she must come home at once. But she'd have hers switched off right now, he remembered, tossing the phone back on to the pile of papers on his desk.

Lorimer ran a hand through his hair, trying to gather his thoughts. How best to proceed with this? He wanted to rush out this very moment and drive to wherever Maggie was, bring her home to safety. But there were other considerations that had not escaped his thoughts. His wife's involvement might change things completely, could even preclude him from heading up the case now that he had a personal interest. That decision was surely up to Iain Macintosh, the Fiscal. He sat back, drumming impatient fingers on his desk top, thinking hard.

*

Molly Newton listened as the detective superintendent took them through the latest revelation. That murder in Edinburgh had been committed by the same perp who'd killed the Donovan woman and Carolyn Kane, effectively ruling out Jake Richardson. She breathed in a sigh of despair at all the man hours spent trawling through irrelevant data not to mention the countless interviews with members of the public.

'The discovery of Celia Gemmell's body only adds to our view that the same man targeted these women who so resembled one another,' she heard Lorimer saying. 'I am waiting for confirmation about who will continue to lead this case,' he said, fixing them all with his blue gaze. 'But it seems I may have a conflict of interest.'

Molly listened, appalled, as he went on to describe Mrs Lorimer's involvement with the young man in Edinburgh who had sought her out at several book signings.

'The bogus security man, styling himself Christopher G. Stevenson – though that is almost certainly an alias – is our number-one priority now.'

Murmuring amongst the team broke out as Lorimer turned to sip from his glass of water. Who would take over if the Fiscal decreed that Lorimer was off the case? Molly glanced at DCI Cameron, sitting next to the boss, his long legs stretched out, arms folded as he regarded Lorimer. *Probably*, she thought. He was close to Lorimer and would keep him well informed every step of the way. But then, perhaps Lorimer would be permitted to continue with the case, given that it had been the Edinburgh DI who had interviewed Margaret Lorimer.

She watched as Lorimer switched on the overhead projector and fiddled with the device, getting the focus right.

'Here's an artist's impression of the man,' he told them, standing slightly to one side so that everyone had a good view of the suspect. 'My wife had several conversations with him and has a good recall for faces,' he added.

Molly stared at the image, seeing a man in his fifties, perhaps, with thinning grey hair and moustache over a downturned mouth and eyes that were couched in small folds of flesh. A military type in his youth, she wondered, though maybe it was the moustache that suggested that.

'Medium height, maybe five feet nine or ten,' Lorimer continued. 'Well spoken but with no particular accent, certainly not recognisably Aberdeen or Edinburgh. Maggie thought he had a nice voice,' he added bitterly. The irony of this observation was not lost on any of them, Molly decided, noticing the small silence that followed his remark. Whoever this guy was, he had an avuncular sort of appearance, not the face of a deranged madman with rolling bloodshot eyes. And, she knew, this might make it all the harder to find him. Her thoughts flashed back to the images of other men who had seemed perfectly nice and she shuddered remembering the face of Thomas Hamilton, the man who had taken all those precious young lives in the Dunblane massacre.

'Until we have further instructions from the Fiscal we do not know if we are going to go public with this,' Lorimer said, tapping the edge of the screen. 'I'd prefer to keep it in-house for now, though, so nothing has to be talked about outside these walls, okay?'

Again an approving murmur met Molly's ears. None of their officers would dream of spilling information that might endanger a case, particularly one as fraught as this.

'Is Mrs Lorimer back home, sir?' someone asked and Molly was surprised to see the boss shake his head.

'No, not yet. She decided to carry on with her book tour since there are just two days left,' he said. His voice sounded perfectly normal, Molly thought, but the shadows under those eyes told a different story.

A knock on the door made everyone look towards it and Molly saw one of the detective constables slip in, walk smartly up to Lorimer and hand him a sheet of paper.

She could not make out the whispered words, but the DC's eyes were shining with excitement as she spoke. And Lorimer's open-mouthed reaction as he read whatever was on that paper made every officer in the room look towards the front, Molly leaning forwards expectantly. Something was happening, anyone could see that.

'Thanks,' he said as the DC took a seat just beyond the table. Then, taking a deep breath he waved the paper in the air.

'This has just come in,' he told them. 'A report from forensics that confirms another match to the mud found on Celia Gemmell's wellington boots.' He paused, letting them all puzzle out what this might mean.

'The water butt outside Patricia Donovan's home was examined as part of an extensive search by our forensic team recently,' he explained. 'And traces of the same mud were found attached to the wooden rim. They conclude that some-one had been standing on top of that barrel,' he continued. 'And a partial print has been found that looks as if it came from the sole of a size-eight hiking boot.'

'The stalker!' Molly blurted out before she could stop herself.

'That's what we can presume.' Lorimer nodded, looking directly at her and making her cheeks flush. 'And it gives us yet one more link between Celia Gemmell's place of burial, the same area she had visited wearing her new wellingtons some time earlier, and whoever had stood on top of that water butt.'

It was all coming together, Lorimer thought, but just as it did, there was every chance he might be taken off the case. He had given the team all of the up-to-date information plus that latest report from the forensic scientists in Gartcosh, and now the main thrust of the investigation was to find out the identity of this middle-aged man who had haunted these women. And who had succeeded in befriending his own wife.

There was a certain excitement now that different strands were being linked, thanks both to the painstaking work of the MIT team and to Professor Dawson's expertise. There was one other person he needed to speak to, however, and just at that moment a knock on his door heralded the very man he wanted to see.

'Solly, come on in. You were there to hear all this latest news?' Lorimer stood up to greet his friend. Solly had indeed been seated at the back of the boardroom, legs crossed, listening intently to the detective superintendent.

'You wanted an update on the profile,' Solly said smoothly, sitting on one of the pair of comfortable armchairs that Lorimer used for visitors. 'But there is something else we need to discuss first,' he said, looking Lorimer straight in the eye.

'Oh?'

Solly heaved a sigh and shook his head slightly. 'Hard to know how to tell you this,' he began. 'Maggie called me and asked if I might help her,' he said. 'I think the woman who has been taking her around Scotland these past few days has had an agenda of her own, shall we say.'

Lorimer frowned. 'Ivy Thornton? What has she been doing?'

'I suspect that she has been trying to deliberately frighten Maggie with a bogus stalker,' Solly said, still looking carefully at his friend to see his reaction.

'She ... what? Good God! I knew there was something about that woman,' he exclaimed, thumping the arm of his chair. 'Never took to her from the outset. Not at all like Maggie's nice agent in Edinburgh. How do you know all this?'

Solly explained about Maggie's misgivings and what she had overheard Ivy saying on her mobile. 'My contacts in the publishing world tell me that she has a reputation for being quite unscrupulous when it comes to getting media coverage for her authors,' he told Lorimer. 'Now I think Maggie is ready to confront her about the nuisance call and other stuff that was designed to make it look as though she had a stalker.'

'This complicates things,' Lorimer muttered darkly.

'Maggie already made the mistake of thinking Christopher Stevenson, or whatever the hell his name is, was sent by me to protect her. Now you're telling me that the Thornton woman's been playing games like this?'

Solly nodded slowly. 'But I do not think that she had anything to do with the man whose image you just showed us,' he said. 'He has been the real stalker, following Maggie around on at least part of her book tour, whilst Ivy Thornton set up a chap in the London publishers named Paul Fellows to make that filthy phone call.'

'I'll have the woman's guts for garters,' Lorimer growled.

'I wouldn't worry unduly.' Solly gave a faint smile. 'Once the truth comes out in the press then her career will be finished. Something rather fitting about doing it that way, don't you think?'

Lorimer nodded. He'd still like to pursue the woman on a criminal charge, all the same, but perhaps Martin Enderby would be happy to take on a scoop if he were to ask him? It would indeed be appropriate if the very journo the Thornton woman had duped were to be part of her downfall.

'Right,' he said, leaning forward and handing Solly a copy of the artist's impression he'd so recently shown the team. 'Let's get on with the other business now, shall we? What do you make of this man?'

Solly looked at the image for a while as though pondering something then sat back and recrossed his legs.

'It isn't the sort of face one would expect to see on a multiple murderer or a man that stalks young women,' he murmured. 'But then we are always dealing with appearance and reality, aren't we?'

Lorimer nodded his agreement. The face he had shown the team was one that was hardly memorable and not in the least suggesting a deviant personality.

'Let me take you through one theory I have,' Solly began, uncrossing his legs and sitting forward a little. 'It's to do with mapping,' he continued. 'The areas where the deaths occurred and where the two were found in parkland interested me particularly. It suggested that our perpetrator might live not too far away.'

'But Celia Gemmell—' Lorimer began to protest but was stopped by Solly's raised hand.

'Hear me out,' the psychologist interrupted. 'Celia worked in roughly the same area of the Southside. Bankbrae is approximately halfway between Shawlands and Bellahouston. Now, your own home is in Giffnock, about the same distance from Shawlands as here, right?'

Lorimer nodded. Helen Street, where the MIT was housed in the large police office, was across the road from one side of Bellahouston Park.

'Say our killer goes on foot from wherever he lives and meets up with Carolyn last summer and Patricia much more recently. Who's to say he hadn't already selected Celia when she was working in Bankbrae?'

Lorimer frowned. 'You think he stalked her?' he asked doubtfully.

Solly gave a vague smile. 'Actually, no,' he admitted. 'I

think his relationship with Celia was rather different. The deposits in her bank account could be the proceeds from a different sort of work.' He nodded meaningfully, catching Lorimer's eye.

'You think she may have been on the game?'

'Yes. Now, bear with me for a moment. Say our man was in the habit of picking Celia up after work at or near the primary school then taking her off in his car. That might explain why her body was found out in the countryside.'

Lorimer's thoughts turned to the rugged blond PE teacher. He was big and strong enough to have overpowered a woman like Celia. And he had admitted to being interested in amateur dramatics. Could he have disguised himself as an older man to stalk Maggie? But what about the place with the ruined house? Did Johnstone have any connection with that? PE teachers were involved in cross-country runs, after all, weren't they?

'But why did he kill her in the first place? Surely, if he was a regular client then he'd have wanted to keep her alive for his own purposes?'

'Ah.' Solly smiled. 'Now that is the question. And why, one might ask, was there no sign of sexual activity with the other victims? Not a trace of semen anywhere.'

'What are you trying to say, Solly?'

The psychologist gave another sigh, the smile fading from his face. 'I'm not quite sure yet,' he admitted, 'but I have an inkling about these women and why he eventually killed them. One, how similar they are in appearance, suggests to my mind that there was a woman in his past whose memory was triggered by seeing them. And two,' he held up his thumb and index finger, 'I imagine this chap is physically incapable of a sexual act.'

Lorimer breathed out slowly. Solomon Brightman had obviously given the case a great deal of thought though these theories were surely tenuous at best. He stifled the impulse to object, remembering so many cases in the past when Solly's expertise had drawn a profile of a killer that had been uncannily correct in many ways.

'You'll have all of this down I writing, I suppose?'

'Oh, yes.' Solly nodded. 'And if someone else takes over from you they will have my fullest cooperation,' he added firmly.

'Hello, you.' Maggie's voice made his heart soar for a moment then he sat back on his office chair, Solly's revelation still in his thoughts.

'Hello yourself,' he replied gruffly. 'Where are you now? Think I've lost track.'

'Dumfries,' Maggie replied. 'I'm actually sitting in the loo next to the green room in a theatre. Only place I could talk to you without being overheard.' She giggled.

'I'll understand when I hear a toilet flushing, then,' Lorimer said drily. 'I guess it's hard to talk when she's always around. Have you said anything to her yet?' he asked. 'Solly's brought me up to speed with all of her shenanigans,' he added sourly.

'No,' Maggie replied. 'Not yet. I think we'll be having a little chat once we get back to our hotel, though. And it's just one more overnight in Ayr then we're back on home territory. A bookshop in Newton Mearns, then home.' There was a pause as each of them considered this statement. Then Maggie spoke again. 'Don't suppose there's any chance you could pick me up from Newton Mearns and take me home?'

'Yes, I'll be there, I promise. Tell you what. Keep your phone switched on for now. Never know when I might need to contact you.' He bit his lip. He'd give anything to drive down to see her right now but meantime they simply had to wait and depend on the assistance of local police officers to keep an eye on Maggie. Tomorrow the decision of whether to allow him to continue heading up this case would be known. But he wouldn't tell Maggie that just yet.

'Got to go,' Maggie whispered. 'I can hear you-know-who calling me.'

And with that Lorimer heard the click that signalled the end of the call.

CHAPTER THIRTY-ONE

It was a lovely theatre, Maggie thought, smoothing down her velvet skirt and smiling out at the audience. Perhaps some of its charm came from the fact that it was in Dumfries, last home to Scotland's national bard. She had been a bit put out earlier as they'd entered the town, Ivy pointing out some derelict shopfronts and charity shops while Maggie had been gazing at the old buildings and imagining the streets as they were in the days when Robert Burns had walked them. For a person who worked in the world of literature, Ivy had little real interest in books other than how to promote them, Maggie had gradually realised. If her career did take off Ivy Thornton would be the last person she'd want around. She was a phony as well as unscrupulous.

There were sufficient numbers in the audience to justify a stop here and the local Waterstones bookstore had set up their stall out in the foyer. Now it simply remained to speak to the people who had come to hear her and read some excerpts from the book. She ought to be an old hand at this by now, Maggie thought, but for some reason she was more nervous than ever. The lady by her side was a celebrated children's author who had agreed to interview Margaret Lorimer on stage tonight and Maggie had warmed to the woman as they'd chatted in the green room. So why should she be so tense? The answer came all too easily: what if Christopher was here, in this audience? Her stomach churned, imagining the dreadful things this man had done. And he'd selected her. Just because she reminded him of someone in his past, Solly had hinted. The thought of him somewhere in the crowded theatre, watching and listening to her, made Maggie feel sick. She'd read about stalkers; how their quest to hunt down the woman with whom they were obsessed was totally relentless. They never gave up and years could pass before they made any sort of move. If the police failed to catch this predator would she have to spend the rest of her life looking over her shoulder? Maggie took several deep breaths to quell her nerves.

Be sensible, she told herself. *What on earth can go wrong?* After all, there was a local chap from CID standing near the theatre entrance who had been given the image that had been drawn in Edinburgh, a picture that had not really satisfied Maggie in the end. It looked like anyone's dad at a Sixth year parents' night, though the moustache was rather old-fashioned.

Now the local children's author was introducing her and Maggie felt a familiar glow of warmth on her cheeks as the white-haired lady showered praise on *Gibby the Ghost of Glen Darnel*.

*

He had shed the moustache and added a pair of thick spectacles, the fisherman's hat pulled down over his hair to complete the disguise. Looking at his reflection earlier in the bathroom mirror of his B&B out in the countryside, he had chuckled at what he had seen: a chap in a tweed jacket and green trousers, the epitome of a country gentleman. Of course he would be sure to keep well away from Margaret's gaze tonight.

But that would make it all the more special when the opportunity came to have her on his own, something he planned to happen very soon.

'Thank you so much, you were wonderful!' Maggie exclaimed as the two women stepped off the stage amidst enthusiastic applause. It was dim backstage after the strong lights of the auditorium, everything dark against the black drapes, the smell of dust reminding Maggie what an old theatre this was. The older woman turned and smiled, tapping Maggie affectionately on the shoulder.

'My dear, thank *you*,' she said. 'It's a while since I heard such a rapturous reception from a local audience. They've seen me too often to turn out in force these days.' She gave a short self-deprecating laugh. 'That was all for you, Margaret.'

Maggie blushed a little, unsure whether or not to accept the compliment.

'I love your book,' the woman added, moving aside to let the sound engineer removed her lapel microphone. 'You're a real talent, you know.'

However, before Maggie had time to reply, her own

microphone was unclipped, the grinning engineer coiling it up expertly and she was ushered towards a signing table where a queue of readers was already snaking around the theatre foyer.

It was only natural that she should scan these faces, just in case. Maggie breathed a sigh of relief and turned to the first child in her queue, pushed forward by a smiling grandmother. Christopher Stevenson wouldn't be so stupid as to show up at any more of her events, Bill had assured her. In fact, he'd be foolish to show his face anywhere near her ever again. Yet, despite these thoughts, Maggie gave a shudder, still wary about the man who had posed as her protector.

He watched her as each new person stood ready, the book open in front of them. She hadn't noticed him standing beside an older lady and her grandson, the proximity affording him the best form of disguise. He blended into this crowd well, the tweeds and hat the sort of gear one would expect to see in this part of the world.

It wouldn't be long now until he brought her home for good, this book nonsense over and done with. Then they could begin a life together, the way it was surely meant to be.

'I'm sorry, too,' Lorimer said, trying hard not to let the disappointment sound in his voice. 'But it's hardly unexpected.'

'Take a few days off,' the Deputy Chief Constable suggested. 'Maybe you could catch up with that clever wife of yours,' she added.

Was that a chuckle he heard? Or was he imagining the woman's expression as she spoke?

'Right,' he agreed. 'We would normally be up in Mull at this time of year. Thanks for calling.'

Lorimer put down the telephone, looking at it intently. Few people had their ex-directory landline number, mainly Police Scotland personnel and close friends. DCC Caroline Flint was fast becoming a good friend, however, he decided. And her tone suggested that he might not sit on his hands while DCI Cameron took over the murder case, didn't it? He gave a wintry smile. She was no fool, the woman who had been promoted from down south to Police Scotland's second most senior post. And she knew him well enough by now to guess that he would be doing his bit behind the scenes, if only to protect Maggie from any more unwanted attention.

Still, expected or not, it was a blow to be taken off the investigation, but a conflict of interest like this could jeopardise the entire case. Legal loopholes sought by any cunning defence lawyer (and there were a few of those in Scotland) might result in the perpetrator getting away with his heinous crimes.

He sighed and sat back on the stairs, pondering what to do with his time. Maggie was in Dumfries tonight and tomorrow would be heading back up through Ayrshire before her final event in Newton Mearns. He'd get there early, Lorimer decided, and listen to her reading from the book. Then they could go out for a meal and a celebratory drink, perhaps.

He stood up and headed into the long open-plan room that began as a study area then doubled as a dining room with a few comfy chairs arranged around the fireplace. The kitchen beyond was separated by a long breakfast bar and Lorimer stopped there to fish a tumbler out of a wall cupboard. The Laphroaig was already on the counter and he poured a good measure into the glass, topping it up with a mere splash of water. Well, he wasn't going anywhere tonight, he sighed, leaning against the angle of the counter and staring into the darkness. Outside the sky was inky blue, clouds covering any trace of moon or stars. Was the frost past, then? Would tomorrow bring a warmer day, letting him stroll around the garden? The thought reminded him that Flynn, their gardener, was due tomorrow and Lorimer gave a crooked smile, thinking of the former drug addict whose life had been so changed by his involvement in a murder case. Joseph Alexander Flynn had been a good friend since those days, always happy to housesit and care for Chancer when the Lorimers took off on holiday.

He drained the glass, enjoying the final swallow, a smooth burning sensation in his throat. The germ of an idea was forming, an idea that included Flynn, if he was willing to cooperate. Perhaps, he told himself, there would be no need to wait another two days to see Maggie after all.

It was something she had been dreading, Maggie told herself, but it had to be done. The woman had been unusually silent on their way back to the hotel and Maggie wondered if Ivy Thornton had guessed what was coming. She glanced across at the woman, noticing the podgy hands gripping the steering wheel. For a moment she reminded her of one of her fourth-year pupils, a large girl named Morven who had always seemed to be munching on a bag of crisps as she waddled along the corridor at Muirpark. One could pity the girl for being over-weight but Morven was a known bully, her size something she used to good effect in playground brawls. Had Ivy been like that as a child? And as an adult had she manipulated other people, intimidating them by the force of her personality and promises of nice hotels and top-class restaurants? She ought to feel disgust for the woman who had deceived her so thought-lessly, but Maggie suddenly felt something quite different as she took in the woman's profile.

She'd talked to Morven often enough, sorry for the pupil and wanting to help, but nothing she'd said had made any apparent difference. She'd watched as the girl looked away, bored by the teacher's attempts to change her attitude, her jaws working, always chewing on something.

What was Ivy's life like back in London? There was no loving husband waiting for her or any significant other, just a job she tried to milk for all it was worth and an expense account she could enjoy at different locations around the country. It seemed such an empty life compared to Maggie's own and for a moment she wanted to reach out and touch the woman's hand, expressing the sympathy that welled up in her heart.

They stepped out of the car into the darkness of the hotel car park, gravel crunching beneath their feet. Maggie shivered, pulling her coat around her neck. It was cold down here in the south of Scotland and there was a bitter wind blowing in from the Atlantic.

'Right,' Ivy said, locking the car and turning towards the entrance. 'Off to bed for me.'

Maggie stepped beside her and, as they approached the front door and the beam of light from within, she caught hold of Ivy's arm. 'We need to talk first,' she said quietly. 'And I think you know what I want to say,' she added.

There was a moment's silence as Ivy's eyes met her own and Maggie saw a flicker of uncertainty.

'Your room or mine?' Maggie persisted.

The frown she was given confirmed Maggie's suspicions. Ivy stopped and she could hear a long, drawn-out sigh. 'Okay. My room,' Ivy said, refusing now to look Maggie in the eye. 'I can smoke with the window open,' she added, a tone of resignation in her gravelly voice.

Maggie didn't take her coat off when they entered Ivy's room but stood with her back to the door, determined to remain standing, instinctively seeking a semblance of authority. How often had she looked down at recalcitrant pupils, giving them advice about their behaviour? This wasn't so very different, she mused, seeing the smaller woman thrusting her coat on to the bed and immediately fishing in her handbag for the pack of cigarettes.

'I know what you've been doing since the start of the tour,' Maggie began. 'I have a friend who spoke to his publisher, Simon Haggerty, about you. Simon did some digging and came up with the name Paul Fellows.'

Ivy froze, the cigarette halfway to her lips. Maggie saw the colour leach from the woman's cheeks. She opened her mouth to speak but no sound came out.

'Paul told us everything,' Maggie continued. 'How he had managed to send these text messages, make that horrible call ... all at your request,' she added sternly. 'Why? Why did you pretend there was a stalker when a real case was ongoing, Ivy? Didn't you think that it would be dangerous?'

The woman turned away, head bent. Maggie watched as she began to cry. Tears had often been shed by kids in a last-ditch attempt to appeal to Maggie's soft side but she was wise to these tactics and didn't believe in them any more now than she had on previous occasions.

'You've been using me for your own ends, haven't you?' Maggie went on. 'Fuelling a fake story about me having a stalker just so that you might engender more publicity.'

Ivy looked up, her tear-stained face suddenly defiant. 'Well, it worked out all right for you, didn't it?' she snapped. 'You've been all over the papers, thanks to me,' she declared. 'If I hadn't worked so hard for you there would be no major coverage in the big weekend supplements or invitations to Edinburgh, would there?'

Maggie felt indignation rising in her throat. Lucy Jukes had arranged the Edinburgh Festival event, not Ivy, and the reviews for *Gibby* had come from a variety of children's authors and reviewers as well as the constant praise from readers. The words of the author who had shared her platform earlier that evening came back to her and Maggie drew herself up before fixing her eyes on Ivy Thornton.

'Don't you dare try to justify what you've done!' she exclaimed. 'Not only did you try to frighten the living day-lights out of me but you may have hampered a real, ongoing police investigation!'

Ivy's jaw dropped at that.

'Yes,' Maggie continued. 'You've been a very stupid woman, Ivy. And, let me tell you, you're not the only person who has helped me these past few months. I've got a very supportive editor who will be furious to hear what you've been up to and my agent will never allow you to represent her authors again.'

'I ...' Ivy began, but she closed her mouth as Maggie glared at her.

'As for what you think you've done to promote me as an author ... let's just see how my book does on its own merit,' she declared. 'There will certainly be no need for you to hang about after the tour is finished. In fact, my husband will be at Newton Mearns so you can disappear as soon as you drop me there.'

Ivy gave Maggie a baleful stare but said nothing.

'I'm off to my own room now,' Maggie told her. 'I think we can remain civil to one another for what remains of our associ-ation but I doubt very much if our paths will ever cross again after that.'

Ivy met her gaze then looked away as Maggie left the room and closed the door firmly behind her.

She sat there on the edge of the bed, trembling with rage. Damn Paul and his big mouth! Hadn't she paid him sweetly enough for his services? What the hell would happen now? Would she lose all her clients? Would Maggie press charges, even? Ivy's mind was full of unanswered questions and for a moment she was tempted to rush after Maggie and plead with her not to take things any further. But it was too late for that now, she thought bitterly, crushing the cigarette between her fingers, dry flakes of tobacco spilling on to the floor.

CHAPTER THIRTY-TWO

Niall Cameron had no ambition to rise above the level of DCI, a position he enjoyed especially in the MIT, but having been seconded to take over from Lorimer had given Eilidh, his wife, other thoughts.

'You can do the job just as well as he can,' she enthused, standing on tiptoe to straighten the knot in her husband's tie. 'This is just the chance you need to show them.'

Niall removed her hand gently and encircled her slim waist. 'I'm happy as I am, Eilidh,' he murmured. 'The salary is enough to keep us and more,' he added with a frown. Was she beginning to yearn for a better lifestyle than the one he had provided for them? Her job as a nurse was fulfilling though sometimes left her pretty exhausted after a twelve-hour shift and recently she had dropped hints about wanting to cut back on her hours. *Fine by me*, he'd told her and it was true. With no children yet, their joint income gave them a lovely life together in their semi-detached house in Knightswood but perhaps

Eilidh was looking to a future where she might give up work altogether? Niall let his hands run across the back of her fleecy dressing gown as he held her for a moment. His salary was easily sufficient to support them both, he reasoned. And, besides, what would he do if promotion came along? Leave the MIT and start again somewhere new? No, he decided, releasing his wife and planting a kiss on her neck. He was content to be doing this job and Eilidh must not hold out hopes he could not share.

'I'll be late home every night,' he warned. 'There's a wheen of paperwork as well as organising where we go next in the case,' he told her. 'Just as well Lorimer and I have been in this together from the start of the whole thing,' he added, almost to himself.

Eilidh simply gave him a look and shook her head. 'Know your trouble, Niall Cameron? You don't value yourself highly enough,' she protested.

'Well, maybe that's not a fault,' he replied mildly. 'I've seen what can happen to some over-ambitious cops. And not all of them stay happily married to lovely wee wives like you,' he said, giving her a wink.

'Right, I'm off. See you when I see you.' And he raised his hand in a wave as Eilidh stood on the doorstep, clutching her dressing gown around her.

It was early enough for the traffic to be reasonable driving across the city and he reached Helen Street before the end of the six-thirty news bulletin. For once there was no mention of a murder victim and he breathed a sigh of relief as the weather

318

lady began to forecast the rain and sleet that was coming their way. Lord Donovan's daughter had taken up a lot of air space as well as columns in the papers, then the story of Maggie Lorimer's involvement with a possible stalker had hit the headlines. However, it was the Edinburgh murder and the man whose DNA had been found linking it to the women in Glasgow that had changed the whole tenor of the case. Niall was certain that they were gaining ground now and that it was simply a matter of time before they located this creature. A pity they were on the right tracks just when Lorimer had been ordered to pull out. He sighed, turning the car into its usual parking space. Still, he'd keep him informed each step of the way as he'd promised.

Professor Dawson's expertise had been invaluable, Niall thought as he pointed the key fob at the car and watched the double flash on the headlights. Finding the burial site with Celia Gemmell's decomposed body had given the team a new impetus and the area was already being investigated by several officers. The woodlands had proved to be a source of interest, the ground a mixture of saplings and garden plants run wild. The remains of a former dwelling house. It had reminded Niall of some of the old hamlets back home, outlines of grey stone and rubble buried in acres of bracken, places where folk had once thrived before those times when economic forces had driven so many of the people away from his island.

He had a little time to scan the day's headlines, though the radio had given him the main news en route to the Govan HQ, then DCI Cameron would pick up where his boss and former mentor had left off. Straightening his back, he stepped briskly towards the entrance, a spring in his step that had nothing to do with the earlier conversation with his wife but everything to do with finding the man whose image was now pinned on the walls of every police office in the country. His first decision, Niall realised, was whether to make this public or to follow Lorimer's advice and not risk driving the fellow further from their grasp.

Meantime he felt he owed it to the former fiancé of Carolyn Kane to let him know that he was no longer a suspect.

Jake Richardson sat listening to the gentle tones of the man from the MIT, who was explaining why he no longer needed to fear being a person of interest to the police. They had DNA evidence that eliminated him from any further suspicion, DCI Cameron said.

Jake Richardson began to weep, real tears silently coursing down his cheeks. 'I never thought ... I ...' he began. 'It was so much my fault ...'

Niall Cameron gave him a frown. 'What was your fault? Are you still beating yourself up because you didn't walk Carolyn home? It was hardly pitch dark,' Cameron said, 'and she was a grown woman, not a little kid.'

'It's not that,' Richardson said and sighed. 'I never told your lot the whole story.' He bit his lip. 'Carolyn broke it off with me that night,' he whispered. 'I was devastated, even though I'd seen it coming for weeks. She knew I wasn't the steadiest of catches,' he admitted. 'And she was right. I was too wrapped up in my own career, I suppose. Never took enough time to plan stuff with her, you know. Like moving in together...'

Cameron listened to the man's sighs. It made sense that Richardson had not revealed this lest he become the police's prime suspect. But had he told other lies, concealed other facts?

'What about Patricia Donovan?' he asked.

Richardson shook his head. 'We had a fling, that was all. Met her one night backstage at the Citizens Theatre. She'd seen my name on the programme and wanted to go for a drink. Old time's sake, and all that. Guess I was flattered. Anyway, she came back here and ... well, one thing led to another. You know how it is,' he protested, as though such behaviour was normal for any man who'd already made a commitment to another woman. Cameron kept his face impassive. *No*, he thought, *I don't know*. He'd been faithful to Eilidh all through their courtship and could not imagine himself ever lusting after any other woman.

'When was this?'

'Couple of years back. It was the last time I saw her. She had my number but never called.'

'Did Carolyn find out about that?'

Richardson shook his head. 'No, but maybe she sensed something ... I'll never know.'

Niall Cameron walked down the darkened close and into the daylight, taking a deep breath of the fresh air. Another loose end had been tied up but it would never bring back either of

321

those women nor diminish the sadness their deaths had created. There were so many victims in this case, families and friends whose lives were forever tainted by the killer's actions. He gritted his teeth, more determined than ever to conclude this case successfully and hunt him down.

Maggie smiled as the sound of her phone woke her from an untroubled sleep. Stretching out a hand, she grasped the mobile and put it to her ear, sinking back onto the pillows.

'Good morning, darling,' she said, a smile on her lips.

'Good morning to you, too,' her husband replied. 'How did it go last night? I was thinking about you.'

'Well, the event was fantastic. I told you about my other panelist?' She waited for Lorimer to remember the author's name.

There was a silence so she continued, reminding him of the woman's identity. 'You know, she's famous! Written hundreds of brilliant children's books. Some of them were made into television series. She illustrated them all herself as well,' Maggie enthused.

'How did the other part of your evening go?' he asked quietly.

'Oh, that.' Maggie sighed. 'Honestly it was quite embarrassing. Ivy really has very little self-awareness for a woman of her experience. I am not sure she even realises the gravity of what she's done.'

'Did you tell her she could be prosecuted?'

'No.'

'What did you say, then?' he asked.

Maggie sighed again. 'I confronted her about it and she couldn't deny it. Claimed I'd actually benefited from her stupid nonsense!' she exclaimed indignantly.

'It was Ivy Thornton who was trying to benefit out of your tour. That was the whole point of it,' he replied. 'She set up this fake stalking to engender lots of media interest and that's what she achieved. But the way she went about it will prevent any decent publishing house ever taking her on again.'

There was another silence as Maggie pursed her lips. Her husband was right and, as always, sounded so reasonable. 'Anyway, I told her she could drop me at Newton Mearns and go back home. Frankly, I'm dreading today and tonight. Wish it was all over. There's bound to be an unpleasant atmosphere.'

'Maybe I can solve that,' he said.

'Oh?'

It was her husband's turn to sigh and Maggie guessed at once that something was wrong.

'I've been taken off the case,' he told her.

'Why?'

'Conflict of interest,' he said slowly.

'Oh. That's all my fault, then. I'm so sorry.'

'Don't be. We've made huge progress and the team's in Niall Cameron's capable hands. Besides, it frees me to come and pick you up even earlier, doesn't it?' he said warmly.

'Really?' Maggie sat up with a delighted squeal. 'When shall I see you?'

'How about later on today? What time is your event in Ayr?'

'Well, I've got an event in the library this afternoon then

Ayr theatre at six-thirty. Most of these are early-evening events because of the children,' she explained. 'How about dinner afterwards then we can go home together?'

'That sounds like a plan, Mrs Lorimer.' She heard him chuckle. 'Though I think dinner could extend to an overnight in our favourite hotel in Troon.'

'The Lochgreen? Oh, I'd love that!' she exclaimed.

'It also gives me time to have a serious talk with Ms Thornton.'

'Do you have to?' Maggie asked, her enthusiasm suddenly deflated.

'I think so,' was all that he said and she nodded silently. It ought to be a police matter, after all, and who better to decide that than her own husband?

'Look, I'll call you later to let you know when I'm arriving. Okay?'

Maggie lay back and smiled. 'See you soon,' she told him. 'Love you.'

'Love you, too.'

Lorimer heaved a sigh of relief. Once he was down in Ayr he could finish the business with the Thornton woman, let her know her position and how she was at risk of losing any future freelance work as well as facing a police prosecution, though Maggie had made it clear she didn't want to press charges against anyone associated with her publisher. Nobody else in the publishing house was to blame; in fact, Maggie had spoken in glowing terms about how good they had all been to her. It just remained to sort a few things out here, like asking Flynn to look after the cat tonight. Then Lorimer would see if he could book them into the Lochgreen.

Breakfast was a quiet affair, Maggie on her own in the hotel dining room, no sign of Ivy. She kept glancing up at the entrance but by the time she had finished her coffee Ivy still hadn't appeared. Perhaps she'd had breakfast in her own room, Maggie decided, standing up and heading across the dining room. It was a bit of a relief not having to see her across the table this one last time, however. And no doubt Ivy Thornton would be equally happy not to have to face her client this morning after the previous evening's confrontation.

There were few people about in the lounge area as she passed through to the wide staircase up to her room and she did not pay much notice to the tweedy gentleman hidden behind his morning newspaper, nor did she see his eyes following her as she began her ascent.

Just at that moment Ivy came downstairs and the two women stopped on an angle of the staircase.

'Good morning, I've had breakfast,' Maggie said briskly. 'Shall I meet you down here in an hour?' She looked at her watch. 'That gives you time to have your own breakfast and settle up.'

Ivy threw her a startled look, obviously unused to this new Margaret Lorimer's authoritative manner.

'Sure,' she mumbled. 'About last night . . . '

'I'll speak to you later,' Maggie said. 'But just so you know, Bill is coming to Ayr to pick me up this evening so you can leave as soon as we get there – I can make my own way from the library to the theatre.' And, not stopping to see Ivy's reaction, she swept up the stair and headed along the corridor, heart thumping.

Once inside the bedroom, Maggie sank into the nearest chair, her legs trembling. It was a horrid situation but thankfully she only had the car journey to Ayr with Ivy then she need never see the woman again.

He watched the small plump woman making her way into the dining room where he had sat earlier in a corner, hidden from any prying eyes. Something was wrong between them, he could see that; Margaret's tone had been so different, almost like a schoolteacher. He grinned at the thought. But the smile was short-lived as he recalled the words he had overheard. The husband was going to come to Ayr tonight and whisk his beloved off again? Well, perhaps it was time to put a stop to the policeman's intentions once and for all. It just meant putting his own plans into action a little sooner than he had anticipated. Looking carefully around him, he folded the newspaper and picked up the small travelling case by his side. There was no need to trail them now, he thought, as he walked towards reception to settle his bill. He knew exactly where Margaret would be going.

The young man behind the desk smiled as he approached.

'Room 101,' he said, thrusting the plastic key across the desk.

'Here we are, just a signature here,' the receptionist said, giving him a sheet of paper with an itemised bill.

He laid the notes out carefully, the cash transaction a necessity, a decent tip making the young man's smile even wider.

'Thanks so much,' the receptionist said as he turned to leave. 'Hope you enjoyed your stay with us, Mr Stevenson.'

CHAPTER THIRTY-THREE

It was a decent enough day for gardening, Flynn thought, whistling along to the music from his radio, his thoughts turning towards what jobs awaited him in the Lorimers' place. Too early to take the dahlia tubers out from the shed where they were lying dormant, but maybe he could see if the greenhouse required a bit of a clean-up. Mrs Lorimer usually brought on seedlings before the summertime but this year she was away on her book tour. *Good for her,* Flynn thought as he pulled out his plastic trug full of tools. He stopped for a moment, contemplating the house with its wreath of winter jasmine still climbing up by the doorway.

He'd been so lucky to stay here with the Lorimers after the road accident that had changed his life. He gave a small grin, remembering Maggie's mum, who had mothered him in a kind but scolding manner. He still missed her easy banter and it was hard for Maggie, too, to have lost the woman who had been so close to them all. Flynn sighed. Still, she'd made something of herself now, hadn't she? Not just a schoolteacher any more but a real author dashing about the countryside giving talks and no doubt selling loads of books. Crikey, maybe he'd be famous one day for being Margaret Lorimer's gardener, Flynn told himself gleefully. Didn't authors make millions nowadays? Perhaps Lorimer would quit the polis an' all.

The door opened as if the thought of the man had conjured him up and Flynn gave the tall policeman a small salute.

'Aye, aye, not at the MIT, the day then?'

Lorimer shook his head. 'Off the current case as it involved Maggie. Maybe you heard about that? Young chap over in Edinburgh? He was one of Maggie's readers, seemingly,' Lorimer said.

'That right? Naw, didnae hear that. So, you off on holiday for a bit then?' Flynn put down the trug and made to return to the van for the rest of his tools.

'Yes, I am as it happens and that's what I wanted to talk to you about. Can you do us a favour and stay over. See to Chancer tonight? I want to take Maggie to a place we like in Troon after her gig then we can come home tomorrow.'

Flynn scratched his chin thoughtfully. 'Aye, why not? Need to go home for a change of clothes, right enough, but I've got a key so ... ' He shrugged. 'Nae problem, big man. I'll feed Chancer and get as much done in the garden as I can before her ladyship comes back, okay?' He grinned. 'Youse havin' a wee romantic night thegether, eh?'

He laughed as Lorimer made a face, evidently embarrassed

at Flynn guessing correctly. 'Right, I'll get some stuff done and head back to the flat at lunchtime, awright?'

'Thanks,' Lorimer replied. 'Good to know we can depend on you.'

'Nae hassle,' Flynn replied. He did not need to voice the gratitude he owed to this man. Lorimer would pay him a decent rate but he'd put in extra hours just the same. Least he could do, he thought, pulling the last of his tools from the back of the van.

Lorimer turned to go back indoors, intent on putting some things into an overnight bag, when he heard the telephone ringing.

In a very few strides he was beside the phone. Surely this wasn't a sudden recall to the Govan office? Not after he had just made plans for this evening.

'Lorimer,' he said abruptly.

There was a silence that went on just a tad too long then he heard what sounded like someone clearing their throat.

'Sorry,' a man's voice apologised. 'Wrong number.'

There was a click and Lorimer stared at the phone, hearing the constant tone that signified the line was now disconnected. He hung up, a frown creasing the space between his eyes. Was that the same person who'd rung here before? Had someone been given their ex-directory number in error? It could be that, but as he strove to recall the man's voice, Lorimer began to wonder.

Looking out he could see the van sitting by the pavement

but no sign of the gardener so he went through to the back door and looked around. Flynn was already at work, thick rubber pads secured around his knees as he tackled the border by the back lawn.

'See if you get any calls,' Lorimer called out. 'Can you log the time and who made them?'

Flynn looked up and gave him a cheery wave. 'Aye, aye, Cap'n. Will do.'

Lorimer retreated indoors with a sigh. Something wasn't right but he could not think why a wrong number should bother him like this. It was second nature to be suspicious, however, given Maggie's experiences in Edinburgh. At least, Lorimer told himself, they would soon be rid of the Thornton woman and the stupid games she had been playing with his wife.

There was no hurry to reach Ayr just yet. Some things required careful preparation and if he was to fulfill his dream of having the dark–haired woman completely to himself at last, he would need to present himself in the best possible way. He reached down into the open case that lay on the passenger seat and unzipped the inner mesh sleeve then lifted out a nylon bag. The toupee was light brown and would serve to make him appear younger and more desirable. Perhaps he would dispense with coloured lenses tonight, though, he decided, putting aside the array of little plastic boxes. Better to let her see his gaze for what it truly was as he declared his love and told Margaret what her future now held. Finding the policeman at home had been a stroke of luck. And by the time Detective Superintendent Lorimer reached Ayr, his wife would already have gone.

Looking at himself in the car mirror, he gave a nod of approval. How could she resist him? Once she'd received the flowers he'd be waiting for her.

He closed his eyes, seeing once again the churchyard and the mourners. But this time there would be no sadness, no tears to spoil his happiness.

CHAPTER THIRTY-FOUR

'I'm off the case, but I expect you knew that.' Lorimer drained his mug of tea and set it down on the professor's table.

Solly nodded, his eyes full of sympathy. 'It's the way of things now,' he said slowly. 'Any conflict of interest can jeopardise the outcome of a case.' He sighed, echoing the very words of Iain Mackintosh, the Procurator Fiscal.

'It's all for the best, really. Means I can go down and collect Maggie. Been worried sick about her since that lad in Edinburgh was killed. Still, it's frustrating to have come so far and then have to hand it over.'

'DCI Cameron will be a safe pair of hands,' Solly assured him.

'Oh, I know that, but I'm not very good at twiddling my thumbs when so much is going on,' Lorimer said.

Solly smiled. 'Is that why you came here today? Before you meet up with Maggie?'

Lorimer gave a short laugh. 'I'm rumbled, aren't I?' He shook his head at the psychologist's ability to see through him. 'Okay, let's see what we have so far, shall we? If I'm not permitted any further access to the case at least I can think about it and try to work out what sort of motive this man had for his crimes.'

'I think he will not see himself as a criminal, of course,' Solly insisted. 'Delusional types rarely have that sort of self-awareness.'

'Or empathy,' Lorimer added.

'Mm, you're imagining this man is some sort of psychopath.'

'Well, isn't he?'

Solly sat back in the easy chair next to his desk and gazed out of the window as though he needed time to consider the question.

From the next room Lorimer could hear the sound of Rosie singing softly as she tried to rock baby Ben to sleep. Abby was in the lounge watching a cartoon, its sound filtering through the large flat. He was suddenly aware of the contrast with his own home where it was so silent.

'I think something traumatic happened to him, possibly something from his childhood,' Solly said at last, breaking into Lorimer's thoughts.

'Oh?'

'It revolves around a woman, maybe a lover, but from what I've read of this type of personality it's more likely his mother.'

Lorimer tried not to make a face. This all sounded a tad too Freudian for his liking, but then again, he was talking to a professor of psychology.

'This woman had an impact on him when the trauma took place, or she may have been the cause of it. Either way, women who resemble her trigger something in his brain.'

'He wants to find a lover that looks like his mother? Isn't that a bit Oedipus?' Lorimer protested.

'I think he can only be happy if he finds a woman who relates to him in the way his own mother once did.'

'Are you saying his mother abused him?'

'Not necessarily.' Solly shook his head. 'What I am suggesting is that he is looking for a type of woman who will show him the same affection that his mother did. It's not so unusual,' he mused. 'Many people subconsciously choose a partner based on memories of a parent. Though from what I've seen of him in photographs, Rosie's father looked nothing like me.' He grinned, stroking his thick dark beard.

'They do say some women choose a father figure. And does the same hold for men? Are we supposed to be looking for our ideal woman based on our own mothers?'

'That depends on the mothers,' Solly laughed. 'And, no, there's no hard and fast rule about that. Only, sometimes a person can be so heavily influenced by a parent that their lives are forever entwined by their memory, whether consciously or not.'

Lorimer made a face. 'How does this help us to find the guy?'

'I don't suppose it does, really,' Solly admitted, 'but it might give an insight into why he has targeted several women.'

'And killed them.'

'For destroying his dream,' Solly replied. 'I see it happening like this. Christopher Stevenson, or whatever he is really called, selects a woman for what she looks like, follows her secretly whilst building up a fantasy about her showering him with love. Now,' he raised a finger and then continued, 'let's imagine that Celia Gemmell got to know this stalker reasonably well. She strings him along, takes whatever she can get from him, then for some reason he realises that she is playing him false. The betrayal would be seriously wounding to his fantasy.'

'So he kills her.'

Solly nodded. 'And he knows where he wants her to be buried. The place in the woods has a real significance for him and I bet you find that it is linked in some way to the woman, mother figure or whoever, that he is still seeking.'

'Classic fixation pattern,' Lorimer murmured.

'Same thing happens when he eventually meets Carolyn and Patricia. I doubt very much if either woman was aware of their stalker. He probably appeared to them quite out of the blue, his stalking methods honed to perfection by then.'

Lorimer looked away, imagining the scenes: a man appearing suddenly by their side in a park at twilight, professing his love for them ... it must have freaked out these poor women. Did they try to run from him? Shake him off? Scream abuse. He thought back to the Facebook posts. Why write them *after* he'd killed those two women? Was it his twisted way of saying goodbye, or was he consigning them to eternal darkness, knowing they were dead?

'Their rejection triggered an instant reaction, of course,' Solly continued as though he had read Lorimer's thoughts. 'And he had to destroy the very embodiment of a dream that had crashed right in front of him.'

'You feel sorry for him,' Lorimer said, looking at his friend, 'don't you?'

Solly gave a tired smile. 'I regret the loss of innocent lives as much as you do,' he began, 'but yes, I feel an element of pity for a man whose mind has been twisted to such an extent. Will we ever know the whole story, I wonder?'

CHAPTER THIRTY-FIVE

Auld Ayr. Whom ne'er a town surpasses. For honest men and bonny lasses.

Maggie Lorimer smiled to herself, remembering the lines from her favourite of Burns' poems, 'Tam o' Shanter'. She had loved it as a schoolgirl and taught it year on year to her own pupils, enthusing over the language as well as the story. A quick glance at Ivy who was busy looking out for a parking space told her that there was no point in quoting aloud for the woman. She had expressed no interest in poetry or anything to do with the bard's heritage. It was such a pity. Perhaps her next PR would be cut from a different cloth, Maggie reasoned.

She had called Lucy, her agent, the previous day before confronting Ivy, explaining the revelations about her. Lucy had been appalled and wanted to reassure Maggie that she was sure the publishers would do everything they could to compensate for her distress. Maybe Lucy Jukes might accompany her on the next outing with the book, Maggie thought. She was to be at the Edinburgh event in August, introducing Maggie to the audience there at any rate. Would Ivy's interference have spoiled her relationship with the London staff for good? Maggie stifled a sigh as they rolled into a car park at the back of Ayr library. She could expect a warm greeting from the librarians, a special breed of people whom she was beginning to rate more highly than ever.

'Hello; welcome to Ayr.' A friendly woman stood at the back door of the library and smiled at Maggie as she walked from the car. 'We've been looking forward to this all week,' the woman went on. 'I'm Janice. Come on through. The kettle's on and there's a pile of home baking ready for you.'

Maggie allowed herself to be led through a narrow passageway and into what appeared to be the staffroom, a cosy place with old armchairs around a table set with mismatched mugs and plates of scones, iced buns and buttered pancakes.

'My goodness, what a lot of trouble you've all taken. This looks like a feast!' Maggie exclaimed.

'This is Aileen and that's Natalie,' Janice said, waving her hand at two other women in the room, one of whom held a large yellow teapot. 'Tea? Or would you prefer coffee?' Janice asked, this time including Ivy in her question as the woman pushed her way into the room and flopped down on the nearest chair.

'Coffee for me, please,' Ivy replied, her eyes already on the table full of home baking.

'Tea, please,' Maggie answered.

'Lovely flowers,' Janice said, handing a huge bouquet of pink and white roses to Maggie.

'Oh, my. That's so kind . . .'

'Not from us,' the librarian said with a smile. 'Local florist delivered them.'

Maggie put the fragrant flowers to her face. They had to be from Bill, she thought, then searched for a card.

Meet me at Auld Alloway's haunted kirk at five. XXX

Maggie chuckled. He knew how much she loved 'Tam o' Shanter' and she smiled at the poetic reference to the kirk. They'd spent a great day out at the new centre in Alloway last summer and the kirk, or church, was not far away. She'd take a taxi from the library, though, Maggie decided. No way was she going to ask Ivy for a lift there as she definitely did not want a scene between the woman and her husband.

There was a noticeboard on the wall outside the staffroom with several small business cards attached, one of which was for a local taxi company. Phone in hand, Maggie tapped in their number. She'd call them straight after the event and be there early to surprise him.

'Sorry about that,' she apologised. 'Now, about that nice cup of tea,' she declared, beaming at the library staff and taking a seat at the table. 'And these scones look delicious.'

He had chosen the best room in the hotel, casting any thoughts of expense aside, telling himself that Maggie deserved it.

Lochgreen House Hotel was a little way out of the town, its gardens and trees giving it a secluded feel. As he approached the building Lorimer gave a sigh of pleasure, seeing again the red-tiled roofs and the swathes of well-tended lawn. Yet his mind drifted like the black-headed gull he watched gliding overhead, and he could not help thinking about the man that had followed his wife around the country.

Who was he? And where had he gone now? What sort of stalker flitted from one woman to the next, their similar appearance like some sort of magnet attracting him? Most of the stalking cases he'd read about in recent years had involved women (or men) whose stalker was obsessed to the point where they followed just that one single person, sometimes for many years. But this man was different. And part of his difference included being a ruthless killer. Lorimer heaved a sigh, half-wishing he was back in Glasgow, finding out if the team had come up with any answers.

Though he was officially off the case, Lorimer knew that Niall Cameron would keep him abreast of any new developments and so he had his mobile charged and in his jacket pocket, ready to hear what was happening back in the city. And, however much he told himself that this was a welcome break from the investigation, Lorimer's instinct was to consider the features of it that still troubled him most and which had resulted in a conflict of interest. This stalker was most likely a middle-aged man who had brazenly offered his services to Maggie as a security guard. That had been taking a risk, but was that part of the challenge for him? He had followed Patricia Donovan into Bellahouston Park (or, more likely, persuaded her to accompany him: they were still at a loss to know why she had not returned home after the exercise class) and the same thing may have taken place last summer in Queen's Park with Carolyn Kane. Had they rejected his advances? Solly seemed to think so and Lorimer trusted the psychologist's instincts. Celia Gemmell, now that one was a mystery. Had he enjoyed a relationship with the woman who was rumoured to be a sex worker? And, if so, what had happened to make her killer lure Celia into these woods out near Hessilhead? That looked as if it had been planned, but he still felt the other two women's deaths might have happened after an emotional outburst of some kind. Solly thought the place could have significance and the ruined house was being investigated to see if there was any link. Lorimer touched his pocket, instinctively willing Cameron to call.

The whole thing came down to a man's preference for a type of woman, a woman bearing a resemblance to his beloved Maggie. Lorimer shivered despite some warmth from the heated seats in the Lexus. The stalker was searching for a particular woman, Solly had said, someone that bore a striking resemblance to a woman from his past, he reckoned. A former lover? He sighed, racking his brains for an explanation. What sort of man would hunt down his perfect woman only to end up killing them? Had Celia Gemmell seen him as one of her customers? Just another lonely man needing the attentions of a woman? Why had she gone with him into these woods wearing these new wellington boots? Had he promised her more money for a sex romp there? Lorimer frowned, recalling that Solomon Brightman had suggested the stalker might be impotent, a man enraged by his own inability to perform the sex act and destroying the very woman he had stalked. But surely that gave rise to the notion of a sudden burst of emotion? An anger that overwhelmed him?

'Have Darkness,' he quoted softly. And Celia had been deliberately taken back to the same dark spot amongst the trees where she'd been before. That was well thought out beforehand. He closed his eyes, imagining a car trundling into the woods, a spade already in the boot, Celia Gemmell in the passenger seat dressed in her pink coat and high-heeled boots. She'd been ready for a night out in the town, not a country ramble. So, what had gone wrong? And why had she been murdered?

Well, they were pulling out all the stops to find this character now and in a few hours Maggie would be safely in his arms, tucked up beside him in the nicest bedroom Lochgreen could provide after enjoying one of the hotel's legendary gourmet dinners.

Lorimer got out of the car and lifted his overnight bag from the back seat. There were things he wanted to do to make their reunion perfect: flowers and champagne. Could the hotel arrange this or should he head off in a little while and purchase them himself? With a smile on his lips, Lorimer headed towards the entrance of the country house hotel focusing his mind on their reunion and what he would say when they met in Ayr.

*

343

'Tea? Coffee?' Janice the librarian offered as Maggie looked up to say goodbye to the last in her signing queue.

'Oh, there's somewhere I have to be, sorry.' Maggie smiled. 'But thanks ever so much for this afternoon. You made it all very easy,' she added, glancing again at the space where seats had been arranged for her audience and the posters fixed to several book stands.

She lifted her mobile and nodded. 'I just need to call a taxi and get my coat from the staffroom,' she explained.

'Oh, is the other lady not going with you?' Janice asked. Maggie shook her head, avoiding the librarian's eyes. She had seen Ivy slip out before she had finished her talk and known instinctively that the woman was intent on putting as great a distance between them as possible. What she would do now was a matter for the publisher to decide but Maggie doubted that she would ever see or hear of Ivy Thornton again unless it was an article revealing the woman's duplicity.

The taxi was a silver Skoda, the driver a local man with a strong Ayrshire accent.

'Alloway's auld haunted kirk? Did ah hear ye right, lady?' he asked, heaving Maggie's suitcase into the boot.

'You did.' Maggie smiled at him. 'I'm meeting my husband there. We're both big fans of Robert Burns, especially "Tam o' Shanter".'

'Ah, well now, there was a man,' the driver murmured as he slipped behind the wheel. *'There was a lad was born in Kyle ...'* he began to sing in a light tenor voice and Maggie smiled as they set off through the town, glad to have found a fellow Burns enthusiast in this particular part of the country. She was already rehearsing how she would retell the incident to Bill when they met.

The light was fading from the skies and Maggie buttoned her coat up to the neck, aware that it would be chilly after the warmth of the taxi. Still, the Lexus would be waiting and she wouldn't have long to be outside in the evening air. The driver had begun to croon 'Bonny Wee Thing' as they drove along the quiet road to Alloway and Maggie settled back in the passenger seat, listening to the song that Burns had written for his baby daughter. What a genius the man had been! To pen songs and poems as diverse as lullabies, satires and the vivid narrative that was so closely associated with this very area ...

Bill must have had romance on his mind, surely, to arrange the old kirk as a rendezvous? They were almost there when the driver turned to give Maggie a quizzical glance. 'Sure this is where you want to be dropped, missis? It's a bleak place at the best o' times but gey dark the night.'

'Oh, it's fine. I'm being picked up by my husband,' Maggie assured him.

'You'll be wanting a receipt?'

Maggie hesitated. Ivy had drummed into her the need to keep all receipts so the publisher could cover expenses.

'Yes, I think so,' she agreed. 'Can you make it out to Mrs Lorimer, please?'

'Hey, are you the lady that wrote that ghostie book? My

wee grandson loves it!' the taxi driver exclaimed, looking at Maggie wide-eyed.

'That's me.' She nodded, surprised that anyone outside a library or bookshop would have heard of her.

'Well, I never,' the driver said, shaking his head as he fumbled for a business card and wrote down her name, the date and the fare on the back.

'Here, can you sign this for him?' he took a second card and thrust it into her hands.

Maggie obliged and then paid the fare, adding a generous tip as he took her case from the boot and pulled out its handle.

'That's for the free concert,' she joked, getting out of the car and closing the door.

'Thanks a lot, lass. Have a good night,' he said, giving a wave before turning the car back the way they had come.

'You too,' she said, though her words were lost in the sound of the Skoda speeding away.

Maggie turned to look at the dark church outlined below a velvety blue sky. Her breath clouded a little in the cold air and she could see the first star above the horizon. Venus, perhaps? A planet rather than a star? She could not remember what heavenly bodies were visible at this time of year. The area around the church was deserted, no sign yet of the Lexus. Maggie glanced at her watch. It was not quite five o'clock so she was first to arrive. Rather than stand still, she decided to walk around the place to keep warm. Leaving her suitcase propped against the railings, she stepped into the entrance of Alloway's kirkyard.

The old gate creaked as she pushed it open, its hinges badly in need of oiling. The sound echoed in the darkness, making her shiver. There was a path winding around the church, ancient gravestones lying along the grass, some completely flat on the ground, others tilted by years of wind and weather, all grey stones marking the last resting place of men and women, long dead.

Perhaps she should imagine a graveyard like this for her next book, Maggie pondered, stopping to examine one of the more ornate headstones that towered above her, a carved angel with outstretched wings looking unseeingly over the graveyard with her stone eyes. *What would Gibby make of a place like this?* she wondered, conjuring up an image of her little ghost boy.

She was almost at the back of the church, past a closed wooden door, when Maggie heard the car arrive. Quickening her step she hurried onwards, taking the path around the church that would surely come out again at the road where she had been dropped.

At first Maggie assumed that she must have left something in the taxi, for wasn't that the same silver car parked nearby? It was certainly not the familiar shape of her husband's Lexus. She looked down at her shoulder bag. The pull-along case was outside and that was all the luggage she had brought for the tour. No, nothing missing. She was wearing her soft leather gloves and her silk scarf was tucked into the collar of her coat. So why had he come back? Puzzled, Maggie quickened her stride just in time to see a figure walk along the pavement and grab her suitcase.

'Hey!' she cried out then began to run. What did he think he was doing? 'I'm here!' she cried. 'I haven't forgotten ...'

Maggie was almost upon the man when he straightened up and turned around.

Her mouth opened but her voice was shocked into silence as she recognised the face of Christopher Stevenson.

'Hello, Margaret,' he said, pulling the case towards her. 'Of course you haven't forgotten me, how could you?' He gave her a smile and drew his hand across his mouth. 'Had to get rid of that moustache. You don't mind, do you?'

Maggie stood motionless, her brain refusing to process what her eyes told her she was seeing. This man, the stalker ... Her stomach felt suddenly weak as she licked her lips and took a quick, nervous breath.

'My husband. He'll be here any moment,' she said, looking around frantically, desperate for a sight of the Lexus rounding the nearest corner.

She jumped as Christopher took her arm, none too gently. 'No, my dear. He won't be coming back for you any more,' he said then chuckled. 'It's just you and me now. Isn't that nice?'

You're mad, Maggie thought. *Completely, barking mad. And dangerous, too.* Yet, some instinct told her to play along with him, humour him a little the way she did with difficult pupils. Her brain worked frantically as she allowed him to pull her towards the car. Resistance might make him snap into a desperate killer, she thought. For now he saw her as a compliant female, someone that posed no threat to whatever mad scheme his twisted mind had devised and it would be to her advantage to keep up the façade. She just needed to trust that Bill would find her ...

'Here, the car's waiting to take us home,' Christopher said, pulling her arm and rolling the suitcase behind him.

Maggie thrust her free hand into her coat pocket, fingers exploring under a paper handkerchief. Yes, there it was, the smooth pebble of rose quartz Bill had given her one day on Calgary beach.

It made hardly any noise falling to the ground and for a moment Maggie regretted her action, wondering if she might have lost her precious stone for good rather than leave a tiny sign for others to follow.

CHAPTER THIRTY-SIX

'We've traced the original owners of that derelict house,' Niall Cameron told Solly as they walked together towards the meeting room at the end of the corridor. The psychologist noted the light in the DCI's eyes and nodded. 'Something significant?' he asked.

'We think so,' Cameron replied. 'The place was owned by a family way back in the fifties. It was passed down to the only daughter eventually and that's when it became abandoned. We're still trying to find out more about what happened to her, but one thing we do know, she died in unusual circumstances, a suspicious death that was never resolved by the Fiscal.'

Solly raised his eyebrows. 'And who was she?'

Cameron gave him the ghost of a smile. 'That's what is so interesting,' he said. 'Her maiden name was Stevenson but her death was registered in the name of Kennedy.'

'Christopher Stevenson,' Solly said slowly. 'That has to be a link, surely?'

'We think so,' Cameron replied. 'We'll find out more in the next few minutes if our officers have come up with any details about this family.'

Maggie sat silently as the car bumped along the rutted track. *Breathe in, breathe out*, she told herself, quelling the rising panic that made her back and neck rigid with fear.

She had to dissemble, make him think that she was happy to go along with his plans. That was the only way she would be safe from whatever manic rage had already consumed four innocent victims.

Before they had left the old kirk, he had taken her handbag and pulled out her mobile, thrusting it into the side pocket of the car. The action had alarmed Maggie. He was cutting her off from anyone who might try to make contact. But, she reasoned, at least he hadn't broken it or chucked it away. Perhaps she could retrieve it later, once they had stopped? But the way he had snatched it had alarmed her, as though he were taking possession not just of the phone but of Maggie herself.

'Nearly there,' Christopher said, casting a glance at her as the car slowed down. He patted her gloved hand and Maggie kept quite still, teeth gritted, resisting the impulse to flinch at his touch. What if he should become amorous ... expect her to do things with him?

She closed her eyes, intoning a prayer to a heavenly father who had promised always to be with her. A feeling of guilt swept over her: was it only in extreme situations that she ever offered up a supplication like this? 'Ask and it shall be given unto you,' wasn't that what the Scriptures said? Maggie swallowed hard. If ever she needed that promise then it was right now.

Help me, she begged silently. *Please, please help me.*

'Here we are.'

Maggie's eyes flew open as she sat looking into the darkness ahead, the twin headlights picking out grey, leafless trees whose branches appeared ghostly in the pale white light.

She swallowed, her mouth dry. 'Where are we?' she whispered.

'My dear, we're home,' Christopher smiled. 'Can you see it?' he pointed towards a shape half hidden by the trees.

Maggie blinked, striving to see what he was showing her.

'It's unfit for habitation now, of course, but we'll rebuild it, won't we? Make it our very own.'

Maggie nodded silently, sensing his arm creeping across the back of her seat. Whatever fantasy this man was having, it evidently included her. *Pretend to like what he's telling you*, a small voice urged. *Don't let him see how frightened you really are.*

She leaned forward, peering out of the windscreen. Perhaps that was the shape of a gable end, after all, the remains of a dwelling house left to become a ruin. A woman's body had been found there, Bill had told her. Had she been brought here to be dumped in the self-same grave? Her heart thumped so loudly she feared the man next to her must surely hear it.

'Was this your home once?' she asked, her voice high and strained. Keep him talking, she thought, anything to avoid getting out of the car.

'Oh, yes. And it will be again, I promise you.' He smiled, taking his hand and brushing a strand of her hair away from her face.

'You are quite beautiful, you know,' he murmured. 'Perfect.' He stretched across and pulled a bag from behind her seat. 'Here.' He handed her a large plastic carrier bag. 'I bought these for you. We could go for a little walk now.'

Maggie opened the bag to see a pair of brand-new wellington boots. She swallowed hard, mouth dry as she remembered a detail from Bill's triple murder case. Lorna Dawson had found the woman's body after examining the mud on a pair of wellington boots. He must be mad to risk coming back here again! But then, she reasoned, no sane person would behave like this.

Maggie froze, every instinct telling her to get out and run, but her common sense battled against that urge. *Stay with him, play along*, the same small voice soothed. *Make him want to be kind*.

'Oh, I don't know,' she said, trying hard to keep her nerves in check, glancing at the man seated so close to her. 'I'm a bit too tired to go for a walk right now. Besides, it's ages since I had anything to eat,' Maggie continued. 'How about you take me somewhere nice for dinner?'

She smiled at him, forcing an expression of false charm that she did not feel.

'Oh.' He drew back, a look of surprise on his face. 'I hadn't thought about that. Are you hungry, my dear?' he asked anxiously.

'Yes,' she said as firmly as she dared. 'I am.'

'Well.' He sat back heavily as if the mundane thought of food was something new to him. 'I suppose I can cook for you. I don't live very far away, after all,' he added, almost to himself.

'We could come back and see the old house when it's daylight,' Maggie suggested. *Anything to play for time*, she told herself, hoping that it would not require an entire night spent in this man's company before Bill found her.

'Hmm.' Christopher gave a little nod and switched on the car engine again. For a moment he seemed to be looking into the darkness, looking at something that Maggie could not see, and she wondered what had happened to this old house and why it meant so much to the man who had taken her captive.

'Sorry, she hasn't turned up yet. We tried her PR but she didn't answer either. Do you know when she might be here? We have an audience waiting,' the young man told Lorimer, looking anxiously at his wristwatch.

'I thought she usually arrived a good bit before an event, at least that's what she told me,' Lorimer replied, frowning. His plan to surprise Maggie before her event appeared to have backfired somewhat, he thought ruefully, the bouquet of red roses clutched in one fist. 'Wasn't she at the library earlier on? Could she still be there? Maybe one of the librarians offered to bring her here?'

The theatre manager shrugged. 'Sorry, all I know is that your wife's PR told us they would be here by six-fifteen at the latest and it's past that now.' The man gave a frown of annoyance. 'I hope she doesn't let us down,' he added. 'This has been on our programme for weeks.'

Lorimer grasped his mobile and tapped on the number next to Maggie's name. The call rang out for a few seconds then went into voicemail.

'Maggie, I'm at the theatre in Ayr. Where are you? Ring me back right away, will you?'

He pocketed the phone, regretting now his visit to Solly. If he'd left Glasgow earlier, decided to meet her at the library instead of the theatre, then she would be with him right now. Instead ... his thoughts began to darken. Where was she? And why had Maggie not rung the theatre if she was going to be delayed in any way? It simply wasn't like her. Maggie was always so well prepared and punctual, a habit instilled by years in the classroom.

No, he told himself, suddenly. Something had happened. And it was up to him to find out where she was.

CHAPTER THIRTY-SEVEN

After the dark woods and the unlit country roads it came as a surprise to Maggie when the car entered the outskirts of a small town. Christopher drove sedately along its streets, turning at last into an estate of post-war bungalows and semi-detached villas, neat gardens picked out by street lights overhead.

This was where he lived? She looked from one house to the next, seeing only what appeared to be a very ordinary crescent of homes. A glance at the man driving slowly over the speed bumps told her nothing more than what she already knew; Christopher's appearance as a normal middle-aged man simply belied the reality of his madness. Who knew, after all, what life lay behind these curtained windows, these identical driveways with their shiny cars? Hadn't she taught that very thing in so many studies of literature? How the outward show of things was often at odds with something dark and menacing within?

The car turned a corner and they drove along a little further before stopping outside a detached bungalow next to a narrow lane, its high hedges shadowing the property. There were no lights on in the house, nor in the one next to it, Maggie noticed, her thoughts turning to how she might escape from this man's clutches.

'I'll fetch your case later,' Christopher told her, clasping her wrist firmly. 'Everything's ready for you indoors, my dear. I even have the heating on a timer,' he added with an avuncular smile.

The moment he got out of the car, Maggie felt for the handle but it was on some sort of child lock, securing her where she sat. Slowly, she removed her seat belt and took a deep breath. It was either make a dash for it and risk his wrath or go along with whatever mad plan he had for them both. Too late, she remembered her phone lodged in the driver's door.

'Out you get, Margaret.' Christopher was there, bending over and offering his hand, as though abducting a woman was perfectly natural. But then, he didn't see it that way, did he, she thought as he helped her out of the car. He was seeing her as his beloved, not as the wife of a police officer who was surely trying to locate her whereabouts at this very moment. *Oh, dear Lord, let him find me.*

Christopher tucked her arm into his own and led Maggie up a short path to the front door. In moments he had the key in the lock and she was led inside, dazed by how quickly everything had happened and how she had lost the opportunity to escape. Or was she following an instinct for survival?

Pretending to be a part of whatever fantasy this man was playing out in his sick mind?

Maggie's heart thumped in her chest as she stumbled beside him.

What was waiting for her in this house? Did he have some sort of room full of whips and straps? Had he taken other women here and kept them prisoner?

The door closed behind them, slamming loudly as though a gust of wind had caught it, making Maggie jump.

'This way,' he told her, half-dragging Maggie along a carpeted corridor and into a room towards the back of the house.

Where was he taking her? Was this where she would feel certain pain? Be subjected to torture or sexual abuse? A feeling of nausea filled her throat and Maggie swallowed hard, her stomach churning.

A click of the light switch and the place was washed in light, making Maggie blink.

'Oh,' she exclaimed, looking around at the room. Whatever she had expected, it was not this room decorated in shades of beige and brown. There was a small sofa, its moquette seats covered in a pale fleece throw and a matching pair of armchairs, their velour cushions stacked at an angle. In one corner an ancient television sat on a wooden stand, in another stood a standard lamp, its yellowing fringed shade reminding Maggie of something a great-aunt had owned way back in her childhood.

'Sit down, Margaret, do,' Christopher said. 'Oh, but allow

me to take your coat. We'll just put it here,' he said, holding out his hands and indicating the settee.

How polite he was, she thought, with a nervous shiver, his manner making this situation quite surreal.

Maggie shoved her gloves into a pocket then fumbled the buttons on her coat, terrified that he would come nearer, desperate to avoid his touch.

'Here,' she gasped, handing the coat to him.

'Cup of tea?' he asked, folding her coat carefully as though it were some precious object.

'Yes, please,' she replied, looking up at him and seeing the way his eyes feasted on her face. Anything to delay whatever he had in mind.

He's obsessed, an inner voice told her. *Capitalise on that.*

'Just milk, no sugar, thank you,' she added, forcing a polite smile. *This is crazy*, Maggie told herself. *Taking tea with a murderer.* She clasped her hands together tightly, stopping them from trembling. The small action prompted another prayer. *Help me. Please, please, help me.*

'I won't be a moment,' Christopher said. Just make yourself comfortable.' And with that he left her alone in this strange room, staring after him.

Looking around, Maggie took note of the faded flowered wallpaper, the low marble hearth with a two-bar electric fire, china ornaments ranged along the mantelpiece. It looked like an old lady's house, she thought, not the sort of place she had expected at all. Was there another person living here? Would she find some poor old soul in a bedroom nearby? No, she told herself, remembering how confidently he had taken her arm. He's not bringing me home to mother. Perhaps he's lived here with someone else. And now he's on his own, trying to find the perfect woman to make him happy.

The sound of ticking made her turn to see the carved wall clock on the wall behind her, the sort of thing she might have found in an antique shop, its dark wood containing a pendulum clock with roman numerals, the casing topped with an eagle's head. With each loud tick, Maggie's heart beat faster. How many more minutes did she have until something dreadful happened?

'And now we know who owns it,' Cameron said triumphantly, turning to write a name on the whiteboard. 'And this,' he continued, pausing to write beneath it with a blue marker pen, 'is his current address in Glasgow.'

Murmurs and a scattering of applause broke out as the officers from the MIT congratulated one another.

'Right,' Cameron went on, 'this is how we are going to apprehend our man,' he told them, tapping a pencil against the artist's impression.

Molly Newton grinned at Davie who was whistling a silent breath through his teeth.

'Who'd have thought it, eh?'

'Lorimer'll be pleased to see this finished tonight,' Davie said at last. 'Shame he's not able to come with us, though. Should be there to see the man arrested.'

'Maybe Cameron will give him a bell,' Molly whispered as they turned their attention to the DCI who had begun to outline the procedure for making an arrest, now that the stalker's true identity was known to the police.

The library was not yet in darkness when Lorimer jumped out of the Lexus and headed to the main entrance where a poster, advertising MARGARET LORIMER, AUTHOR OF *GIBBY THE GHOST OF GLEN DARNEL* was displayed.

He tried the handle, shaking it in exasperation, but the big wooden door was evidently locked.

Racing around the building, Lorimer skidded to a halt as he saw the figure of a woman descending the back steps.

'Oh!' she exclaimed, putting a hand to her chest as she caught sight of him.

'I'm Lorimer, Maggie's husband,' he called out. 'Please, can you tell me where she's gone?'

The woman drew back, doubt clearly evident on her face at this encounter with a strange tall man.

'Here,' Lorimer showed her his warrant card. 'I think something might have happened. Maggie didn't turn up for her event at the theatre. Do you know where she went when she left the library?'

'Goodness.' The woman shook her head. 'She took a taxi,' she replied. 'But I thought she was meeting you . . . ?'

'Which taxi firm?' Lorimer demanded, standing his ground, determined to find out every detail that could lead him to his wife.

'Oh, we always use Jock. Wait a wee minute, his card's on the noticeboard.'

Lorimer waited impatiently as she unlocked the back door with three different sets of keys. On any other night he could have admired the library's security but right now every second's delay mattered. At last he followed her back into the library, watching as she turned on the light and unpinned a business card from a long corkboard in the hallway.

'Here it is.' The woman handed Lorimer the card.

'Thanks,' he replied, his mobile already in one hand. 'Sorry to have delayed you,' he added, hurrying out into the darkened car park once more, leaving a bewildered librarian staring after him.

CHAPTER THIRTY-EIGHT

'Jock's Taxis,' a broad accent exclaimed.

'This is Detective Superintendent Lorimer. I need to speak to the driver who picked up my wife earlier this evening,' he said.

'Mr Lorimer! Ah, nice to talk to you, sir. I wis that happy to make your wife's acquaintance. Her being the famous writer an' all,' the man began. 'But why are you askin' me this? When I dropped her off Mrs Lorimer said you were meeting her. She didnae leave onything in the car, did she?'

'Where? Where did you take her, man?'

'The auld kirk, where you said she wis tae meet ye.' The voice sounded aggrieved. 'Alloway's auld haunted kirk. Did ye no' get there on time, like?'

'When was this?'

'Just afore five. I wis no sae happy tae let a bonny lass like that stand on her ain, ken, but she telt me ye were going to pick her up. Why ... has something happened ...?'

Lorimer said a brief thanks and pocketed his phone, racing back to the car, a deep frown settling between his eyes.

Maggie had thought he was going to meet her in Alloway? Who had put that idea into her head? Was this some last stupid trick of Ivy Thornton's? Had the woman deluded his wife into missing her final event?

Or, he thought, a deeper dread settling in his stomach, had the stalker managed to lure her there?

It took less time than the silver taxi had taken to speed away from the library and drive down to the old church near the Burns Centre, gunning the Lexus as fast as he dared. Soon the town gave way to countryside and the dark shape of a spire appeared against a cobalt-blue sky.

Lorimer stopped by the pavement and felt in the glove compartment for his heavy rubber torch. Switching it on, he left the warmth of the car and played a beam of light along the stones of the churchyard. Had she waited here for him to arrive? Then what? Jock had insisted that no further requests for a taxi had come from Mrs Lorimer. So where had she gone? And who had picked her up from here?

Slowly he walked around the church, looking for any sign that Maggie had been there, but there was nothing. He came back out, pushing the creaky gate behind him with a dull clang and leaned against the railings. Where had she gone? Ivy Thornton was not answering her phone and Maggie's was still going to voicemail.

He looked one way and then the other, his torch flicking across the cracked pavement and into the gutter.

An owl hooting made Lorimer turn suddenly and look up but he could see nothing in the thick tapestry of branches except rags of clouds drifting across a pale moon. With a sigh he turned back, the torch making a circle of light near his feet.

It was at that moment he noticed it.

Bending down, Lorimer scooped up the shiny pale pebble and laid it in the palm of his hand. It was Maggie's little bit of quartz from Calgary! He looked down again, trying to create some sort of sense from the discovery. Had she lost it? Or was this a way of leaving something for him to find?

Heart racing, Lorimer closed his fist around it. She could be a sentimental woman at times, keeping little treasures to remind her of happy times; no way would she discard this without a good reason.

So, where had they gone? He imagined her being bundled into a car, thrown into the boot, even, and taken away . . .

Where had he taken Celia Gemmell? Lorimer suddenly decided to follow his first thought and head further north to the wooded area near Hessilhead. Maybe, just maybe, he had replayed the same journey of a year before. Gloom settled on Lorimer's mind. What would he find there? Another shallow grave? What was it Solly had said? The man was deluded into thinking that Maggie could love him. Well, if he had taken her captive, how long would it be until he saw how wrong he really was?

*

365

'Hello, are youse looking fur ma neighbour?' An old man pointed to the door opposite his own flat. 'He's no here, the noo. Holidays, awright fur some,' he added glumly.

Molly and Davie approached the man standing in the lighted doorway. He was dressed in a knitted pullover that had gravy stains down the front and a pair of grey slacks that were baggy at the knees.

'Police Scotland,' Davie replied, looking the old man up and down. 'Do you know where he is and when he'll be back?'

'Polis, is it?' The old man seemed to brighten up at the sight of Davie's warrant card. 'Well, well, whit's the man been up tae? Too squeaky clean, they types, if ye get ma meaning, son.'

'Do you know where he is, sir?' Molly asked, barely concealing her impatience.

'Aw, he's mibbe in the ither hoose the noo, or away his holidays. Wait a wee minute, hen.' He shuffled away from them into the flat and stopped a little way along the hall. Molly could see him stoop down by an old table that had a lower shelf covered in papers.

'Here ye are,' the neighbour said at last, holding out an old envelope. 'Wrote doon his address wan time when the postman had to redirect some mail.'

Davie took the envelope from the old man and showed it to Molly. 'Think he might be there?' he whispered but she did not reply.

'Thank you, sir,' Molly said, handing the old chap her business card. 'If you do see your neighbour, please can you call us? It's important and we would prefer it if you do not let him know we have been here.'

The old man's eyes widened and he nodded silently, watching as the two police officers departed from his doorstep.

Niall Cameron listened as his detective sergeant reported on their findings. 'We'll send our own people there,' he said at once. 'It's not that far from where we found the Gemmell woman's body. Makes sense that he had a place in that area.'

He laid the mobile on his desk but immediately it rang out again and he saw the name *Lorimer* illuminated on its screen.

'Cameron,' he began.

'Niall, it's me. It's the stalker, I think he's taken Maggie. I'm on my way to the place where Celia Gemmell was buried,' Lorimer told him.

'What? Where are you? What's happened?'

Lorimer gave his DCI the facts about Maggie's disappearance and his fears that she had been snatched.

'We're heading in the same direction,' Cameron said grimly. 'But we've found out his real identity, Lorimer. I don't know how he's done it but the man styling himself Christopher Stevenson has been running rings around us all this time.'

Lorimer drove deeper into the woods. It was hard to believe that someone like that had been leading a double life for so long. Solly might feel some pity for the stalker but right now all that Lorimer felt was a cold rage.

He stopped at the same spot he had parked before when Professor Dawson had made her brilliant discovery. He cut the engine, leaving on the car headlights so he could see the path ahead. Crime scene tape still fluttered around the place where Celia's body had lain, a stark reminder of what might happen to Maggie.

Hefting the torch again in his right hand, he walked slowly towards the old ruined house. If need be he could use it as a weapon as well as to light his way.

Lorimer kept to the grassy area, shining the beam on the moist ground. Then he stopped as fresh tyre tracks appeared on the ground. Someone had been there, and by the looks of it, fairly recently. He flashed the torchlight upwards and around, but there was nothing to see. Stepping to one side, he trained the light back on the tracks, noticing now that there was a curve where a vehicle had been turned around and a second set of tracks heading out of the wood. He gritted his teeth, realising that the Lexus must have driven over the same set of tracks on his way into the wood. But at least he knew now that officers were on their way to the nearby town where the stalker had his weekend residence.

It took just a few minutes to drive out of the woodlands and back to the main road that led towards Lugton and Beith. Cameron had outlined his strategy for taking the man into custody and there was a team of officers heading that way already, but Lorimer was determined to reach the stalker's address before anything happened to Maggie.

*

'Here you are, a nice cup of tea,' he said, laying down a tray.

Maggie looked at the hand-knitted tea cosy and the bone china cups and saucers then up at the man's beaming face. It was like being part of a scene from a different era. Was this what he had planned? Was there something from this man's past that made him seek out a woman with dark hair, someone significant? Solly thought so, Maggie reminded herself.

Christopher rubbed his hands in glee. 'Shall I be mother,' he said coyly and Maggie nodded silently, still letting him think she was a willing party to his weird fantasy.

For a moment he looked at her, eyes narrowing. 'You're very quiet,' he scolded her. 'Not like you at all. After all these talks? I thought you would have plenty to say,' he chided.

Maggie forced a faint smile. 'I'm rather tired,' she told him. Then, fearful that he might suggest bed, she added, 'I'll just go and wash my hands, if I may. Where's the bathroom?'

She made to stand up and he moved swiftly towards her, grabbing both her hands in his. 'I'll show you, my dear,' he said, pulling Maggie to her feet and leading her out of the room and along the hallway to the end of a corridor and indicated a white-painted door.

'In there,' he said. 'Don't be too long. We don't want your tea to get cold, now, do we?'

Maggie entered the toilet and closed the door behind her, pushing the snib into an old worn hole in the wood to lock it. With a sob of relief she sank on to the toilet, head in her hands.

Could she remain in here? She looked at the lock again in dismay. One heave and he could force his way in. No, she decided, it was better to have this short break from his staring eyes to gather her thoughts. If she were to pretend to feel ill ... an idea took hold, something that might prevent him touching her, tonight at least.

She gazed around her. The small room was half tiled in pink, the rest of the walls painted pale grey, not a man's choice, she thought, wondering who had lived here before her captor. And what had become of her.

Maggie splashed her face with cold water and dried it, wiping smudges of mascara from beneath her eyes. Then, flushing the toilet, she heaved a sigh. There was only so much time she could linger here and besides, she sensed the man's presence in the corridor outside.

Opening the door and pulling the light cord, Maggie almost collided with him.

'Oh,' she said. 'Sorry I took so long.' She made a face. 'Time of the month,' she added, improvising quickly.

He drew back for a moment and let Maggie walk past him back to the small sitting room, an expression of mild disgust on his face.

Seated opposite him once more, Maggie raised the cup of tea to her lips and took a small sip, wondering for a moment if it was safe to drink. Could he have dropped something into it while she had been out of the room? She'd seen plenty of TV crime shows where things like that had happened.

'What are you thinking, Margaret?' he asked her, leaning forwards and forcing her to look into his eyes.

Maggie shuddered, despite herself.

'I . . .' she began but just at that moment a heavy pounding came to the front door, making Christopher jump up to his feet.

'*Police! Open up!*' A voice came from beyond the door, a voice Maggie knew so well. He'd found her! And there were other officers with him, surely?

'What did you do?' Christopher snarled, grabbing Maggie by the hand and dragging her out of the room, along a passageway and into a well-lit kitchen.

'Nothing!' Maggie protested, looking around wildly to see if she could find a weapon of some sort. Something heavy to strike him with . . .

There was a back door, Maggie saw, hope rising for a second. A glass door with patterns of leaves. Could she force her way out?

'How did they find us?' he snapped, his face contorted in a sudden rage that made Maggie cry out in alarm.

'Stop it!' she cried. 'You're hurting me!'

For a moment he paused, regarding her with a strange look in his grey eyes. 'Yes,' he said softly. 'I will hurt you.' Then, still clutching her hands, he turned towards a worktop where a magnetic strip of knives gleamed against a dark green wall.

'No!' Maggie screamed, her nerve snapping at last. Struggling against his grip, she pulled as hard as she could, but this only served to make him lift one hand and belt it across her face.

She cried out, the pain searing her cheek. For one moment Maggie stumbled then, as she regained her balance, she lashed out a foot, aiming for his ankle. No way was she going down without a struggle, she told herself.

Maggie knew a moment of pure anger. How dare he lift a hand to her! Nobody in her life had ever done that. She backed away a little, eyes glancing to left and right, desperately searching for some weapon.

And there it was. An old-fashioned copper kettle, its handle grey with age.

Grabbing it from the work surface, Maggie swung the kettle as hard as she could, catching her assailant on the face. The crack as it met his jaw gave her a moment's satisfaction but the roar of pain made her step back once more.

She quailed, seeing the fire in his mad eyes.

'Get away from me!' she screamed, aiming the kettle at him again.

This time, though, he ducked then lunged towards her.

'No!' Maggie shouted, stepping sideways so that he staggered against the sharp corner of the counter.

A guttural noise came from his throat, more animal than human as he crept forward once more, determined to corner his prey.

Maggie threw the kettle at him with all her might but it fell with a dull clang on the kitchen tiles as he leapt towards her.

She tried to protect herself, arms held aloft, but the killer grabbed hold of her hands, his grip hurting her wrists.

Maggie pulled as hard as she could, yelping as she felt his fingernails digging into her soft flesh.

She had to get away ... but now she felt her feet skid

on the tiled floor as he dragged her back towards those deadly knives.

Sudden light streamed against the glass door of the kitchen, blue flashing light that Maggie recognised at once.

The killer saw it too.

'They won't take you away from me!' he shouted. 'They won't . . . '

Maggie gave one final pull and felt his hands slip out of hers. She half ran, half staggered from the room, desperate to gain the end of the corridor and the front door.

With a snarl, Christopher pulled a carving knife off the rack and made to follow Maggie out of the kitchen.

At that moment the crash of splintering wood reverberated through the hallway and a figure pushed into the house, past Maggie and towards the knife-wielding stalker.

'Get out! Now!' Lorimer commanded, not stopping to glance back.

Maggie stumbled out into the night air, sobs choking her.

Lorimer stood his ground as the man lunged towards him then, with a speed that took the man by surprise, he side-stepped and grabbed hold of the man's wrist. With a yelp, the stalker dropped the knife and Lorimer pushed him against the wall, pinioning his arms behind him.

'Over here!' someone called out and in moments the place was full of officers from Lorimer's team, handcuffs fastened on their culprit.

'Steven Dewar,' Niall Cameron told the head teacher, 'I

am arresting you for the murders of Celia Gemmell, Carolyn Kane, Patricia Donovan and Edwin Ramsay.' He continued to state the words that gave this man his rights under Scottish law as Lorimer slipped past them, his eyes searching for Maggie.

He found her sobbing quietly in the arms of Molly Newton, the detective patting Maggie's back as though she were a child in need of comfort.

'It's okay,' he heard Molly soothe. 'It's over now.'

Lorimer met Molly's eyes over his wife's heaving shoulders and she gave him a quiet nod. It was over at last, he thought, suddenly exhausted by the race to find his beloved Maggie.

'Let me take her home,' Lorimer said softly and then, as Maggie turned towards him he heard a plaintive cry.

'Margaret!' a voice cried out. 'I'm sorry . . . '

They both looked towards the officers escorting Steven Dewar away from the bungalow. What Lorimer saw was a middle-aged man slumped between them, his thin grey hair blown by the wind, all signs of resistance gone. Whatever fire had ignited his wrath had now burned out, leaving just the shell of a human being. Lorimer stared at him. It was hard to imagine such a pitiable figure could have killed and killed again.

The sound of the van door slamming shut cut off any further words but, as Lorimer pulled Maggie into an embrace, he felt her whole body shuddering.

CHAPTER THIRTY-NINE

They had managed to eat some of the late supper brought up from the hotel kitchens that a smiling waiter had laid out on a circular table, the white linen now stained by red wine that Maggie had spilled. Now they lay in the massive bed, Maggie curled into his side, waiting for the tale to end.

'We'll find out more in due course, but it turns out that Steven Dewar inherited the Beith property from the aunt who brought him up after his mother's death,' Lorimer told her. 'The team found out that much from registry documents. The mother's name was Kennedy and Dewar was his aunt's married name. There's some mystery involving that old house in the woods and why he was so insistent that it would be his new home. I'm guessing that's behind the motivation he had for stalking these women.'

'And me,' Maggie reminded him drowsily.

Lorimer sighed, grateful to have her safely beside him. There was a lot to discover but it would be up to Cameron and the team to carry out these interviews now, his own part in the night's activities being off the record lest it interfere with the eventual outcome.

'Close your eyes and give me your hand,' he said, stretching out to pick up a small object from the bedside table.

Maggie's eyes flew open when she felt the smooth stone on her palm. 'You found it!' she gasped, delight on her face.

'Your lucky pebble,' Lorimer agreed. 'Saved your life tonight, maybe.'

Maggie remained silent, pondering what to tell him. Would her husband understand the little voice that had guided her through this dreadful evening, making her stay calm throughout much of her ordeal? Would he think she were mad if she told him that she felt certain someone had been watching over her, in answer to her fervent prayer? Perhaps one day he would understand how these moments of faith had sustained her, Maggie thought to herself. She had put her trust in a false guardian angel once, but, she reminded herself, it was the man beside her that had saved her life back there. Breathing a sigh of sheer relief, Maggie closed her eyes again, an inner prayer of gratitude for the husband she had and for the grace she had been given.

'He won't speak to us,' Niall Cameron told Solly. 'Just sits and weeps into his hands, shakes his head a lot but says absolutely nothing. It's like he's suffering.' The DCI sighed. 'I almost feel sorry for the fellow.'

Solly nodded sagely. He had watched the attempts

to interrogate Dewar from behind the glass wall in the MIT, pondering what was going on in the head teacher's twisted mind.

'Would you like to ...?' Cameron raised his eyebrows questioningly.

Solly nodded. 'I'll see what I can do,' he replied. 'But don't expect miracles.'

He followed the DCI along the corridor and into the interview room where the duty solicitor sat a little way off from the figure now dressed in jeans and a prison pullover. A uniformed officer stood sentry at the door and moved aside as Solly and Cameron entered the room.

'This is Professor Brightman,' Cameron began, 'entering the room at nine-thirty a.m. on April tenth.'

Solly sat down opposite the two men, a small frown on his face. It was not ideal to be seated like this, facing the man as if he were his opponent, but that was how things were done here and he had that obstacle to overcome if he were to make any progress at all. Besides, the chairs were like that for safety purposes. It wouldn't be the first time that a prisoner had thrown a piece of furniture at an officer. Still, this chap looked as though all fight had left him hours ago.

The professor shuffled his chair a little to the side and sat down again, the angle affording him sufficient view of Steven Dewar's face and minimising the impact of his apparent authority. How often, he wondered, had this man sat behind a desk scolding recalcitrant schoolchildren?

'Steven, can you tell me a little about your mother?' Solly

leaned towards the man and murmured just loud enough for the audio recording.

Dewar sighed and stirred a little but still he said nothing, eyes staring at the tabletop.

'She must have meant a lot to you,' Solly continued softly. 'And your home in the countryside, was it a happy time, Steven?'

For a moment the man's eyes met his and Solly saw tears forming. *No*, he thought, *not a happy time at all*.

'What happened to her, Steven? How did she die?'

But Solly only saw more tears roll down the man's stubbled cheeks, his silent weeping testament to the trauma that had been at the heart of all this business.

'You wanted her to love you,' Solly whispered, 'didn't you?'

Then a nod and a sigh, more progress than anyone had made over the preceding hours.

'Did Celia promise to love you, Steven? Then did she let you down?'

As he saw Dewar clench his fists together, Solly imagined those hands choking the life out of the woman who'd been a kitchen assistant at Bankbrae Primary School. He had suspected that Celia's presence there had been the trigger for what had become this series of crimes, the woman who so resembled Dewar's long-dead mother provoking memories that had been suppressed for decades.

'Is that why you had to kill her, Steven? Celia betrayed you, didn't she?'

Again, a slight nod.

'Please speak for the tape,' Cameron told the man.

'Yes,' he said at last, his voice hoarse from weeping. 'Yes, she had to be buried there ... '

'And your mother? Did she end her life there too, Steven?'

There was a prolonged silence in the room as the man looked down at the table, whatever he saw in his mind too much to utter. Perhaps, Solly thought, he might be persuaded to tell the professional psychiatrists in time. But right now, this man was too broken to continue, the tears that flowed down his ruined face coming from a grief that was all consuming.

'We'll never know the whole story, I suppose,' Solly told Cameron as they walked back upstairs to the DCI's office. 'Forensic evidence certainly links him to all of the murders and you have enough to make a case. But, question is, will he be fit to plead?'

He heard the detective heave a sigh. 'I doubt it,' Cameron replied. 'He's being assessed by psychiatrists and what background information we have suggests that he'll be sent to Carstairs rather than Barlinnie.

'What do you think made him do these things, Solly?' Cameron asked as they stopped at the top of the stairs.

'Something bad happened to him as a child, I'm certain of that,' Solly replied. 'How his mother died is central to it all, I feel. But,' he gave a laconic shrug, 'unless there are any relatives still alive to fill in that story, perhaps we'll never know.'

*

If she had smiled at him, taken his hand, then he would never have done it. But she had ignored him as usual, striding ahead on the sands, her feet too fast for him to keep up. He recalled the rocky outcrop that had slowed her down, the sound of gulls overhead then her exclamation of annoyance as she'd slipped and fallen, a curse on her lips.

He'd wanted to help her up but she'd glared at him as though it had been his fault, shouting at him that he was stupid and accusing him of holding her back.

The little boy had felt a burning white rage inside as the woman had continued to scream at him. He hardly noticed the rock in his hand or felt the impact of it as he smashed it against her skull, over and over, silencing her voice for ever.

Afterwards they had all been so kind, taking his hand and leading him away from her body. Had she slipped down on to the rocks, they'd asked, and he'd nodded dumbly, only too ready to comply with whatever story they wanted him to tell.

The house had fallen into disrepair over the years, of course, none of the family willing to live there in that darkened wood, neds eventually setting fire to it, nobody wanting to repair the damage. But he'd visited it after meeting Celia.

Steven sat in his room drinking lukewarm tea from the plastic cup they'd given him. They wanted to know all of the details, of course, how he had seen their photos in the newspapers, followed them thinking that perhaps, this time, one of them might turn and smile, take his hand, and lead him to a better place.

CHAPTER FORTY

The crowds in the tented theatre turned to stare at the dark-haired woman and her companion as she walked confidently between the rows towards the raised platform at one end.

'Go on, you'll be fine,' Lucy whispered at Maggie's side.

It was bright outside, the August sunshine making dappled shadows across the canvas, echoing the shapes of trees along Charlotte Square.

As she reached the platform, Maggie heard the applause and to her surprise the entire audience was on its feet, giving her a standing ovation. She opened her mouth in astonishment, but then felt Lucy's hand on her elbow, guiding her towards the seat.

'Everyone knows about the stalker,' her agent had told her earlier as they'd sat in the authors' yurt, preparing for Maggie's first event at Edinburgh International Book Festival. 'Martin Enderby did a great piece in the *Gazette*, remember.' And

Maggie did remember. The journalist had made his peace with Detective Superintendent Lorimer, coming to their home once again for an interview that Ivy Thornton would have loved. Ivy's fall from grace had not affected Maggie's relationship with her commissioning editor; they were already talking to Lucy about a possible option by a TV company.

The audience was seated once more and Maggie beamed out at them, her eyes scanning the rows for familiar faces. Yes, there was Sandie from school and Rosie and Solly ... but so many strangers! She looked from row to row until she spotted him, seated at the back, long legs stretched out in front of him. And, as her husband gave her a lazy smile she saw him signal, thumb upward, telling her that everything was fine, just fine.

Maggie took a deep breath and listened as Lucy introduced her. She smiled out at the audience, many of whom were no doubt intrigued about the woman who had been prey to a murderous stalker. But, Maggie told herself firmly, that was not her story to tell, not today.

'Hello and thank you all for coming,' she said warmly, holding her reading copy open on her lap. 'I'd like to tell you about my book, *Gibby the Ghost of Glen Darnel*.'

ACKNOWLEDGEMENTS

Ah, this has been the hardest book ever to write! Health issues meant that I was unable to sit at my desk for long spells and my publishers, Little, Brown, have been not just wonderfully understanding but very kind and concerned over these past months. Thanks are due to the entire L,B team but particularly my editor, Lucy, whose own wedding plans never once detracted from her keeping in touch to see how I was and who kept reassuring me that missing a deadline didn't matter, just to get well once again.

There are, as ever, so many professional people to thank for help in researching a crime novel, among them DS Mairi Milne, whose thirty years as a serving officer has recently come to an end. Well done, Mairi, I am so proud of my former pupil!

It was a joy to collaborate with Professor Lorna Dawson, CBE, the eminent soil scientist who agreed so willingly to be herself in the story. May we have more fun with that in future cases with Lorimer! I am deeply honoured to have Lorna in this book as well as having her first-hand expert knowledge of soil science, a completely fascinating subject.

More thanks are due to Lucy Jukes, agent of many real and well-known children's authors, for representing my Maggie in her (your) fictional children's agency and for being kind enough to let me write her into the book. I love blurring the edges of fiction and reality and such cooperation is a joy.

Thanks to Dr Jenny Brown, my amazing agent, whose encouragement means so very much. It was easy to become despondent when I could not walk and when additional problems like repetitive strain injury sometimes stopped me writing the story. In the months since my knee collapsed beneath me, requiring two lots of surgery, it has been a time to value more than ever the kindness of family and friends as well as that of strangers. Thanks to the many folk that have helped me during this time: the staff in airports whose friendliness made the wheelchair journeys bearable; the lovely nurses and doctors who looked after me in Ross Hall Hospital; Hannah, the physiotherapist whose encouragement gave me hope; Caro Ramsay, my brilliant osteopath-cum-fellow crime writer whose emails in Canada helped us to tackle the initial problem correctly and who continues to take care of me.

Best thanks of all are due to Donnie for his wonderful care back in October 2017 till now. I am truly blessed among wives.

When Dorothy Guildford is found stabbed to death in her home, all signs point to her husband, Peter. The forensic psychologist is convinced there's more to the case that meets the eye but Police Scotland are certain they have their man.

While DC Kirsty Wilson searches for evidence that will put Peter away for good, she is shocked to discover a link with a vast human-trafficking operation that Detective Superintendent William Lorimer has been investigating for months. But before they can interrogate him, Peter is brutally attacked.

With one person dead and another barely hanging on, the clock is ticking for DC Wilson and DSI Lorimer. And the stakes grow higher still when one of their own is kidnapped . . .

THE FIRST LORIMER CASE

When three young women are discovered strangled and mutilated in a Glasgow park, it is up to DCI Lorimer to find their killer. Frustrated by a lack of progress in the investigation, Lorimer is forced to enlist the services of Dr Solomon and Brightman, psychologist and criminal profiler. Together they form an uneasy alliance.

But when a homeless man is brought in for questioning, the investigation takes a bizarre turn. Soon Lorimer has to scratch the surface of the polished Glasgow art world and reveal the dark layers hidden beneath . . .

*

'Gray never rushes her story, preferring to slowly, delicately build a multi-layered, international web of drama and deceit that requires the concentration levels to stay on high from the first page until the last'
Daily Record

'Convincing Glaswegian atmosphere and superior writing'
The Times

Alex Gray

KEEP THE MIDNIGHT OUT

Two murders, twenty years apart. Time for revenge...

When the body of a red-haired young man is washed up on the shore
of the beautiful Isle of Mull, Detective Superintendent Lorimer's
tranquil holiday away from the gritty streets of Glasgow is rudely
interrupted. The body has been bound with twine in a ghoulishly
unnatural position and strongly reminds Lorimer of another murder:
a twenty year old Glasgow case that he failed to solve as a newly
fledged detective constable and which has haunted him ever since.

As local cop DI Stevie Crozier takes charge of the island murder
investigation, Lorimer tries to avoid stepping on her toes. But as the
similarities between the young man's death and his cold case grow
more obvious, Lorimer realises that there could be a serial killer on
the loose after all these years.

As the action switches dramatically between the Mull murder
and the Glasgow cold case twenty years earlier, Lorimer tries
desperately to catch a cold-hearted killer. Has someone
got away with murder for decades?

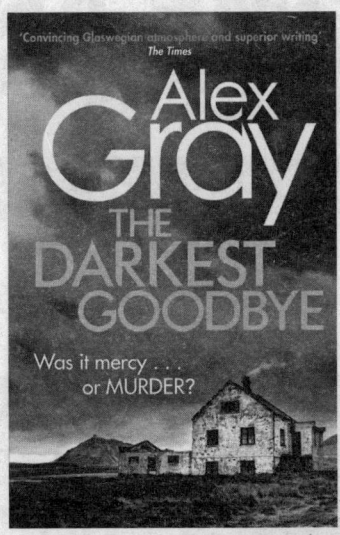

'Convincing Glaswegian atmosphere and superior writing'
The Times

Alex Gray

THE DARKEST GOODBYE

Was it mercy . . .
or MURDER?

'Brings Glasgow to life in the same way
Ian Rankin evokes Edinburgh'
Daily Mail

When newly fledged DC Kirsty Wilson is called to the house of
an elderly woman, what appears to be a death by natural causes
soon takes a sinister turn when it is revealed that the woman had
a mysterious visitor in the early hours of that morning – someone
dressed as a community nurse, but with much darker intentions.

As Kirsty is called to another murder – this one the brutal execution
of a well-known Glasgow drug dealer – she finds herself pulled into a
complex case involving vulnerable people and a sinister service that
offers them and their loved ones a 'release'.

**Detective Superintendent William Lorimer is called in to help
DC Wilson investigate and as the body count rises, the pair
soon realise that this case is about to get more personal than
either of them could have imagined . . .**